BOOKS BY KB FISHER

ASHER HUXLEY

The Two of You
Admit Two

STANDALONE

Of Storm and Shadows
Promoted with Tenure

THE TWO OF YOU

KB FISHER

First Edition: September 2025

Paperback ISBN: 979-8-9880200-6-6
eBook ISBN: 979-8-9880200-7-3
Library of Congress Control Number: 2025915765

For TAMMY—
my best friend and Jedi master who supports my chapters,
regardless of the plot twists

Acknowledgments

I thank my wife, Carissa, for calling out my bad ideas and watering the good ones. Without you, there's no telling where my thoughts alone would lead me. Ever since Asher set foot in New Orleans, you've been there to ensure that he gets where he's going. Thanks to you, he's exactly where he needs to be.

I also thank my editor, Dylan Garity, for trusting in Asher's journey (and my own). Because of you, it looks like I know what I'm doing. Thank you, and I look forward to seeing where this series takes us.

part one
CLOSURE

Chapter 1

The homeless man sauntered along the river walk and deeper into the blanket of morning fog. The lingering Mississippi moisture broke against his raw, sunburned skin.

Change was getting low.

He paused and reached into the pocket of his grass-stained jeans, searching for what remained of the previous day's efforts—but his fingers widened the hole that had formed in the bottom of the fabric. The man yanked the pocket inside out. Lint clung to his sweaty palm.

"No. Not again," he said, turning and looking to the ground behind him. The walkway was cloaked in a dense haze. He began retracing his steps but soon realized it was all in vain, his sight too limited in the damp Louisiana sunrise.

A trashcan overflowed on the nearby grass, between the path and the river. He adjusted the bag on his shoulder, then rummaged through the sodden pile of waste there.

As he reached for one of the empty foam cups, a barge sounded its horn on the water. He fumbled the container, and his stomach spoke with an empty growl. He snatched the cup from the ground and strode farther into the gray. A crowd of tourists were beginning to wander along the riverfront, perhaps making their way from breakfast somewhere on Decatur.

New day. New people. A fresh opportunity for change.

"Anything is appreciated," the man said aloud as he held out the makeshift collection, overstating his shuffle across the wet redbrick path. "Anything at all."

He could always tell the difference between the locals and the travelers. To the natives, he wasn't there; he had altogether ceased to exist. For the couples and families vacationing in the city, he was the evident source of their shame. He could see the embarrassment carved into their eyes when they walked by but didn't offer him a spare something.

An elderly woman, hardly visible through the mist, rested on a bench with a gentleman at her side. Probably her husband. She flung open her purse, then unsnapped her wallet—before dropping the bag onto her spouse's lap in haste. She said nothing. Most of them didn't; they didn't know what *to* say. She just held out a five-dollar bill with a sheepish grin, avoiding his eyes.

He extended the cup, and she dropped the money inside.

"Thank you, ma'am," he said with a nod. "Thank you."

As he walked farther down the riverbank, breaking through the fog as it momentarily parted over the brick pathway and dripping St. Augustine grass, he heard the mumble of the woman's husband behind him. Objecting to her random act of kindness, most likely. It was always the same—someone eager to help, their friends or relatives not so much.

He shuffled farther and again into the fog that was broken only a few strides back, approaching the abandoned pier he knew was just ahead. But as he did, something lured his attention. Something nearer to the river. A sound of sorts.

The fog was heavier, now. His other senses grew heightened.

He shuffled closer to the bank.

And there it was—the barred dock, gated by a chain-link fence covered in lovers' padlocks. A weathered wooden sign in the center of the locks looked like it had been carved by hand—"LOVE WINS," the board read.

He stepped nearer to the gate, and the noise grew shriller. A throaty hissing. Grunting. Like a pig's rooting.

He inched forward yet again, closer to the black figure hovering in the gloom near the water. No—the *figures* hovering.

He looked back over his shoulder, curious as to whether anyone else could hear the weeping cries. Then he turned again to the river's edge.

As he pushed forward, a wake of black vultures scattered into the lowly clouds, their wings stirring the mist into swirling funnels like jets banking through a woolly sky. Then it dawned on him—he had disrupted their feeding.

As he stepped farther beneath the rickety pier, the man's own worries disappeared with the fowl and into a shifting haze. Flies, drawn from nowhere, crawled over a body en masse.

"Hey! What's goin' on down there?" A voice from behind startled him—and his feet slipped from the jagged, slick rocks. Before he knew it, the homeless man found himself splashing into the turbid Mississippi.

Face-down on the rancid and rotting corpse.

Chapter 2

Black and dark—anything else no longer did the trick.

"Do you mean two Americanos?" the barista asked. "Café noirs, maybe?" She sported crystal-green eyes and had her dirty-blond hair in a tattered bun. Freckles lay strewn across the bridge of her nose, backlit by a smooth almond crème complexion—not a day over twenty. But the girl spoke as if she saw right through him. Like she was a few decades older than she appeared.

"Sure," Asher said. He felt a tug at the corner of his mouth, although the expression faded in no time. "American, French. As long as it gets the job done, I'm sure it'll be great."

The girl leaned forward, over the counter. "American?"

"What's that?"

"You think Americanos are American?"

"Uh, sure. Americano . . . café Americano . . . American coffee? That's what you're referring to, ain't it?"

"Well, whether or not it's American coffee depends on who you ask." Asher found that her willingness to correct him made the freckles more attractive, but he pushed the thought away no sooner than it arrived. "Americano *is* an Italian word, and the drink's based on Italian espresso. To go?"

He nodded.

She grabbed two cups from behind the counter. "As it turns out, American soldiers back in the day couldn't handle the strong stuff." She uncapped a marker. "Can you believe that? Soldiers—unable to handle a little caffeine."

"Is that right?" The detective slid the aviators from his eyes. "Couldn't handle it? Really?" He hung the glasses from the crook of his black button-down shirt and curled a tuft of espresso hair around the back of his ear.

"Hey, don't shoot the messenger." She glanced up, but only for a second—at the badge clipped to the front of his belt. "One way or another, some people just aren't able to hang. You know?"

"Well, I'll leave my fate up to you." He removed his wallet from his back pocket. "Don't go easy on me, though. Give me the good stuff."

"Yes, sir. Two café noirs it is, then." The girl waved off the payment. "Don't worry about it."

"You sure?"

"Of course I'm sure. You plan on being back, don't you?"

He nodded.

"Alright, then."

Looks like this might be the place.

There was no going back to the other shops. Not after what had happened. Café Beignet, PJ's, Dunkin', Café Du Monde— all of them were off limits. Asher needed a new go-to, now that he was alone. Somewhere that didn't remind him of how big he had missed the mark.

He sat at one of the high-tops near the window and waited for his order. A trail of chicory lingered in the air around him. He reached into his leather jacket and removed his phone, then placed it on the table.

Asher Huxley had been heading up the New Orleans Homicide Unit for a little over two years, now. Already, he had experienced more than he'd bargained for. More than most men dealt with over the entirety of their run in law enforcement, he suspected. The question was whether or not it was worth it.

How far are you willing to go for your career, Detective? His reflection stared back at him from the metal chair across the way.

Perhaps he had already gone too far. The more he thought about it, day in and day out, how had he not?

Dawn had hardly shown its face. A yellow Edison bulb hung low over the tabletop, with three more over the counter at the register.

He stared out of the window and into the shadow-filled alley, a bulb flickering, struggling, from somewhere he couldn't see, its light hesitant between the night and rising sun.

The door chimed, and Asher sprang from the table, kicking back his chair against the wall, reaching for his pistol and backing away from the window. As he did, the barista froze—and looked to the three teenagers walking into the shop.

No sooner did the embarrassment reach his face than his phone began to vibrate, crawling its way to the edge of the tabletop. At first, he ignored it. He pulled his chair back to the table, concealed the pistol with his jacket, then lifted his hand in apology to the girl behind the counter.

The kids stepped through the shop as if walking on tenuous ground, glaring at the detective like he was some mad degenerate. It was stamped all over their faces: *What the hell was that?*

"How's it going?" Asher asked as they walked by. But not one of them said a word.

He sat down and pushed his hand back through his hair before answering his phone. "Yeah, what is it?"

The barista walked out from behind the counter with the two coffees and set them on the table in front of him. "PIRATE KING COFFEE" was written in a circle, around a logo that included a shield and two swords, flanked by a pair of skulls and a crown on the side of the black cup. "LAFITTE" was stamped below the armor.

"Hey," Pierre said through the phone. "Where you at?"

Asher rested the phone between his ear and shoulder, and reached for his wallet. The girl waved her hands in front of her yet again and whispered, "Nope. I'll see you next time." She double-tapped the tabletop with her ring as a farewell.

"I'm at Jean Lafitte's, grabbing a coffee. What's up?"

A pause lingered in his ear. The chief never paused; he only dished out orders, one after another. "How quick can you get out here to the river?"

"Where at?"

"Back behind the brewery, out at the Love Wins pier."

It didn't sound like his boss; something in his voice was a bit off. Something worrisome. Something . . . personal, perhaps?

Whatever it was, Asher didn't care for it.

"Yeah. I'm on my way."

Pierre didn't bother to respond—he just hung up. At the very least, Asher usually got a "dickhead" or "numbnuts" out of him. Something to convey the boss's frustration with his lead detective. But this time? Nil.

Something was off-center.

Asher grabbed a five from his wallet. He picked up his two coffees and walked to the register, dropping the money in the tip jar and lifting his drinks to the barista as she served the kids.

"Gotta run," he said.

She flared her nose and smirked. It made her freckles dance.

Asher put his back to the door, then stepped out into the humid alley.

Chapter 3

There were never this many first responders at a scene—not before the head of Homicide arrived, anyway.

Asher threw the pistol grip of the Vette into park behind one of the three firetrucks, their red and white lights dissecting the dismal gray morning, blocking the one-way parallel parking adjacent to the river. No less than a dozen patrol units crowded the railroad tracks and grassy median. EMS were already leaving the scene with their lights off.

No one to save? No hurry.

But the rest of them? The uniforms and firefighters, the plain-clothes officers who looked out of place even to Asher himself? They all appeared to be sticking around—whether they were needed or not.

Looks like I'm late to the party.

He made his way across the still-damp grass and onto the brick path of the river walk with a coffee in each hand. Pierre greeted him there.

"Well, it's about time you do something right," the chief said, reaching for one of the cups.

"I don't think so." Asher lifted the drink into the air. "Yo, Xavier!" he called down to the water.

"Oh, fuck off," said Pierre.

Xavier looked up to the path from the riverbank, lifting his chin to Asher. "I'll be right up."

"What we got?" Asher asked Pierre. "Must be something special for such a production. It's lookin' borderline Hollywood." He sipped his brew.

"Well, we're not really sure if, uh . . ." The chief ran his hand down his cop-ish, washed-out mustache. Then he pulled a torpedo from the inside pocket of his black peacoat, slipping the cigar between his teeth before searching his pockets for a lighter. Pierre squinted, although the sun was at his back. "Before you head down there, Asher, you should probably—"

"It's about time," Xavier said. Asher handed him the coffee.

Pierre pinged the metal lighter against his other hand and lit the cigar, then gave Xavier a sideways glance. He slapped the lighter shut.

"So, what we got?" Asher said, popping Xavier in the chest with the back of his hand.

Smoke drifted from Pierre's mouth and straight into Xavier's face as he tipped back his coffee. The man didn't flinch, though; it came with the territory.

"I think you should come take a look," Xavier said, looming over Asher. "Ain't no point in arguing over spilled milk, until you see the mess for yourself." Xavier was a brown-skinned tower of a man—and the new lead technician of the forensics team.

"Alright," Asher said. "Let's get it."

He and Xavier made their way down to the water, but Asher soon noticed that Pierre wasn't with them. They glanced back to the path.

"You coming?" Asher said.

The chief pulled another drag from his cigar, a deeper and lingering breath that forced Asher to stall and wait for an answer. "No." He looked out to the river and blew the smoke toward them. "I think I got the gist of it."

As they reached the edge of the river, below the creaking wooden pier that seemed as if it were held together by a few propitious nails, Asher saw the navy-blue tarp at the water's edge.

"Well?" Asher gestured with his cup. "Let's see it."

Xavier moved closer, swirling his coffee in hand, looking back at his friend, then again to the tarp. Slow.

As he did, Asher took greater notice of everyone around them than of the sheet as it quivered over the waning shore. The blue uniforms stood behind them with their hands on their belts. The firemen were nowhere near their trucks, instead sitting on the benches in the grass. All of them watched on.

"Why do I get the feeling there's something I need to know?" Asher said.

Xavier glanced at him again, then crouched and pulled two of the metal stakes from the muddy ground. He peeled back the tarp from the body. Asher half expected him to say something, for someone around them to throw their two cents into the mix and brief him on what they were thinking. Anything.

But the silence grew deeper. The precinct talkers, the trainees. Pierre back on the path. No one spoke—except for some still-famished birds watching them from a distance.

It took a minute for it to click for Asher, because of what the river had done to the body. But then it all came into focus, like he was the butt of some dramatic gag for a crowd of quick-to-judge spectators. Just standing there like an idiot for everyone to see.

Only it was no joke, it was life. And they were more than just onlookers; they were colleagues.

Everything around him faded. Asher stepped closer, and felt the blood drain from his face.

Chapter 4

"I already know what y'all are thinking," Asher said. "Let's not get ahead—"

"You're thinking it, too." Xavier remained crouched next to the body, holding back the tarp. "You just don't wanna say it, either."

"Either?"

"Yeah." Xavier peered over Asher's shoulder, up to the chief, who was still watching from the river walk. "Just like him—scared of what this means if there's no one left to provide the two of you with answers."

Asher turned and looked at Pierre. Their eyes met in secret, with a mutual understanding—an unspoken nod to what the moment meant for the uncertainty of their careers.

"Alright, everyone!" Pierre shouted. "Let's get moving. Show's over." He swirled his cigar overhead.

Asher turned back to Xavier and the body. "What do you mean, 'answers'? There are no answers. Just facts. Just what happened and what didn't happen. You know that."

"Sure," Xavier said unconvincingly.

Asher crouched next to the body. "Let's not get carried away."

But he did need answers. He needed to know *why*—beyond

what had been said while he was held at gunpoint by his "partner." And he needed the *who*—who the hell let her into the department? Maybe the chief had more to worry about than his lead detective.

The problem was that Asher was terrified of the answers. Needing and wanting them were more than mere worlds at a distance; they were alternate truths in and of themselves.

The decedent was largely unrecognizable at first glance: bloated, half-eaten and sloughing skin, eyes gone with the beaks of whatever scavengers had arrived first, intact pants, no shirt. There were a few things that stood out, though—once Asher let out a controlled, unnatural breath over the course of eight lengthy seconds.

Female. Middle-aged. Brunette. Those were the observations any detective would've made. Any cop other than Asher.

No, what drew him in were the subtle features. The holes, in particular. A larger one on the right side of her chest, inches below the collarbone. The other two in the corner of her left eyebrow, as small and inconspicuous as they were. Once he noticed those, it was hard to act like it wasn't her.

But it can't be. Not really.

Asher leaned in and waved the flies from the gaping, picked-over mouth of the corpse.

"So, what's the plan?" Xavier asked.

"Plan?"

"Yeah. *Plan.* You know as well as I do, once this gets out, you and Pierre are gonna have a lot more to deal with than some attention from colleagues." Xavier lifted his chin to the crowd of uniforms, who were being swallowed by a growing mass of media. "What then?"

Pierre spoke loud enough for everyone to hear, addressing what on-duty officers remained. "Get 'em out of here."

"Then we do our job," Asher said. "It doesn't matter. There's nothing else *to* do. But we're not releasing information that hasn't been confirmed yet, if that's what you're thinking. Not if I can help it."

He stood up and looked back to the Quarter—in the direction of the shootout only two weeks prior. The one that had managed to kill his marriage and forever ruin his idea of what it meant to know someone. At least, it felt like two weeks ago. The days were melting together into an endless dream. A nightmare with eyes wide open.

Pierre walked toward them and down to the water. "So? What ya thinking?"

Asher didn't miss a beat. "You first."

The chief took a drag, then let it out slow. "We need to stay ahead of this and get an official ID and autopsy ASAP, before we shoot ourselves in the foot trying to answer questions we ain't got the answers to."

"Yeah," Asher said. "That's what worries me." He kept the details of his concern to himself, at least for the time being. He did his best to stand up straight, to pull back his shoulders and act like he had it all under control, but he must've appeared different on the outside.

The chief slapped him on the shoulder. "Cheer up." He stared at the body, buried his hands in his peacoat, and rolled the torpedo between his teeth. "No more worrying about Cassandra."

"Well . . . maybe," Asher said.

If only it were that simple. But it can't be. Not really.

Asher's jacket vibrated against his chest, accompanied by

the theme song from *Halloween*. He removed his phone as some birds screamed bloody murder in the distance.

An image of Michael Myers flashed across the screen.

Asher swiped right and answered the call. "Well speak of the devil."

Chapter 5

The coroner's office had become a second home to Asher—but not all homes had a welcome mat at the front door.

As he walked down the barren and dark hallway of the basement, the memories of his last visit there appeared from the corners of nowhere. Asher wanted nothing more than to remember Sofia as the woman he'd married for her strength and beauty, her smarts and her wit. Instead, the image of his wife's disfigured body, lifeless on a steel table, took precedence over all other memories of her.

Not to mention the pistol pressed against the side of her head—the final picture of his wife alive.

Get it together, Ash. Now isn't the time. Life goes on.

He dropped his aviators onto the bridge of his nose before pushing through the double doors and into the even colder exam room and adjoining morgue.

"Well if it ain't the worker of miracles herself," Asher said dramatically.

Agnes, the New Orleans chief medical examiner, tapped her Marlboro Red in the ashtray on her desk. "Always the charming type." Her dreads swung all too close to the pile of smoldering cinders.

"Still trying to pollute a perfectly good exam room, are we?"

"Hey, I'll stop smoking when you stop bringing me bodies. How's that?"

Asher lifted his hands in defense. "No promises on that front."

She took a last drag and smothered the cigarette in the glass tray. "It's been an interesting morning, huh?"

A metal gurney in the exam room, separated from the freezer boxes visible in the next room over, stuck out like a hammered thumb. Agnes glanced that way, so Asher did as well.

"Yeah, you could say that," he said.

"I'd say I'm sorry, but I'm not sure that'd be the appropriate response." She walked over to the rolling table, covered with a white cloth that harbored the obvious beneath it. "Actually, I'm not sure what to say, given the circumstances."

Agnes lifted the sheet—exposing what might or might not have been Cassandra's body, naked and exploited without mercy by the elements.

"Given the obvious, I think the autopsy should be straightforward."

"And what's the obvious?" he said.

Asher knew what Agnes was referring to, but he also knew that she was oblivious to his doubts. No one was the wiser when it came to his former partner and what she was capable of— including the not-so-subtle "visit" at Café Du Monde after the shooting, once she had gone missing. That one was in his back pocket until the time was right—now that they *might* have the body.

Making himself look like a fool was one thing, but the department? After what had happened? No way.

Agnes stretched on a pair of latex gloves and walked to the

steel table, locked in place over the metal drain at the center of the room.

"I think y'all got it right," she said. "There's the location of the gunshot wound, which matches your and Xavier's accounts of the shooting, and then there's the piercing." She pointed to the corner of the eyebrow. "But that's just the beginning. As soon as she got here, it was one thing after another, and all of it screams you know who."

Only it can't be.

"And what's that?" Asher said.

"Well"—Agnes grabbed a clipboard from the workbench nearby—"we can calculate a postmortem submersion interval to estimate an overall postmortem interval. Basically, use time in the water to represent time deceased. I still need to do a microbial succession of the gut when I complete the rest of the autopsy just to be sure, but at first glance, I can at least give you a reasonable ballpark of how long she's been dead."

"I'm guessing the skin plays a role in all that? Or at least what's left of it?"

"Of course," Agnes said. "We can use an aquatic decomposition score based on the level of bloating, skin slippage, and what, if any, skeletal components are exposed and to what extent. Accounting for the environmental factors that Xavier and forensics provided, we can come up with an overall score."

"And then time deceased."

"Exactly."

"So, what are you thinking?"

"Based on an initial score, without getting too far into the weeds, I'd say she's been in the water for about ten days. Roughly. Not to mention, the sex and estimated age line up with your girl."

Two weeks since the shooting, less four days since the café? That was ten days.

"But it's been about two weeks since everything went down," Agnes continued. "I'll leave sorting that out to you, hun."

"Well, she was shot two weeks ago. That doesn't mean she died two weeks ago."

"Of course."

"Say." Asher stepped closer to the body, looking for any idea as to how he could put his uncertainty to rest. "You plan on running the DNA, or confirming dental records by any chance?"

"DNA? I didn't plan on it. Not with a decedent this far gone. Why? I do plan on looking at any dental records, though. Fingers crossed that they're out there."

"I just wanna get this right, is all. You know?"

Agnes seemed to waver on it for a second. "I'm not sure about the whole DNA thing, but sure. I'll take a look at the dental records. That shouldn't be a problem."

"Please," Asher said. "DNA would be a shoo-in, no?"

"Yeah. But after being in the Mississippi for that long, I highly doubt that I can—"

"Please?"

Again, she seemed hung up on the idea, but Asher put on his best just-for-me face.

"Alright, hun. I'll see what I can do. But between you and me, I think it's overkill."

"Of course. But like I said, this needs to be solid. We're fucked if we don't get this right."

"Oh, before I forget—" Agnes dropped the clipboard onto

the desk and grabbed a clear evidence bag. She tossed it to Asher, then sat on the edge of her desk. Grinning.

The detective caught it against his chest. What else could there possibly be?

He turned over the bag and saw Cassandra's department-issued ID. "New Orleans Homicide" was stamped in block blue letters across the top, with the sheen faded and cracked.

"They found it in her back pocket."

Chapter 6

Asher popped out the ashtray and flipped the kill switch. He trusted no one, at no time and nowhere, when it came to the '67—even in the Garden District.

As he walked to the front porch of his home, he leaned over and snagged a few pecans that had fallen from the tree in the front yard and were resting on the tips of the thick emerald grass. "It's the gift that keeps on giving," Sofia had used to say.

He pried open one of the shells and slipped the fruit into his mouth. It brought him back. All the way back to the late evenings with his wife in the living room, shooting the breeze with Xavier over a hot cup of French Market. A basket of pecans was always on the coffee table.

But that was then.

He walked inside and tossed his jacket onto the island—right next to her coffee mug. The one with "Hubby's #1 Biologist" stamped on the side, with her desert nude lipstick dried on the ceramic rim. It had been two weeks, and he hadn't touched a single item of his wife's belongings. He couldn't bring himself to start the process of removing her from the life they had built for so long; her funeral was more than enough for the time being.

Asher opened the fridge and reached for a bottle of water.

"Maybe rethink the coffee," his therapist had said not long ago. "It tends not to mix well with anxiety." Every cup had become a battle with his former self.

He was now back on the slope, though—as slippery and addictive as it was. And he was already a cup deep for the day. So, why not?

"Screw it," he said aloud.

He shut the fridge and pulled a filter from the cabinet above the coffee pot, then filled it with grounds from the red can of chicory above the stove.

"What more could possibly go wrong?"

As he pulled his holster and gun from the small of his back and set it on the counter next to the wine rack, it hit him flush in the chest: it was date night. A wave of guilt, of remorse for not being more present in his role as husband, of feeling he had let down the one person he was responsible for protecting, imbued him with a new type of hurt. A new form of agony not familiar to his everyday, anxious, pain-laden self.

It was a melancholy sort of anguish with which he had little familiarity.

And the sorrow made way for worry.

While he stood there with one hand on his pistol, the other braced against the counter, lost in the black bottles of wine, he saw himself from across the room. From behind, as he was in that very moment. What was supposed to be real now felt more like a motion picture. It was as if he were watching his life play out, while not participating in decisions and his own reasoning. At least, not really.

He saw it all from a distance but somehow only felt the dark of recent weeks.

Beep. Asher grabbed his gun from the counter, and the holster dropped to the floor. He thumbed the safety and aimed the pistol in a general, downward direction. The cold metal sweated and shivered in his palm.

Beep . . . Beep . . .

The light of the coffee pot flashed with each of the alerts.

"Fuck me," he said, thumbing the safety back into place.

A string of heavy thuds sounded from the front door.

Chapter 7

"Who is it?" Asher said, leaning next to the door with the .45 hanging at his side.

"It's me. Who else would it be?"

There was only one person it should've been; everyone else had moved on.

Asher eased the door open just enough to peer outside.

"It's date night," Xavier said, like Asher should've been expecting him. He was gripping a plastic bag of what smelled like crab. "You didn't think I'd forget, did you?"

Asher slid the pistol around his back and into his waistband. Then he stepped aside. "Date night? What do you know about date night?" He shut the door and locked the deadbolt before swinging the latch closed at the top.

"Oh, come on. I interrupted y'all's date night with bullshit from work more times than I care to admit. You up for some soft-shell po-boys?"

"Is that a serious question?"

A few minutes later, Asher was sitting at the island and watching Xavier cook dinner. Normally, he wouldn't have let it happen. It was his house, his guest, and Asher loved cooking; he had a knack for it. But he also knew that Xavier would take it to heart if Asher didn't let him cook for him. Especially now.

"So," Xavier said, "how you feelin' about today? I know it ain't easy either way, but do you at least have *some* relief knowing she ain't out there, running around anymore?"

"Maybe a little, but I'm not holding my breath. I've made that mistake before. I'll breathe easy once Agnes gets back to us with the official autopsy."

Xavier popped open a beer for himself, then poured Asher a glass of red wine and set it down on the island. Oil warmed in a pan on the stove.

"Alright," Xavier said. "Let's assume what's likely: it's her. What then? What's that mean for you and Pierre? And you"—he lifted his beer—"personally?"

Asher palmed the glass from the bottom and sipped his wine. "Then we move on. Like I said earlier today—we do our job. Just like we always have."

Xavier leaned back against the counter, waiting for Asher to say more. Maybe the answer wasn't what he'd expected. Or perhaps he felt it was unfinished?

"And what does that mean?" Xavier asked.

"What do you mean?"

"You think things will just go back to normal? After everything that happened over the last few weeks? The last few *years*?" He chuckled a bit.

"Probably not, but there also ain't much I can do about it." Asher took a bigger sip now, knocking back the rest of the glass.

"You good, man? You gonna be alright?"

Is anyone really alright?

"Of course I'm alright."

"Well, either way this goes, whether it's Cassandra or not, shit's gonna hit the fan here pretty soon. I know I'm preaching to the choir, but I'd be remiss if I didn't at least say it out loud."

Xavier prepped the crab at the sink. Asher poured himself another glass.

"Must be some good stuff," Xavier said.

"Yeah, well, *either way*, I'm fucked. Hell, me *and* the chief, most likely. All I can do is hold on and enjoy the ride. You know?"

"Can I ask you something?" Xavier said, not turning to face him. "Without it being a big deal?"

"Have I ever kept you from speaking your mind before?"

"No, you haven't."

Only then did he look over to Asher, who was seated back at the island and nursing a topped-off glass. "Shoot."

"Okay . . . So, you think giving it just a few days was long enough? I mean, you weren't exactly laid up on the sofa with a cold."

Asher tipped back another sip, disappearing nearly half of what he'd poured. He set it down and began swirling it in a tight circle, unblinking, lost in the drink as it splashed up the sides of the glass, then bled back down into a pool of scarlet.

"What are you saying, man? Am I not doing my job?"

"Like I said, I'm not looking to make it into something it ain't; I'm just worried. Taking a couple days to yourself and then rushing back to the precinct would be a lot for anyone. No one would fault you for taking more time to yourself if that's what you need."

"Taking more time would only drag it out. I'd be sitting here overthinking everything and doing nothing. And that isn't what I need. What I need is a distraction. Either way, Sofia's gone. Ain't no time at home gonna bring her back."

"Yeah, I know. I just wanna make sure that your head is in the right place. That's all. And that you aren't too focused on the wrong person."

"The wrong person?"

"Yeah. She may be gone, Ash—but if I know you, you're gonna obsess over Cassandra until you drive yourself crazy. Who knows if you'll ever have all the answers you're looking for?"

"And you don't think I will? Have all the answers?"

"Do *you?*" Xavier pressed. He stopped messing with the crab and turned toward Asher. "Look, all I know is if it were me"—he glanced around the house, at Asher and Sofia's home, not touched since the day she died—"I'd be more worried about what I can control. No, she ain't coming back. But what happened . . . happened."

"What does that mean?"

Testing the temperature, Xavier dropped a pinch of batter into the still-warming pan. It sizzled, and he dusted his hands. "After everything that happened, maybe you should focus on you for a while, on your home and coming to terms with losing your wife. To be honest, I'm just wondering why you seem more worried about this autopsy than you are about the obvious."

Xavier lined a plate with paper towels and set it on the island, nudging Sofia's coffee cup to the side. Without pause, Asher leaned forward and, with a single finger, slid the mug back into place.

Chapter 8

ust as Asher gripped the doorhandle to step inside, a downy woodpecker with white-peppered wings hopped along the fence abutting the home office. Sofia came to mind as the sun ignited the bird's fiery red nape. Woodpeckers had been her favorite.

He pushed open the door and stepped into the wide-open foyer of the quiet and dim antebellum-style home. Justin must have been with another client; his door was shut, and Asher could hear a faint back-and-forth through the papery walls.

So, he fashioned himself a cup of coffee while waiting.

Before long, the office doors opened, and a young man emerged. He shuffled out of the room with his eyes glued to his phone, nearly walking straight into Asher as his mug splashed, full to the brim.

"Oh, shoot," he said. He palmed his phone and sidestepped Asher. "I'm so sorry. I didn't see you there."

Who was this? Asher didn't recognize him, although he rarely saw Justin's other patients.

"No worries," Asher said.

"Everyone waits until I'm indisposed to start blowing me up, you know?" His attention returned to the cell phone. "Just the same ole same ole." He looked like he was in his early twenties, and his voice was young and shrill.

Asher thought the client would leave, but instead of turning to the front door, the kid walked the other way and toward the main house. He stopped at one of the several inside doors and knocked with a few gentle raps that echoed off the oak floors.

A woman with a sun-kissed complexion and a cascade of unassuming mahogany hair opened the door and stepped aside. "Hey, come on in."

"Hey, Aunt T," the boy said. He entered what looked like a kitchen on the other side, with his attention back on the screen in his hand.

"Morning, Ash," Justin said from behind, standing in the doorway of his office. "You about ready?"

Asher sat on the sofa. Justin pulled at the knot of his silk knit tie and set his glasses on the coffee table between them, his butter hair bright against the light of the fire beside them. The psychologist's appearance was spot-on and dapper as always, with his lawyerly suit.

"Looks like you're back in the deep end, huh?" Justin gestured to Asher's coffee with his pen.

"Hey, it's the only crutch I've got. At least let me have this one."

"Of course, Asher. I'm only messin'. So, tell me—what's goin' on with work? From what I'm seeing in the news, y'all might have made some progress with Cassandra? Is everything alright?"

"Ha. Yeah, well. I'm not sure if alright is the word I'd use." Asher shifted on the cushions that fought to swallow him whole. "We may or may not have found Cassandra's body."

The therapist's expression ignited.

"We found someone out on the bank by the river walk. From what we can tell, it's most likely her, but we still need an official autopsy and ID before we can say for certain. Let's just say that whoever it is, they no longer resemble what they used to look like."

"Well, that's something, ain't it? You feel like that's a good thing, or no?"

"None of it's good. My partner went off the deep end and tried to kill me; her husband—that I didn't even know she had—killed my wife, and now the department looks corrupt. Honestly, it's a bit hard to see the bright side in any of it. And the fact that we don't even know if she's dead or alive after Xavier shot her is just icing on the cake."

Justin let that linger for a beat. Then he picked up the yellow legal pad from the table. "And the symptoms? Your anxiety getting any worse? Staying the same? Better?"

Asher's phone danced in his jacket pocket. He snuck a quick look at it. It was Pierre. "That's actually something I wanted to ask you about. I've been having these strange feelings that come and go, like everything that's going on around me isn't real. Almost like I'm watching myself in a film, seeing everything from a distance but not actually experiencing anything."

"Huh. You losing time at all?"

He set the phone on the end table.

"Losing time?"

"Yeah. Are you blacking out and not knowing what happened?"

"No, nothing like that. I mean, sometimes the day will go by really quick, and then it's over before I know it. And I don't really feel like I did anything. I just kind of walked through it."

"And your memory?"

"It's been better. I'll forget things I probably shouldn't. Maybe more often than I should."

"Alright." Justin clicked his pen and scribbled with a frenzied hand. "So, I'd like to hear some more about the symptoms to see how it's related to your generalized anxiety, but it sounds a bit like derealization, probably because of the recent trauma. The good thing is that—"

"The trauma?"

The phone started up again, walking in a tight circle on the table next to the sofa.

"Yeah. The trauma. You just watched your colleague of several years put a gun to your—"

"No, that's work. I deal with work on a regular basis."

He sent the call to voicemail.

"I wouldn't say that being held at gunpoint by someone you knew is 'work,' but even so, you just lost your wife, Asher. No matter how you look at it, that *is* traumatic. And symptoms of derealization, stemming more broadly from dissociation or disconnect in general, are relatively common under these kinds of circumstances. When you have such nonstop anxiety for so long, especially with your history of GAD and panic attacks, not to mention your career, you can start feeling detached from the things around you."

His phone let out a single brief tremor. Asher picked it up— to a text from the chief.

"I can't help but wonder," Justin continued, clicking his pen, then setting it down on the arm of the chair and crossing his legs, "if perhaps you need some more time."

"More time? Time for what?"

"You," the therapist said. "It's only been a matter of weeks,

Asher. Days, really. And with these new symptoms, maybe you need some more time away from work to put this all into perspective and come to terms with what happened. I don't want you interpreting these new feelings of detachment as anything more than what they really are. They're just feelings."

Asher opened the text message from Pierre: *Got a fresh one. Good Friends Bar. Get down here.*

"I'm not quitting my job."

"I'm not suggesting you do."

"Then what do you recommend?"

"More time away from this twenty-four-seven grind you have such an affinity for."

"I can't. I have no control over my work schedule. I'm either on or I'm off. There isn't really an in between."

"Okay, then we balance it. I'd like you to start coming in every other day, weekends included."

"Every other day? Isn't that a bit much?"

"To be honest, I think it's a bit much to be held at gunpoint, be shot at, have your coworker deceive and abandon you, and watch your wife be murdered all in a matter of seconds. No, Asher—it isn't a bit much in the slightest."

Now, read the following text from the chief.

The weight of it all came crashing down, and Asher gave the man a slow, grudging nod.

Chapter 9

The victim was posed, naked and on display, laid bare on the balcony at the corner of Dauphine and St. Ann—as lookers-on gawked and pointed from less than a block away. Unbelievable.

Asher called up to the balcony. "You guys wanna cover that up? Or we putting on a show for the whole goddamn city?"

Xavier exited the second floor with a blue tarp. "Already on it," he called down.

Asher mumbled to himself, "Take your time."

"It's been a fucking madhouse." The smoke from the cigar found Asher before the chief did. "Thanks for stopping by."

"No problem at all," Asher responded with his effortless bite of derision and associated smirk. "I was getting restless just sitting around anyways."

Pierre glanced up to the balcony, seesawing the torpedo between his teeth. "I've got it covered down here, but you should head on up." His sideways glance was suggestive. "You ain't gonna wanna miss this one."

Finally, the scene was covered from view of the street.

Asher walked into the bar and past the '70s cigarette machine. As he reached the archway in the corner, he looked up to the pitch-black stairwell in front of him. It reeked of dried urine and cheap draft beer.

Well if this isn't some seedy shit.

An exit sign struggled from above.

As he reached the top of the stairs, flashes of light from Xavier's camera touched the hallway. Asher walked inside and was instantly struck by how banal it all seemed at first glance.

To the left, a bed appeared freshly made, its hospital corners folded and tucked without a wrinkle. Tight and seamless. To the right was an armoire with a TV inside of the double doors. No more, no less. Not a single picture adorned the walls, no mirror, nothing.

He opened the closet. A lone suit hung in the middle of the space, flanked by a number of hangers, ironed and folded to a T with a salmon tie hanging over the slacks inside of the jacket.

"Eerie, ain't it," Xavier said as he walked inside from the balcony.

"That's one way to put it," said Asher. "But yeah—it's far too clean, if that's what you're getting at."

He walked past the bed and into the bathroom, which was much the same—all white and minimal everything, including the towel hanging next to the vanity. Nothing else. Asher turned back and headed for the balcony.

As he approached, he saw that someone else was out there. Someone he didn't recognize.

"Who's that?" Asher said.

"Who?"

He gestured outside. "Him."

"Oh, just my new shadow," Xavier said. "A young forensics trainee straight out of LSU grad school. The chief told him over and over again that we weren't accepting anyone new, but he wouldn't let up. Damn near drove Pierre over the edge until he gave in. Said he'd work without pay if he had to, just to get the experience. Don't worry, though; it's just a probationary thing."

"The chief? Give in?" Asher said. "Since when is that an option?"

"I know, right? I'll take care of it."

"Yeah, well, as long as he doesn't fuck up my crime scene, we shouldn't have a problem."

They stepped onto the balcony, and the new guy rose from his seat at a languid pace. He set his notebook in the wrought-iron chair, then held out his hand to Asher. "John," he said. His wiry glasses were smudged and bent.

"You think that maybe sitting down in the middle of a crime scene ain't the best idea, John?" He stepped to the railing and glanced down at the notebook in the seat. "That yours?" Asher turned toward him while pointing at the book.

"Yes. It is." The trainee grabbed it from the chair—and then leaned against the railing.

Asher glanced at his friend, and Xavier shook his head in the smallest of ways.

Relax, Xavier mouthed, gesturing for Asher to calm down.

Asher turned to the decedent, who was sitting spread-eagle on the floor with his hands cuffed to the railing in front of him, facing the street. His head bent backward and looked up to the balcony's overhang. His mouth gaped open.

"Looks like he was strangled," Xavier said. He lifted his camera and snapped a few pictures of the man's throat. "The pose, though—"

Asher knelt to the violet, blood-pooled ligature marks running across the deceased's throat. He could still see them: the murder-suicides he and Cassandra had worked side by side, and the first couple, who were found in their hotel room. The furrows in the poor girl's neck after she was strangled with her own necklace and left for dead.

"Why the cuffs?" John said. He stepped closer to the body, almost in a daze, like he was lost in the familiar. His eyes narrowed, and his shoulders dropped.

"You tell me," Asher said.

The trainee's pinhole stare moved down the dead man's body and between his legs. His own chest began to rise and fall more noticeably. Then he, too, crouched next to the body, leaning in until his windbreaker was all but brushing the thigh of the corpse. He kept silent, though.

Asher glanced up at Xavier, and his friend shook his head once more.

A weak glimmer from inside caught Asher's attention. They walked back into the room. "Give me a pair of those," he said to Xavier, reaching for the box in his friend's hand.

He stretched on a pair of blue latex gloves that suctioned his hands like a film of sweating skin, then knelt down and eased up the bed skirt with his finger. Under the bed, he found a black-and-gold pen. "I'm guessing you weren't leaving this for me?"

"What is it?" Xavier said.

"You got the picture?"

After Xavier took the photograph, Asher picked up the pen and placed it into a clear evidence bag.

"Really?" John said from behind them. "You think a pen is gonna tell you something about this?"

Asher lifted the bag and smoothed it out to get a better view. "Well, it's a pen from The Walking Murder Tours Company." He ran his fingers over the plastic a bit more. "And it's cracked."

John rolled his eyes—and turned back to the body.

Chapter 10

 few minutes later, the chief shouted up to the balcony from down on the street. "Yo, Asher!"

He walked outside and saw John back against the railing, staring at the body in a daze. Asher pulled back the tarp where it hung from the overhang against the building. "What's up?" he yelled down.

"Get down here. There's someone who needs to talk to you."

Asher walked back into the room and passed Xavier. "Get that idiot off of the balcony." He spoke in an agitated way—not to Xavier himself but in light of his poor excuse for a trainee.

He walked back through the empty bar and out the front doors. Pierre was standing in the middle of the street with two other men Asher didn't recognize.

"This is Bryson," Pierre said. "He owns the bar." The bald man in skinny jeans shook Asher's hand. "And Clint's one of the bartenders who was working last night." He, too, greeted Asher with a handshake, then pinched at one of his pierced ears. "Clint might have some information for us."

"Is that right?" Asher said.

The owner widened his stance and folded his arms, like he

was only there to ensure his employee didn't say anything stupid.

"Maybe," said Clint. "It might be nothing, but even if it is, I thought y'all should know."

"Shoot," said Asher.

"All throughout last night, there was some guy who kept going up to the second floor over and over again, always looking back over his shoulder, acting a little off. Like I said, maybe it was nothing. I just figured it couldn't hurt to let y'all know."

"Who usually has access to the second floor?" Asher asked.

"Mostly employees," said Bryson, "but there's a few regulars who go up there, too. There's a private lounge across from the room where we found the . . . you know."

"And our victim?" Asher said.

"I've seen him in the bar before, but I couldn't tell you his name," Clint said. "But the guy I'm talking about, the one who was acting weird, took him up there after a while. But—"

"I don't get it," Asher said. "So the second floor is private or not? Who's allowed up there?"

"It isn't private," Bryson cut in. "But few people know about it. Like I said, it's mostly regulars who go up there, usually to get away from the crowd."

Clint continued. "But when that guy came down toward the end of the night, right before last call, that regular wasn't with him. At first, I didn't think anything of it, but after we closed up—well, that's when we found him. Early this morning."

"So, this new guy who went up there with him," Asher said, "what did he look like?"

"It stays pretty dark in there while we're open, but from serving him several times throughout the night, I wanna say he had messy, brownish hair maybe. Lanky build. He was definitely pretentious and a bit . . . over the top, you could say."

"Over the top?"

"Yeah. He was just really outspoken and demanding, sending back drinks and getting impatient later on in the night. Oh—" It was like the bartender suddenly remembered something of value. "This might sound a bit weird, but he had, like, really wide, unblinking eyes. Like he was always running at a hundred, you know? Just really high energy, I guess."

That October ring of piano keys sounded from Asher's pocket. He swiped and answered the call. "Yeah, what's up?" He stepped away from the three of them.

"When can you get down here?" Agnes asked.

"I should be able to head that way soon. Why?"

"Those requests you had on ya girl's ID? Sorry to break it to you, but it turns out those are two miracles that yours truly ain't pulling off, hun."

Asher dropped the phone to his side.

Everything around closed in on him, and the city streets suddenly felt like a dream. He was there, standing outside the bar below the balcony, sidestepping the puddles and what trash remained scattered at the curb from another French Quarter night—but he didn't *feel* there. He felt nothing, other than an impending sense of indifference enveloping him.

This was no place for indifference, though. Not now.

He lifted the phone. "I'll be there." Then he slid it back into his pocket and turned to the men.

"Sorry about that." Asher held out his card to the bartender. "Get in touch, yeah?"

Pierre pulled the cigar from his lips. "Where the hell are you going?"

"Loose ends, Chief." Asher turned and walked away. Straight into the two of them, lying in wait behind the van.

Chapter 11

Both of the women shoved their tape recorders in his face.

"Detective Huxley, what can you tell us about the recent homicide?" one of the journalists asked.

It threw him off; not only had they come out of nowhere, but the lazy eye of the lady speaking made it seem like she was addressing someone else entirely.

"Look, we've only been on the scene for a couple hours. There really isn't much that I can—"

"No," said the other one, "the body out by the river." She wobbled closer. "What can you tell us? Is that the detective who went missing after your department—"

"Hold up," Asher said. "As of now, nothing has changed with that case since our department released our report on the shooting. Now, we've recovered a—"

The first one started in again. "So you're not willing to inform the public on who was found out at the Love Wins pier? Is that what you're saying?"

Aside from media flocking to the pier when they'd found the body, this was his first run-in with a news crew regarding Cassandra's remains. The previous two weeks had been nothing but coverage on the shooting itself and where his wounded ex-partner had run off to. And now, the fact that they were already putting words in his mouth gave him the uneasy feeling that this was the first media ambush of many.

"No, I'm not saying that at all. Our department has already released a statement that one of our detectives—"

"Your partner. Is that correct?" the second one said.

"My *former* partner, who we suspect of foul play, was shot and evaded our pursuit after a hostage situation involving myself, one of our forensics experts, and two victims."

"Sure," the second lady continued, "but is it her? Is it your partner who y'all found out at the river?"

"As of now, we haven't confirmed an ID, so the city should continue to follow our guidance on the matter: this is a highly dangerous and trained officer who is armed and may or may not still be out there. The public should continue to remain alert and operate under the assumption that this person *is*, in fact, alive and still within the city of New Orleans."

Asher stepped forward in an effort to move past them. "Our department will release any further details regarding motive and the shooting itself pending an official inquiry, as soon as we—"

"Do you agree that your department should be investigated for this?" Her eye was growing restless. Wandering. "Doesn't someone need to be held accountable?"

And there it was. At the end of the day, all that mattered was the blame. Not a single thought on the well-being of the other parties involved.

"Rest assured," Asher said, "our department is conducting an internal investigation. But just like any other case, we don't release information regarding ongoing investigations. Once we have answers that are supported by evidence, the public will know about it. Now, if you'll excuse me—"

He stepped past them.

"An *internal* investigation?" one of them said to his back. "Really?"

The other added, "Well isn't that convenient."

Chapter 12

sher entered the exam room to find Joe Bonamassa's "Blues Deluxe" crying in the background and Agnes hunched over beneath a dome of white light at the center of the room, elbows deep in what she did best.

"Hey, pretty lady," Asher said as he approached the autopsy table.

"How's it going, hun?"

"Joe B, huh?" He pointed up to the music. "You're tugging at my heart strings, listening to my favorite tunes and all."

"Is that right?" Agnes turned to the work bench behind her, placing what could've only been a heart on the gleaming metal scale there. "You should've stopped by earlier for a little Kenny Wayne, then." She pulled the disposable gloves from her arms.

Asher's stomach turned sour, and he found himself clenching his jaw, shifting and gritting the enamel until a shiver filled the inside of his spine at the sight of the bloodless heart, swinging in the slightest way on the cold and pristine scale.

His bitterness toward his ex-partner was heightened once he recalled that he no longer had his other half to confide in once he would arrive home. The anger huffed at the back of his neck.

"Uh"—Asher grunted in pain—"you're teasing me, woman. When did you become such a blues fanatic?"

"Ever since this stubborn excuse for a detective started bringing me bodies, blabbing about this guitarist and that." She winked and pulled a Marlboro from her trenchlike lab coat. "Can you believe that?"

Then he turned to Cassandra's body on the table. Or at least, that was the prevailing suspicion about the corpse, from everyone who wasn't in Asher's shoes.

"So, how's it going with this one?" he said.

"As expected. I should be done with the autopsy hopefully by the end of the day. So far, it all checks out."

"And the DNA? The dental records? What's going on with those?"

She took a drag and adjusted the volume on the radio. "I reached out to every major dentist in Greater New Orleans, not to mention several outside the city, too. But there are no records."

"Maybe I can ask Pierre if she was required to—"

"I already did, and she wasn't. As you know, Homicide originally hired her as an outside contractor, so she wasn't required to provide dental records, prints, nothing. Unfortunately, it looks like that took a back seat once she was officially brought on as detective."

"Well, isn't that convenient."

"Ain't it?"

"And the DNA profile? I know that usually takes a while, so why the shit news so quickly?"

Asher studied the remains and the extent to which the elements had taken a toll. No one, himself included, could ID her just standing there, but when Agnes wrapped it all together in a tight little bow, what was circumstantial turned compelling piece by piece.

Then again, no one other than Asher had felt the barrel of her pistol beneath their chin. He simply wasn't sold just yet.

"I tried, hun. Between that Mississippi water, the heat, and whatever was feeding on the woman for more than a week, the PCR is complete garbage. Every sample turned out to be trash. The bacteria and fungi in particular contaminated the tissue that was already fragmenting from the environmental stressors."

"English, Agnes. Please."

"Oh, yeah. Right." She translated to herself, then shared the thought aloud. "I can't create more copies of the DNA to analyze because it was broken into smaller pieces by the harsh conditions she was in, and those pieces are contaminated with DNA that isn't hers."

"See? Isn't that an easier language?"

She rolled her eyes with a lopsided smirk and balanced the cigarette on the edge of the ashtray. "Hey," she said softly, sitting on the desk and leaning forward, "what's going on? You're not getting all twisted up over this because of who it is, are you? You should know better than anyone, that's a bad idea that leads to something even worse."

"And what's that?"

"Letting your emotions get in the way of the facts."

"My emotions are founded on facts. I was there, Agnes. Can anyone else say the same?"

She looked past him, to the body and the gunshot wound on its chest. "Xavier?"

Thanks to Xavier, Asher was still walking. But no one felt cheated the way Asher did. No one else had been forced to watch the murder of their spouse as a direct result of their own ignorance. No, that one was on him.

"So what's the next move?" he asked.

"Easy. I wrap the autopsy and write up the certificate of death. The manner of death will be homicide, and the cause of death is injury from the gunshot wound. Blood loss plus respiratory failure from the pneumothorax."

His uncertainty surrounding her language returned, and it must've shown on his face.

"A collapsed lung, Asher."

He nodded. "Gotcha."

Asher considered sharing his side of things with Agnes, but the more he thought about it, the more he realized that it wouldn't make a difference either way. After all, he didn't actually *see* Cassandra at Café Du Monde that day.

If she was still out there, her supposed "message" at the café wouldn't help the investigation either way. So why say anything? If she was dead, then it mattered even less.

"How much you love me, girl?"

It wasn't the first time he had pulled a favor out of her, and they both knew that it wouldn't be the last.

"Come on. What is it?"

"I need this ID. Please tell me there's something else you can try. Anything."

She grabbed the cigarette and again set flame to it. She took her time, smoking, looking, seemingly thinking on it every which way she could. Then she walked to the exam table. Her eyes traced the corpse from left to right, every inch, as if she were walking through the autopsy in her head.

"Okay," she said. "I think I have an idea."

"Yeah?"

"But it's the last one." Her back remained turned to him.

"Come back in the morning, sometime after ten; I'd like to have it done before you get here."

She had never come off this reluctant before. This hurried. Whatever it was, it seemed wise to leave it be.

"It's a long shot at best."

"Alright," he said, and turned to the door. "Thanks, Agnes. I appreciate it."

The wintry chill followed him from the morgue and out of the building once more.

<h1 style="text-align:center">Chapter 13</h1>

No sooner did the door click shut behind him than Pierre stepped out of his office. "Get in here," he called to Asher from across the precinct floor.

It was deep into the evening, and the building was all but empty. No phones ringing off the hook, no chatter of computer keys and printers, no heels echoing on the cold tile floors. No Xavier.

Definitely no Cass.

Asher walked into the chief's office and shut the door.

"Take a seat," Pierre said.

The room simmered with smoke and the raw, obscured scent of double barrel whiskey.

"Drink?" the chief asked. He walked to the corner and poured one on ice.

"No, I'm good. What's up?"

Pierre returned to his desk and the walloping leather chair behind it. "I just got off the phone with Agnes, and it's time to close out the search, Asher. Everything we've got points to the fact that it's her." He grabbed a cigar while inching the rocks glass back and forth in its own sweat. Fidgeting.

"To be honest, I'm not so sure. What are you basing this

on, anyways? Don't you think we should be more certain about it before we move forward?"

Asher shifted in his chair and let the smoke envelop him; there were just too many what-ifs floating around for him to get comfortable.

"What if it isn't her?" he continued. "What if she's still out there, and we say that she isn't? And someone else gets hurt? What then? The public isn't gonna—"

"Woah, woah, woah. Calm down there, Energizer. What I'm basing this on is everything that Agnes found in her examination. The age and sex match, where the decedent was shot, the piercing. Fuck—the goddamn *ID* in her back pocket. You're telling me that none of that's good enough for—"

"Oh, come on. If this was any other case, you'd be so far up my ass about circumstantial evidence I'd taste the tobacco." He rose and leaned against the wall. "Tell me I'm lying, Chief."

"Then what do you suggest, Asher? The woman was in the river for nearly two weeks. According to Agnes, there's only so much she can get from a body that's that far gone. What do you want?"

"DNA, prints, dental records. Something. Hell, *anything*."

"She just told me that there are no dental records, and we definitely don't have any on file here, and the DNA is shit. And prints? What prints? There's hardly anything left to get prints *from*."

Asher bit his tongue to keep from saying what was so close to slipping out. From uttering the one thing that undoubtedly no one would buy. Not from him. Not now.

Pierre continued, "So, what's left? What else are you wanting to do, then?"

"I'm heading back to the coroner's office in the morning to

see Agnes. She isn't quite done with the autopsy, so there's one more thing she's gonna try that might help out with the ID. I just wanna make sure that we're on the same page, here: if we close this thing out, and we're wrong—" He chuckled to himself.

"Then what do you recommend?"

"I don't know—a deeper dive into the autopsy? An outside opinion with another examiner?"

"You alright, Detective?"

Oh, come on. Him, too?

"Do what?" Asher said.

"Are you okay? You think maybe you need a few more days to—"

"No. I don't. And I'm tired of every conversation being about me needing more time. Didn't you tell me to come back whenever I was ready? And that you thought I wouldn't be out for long?"

"Hey"—Pierre bit down on the roll of baccy—"it's just a question. No need to get all twisted up over a fucking question. But I will say, if you're okay with being back in the field, and you're really doing as well as you say, then you should have no problem with taking on a new partner."

"Oh, hell no. Not now, Chief."

"Yes, now. Now is as good a time as any. Not to mention, it's department policy." He dropped a heap of papers onto the desk, what looked like the guidelines and procedures manual for department detectives. "Plus, don't you have another case you should be working right now? As horrible as it is, Asher—and please don't take this the wrong way—what happened with Cassandra isn't the only thing going on around here."

Asher turned and yanked open the door to leave.

"Asher." Pierre cut short his exit, dropping the cigar in the near-empty glass of whiskey. "I know you're an obsessed and stubborn little shit, so you'll probably ignore what I'm about to say, but I'm gonna say it anyway: take care of yourself for once, will you?"

As much as he appreciated Pierre's concern, it was a slap in the face. Intentional or not. After a brief pause, the detective stormed out of his boss's office, perhaps shutting the door with more force than he intended.

Chapter 14

You—

Your feet met the crosswalk at North Rampart and Kerlerec. Vapor remnants of a dying rain floated from the blacktop as if the streets themselves were burning in the morning blur.

A horn and the cry of brakes sounded from beside you, growing closer until tires screamed and a man shouted in passing. "Get the fuck out of the road, asshole!"

You kept walking—toward the man sitting against the fire hydrant across the way. The vehicle sped around you. The person shouted once more. You didn't mind, though; that man on the other side of the road needed you.

As you approached the guy, his likeness to your father was chilling. The ragged beard, his hardened and wrinkled hands, the oversized coat. But luckily, it wasn't him.

Besides, what would you have said if it was him, sitting there alone?

You turned the corner, and the Banksy Umbrella Girl took you aback, painted on the white cinderblock wall in black aerosol, across from the man who seemed like he had nowhere to go. Nowhere else to be. Her hand stretched outward from beneath the shadowy umbrella, feeling the dry air as rain descended from inside the cover of her stormy canopy.

It touched you, how such a simple reminder of that tempest could evoke so much emotion—just as the miasma of the man's sordid skin wafted your way.

You turned toward him and greeted him with a helping tone. "How's it going, my friend?" From what you could gather, he was in dire need of a hand.

"Oh, it's going," said the old man. "It's going."

You leaned against the telephone pole, rotting and stapled with sodden papers of those gone missing, positioned next to the hydrant. "Ryker." And you held out your hand in greeting.

"What can I do for you, Ryker?"

As if the man was in any position to help another. No, he needed you—more than he could possibly know.

"What can you do for *me*?" you said. "Oh, no. I'm good, my friend. I just noticed you from across the street is all. Is there anything I can get you? Anything that I can do to help you out? I apologize if I'm overstepping my bounds."

"Not at all," the man said. "I like the suit."

The wind caught your tie as you pinched loose the top button of your sports coat.

He gave you a compliment after standing there for a matter of seconds. You could already tell—he was an exceptional class of people. And this old man deserved better.

So far, he had yet to utter a single excuse for why he was here, camped out on the sidewalk. Your father was well-versed in excuses. "The city is for dreamers like us," he used to say. "Where we happen to sleep is nothing more than a location, son." But you called bullshit on that one, in retrospect. Now that you were older and in possession of a permanent address.

"When is the last time you ate something?" you said. "A hot meal."

"A *hot* meal? Oh, two or three days ago, maybe? That kind of thing is in short supply for people like me. You know?"

"I see." You removed the gold-plated money clip from the inside of your jacket and slid a ten from the fold of fifties. "Here. I ain't got much, but this way, you can at least grab something to eat."

"Aw, man. Thank you so much." He snatched the bill with a magician's pace. "I don't know what to say."

"You stick around here most of the time?"

"Not always," the man said. "I'm actually over by the Square more often than not, doing my best to scrounge up a coffee or a bite to eat."

"A coffee, huh?"

"Gotta keep moving somehow. Speaking of, there's a really good coffee shop over there behind, uh . . . man, what's it called? Oh, yeah—behind Café Beignet, on Exchange Place. A shop called Jean Lafitte Trading Company."

"Is that right?"

"Oh, yeah. I'm over that way more evenings than not," he said. "Best coffee around, in my opinion." He held up the bill between the two of you. "Speaking of . . ."

You laughed to yourself. "Well, I know where *someone* is gonna be headed soon."

"You bet ya."

"Take care, my friend."

"Yes, sir." And with that, the old man leaned back against the silver-and-blue hydrant.

The money didn't matter, though. Hell, the pleasantries were a means to an end. All that mattered was that now he felt comfortable with you—and you knew exactly where to find him.

Chapter 15

Asher pulled the knob on the machine, then grabbed the pack of Lucky Strikes once it tumbled into the opening at the bottom. As he came up, he noticed a figure start up the stairs, looking over their shoulder—paranoid, just like the bartender had said.

Now was his chance to make something happen. To put a stop to what was about to occur yet again, before another victim was lured to the second-floor balcony.

He pulled the string of plastic from around the pack of smokes, placed one of the cigarettes between his lips, and lit it as he walked up the stairs, swaddled by the dark inside of the grimy hallway. The corridor was set alight by the jumping flames at his mouth's edge.

The figure paused at the top of the stairs, but all Asher could make out was a silhouette that appeared to turn toward him, before walking into a room there.

He climbed the stairs one sticky tread at a time. The smell of tobacco lessened the stench of yellowed urinal that filled the space around him.

Should he have waited for backup? Cass wasn't going to make it there for some time. Xavier, too. Where were those two at, anyway?

He reached the top of the stairs, alone and hesitant, then stepped to the side of the doorway, where he was out of view from whoever was in there. He heard two voices going back and forth in a playful way. Almost amorous, by his ear. Then they grew louder, seemingly struggling and at each other's throats.

Asher pulled the 1911 from the four-o'clock position of his back and flicked his cigarette into the dark of the stairwell. His thumb clicked off the safety on the side of the pistol. He turned the corner and stepped into the room, only to see one person standing next to the bed; no one else was there.

A silver badge reflected from their waist in what little light danced inside of the room.

"Don't move," Asher said.

He couldn't see them. At least, not clearly. They stepped forward.

"Don't," Asher repeated.

Just then, he heard Xavier at the door. "Behind you," his friend said as a heads-up.

"Where's she at?" Asher said.

"Who?"

"Cass, man. Who else? I need someone at the first-floor exit."

"Who?" Xavier said again. "What are you talking about?"

Asher turned around to see Xavier standing in the doorway with his gun drawn, soaking wet from the rain.

"I *said*, where is—"

"Asher—" Xavier shouted. Asher turned back to find the figure lunging toward him with arms outstretched. A pair of massive, freezing hands gripped his throat, and he fell backward against the wall. The face before him was blank and blurry.

Then he felt the barrel shoved beneath his chin, cold and

smelling of charred sulfur and smoke. Before he could react, before Xavier had a chance to pull the trigger and stop it, the brief but deafening gunshot exploded.

In a fraction of a second, the pressure filled his head, and a wave of pain escaped through the top of his skull. Unmoving, somehow, he felt the pieces fall over him, covering his lifeless body in a mess of his former self.

He shot up in bed, struggling to breathe, gasping for that ounce of air that was nowhere to be found.

It was just the sweat—and an all-too-real dream.

Chapter 16

What could Agnes have been doing with the autopsy that she wanted to "have it done" before Asher got there? And why was everyone so concerned with the amount of time he'd taken off work, with how he felt about his partner's death after what she'd done to him, not to mention their worry with Asher seeing her body this way or that?

Cassandra had been his colleague—not his wife.

Asher walked into the exam room. As it turned out, Agnes wasn't finished with her assessment like she had hoped she would be. The feel of the room had shifted. He couldn't place it, but the space had become more solemn, lifeless. More so than usual, even.

Once he greeted Agnes, who was hunched over the exam table, ostensibly unaware of the fact that he had entered the room, he began to realize why the air was so stale. So palpable.

It was her task at hand.

Hesitant to break the quiet, he spoke lightly. "Hey, pretty lady."

She remained focused, her attention on the half-degraded limb in front of her, next to an ink pad and fingerprint card on a rolling metal tray. "There he is." She spoke flatly. "Sorry I'm not done with this, hun; it's proving to be more of a struggle than I had anticipated."

"No problem." He stepped back and sat on a stool in view of the mangled palm and associated digits. "As far as you're concerned, I'm not even here."

Her focus remained unbroken.

Asher, too, took an interest in what she was doing, but a minute passed before he realized that she was attempting to pull prints from the disheveled and sloughing skin of his former partner's fingers. Digits that were, perhaps, too far gone for what looked to be a delicate and nerve-wracking task.

But the difficult tasks were Agnes's specialty, and Asher knew that if pulling a single print was in any way possible, she'd at least give it a shot. He still didn't understand her desire to finish before he arrived, though. What? Was he supposed to break down and flood with emotion because of who it was? Over someone who attempted to murder both him and his wife after the long-con of an entire homicide department?

Hell no. Cassandra was likely dead.

Asher only wished that, somehow, she could be forced to watch every second of the painstaking autopsy—*if* it was her.

After a few more minutes, he realized Agnes was taking much more than a simple print, though. "What are you doing, exactly?"

Only then did she glance up and cut a smirk. "You're 'not even here,' yeah?"

"Whatever the hell you're doing, I can't stop watching."

After circling a small incision around the end knuckle of the woman's index finger, Agnes gradually, precisely, pulled a fine layer of skin from the fingertip, like a translucent thimble—and placed it over the tip of her own finger inside a blue latex glove.

"The official term is degloving, hun. But for you? I'm slipping the skin of her fingertip over my own so I can apply enough pressure to pull a print."

"Degloving? Is that really what it's called?"

"Technically? We've always called it epidermal gloving. Personally, I like to call it the pain-in-the-ass method of printing."

"Well that I can understand. It's a touch morbid—"

"But you can't turn away."

"Exactly."

Once the skin rested over the tip of her finger, she gently rolled it onto the sponge of black ink, then transferred the print to a card. At least, what was left of it.

Asher moved closer and squinted in displeasure.

"Really?" he said. "That's it?"

It was a poor excuse for a print, but it wasn't Agnes's fault. The woman was out here covering herself with someone else's skin. She was trying, but the end result left him no less disappointed.

"Yep. That's it," she said. "I was only able to pull two, and both of them are partials. You're free to run 'em, but I don't see either of them being enough for an ID, hun." She eased the skin from the tip of her finger and placed it inside of a tiny evidence bag. "I'm sorry."

"So, what now?" he said, expecting she would offer up at least one additional idea to obtain a more trustworthy ID.

"Now, it's time for me to focus on the case you *haven't* solved." She gestured to mortuary cabinet A2, which presumably held the body of the latest victim, strangled above the bar. "And maybe, just maybe"—she pulled the exam gloves from her hands and dropped them into the hazardous waste—

"it's time for you to do the same."

She turned on the faucet with her elbow and began scrubbing. Asher sat back on the stool, staring at the hand with the naked fingertip, choking on what he wanted to say but couldn't.

Or could he?

Chapter 17

The precinct was as unforgivingly frigid as any other day when Asher walked through the door. The accumulation of unfiltered grime and what appeared to be some sort of black growth clung to the rusted air vent above him. Dripping.

He would never have confessed it to himself, much less anyone else, but this place could be toxic in more ways than one. It was all he had left, though. His lifeline to a sense of purpose. Asher knew how bad it was for him at times, but he justified the line of work in his head: providing closure to families and their loved ones, solving puzzles that refused to fade with the daylight, keeping himself busy and out of trouble.

Revenge for Sofia.

Xavier waved Asher over to his desk in the middle of the floor. Why Xavier—lead of the entire forensics team—had never had his own office was beyond Asher. He felt bad for the guy.

Xavier didn't seem to care, though; over the years, Asher had realized that his friend was in it for the work, for the enigmas and challenges. Much like Asher himself.

He walked to his friend's desk and dropped his briefcase to the floor. "How's it hangin'?" he asked, then took a seat.

"Better than ever," Xavier said.

"Any progress? I could use some good news right about now."

Xavier opened a manilla folder to a working profile of their latest decedent. "Good. I got you covered, then. We've got an ID on our guy from the bar. Name is Cameron Spencer, but he goes by Cam."

"Cam? How'd you come across that tidbit of information?"

Xavier opened a desk drawer and removed an evidence bag, holding the pen that Asher had found under the bed at the scene. He slid it over. "Get this," he said. "I called The Walking Murder Tours Company and spoke to one of the managers. The business? It's owned by none other than—" Xavier gestured, waiting for Asher to finish the thought for him.

"Well," Asher said, "it's owned by Cam Spencer, of course."

"Bingo."

"Okay, so what does that tell us about the murder?"

"Not much, unfortunately. If anything, I think you should head on over to their office and talk with anyone and everyone who's willing to speak with you. There's a reason that pen was there. The obvious? It was our victim's. On the other hand—"

"It could belong to the one person we're looking for."

"Exactly."

"Alright. I'll be sure to give 'em a visit. What about prints?"

Xavier shook his head. "No, there's none on the pen. The only way the pen is gonna help us is if we confirm exactly whose it is. And I say we start with the obvious."

"Sounds like a plan."

"What I'm really interested in, though, is why the decedent was posed. And what's up with the cuffs?"

"Same," Asher said.

"What are you thinking? Control?"

"Possibly. If he was looking for some sort of command over the victim, the question becomes who and why. Who is the victim to him in particular, and what's the MO?"

"Humiliation? We haven't seen this type of display before. Not in public."

"No," Asher said. "This was more personal than that. This was well thought out and premeditated, down to a T."

"And you know that because?"

"I don't *know* anything, but there are plenty of ways to humiliate someone *before* they're dead. Are there not? There's too many pieces to this one: the strangulation, the cuffs, the balcony, the position of the body. Hell, the flawless room with no signs of a struggle."

"Well, if that's true . . ."

They eyed one another in a suggestive and this-isn't-good sort of way. "Then this is just the start."

They continued to obsess over the pen in silence, before Xavier pulled another evidence bag toward them. This one held the handcuffs.

"What about those?" Asher asked. "Any prints? DNA?"

"No. Nothing other than some hair from the decedent himself."

"Well, shit."

"Yeah, tell me about it."

Again, Asher grabbed the bag that contained the pen. "There's something more to it, though."

The pristine room, the pen at the edge of the bed with nothing else out of place—a pen that linked the decedent to his own company. When it came to his puzzles, Asher was more than doubtful of coincidences. Happenstance was usually nothing more than a suggestion to look closer. More times than not, it all came down to how far he was willing to dig.

"What are you thinking?" Xavier said.

"Well, it's either one big fuckup by whoever did this, or it's an even bigger waste of our time. I think you're right, though—either way, it's time for an in-person visit."

He tossed the pen next to the cuffs. "This doesn't feel like a one-off, though. I can tell you that."

"I agree," said Xavier. "Now, if only we had a psychologist to point us in the right—"

"No," Asher said, "fuck the psychology." He stood up and pointed to the folder. "Can I get a copy of that?"

"Of course."

Deep down, Asher knew that his friend had never meant to thump the nerve that was already pinched. The one that kept him writhing in pain and endlessly conscious, night after night. Not intentionally, he didn't. And Asher didn't mean what he had said, either. The psychology and profiling were important, but it was still all too fresh. He didn't want to dwell on it, much less wish Cassandra were there.

He didn't need her. Certainly not now. Never, as it turned out.

"I can't put my finger on it," Asher said. "But I have a feeling—it's the pen. There's a reason we found it where we did."

"Oh, I know. Like you always say . . ."

"No matter how slick—"

"They all leave something behind."

Just as Asher turned away, a crash sounded from Pierre's office, and the chief shouted something incoherent.

Chapter 18

Before knocking, Asher stood outside of Pierre's office in silence, listening to the chaos from inside and debating whether he should just let it be.

So naturally, he knocked.

"What the hell is it now?" Asher heard the man grumble from within, this and that crashing around in the midst of what could only be bad news. "Well come on in, I guess." Pierre's tirades were expected from time to time, but this was a new level of pissy with which Asher was unfamiliar. That made him curious.

He opened the door to find his boss pacing about in the middle of the room, the desk phone on the floor against the wall, off the hook and broken. The ground was powdered by an upended tray of ashes. A fine, gray dust lingered in the air.

"What is it?" the chief said with a deep grit in his voice.

Asher remained in the doorway, just in case he needed a quick exit from whatever this was. "Nothing. I'm just checking in on ya, that's all. You good?"

Pierre removed his peacoat and tossed it onto the desk, where it then slid to the floor. "No, Asher, I'm not 'good.'" He loosened his tie and rolled his sleeves to his elbows.

"Anything I can do?"

"I just got an email from Internal Affairs—saying that I'm under investigation as a responsible party for the whole Cassandra debacle. Look." He turned his monitor to Asher. "Can you believe this shit?"

Asher leaned over and read the brief but direct letter. Sure enough, they were not only looking into the chief's history but the workings of the entire department over the past ten years. The hiring, the firing, the ratio of cases opened to those closed, what cases had gone unsolved and why. The message was short and sweet: *we're looking into your whole operation, so get comfortable.*

Pure torture of the unknown.

"Well, that's nice," Asher said. "Looks like we're finally getting recognized for our work."

Apparently, his boss didn't appreciate the quip. "Oh, shut the hell up. You know what this means, right? What this says for the whole department? We're *all* under the microscope, now. Like little fucking ants, frying under one of those—" He waved his hands, grasping at the thought as it escaped him.

"Magnifying glasses?"

"There you go. You know what the hell I'm talking about. And it'll be all of us, Asher. Everything we do and everything we've done. And you know what?"

Asher did not, in fact.

Pierre prodded an index finger in his direction, but not exactly at him. "It means that you're probably next—that's what."

"Next? What the hell would they be looking at me for? What do you mean 'next'?"

The chief paused and began laughing in a genuinely amused way, like a toddler finding that hidden spot behind his parent's knee. "Really, Asher? Why would they look at you? Shit, you were the woman's partner, dickhead. As far as they're concerned, both of us are probably negligent in whatever conspiracy they have cooked up their heads. Who knows?"

"So, what do you propose we do? I mean, they can look at me all they want; there's nothing there. Not for me, and I'm pretty sure not for you either. However she did it, it's not like we were wise on something everyone else was blind to."

But did Asher believe what he was saying? Or was he attempting to console himself in the absence of good reason for what had happened? Negligent or not, he wasn't ready to entertain the idea of being on the other side of his work. Not in any manner.

Are they not aware that I'm grieving my wife, for fuck's sake?

He was getting ahead of himself, though. Like Justin had always said, time and time again—focus on what you *can* control.

The attention from Internal Affairs, thus far, was Pierre's and Pierre's alone. But the idea of a formal inquiry sat at the back of his throat, choking his ability to swallow, just like those cold hands in his dream, right before his head painted the wall behind him.

"That's beside the point," the chief said. "There's always a running tab—and someone's gotta pay."

The room transformed into a silver screen. Asher was nothing more than a viewer, watching his career from a distance as it grew more uncertain by the day.

Chapter 19

Asher ran by the biology office first to let them know that he was there to collect Sofia's belongings. Due to the circumstances surrounding her passing, his wife's office had been locked and posted as off-limits to anyone and everyone on campus.

Leading up to this, he hadn't been able to work up the nerve to visit, not even to glance inside the room from the hallway. It was too much, too fast—and he needed time. Now, he felt time was working against him. The body out by the river was probably Cassandra, Internal Affairs was snooping around the department looking for who knew what, and the chief had assigned him the new case above the bar.

Asher's ability to escape it all was fleeting, but even so, he needed a stint here and there to himself and away from the hustle—though the hustle was precisely what kept his mind straight. Still, he needed space and a moment to breathe, to escape whatever daydream he was wading in and out of. Time to think.

And that meant cutting his losses, both the bad and the ugly. Although, he knew that walking away, and moving on from what had happened, would in no sense be a simple task.

As he reached Sofia's office on the third floor of the science building, he found the red notice still taped to the door. He'd written and placed it there himself not long ago. He pulled the gold key from his pocket, unlocked the heavy wooden door, and walked inside.

From what he could tell, the office was precisely the way his wife had left it. It even smelled like her: the raw and smooth air of shaved coconut, mixed with the subtlety of rich hibiscus.

The phantom caress of her blond hair dragged against his throat and the divot there, and down his chest and stomach.

Even her chair was in place, just where she had left it, with its faded and torn arm stuck beneath the edge of her corner desk. He dared not move it.

There wasn't much to collect, aside from a few personal effects about her desk and the diplomas and pictures of her working off of the West Coast that hung on the wall. He picked up a cardboard box from the floor, removed the papers from inside, then set it on the table. As he did, his eye was drawn not to the monitor, littered with curling multicolored notes and reminders in pencil, black ink, and everything in between—but to the flowers beside it.

A flask, wide at the bottom and tapered to the top with measurements in fifty-milliliter increments, was dry now. Remnants of a waterline lingered just below the leaves. Many of them were dried and had fallen to the desk and floor, along with the withered petals.

A lone stem and flower rested next to the keyboard, broken from the bouquet and as dead as the rest.

Sofia hadn't liked daisies.

The thought of his wife, and her willingness to go astray, cut deeper than any murder or other wrongdoing could reach on their own. The affair brought with it a sort of sorrow that Asher suspected—or if he was being honest, a sorrow he *knew*—would never fade. Not really. Although, that was precisely the advice everyone around him had put in his ear: get over it and move on. Xavier, Justin, the chief. Somehow, someway, he was expected to just push past it. At least, that was the crux of it, in so many of their seemingly well-intentioned words.

It wasn't anger, though. Asher could never be angry at what Sofia had done. Not when her wandering was likely, in part, his own doing to some extent. No. It was more disappointment than anything else. A sense of failure on his part. And that heaviness—he dragged it behind him and, perhaps, he even deserved it.

Asher grabbed the bouquet of once-living daisies and pulled them from the flask, their parts falling to his feet, crumbling and not floating to the ground as perhaps they once had. Then he dropped the frail and cracking stems into the trash.

The flowers reminded him of his wife—dead, just like her fictitious lover, Damien. The same man who'd murdered her. Cassandra's husband, as Asher thought of him.

He was the last man Asher had shot and killed.

The only man.

Chapter 20

It was the morning of his two-day follow-up, just as Justin had recommended.

Asher walked inside of the household business to an empty foyer. The therapist's door was closed, as it was most days when he arrived, although he heard no one from inside of the office itself. Instead, far-off voices echoed through the door across the room, which led to the kitchen and private portion of the house. Voices that Asher suspected were Justin and his wife.

He pulled a coffee cup from the table there and dropped a pod into the machine.

"He needs somewhere to stay, Justin. Of all people, you're not gonna let Billy—"

Crashing dishes, or maybe silverware, interrupted her.

"And why is that on me?" Justin said with a sharpness to his voice. "I didn't make him . . ." Then Justin's voice faded until Asher could no longer discern the words.

Asher lowered the handle and pushed the flashing blue button on the morning miracle machine. It warmed to a low grumble, and a ghostly steam hissed from just above the mug.

Sounds like maybe Justin is in need of a session or two himself. He slid the aviators to the top of his head and widened his stance, lingering over his morning brew, taking in the notes of his addiction without any sense of shame or reluctance. *Or maybe it's just the sound of marriage awakening in the early-morning hours. Yeah . . . that's it. It's nothing more than the sound of holy matrimony at work—*

Another crash filled the air. *Or shit, maybe that was just my own marriage—thanks to me.*

"It isn't on you," the woman continued at hardly a mutter, "but he's family. And family doesn't—"

"Oh, it's you again." The voice crept up from behind the detective.

Asher turned around to that same young man standing in the doorway of Justin's office, leaning against the wall with his hands fiddling in his pockets.

"How's it going?" the kid asked.

"Oh, hey," Asher said. "How's it going?"

He stepped forward and held out his hand, leaning in but without expression. "I'm Waylon," he said. Then he lifted his chin to the kitchen door. "Justin's nephew." They shook hands, and Waylon bobbed his head from side to side like one of those channel markers in the Mississippi. "Well, his nephew-*in-law*, actually."

"Gotcha," Asher said.

"Sorry if I startled you."

Although it was expressionless, there was an oddity about the guy's face. Somewhat of an unconscious habit, or an anxiousness in it. A nervous tick, perchance?

Repeatedly, Waylon batted his eyes in a seemingly endless and frantic rhythm, one with no apparent rhyme, reason, or regularity to it. He blinked hastily, then slow, with force, as if something unknown was clawing at the back of his eyes in the most anguished and desperate of ways. And in between the flashes, Asher caught a slight roll of those hooded black-and-white spheres—all of it unintentional, by the look of it. Nonetheless, it was plain as day, whatever it was.

Waylon's attention wandered as if he hoped Asher wouldn't address the obvious, much less notice it.

"No worries," Asher said. He turned back to the table and pulled his coffee from the drip tray. "You work here?"

It was the only logical question; Waylon was in Justin's office, after all.

"Something like that," Waylon said. "A little cleaning, a little organizing. Just putting together some odds and ends here and there, you know?"

"Gotcha," Asher said. He took his coffee black—now that his world, turned upside down and shaken empty, was much the same. He turned back, and Waylon's attention found his badge, as almost everyone did at first meeting him.

"So, you're a cop, huh? I think I noticed that the other day. Sorry I didn't introduce myself; I was having a bit of a rough one."

"NOPD, yeah."

"That's cool. I almost joined the academy myself, but then I changed my mind once I realized how nerve-racking of a career it is. I guess that depends on what you end up doing, though."

Asher sipped his coffee. Then, without really thinking about it, short of considering the fact that he was there for his appointment and going to remain indoors for the next hour or more, he slipped the aviators back down over his heavy eyes. The other man's blinking messed with his own sense of calm— if there was such a thing these days.

"True," he said in response. "That's what the coffee's for." He lifted the mug.

Waylon pointed with an I-see-what-ya-did-there in Asher's direction. "That's a good one."

The kitchen door squeaked open from across the room.

"Hey, Asher," Justin said. "You got you a fresh cup? You ready to go?"

Asher lifted the coffee yet again. "I'm all ready."

"It's about time the two of you meet," Justin said. "Waylon's helping me out around the office part time, so I figured y'all would run into each other eventually."

"Nice to meet you," Waylon said. Then he walked out through the kitchen door.

"Yeah. You, too," Asher said.

"Come on." Justin gestured to his office, and they made their way inside.

Chapter 21

"Finally got you some help around the office, huh?" Asher sat on the sofa, Justin in the chair across from him per usual.

His therapist kept his mouth shut, as if Asher hadn't said a word. Ignoring him? Or maybe his mind was elsewhere?

Asher found it all too interesting: Justin's nephew-in-law was working for him part time, even though he ran such a small, private practice, out of his home. What could he possibly need help with?

"So, Waylon's your nephew?" Asher knew good and well Justin had likely heard him the first time. Putting two and two together—the new help that probably wasn't needed but was more of a favor, combined with the marital tension surrounding some family issue of sorts—stress was the most likely culprit for the ensuing quiet on Justin's part.

That was one thing Asher had come to recognize from a mile out: the strain in others was painted in their faces and busied, toying hands. He saw it in others because he had grown to see it in himself.

"Come again?" Justin said.

"Waylon—that's your nephew, yeah? He's helping you out around the office, now?"

"Oh. Yeah. That's Tammy's nephew. Her brother's son. Just giving him a leg up where I can. When the wife suggests that you help out, you tend to do it." Somewhere in his expression, hidden by the effort to remain professional, was a lone percentage point of exasperation. "Family, you know?"

It was nice to see Justin navigating a challenge of his own, even if vaguely from a distance. It broke the screen that Asher had placed between them. One that painted the man without issue, giving advice without proper experience in the trenches.

"So," Justin said. "How's it going? The derealization any better since last time?" And just like that, the man flipped a switch.

"Since last time? Two days ago? Not really. I mean, it's nice to have a word for it now, but I can't say anything's changed."

"And the sleep?"

"About the same. Not the greatest."

"Alright." Justin began scribbling. "So, there is something I'd like to try today. Or at least, something I'd like to introduce. It's more of a practice than anything else, so there will only be so much that I can do here in the office. But just like our behavioral therapy, it's what you tend to do when you leave here that's gonna make a difference. Actually, what I wanna discuss was the springboard for cognitive behavioral therapy in a way, which we've already been exploring."

"Alright."

"You ever heard of Stoicism?"

"Not being overly emotional or caught up in your feelings?"

"Well, that's often the modern-day take on it, but what I'm referring to is the formal philosophy of it. Basically, Stoicism with a capital 'S.'"

"Well, in that case—no. Not really."

Justin got up and turned to the turquoise wall of books behind the sliding ladder, beneath the line of backward-pointing, amber lights at the ceiling's edge. He reached up high and pulled a small book from one of the shelves, then walked back to his chair.

He set it on the coffee table between them. "I want you to read this in your spare time."

"Spare time?"

"Yeah, spare time. And yes, you do have spare time."

Asher grabbed it and ran his hand across the matte cover—*Meditations*, by Marcus Aurelius, translated by Martin Hammond.

"We've already touched on it a bit, but I wanna dive a little deeper. You remember our discussion from before, on how it's not what happens to you but how you respond to it that matters?"

The detective crossed his legs and nodded, flipping through the pages with a loose hand, looking but not really noticing the contents.

"In essence, that's Stoicism. And *Meditations* is gonna be your best starting point. It's just as relative today as it was in the second century."

"And how can this help the derealization, or the anxiety?"

Asher was still uncertain about what it was, at its core, that he was facing. It just didn't jibe—the idea that he could better his anxiety and whatever it was that was causing him to slowly loosen his grip on reality, in this fog he waded in and out of at a moment's notice.

Wouldn't thinking about it, getting even more in his own head, worsen it all? What was the "behavior" aspect of it, if it was based in practice? Shouldn't his actions, his habits, be the focus?

Justin continued, "I want you to contrast what you're going through with the idea of pain."

"Pain?" Asher said. "What do you mean the *idea* of pain?"

"What do you think of it? Is pain a negative or a positive thing?"

"Is that a serious question?"

"You tell *me*."

"I think you'd be hard-pressed to find anyone who enjoys pain, or thinks that it's a positive thing."

"Maybe." Justin pointed to the book in Asher's hands. "But according to Marcus, 'Pain and pleasure, wealth and poverty—all these come to good and bad alike, but they are not in themselves either right or wrong: neither then are they good or evil.'"

Right and wrong, sure. But good and evil? According to whom? To what?

Justin continued, "It's how we react to pain; it's what feeling we assign to it, and the value that accompanies that feeling, that's negative."

"And the fog? The random sense of unreal? Like I'm watching but not there?"

"Same thing," Justin said. "It's a feeling. You may not be able to control it, but you *can* control how you think of it. It's neither good nor bad. It simply . . . is. Why would it be anything else?"

"Because it's unpleasant. And it messes with me in a negative way."

"No. You *tell* yourself that it's unpleasant, you place an unpleasant value on it, and you *allow* it to mess with you. Those are entirely different paths of thought."

Asher felt as though he were treading water, swallowing

twenty-foot seas while clenching a pocket knife between his teeth in the salted ocean—and Justin was suggesting he find shelter.

Justin looked to the tiger eye bracelet and leather, brown-banded watch on the detective's wrist. "I like the bracelet."

"Thanks."

"I want you to give this a try, Asher. The next time you're in that fog, lost in whatever it is that's unreal, like you're in some foreign dream—move your fingers over that bracelet. Recenter yourself with what *is* real. How they feel, their color, their shape, how many there are. Bring yourself back to what you know to be true—and discard the rest. Do it consciously. As an active choice, that is."

Asher pinched the bracelet, pulling it as far back as he could, then let it snap back to his skin. But what did he feel? Pleasure? Pain? . . . Nothing?

"Decide, on purpose, that what you're feeling is neutral. It isn't good, nor is it bad. Period."

When he grabbed the beads again, rolling his fingertips from one sphere to the next, pulling the band taut and counting, the only thing that came to mind was the fact that they were a gift. It mattered not one bit how hard he tried, how much he willed himself in the moment—no amount of decision, neutral or otherwise, would bring back his wife.

And that . . . that, in fact, was pain in its most decisive form.

Chapter 22

The entrance to The Walking Murder Tours Company was a set of peeling, aqua-green French doors at the end of a shoulder-width alley on Royal Street, not far from LaLaurie Mansion. The stucco walls of the passageway were cracked and shedding, beneath which the brown-red masonry bled with a heavy dampness in the sultry shadows of the two flanking buildings.

At the front door, a touristy sign reading "ENTER AT YOUR OWN RISK" hung behind the glass. Asher wondered what it read on the other side, when the place was closed. What was the flipside of entering at your own risk? "LEAVE, OR ELSE"?

As he opened the rickety, pallid door and stepped inside, a windchime of what appeared to be faux human bone clanked and clacked above his head, strung to the door and adjoining wall to alert whoever was working inside.

"Welcome," a thirty-ish woman said in a bland voice from behind the counter. From what Asher could gather, no one else was there. Although, he did hear someone, or something, behind the back wall of the room. "I've been expecting you," she continued.

The comment caught him on his heels.

"I'm sorry?" he said, pausing in front of the counter. She glanced up from whatever she was reading and sipped her tea. Her attention moved over his hip and the badge there.

"NOPD, I'm assuming?"

At least he knew he was in the right place.

"You're here about Cam, yeah?" she added.

"Yes, ma'am."

The woman's appearance was one of a kind, to say the least—her deep ruby hair was held back by a white bandana tied in a bow just above her left eye, a vertical black piercing glistening from the center of her bottom lip. She wore no makeup, and her wife beater was cut about an inch down the center of her chest, hinting at the glowing skin painted between her breasts.

She got to her feet and met Asher in front of the counter. Her pockets reached down past the bottom of her cutoff denim shorts.

"Ambyr-Shae," she said, extending her hand. Asher was by no means abnormally tall, but he towered over her stunted height. "I'm the co-owner, alongside Cameron."

They shook hands. "Detective Huxley."

"So, what can I do for you, Detective?"

"You have a minute?"

"Sure thing."

He pulled the evidence bag from the inside pocket of his leather jacket and handed over the company pen. "You recognize this?"

"Of course," she said. She turned and grabbed a basket from the desk, filled to the brim with the very same pens. "We hand 'em out like candy. They're free to anyone and everyone who stops by. We bring 'em on the tours, too."

Well isn't that a peach. Asher felt the lead slipping from between his fingertips. He should've expected it, though; it was a company pen, after all.

She too seemed to sense how useless the so-called evidence would be. "Sorry."

"No worries," he said. "Tell me, though—did Cameron write with one of these? Did he always carry one around with him when he wasn't here?"

"Actually, no. He was very much a computer guy, always bringing his tablet or laptop with him wherever he went. And if he didn't have those, he was usually typing away on his phone. Very new school, you could say."

There was no way he could prove that it was someone else's from the woman's statement alone, but at least it was something. With no prints, he just needed to figure out who it belonged to, or perhaps where it had come from if it wasn't the owner's or any one person's in particular.

Good thing the pens weren't scattered throughout the city like fleur-de-lis.

Great.

"Gotcha," Asher said.

"Is there anything else that y'all were able to figure out about what happened? Or do you at least know how he died?" The woman came off as if very little, if anything, truly affected her.

He slid the evidence back into his jacket. "Based on what we have so far, he was strangled, but we're still waiting on the autopsy. And you? You notice anything strange leading up to his murder?"

"Not really. I mean, other than the obvious."

"The obvious?"

The woman's face twisted into a telling suggestion, a forewarning of something to which Asher was not yet privy. Her tongue played with the metal ring in her lip. "Well, he was found in a bedroom above that gay bar, right? What was it called?"

"Good Friends Bar."

"Uh-huh." She grabbed a notepad and pencil from behind the counter. Then she wrote a string of numbers. "Well, you might wanna reach out to his wife." She handed over the phone number. "She and the kids would like some answers."

Chapter 23

gnes continued looking down at her writing. "There's my man." She spoke from her chair as a steady line of smoke connected her desk to the ceiling like a pale rope just waiting to be cut. "You miss me?" Her dreads fell across the table.

"Oh, come on," Asher said, "you're all I think about." Apparently that was theatrical enough to get her attention. "So"—he glanced into the adjacent room of freezer boxes and gurneys—"any progress with the new one?"

"Oh, yeah," she said, dropping a folder onto the desk. "I'm all done, as a matter of fact."

He picked up the stack of papers. "You work quick."

"Well, I can slow down if you want."

He appreciated their back-and-forth. Now that his wife and Cass were gone, life presented little room for the banter he so much appreciated. Actually, now that he thought about it, Agnes was the only woman around who took part in it. And then there was Xavier, of course.

Were they really it? Just the two of them?

"Only if you wanna see me fired," he said.

"What? You mean a second time?"

He tried desperately to hold back the smile, then failed with grandeur. "Alright, woman. Give it to me straight. What are we looking at?"

Agnes stepped out from behind her desk and brought him to the next room over, with the cold bodies and even colder steel that held them. She unlatched mortuary cabinet A2 and pulled at the foot of the sliding, polished table. The body jostled as it came to an abrupt stop between the two of them. Then she pulled back the clear layer of plastic that was all but suctioned to the corpse.

"First, there's the obvious," she said, pointing to the decedent's neck. "The deep lacerations alongside bruising and hemorrhaging point to strangulation with some sort of cord."

"Yeah." That was a given.

"Which leads to the petechial hemorrhages in the sclera." She parted the man's eyelids with her thumb and forefinger, revealing the scatter of red dots about the white part of the eye. "Pretty standard stuff."

"You mean, déjà vu type stuff."

"Yeah, no kidding." Agnes gestured to the folder in his hands. "There's also a small amount of pulmonary edema, which isn't entirely unexpected, but it also isn't something we regularly see with asphyxiation, either."

Asher shuffled through the photographs in the folder, which contained images of the lungs and their inflammation and buildup of fluid. "So, what does the edema point to?" The folder also included microscopy images of the pulmonary tissue, stained with that textbook toluidine blue.

"It could be a number of things: trauma, heart failure, medication. There's no evidence for any of those, though. More likely than not, it's the strangulation. But edema alone, in this case, doesn't point to anything definitive."

"And the tox screen?"

"It's clean. Nothing but a little alcohol." She opened a black bag at the foot of the body, then handed Asher a small clear baggie. "Check this out."

He held it up to the light. "What's this?"

"Mistake number one," she said. "Rope fibers."

He looked past the bag and straight into her waiting smile. "You're kidding me."

"Nope."

"Talk about a fuckup on his part . . . You able to tell what they're from? Or what kind of fibers they are?"

"Not yet, but I'll know soon enough."

"Yeah, well, give me a call when you do. These are better than the pen."

"The pen?"

"Yeah. We found a pen at the scene—a company pen that belonged to the decedent, we think. So far, it's a brick wall, though." He shook the bag, struggling to look away from the threads of rope. "But this . . . this is nice."

"What else did y'all find?" Agnes said.

"Not much. A better question is 'what did we *not* find?'"

"Oh?"

Finally, he handed her the baggie, but the potential for what the fibers could mean made him itchy. It wasn't dissimilar to having an ID on the killer—with orders to await further instructions.

"Yeah," he said. "The room where we found him, connected to the balcony, was virtually untouched. We've got nothing, really, other than a pen that was under the edge of the bed. But maybe that's something in and of itself. Maybe there's something we're missing. Something that convinced the victim to go along with it?"

"Maybe," she said. "It wouldn't surprise me. Based on the condition of the body, I don't see any signs of a struggle. There's no superficial defense marks, no bruising other than the neck."

"Well, what do the fibers appear to be, if you had to guess?"

"They look new. Other than that, all I can tell as of yet is that it's not hair. It's far too coarse, and there's no follicle. Straight hair is typically round in cross section. At the most, wavy or curly hair can have more of an oval or flattened shape."

"And the fibers?"

Asher needed this one—to prove to the public, to the cameras and the naysayers, that he was, in fact, fit for the job. That the recent mess was a one-off, and he belonged there in the thick of it.

He needed this one for Sofia. To move forward. To get over it. To let go.

He pinched a single bead of his bracelet. Harder, until that feeling—the pain or something else, whatever negative or positive or neutral emotion he was supposed to assign it— reached the bone in his fingers.

"The fibers have several ridges in cross section. They're almost . . . hexagonal?"

Chapter 24

As he stepped into his office, Asher dropped his briefcase onto the small, borderline antique metal desk. A hollowness rang out over the cold tile of the simplistic room.

He pulled the string on a corner lamp, and the picture of him and Sofia in the Quarter seemed to jump out of nowhere—strolling down Decatur as if their marriage couldn't possibly one day be derailed by Asher's career and her own infidelity. Or maybe it hadn't been the career, just his unhealthy fixation with it. His obsession with the anomalies of his work.

Who could say? Maybe he was just a shitty husband. Period.

He filled the seasoned, miniature coffee pot next to the lamp with water and French Market grounds, flipped the lid shut, then thumbed the button. It was late in the evening, but he was too high strung to just sit around while Agnes was working on the source of those fibers. He needed to dive deeper into the autopsy report.

As he took a seat, Xavier appeared in the doorway. "Hey, hey. I didn't think you'd be in the office today."

"Yeah. Just came in to look over the Spencer autopsy from Agnes. You heading out?"

"No, I'm looking over things myself."

Xavier sat on the other side of the desk.

"Get this," Asher said. "Agnes has fibers from the decedent's neck. Several of them."

"Holy shit."

"Yeah."

"So, what are they?"

"Well, that's the ultimate question, ain't it? They're definitely fibers and not hair, but other than that, she said she's working on it."

"A cord? Rope?"

"Most likely. And get this," Asher continued, "the decedent, Cam Spencer, was married with kids."

Xavier leaned back in the chair, bug-eyed.

"I know, right?"

"You talk to the wife?" Xavier said.

"No, but I need to."

"What are you thinking?"

Asher pulled a Styrofoam cup from the shelf beneath the coffee pot.

"Make it two," Xavier said.

"What am I thinking?" Asher responded. "Well, the wife is also the mother of how many kids? Two?"

"Pulling her hair out day and night while Daddy is out partying with the boys—"

"Only, the boys aren't so innocent. They're grown-ass men with hard-ons for hard-ons. A stiffy with a ring, in this case."

Asher set down a black coffee across the desk, then poured one for himself. The machine hissed and huffed its final breaths.

"But you know she ain't gonna talk—even if she wasn't the one to get her hands dirty," Xavier said. "She wasn't there, so she's untouchable. Right?"

"Yeah. Of course." Asher lifted his coffee, and they knocked cups. "When has a murder-for-hire ever gone sideways?"

But Asher didn't drink. He set the coffee onto the desk—as an unreal sense of reality fell over him, like a shallow and bleary and hazy film; the thought of not one but two suspects carried with it a smothering heaviness.

Chapter 25

You—

"Well I'll be damned," said the old man in his oversized coat, sitting on a bench in the middle of the dusky alleyway. Rocking, tapping his leg in hunger, perhaps in thirst. A lamp post with a dying ocher light stood between the two of you.

Looking at him, you could feel that fretting and famished tick of his like it was your own, walking these very same streets as a kid. Your stomach in knots.

"Long time no see, my friend." You could already tell from a distance that he needed you.

It appeared as though your helping hand from before wasn't good enough. There he sat: no food, no drink, not even the coffee he had mentioned that was so good right here at Jean Lafitte. Was the money all gone? Should you have done more?

"Out here in front of your favorite coffee joint, huh?" you said. "You buy a cup?"

"Oh, no," said the man, and he lifted his shoulders, tense and seemingly gloomy from another evening of the roaming life. "Thanks again for the help. Dinner last night was one of a kind." He tried his best to fashion a grateful expression.

"And tonight?" you said. "What's on the menu?"

But the old man said nothing; he shook his head and sat back deeper on the bench. He buried his hands in his coat and crossed his legs, caving into himself. Your body felt the hurt of what he was going through, like pure muscle memory, returning you to those childhood days of trembling hands and a growling, desperate stomach.

"I'll tell you what"—you slid the bookbag from your shoulder then reached inside—"it might be a little cold, but—"

"No, no, no," said the man. "You've already done enough. Really."

You understood wholeheartedly where he was coming from—and the shame that accompanied handouts, like sifting through the trash for dinner before you're old enough to have hair on your balls.

You stood there, holding the po-boy in one hand and your bag in the other. "Please. Let me help."

He needed you.

You couldn't handle the sight of his suffering. He just sat there, squirming, when you could so easily choke away the pain, relieve the man of his circumstances. The old man in front of you now had no one, from what you could tell. No one but you.

"I insist." You stepped closer, and he took the sandwich from your hands.

"Thank you."

"Of course, my friend. Just promise me one thing," you said.

"Okay."

"You enjoy that tonight." You zipped the bag and slid it over your shoulder. "That's for you and only you, you hear?"

"Yes, sir. Thank you." He ripped open the greasy paper and leaned forward, shoving the cold sandwich into his mouth.

~

You stood at the corner of Exchange Place and Conti Street for hours, waiting for those shrimp to do their job.

The man was lying down, not far from the bench where you had found him earlier.

You started down the street toward him. It was late enough. Dark enough. You were alone enough to help him out in the way he deserved.

You walked past the bench and found him lying inside of a recessed doorway, a few shops down from Jean Lafitte Trading Company. The thick air was deafeningly quiet. You glanced left. Then right.

You poked his side with the tip of your oxblood Oxford shoe just to be sure. His chest, wheezing and shallow, was the only part of him that moved. The only hint of sound in the night. You slid your sports coat from your arms and hung it on the doorknob next to him. Unwrinkled.

Then you nudged him once more for reassurance.

You knelt on the cardboard beneath him. Your hands found his throat. You leaned. You squeezed. He trembled, but only for a moment. As his body fell slack, you instantly felt better, relieved even, now that there was one less soul suffering on these unforgiving city streets. You did it—and your shoulders fell a bit, too.

You pulled the dated, rusted scalpel from your bookbag. You glanced left. Then right.

Your tie hung down. You threw it over your shoulder. Then you rolled the man onto his stomach.

You grabbed what little hair he had left and pulled back his head, ensuring the pressure wouldn't find your suit. The blade jerked a bit in your hand as it punctured, popped, the skin of his neck. You pulled the handle.

In the quiet, a sudden and sharp hiss fizzed from the poor man's throat. In the near dark, shimmers of black and deep purple spurted onto the stone ground of the alleyway. Near and far.

And just like that, beneath the amber of a flickering light, the old man's pain spilled over the city streets.

Where he had endured for far too long.

Chapter 26

"I hope you're ready to work overtime," Xavier said.

But Asher was preoccupied—focused on the body in the middle of the alley, dragged in a slide of red from the doorway about ten feet away. Focused on the sheer volume of blood that covered the ground, frozen in time as it flowed from the man's severed neck into the shallow and skinny strip of a drain running down the center of the path, into a metal grate there.

"Always," said Asher.

The inside of the decedent's torso was exposed to the night air. Its contents were separated into piles around the body, like a rat pinned to one of those metal trays in freshman bio.

Then there was the man's head, gawking from a nearby bench.

"Where to begin?" Xavier said. "I don't even—" He stood there just looking, walking toward the body then backing up, changing his approach. "I don't even know where to step, man." The ground was colored a deep reddish purple, and there were few places to move without treading into the thick of it.

"This way," Asher said as he stepped around the adjacent side of the alleyway, then closer to the body via a few dry spots of stone. Xavier followed.

"All done," Dustin said from the head of the road. A cigarette burned orange from the corner of his mouth. He pointed over his shoulder to the yellow tape he had run across the path. "I got that side, too." He gestured to the far side as well, behind Asher and Xavier.

Dustin was a senior patrolman with the NOPD. Somehow, he always happened to be at the right place at the right time; he was first on the scene more often than not.

Asher lifted his hand in thanks.

Xavier ran his flashlight from the doorway and across the ground to where the body, in part, lay on the drain. "I don't get it," he said.

"What's that?" Asher responded.

"Why move him? There's just as much blood over there as there is here, in the middle of the road. Why drag him out here? Why not just kill him off to the side and let it be?"

The detective focused his light on the doorway, then on the pieces of the body, then the head resting on the bench.

"Attention maybe?" Xavier suggested.

"Anger," said Asher, without so much as a thought.

Xavier crouched not far from the body and photographed the display. The white light ignited the scene in transient flashes of bloodshed.

"We're gonna need more light," said Asher. "Lots of it."

As the flashes continued, Asher could hear voices approaching from behind him. "Goddamn," one of them said.

"What the hell?" said another.

Xavier paused and turned toward them. "Y'all wanna get some light on this thing, or you just gonna stand there with your mouths open?" It was two of Xavier's technicians with forensics.

"Grab the standing lights from the back of the truck."

"I'm on it," the man said, turning away from the scene. But the woman wouldn't look away. Or couldn't? She remained fixated on the puzzle of a body in front of her.

"Hello?" Xavier said with impatience. "The lights?"

The guy tapped her on the arm. "Hey, let's get moving," he said.

"Oh. Right." Then she snapped out of it. She walked backward before turning away from the Hollywood-like scene altogether.

Xavier shook his head.

"I thought they were two of your more experienced ones," Asher said. Rarely did he get involved to the point of knowing the technicians' names; that was Xavier's party. As long as they did their job, that was enough. But he did notice, here and there, which ones had been around longer than the others, and which ones were in any way useful.

"They *are* the experienced ones. At least, they're supposed to be."

Asher shined his light down the alley. "Speaking of . . . where's the new guy. What's his name?"

"John?"

"Yeah. Isn't he supposed to be shadowing you?"

"He called in today. Something about not feeling well."

"Well, ain't that a peach."

"Yeah." Xavier crouched down and clicked a few more photos. "Typical newbie shit."

"Let's wrap up the photos and get a sketch going with some measurements." He looked up to a rumbling sky. "There's no telling how long we have out here in the open."

"Sounds like a plan."

Asher walked to the bench and narrowed his beam of light, looking closer at the head that seemed to be resting there, looking on without a care in the world, just watching them work. He could taste the iron at the back of his tongue as it clung to the wet air, even though they were outdoors and the mess surrounding them had largely dried. The metallic taste lingered there in his throat and sinuses. But not for long.

The smell of blood mixed with the raw cut of tobacco that blew at his back—and with the crackling of burning paper, steady at his elbow.

Chapter 27

"Well, that's one way to get ahead," said the chief, snickering to himself. Asher turned around, and another cloud of cigar smoke hit his face.

"You ever seen anything like this?" Asher said.

Pierre rocked the cigar between his teeth and glanced around in derision. "What? You mean a body that's been cut up and spread around like some sort of art exhibit? No, I haven't."

As off-putting as the murder was, as appealing as it could have been from an investigative standpoint, Asher had reservations about committing to the case. This wasn't some random, off-handed murder that'd be solved in the background like most of the department's cases that were worked by other detectives—the ones who did the bare minimum, "solving" firearm accidents and suicides so they could crow to family and friends. No, this had more-to-it written all over it.

And the timing couldn't have been worse.

"Looks like this is right up your alley," Pierre said. "Ha. Alley . . . get it?"

"Yeah, well. I'm not so sure."

The chief set flame to his cigar, even though it was still smoldering. Asher had come to learn that it was his way of buying time while he considered things.

"You know those will kill you."

Pierre gestured to the head that continued to look on from the bench. Lax and unmoving, like a union supervisor. "And so will looking at this shit." He widened his stance, and his tone shifted to something more bosslike. "What's this crap about you not being sure? I called you out here for a reason, and it wasn't for show-and-tell."

"This case. I'm not so sure it's for me, with everything else I've got going on right now."

"Not *for* you? What the fuck does that mean?"

Xavier interrupted them. "You about ready to start mapping this thing out?" He spoke to Asher while holding up his clipboard and pencil.

Pierre slurred through the cigar and spoke for him. "He'll be over there in a minute."

"You really think it's a good idea for me to work two cases right now? We still don't have a wrap on the Cassandra mess."

He moved closer and into Asher's personal space. "Agnes did her job, Asher. She looked at that thing every which way she could and gave us her best assessment. And as far as Internal Affairs goes, they're reaching out to me because I'm the one who hired Cassandra. So, just let them do their thing."

"Fair enough—but don't you think someone else can work this until—"

"No. They can't." He extinguished the cigar between his fingers, then placed it into the inside pocket of his peacoat for safe keeping. His voice lowered. "You remember our deal, yeah? What we agreed to when I brought you on?"

Asher didn't need to answer the question; it was rhetorical. Pierre had him under his thumb.

"That's right," Pierre said. "The deal was, you're lead as long as you work the difficult cases. Right?" His voice dropped even further. "And in exchange, you don't have to be too involved with supervising the rest of the department. Or as you so gracefully put it, 'babysitting the idiots.' That right?"

Of course it was right. An offer to work in near complete isolation from the others was the one thing that had persuaded Asher to take the promotion. Cassandra had been hired because it was department policy that all detectives be partnered up, and Pierre thought someone with a psychiatric background could be of use. And Xavier was the only other one he could tolerate.

Even with the department's recent calamity, Pierre and Asher had a mutual understanding—he was their best bet for the seemingly impossible cases.

Asher's track record wasn't perfect, but whose was? What mattered, and what the chief needed, what the department needed, was a lead detective who didn't shy away from the career-ending cases. A thinker with initiative who wasn't in it for the kiss-ass publicity. To Asher, they weren't high-profile cases; they were attractive problems that needed solving.

And to Asher? The less attention, the better.

"Look," Pierre said, "I get it. I do. I don't know what it's like to lose your person, partner *or* spouse, but I do get it. You're in a messed-up place right now. But I need you on this, Asher. The *department* needs you on this. You yourself said that you were good to come—"

"Yeah, I know. I said that I'm back, and I'm back. Ain't I?"

Pierre looked to Xavier, who was stepping through the scene like he was skirting landmines after being dropped deep in Viet Cong territory. "Then, good," the chief said. "This is right up your alley."

Chapter 28

Asher rounded the corner and started down Exchange Place with no one else in sight. The only light was from the half-shaded and dusty moon, floating above a buzzing lamp post just outside his newly preferred coffee shop.

As he reached for the door, he overheard a heavy, hollow gasping farther down the alleyway, shaded by the outline of second-floor fire escapes and crooked balconies. A busyness shuffled about, somewhere out there in the dark.

He glanced farther down the road and into the shadows, but there was no one there. So, he turned back and entered Jean Lafitte for his later-than-late-evening coffee.

A second later, as if time had skipped a beat, Asher was outside of the café. He leaned back with the bottom of one foot against the building and tilted back his black espresso. Then the noise—it returned, doubly shrill. The panting. The shuffling.

Oh, if pain had a sound.

He turned down the road. He didn't make it far before he glimpsed a figure, hunched over off to the side in one of the doorways there. Asher took a beat and sat down on a bench in the middle of the alley. Out of sight from whoever, whatever, was rustling about at such a late hour.

More coffee.

But as his eyes adjusted, and the moonlit scene came into focus, he couldn't believe what he was watching: the figure slicing and sloppily carving whatever person lay beneath them. At least he assumed it was a person, mangled and featureless as it was.

The shadows lingered over the character as if the light faded there, just for him.

Asher unlocked his phone to text Xavier, but as soon as he did, the screen flashed black with a single tremor in his palm. Dead. He watched himself sit there, knowing what he had to do but unsure of how to go about it; he was alone and without backup knowing where he was.

Seconds felt more like minutes.

The lock of a door clunked against some metal frame, and then he saw the barista inside of the coffee shop flip the sign at the door to "CLOSED."

And just like that, she was gone.

Asher slipped the phone back into his jacket and pulled his pistol from the holster at his back. The figure was now mumbling to himself, panting in a heavier way. Busier. More frantic. Asher rose from the bench with his pistol in one hand, aimed broadly at the ground in front of him. His coffee in the other. Slowly, he moved against the building and faced the figure.

He nudged the safety with his thumb as he sipped his coffee—only the coffee was no coffee at all.

No. It was something else entirely. Something metallic. Something viscous.

A shimmer of white light reflected from the skinny, finger-deep drain in the middle of the alleyway. Asher stepped toward it, only to see blood flowing down the street and into a metal grate. He turned around and glanced up at the balcony above Jean Lafitte.

There, leaning against the railing, stood a dark and blurry figure—as a glint of light shone from the silver badge on their hip.

Should he chance it? Should he call up to whomever it was? Use his flashlight?

He turned on his light and pointed it up at the balcony, but as the beam shook in the detective's hand and shifted on the brick wall of the building, no one was there. That was when he heard it: the tread of heavy boots growing closer. The wheezing breaths. Feet splashing across the stone path. Growing louder. And louder. Asher turned back to the figure in the alley, now barreling toward him in full stride.

With a knife in hand.

By the time Asher began to lift his pistol, it was too late. He jolted awake and clawed at the pain shooting through his chest and back, grasping for the wound that had never existed in the first place, as a chilling sweat enveloped him once more in the comfort of his own bed.

Chapter 29

Asher rounded the corner and started down Exchange Place. The alleyway was buzzing with locals, tourists, and the like.

He needed to revisit the scene to see if they had missed something in the dark—and get his much-needed morning coffee.

As he reached for the door, he glanced down the alley at all the shops with their inset doorways. Benches lined the center of the path, and the street was chock-full with the chatter of voices and city clamor lingering in the background. He turned back and entered Jean Lafitte for his early-morning coffee.

And to dig deeper into the case, of course.

A couple sat off to the side in a sitting area of couches and armchairs, surrounded by merchandise and pirate décor. Asher turned the other way, toward the register and coffee bar.

"Good morning," said the barista. Even behind the tint of his aviators, her freckles were just as nice as he remembered. "Café noir, right?"

Asher spoke with a pleasant drip to his voice. "Yes, ma'am."

She smiled and pulled a large cup from behind the counter. "Have a seat," she said. "Can I get you anything to eat?"

"Oh, no thanks. Just the caffeine this morning." He, too,

couldn't help but grin. But no sooner than he did, he felt guilty about it—so he turned away.

He sat at the high-top in front of the window and watched the morning as it stirred awake.

Why here? Why kill someone in the middle of an alley in one of the busiest cities in the South? He glanced around the shop. *And a few steps away from the one place I've decided to get my coffee, now?*

The whole thing reeked of coincidence; as a detective, he despised coincidence. As an ex-partner? Happenstance was suspect at best.

He moved closer to the window, peering outside in the direction of where they'd found the body. In doing so, he noticed something that they should've already caught, although it had been dark at the time. Still, that was no excuse.

The shop across the alley, in addition to several other storefronts farther down, all had at least one security camera either hanging over the door or positioned in the window, pointing outside to the street. He stepped back and again glanced around the shop, this time looking for the obvious. Sure enough: one camera behind the cash register, one over the front door, and one in the far corner of the sitting area overlooking the merchandise.

But what about—

"Here you go," said the barista. She set the cup on the table.

"What do I owe you?" Asher said.

"Really?" She folded her arms and tilted her head in a seductive but playful way. "We're gonna do this back-and-forth again?" Then she rolled her eyes, and her nostrils flared. Leaning in, she tapped her hand on the table. "Your money is no good here, Detective."

She walked away while looking back at him over her

shoulder. But before she reached the counter, Asher stopped her. "Hey," he said, "does your boss happen to be around?"

A worrisome look crossed her face.

"No, it's nothing to do with you. I promise." He sipped the perfectly prepared black coffee. "I just need to speak with him about the investigation I'm working." He pointed over his shoulder.

"Oh. The murder." Her smile returned.

He nodded. Another sip.

"Sure," she said. "One sec." She walked to the back of the shop and into a small office.

Right away, a towering man with graying hair and a long, braided beard stepped out of the room. "What can I do for you?"

Asher removed his sunglasses and tucked them into the crook of his shirt. "These cameras"—he pointed above the front door—"happen to work?"

The man looked to the badge on the detective's hip. "Of course they do."

"What about out front?"

"Yeah," the owner said. "We got one over the front door."

Asher sipped his coffee. "Good."

The man gestured to the alleyway. "You working the case out front?"

Asher nodded, trying to get a read on this guy. Not giving too much but being cordial enough to get what he needed when he needed it. "Can we look at the footage?" Never too careful.

"Um, sure." He pointed over his shoulder. "It's back here in the office."

"I appreciate it," Asher said. They turned to the back of the shop.

"Let me know if you need anything," said the barista.

The owner added to the sentiment. "Yeah, just say the word. You're welcome to some more coffee or anything from the bakery. Free of charge."

"Yeah, thanks," Asher said.

The back-room office was a disaster—yellowed paperwork falling from piles on the tiny desk, a calendar on the wall outdated by two years, a torn leather chair with golden rivets in the corner of the room. A green ledger book lay open on the desk, covering a heap of check stubs and shipping forms.

"Oh, sorry," said the owner. He stuck out his hand. "Gene Lafourche."

They shook. "Detective Asher Huxley. Homicide."

Gene sat down in a rickety wooden chair and logged in to the computer. "So, what are we looking at? You looking for a specific time and date?"

"Yeah, let's take a look at the camera outside, yesterday, maybe sometime between dark and midnight?"

"Sure." The owner accessed the video from the day prior and dragged the timestamp forward until it reached dusk.

They watched the recording in various blocks of one minute or so, spread out over several hours. The problem was that the alleyway had been so busy, it would take some time to go through all the footage to find anything worth looking into.

Even worse, the exact spot where the body had been found was out of frame. Things were further complicated once it became dark and the faces of bystanders grew muddled.

"I'll tell you what," Asher said. "If you don't mind, is there any way that I can get a copy of this?" The guy seemed cool enough. Hopefully, he'd give it up without making it any more complicated than it needed to be.

"Sure," said Gene. "You want the indoor footage, too?"

"No need. Just this." Asher pointed to the screen. Then he handed Gene his card. "The sooner the better, of course."

"Absolutely. And if there's anything else you need along the way, just holler."

They shook hands again in good faith. "I appreciate it."

It was almost too easy. *It's too bad that getting evidence isn't always so*—

"Oh, yeah." The owner sat back in the chair and folded his hands on his stomach. His eyes narrowed like he was thinking. Then he pointed to the ceiling. "There might be someone you wanna talk to while you're here."

Chapter 30

Gene walked Asher out the back door of the shop and into a hallway that connected to a stairwell.

"I'm not sure if he's home," Gene said, "but if he is, he might know something." He stopped at the top of the stairs and knocked on the door that was riddled with worn political stickers, some of them law enforcement. Republican propaganda, mostly. One of the stickers read: "Back in the day, we had Republicans and Democrats. Now, we've got men and pussies." Another: "Roses are red, violets are blue. I'm blue too, so fuck you."

"Interesting fella," Asher said.

The owner grinned over his shoulder. "Oh . . . just wait." He knocked again, and the door flew open.

"Oh, hey Gene." The man stared past the owner to Asher, as if the detective had stumbled into the wrong neighborhood. "It's a little early ain't it? Rent ain't due for another"—he brought his watch up to his face, then seemingly realized the dial was showing hours and not days—"well, you'll get your money."

"James, this is Detective Huxley with NOPD." The owner turned to Asher. "Detective, this is James Cormier."

Asher moved up a step and held out his hand. "Homicide," he added. The man inside of the apartment looked at them as if he were in the middle of a bad trip, then turned around and walked back inside without shaking hands.

A heavy and Hendrixy blues song was blaring in the background. Asher couldn't place the artist, but he liked it.

"Well, ain't no bodies in here," said James. "You want a tour?" He turned down the music. "Don't mind the smell, that's just Mr. John Wayne over there." His clownish orange cat hissed from the corner. "But don't worry—ain't no crawl spaces around here."

"A tour won't be necessary," Asher said. "I'm here about the murder that happened out front yesterday. But I'm sure you already knew that."

"Nope," said James. "Ain't left the house for—" He glanced at his watch once more. "What day is it? Hell, I been here for about three days, give or take."

Give or take? How useful.

The short man sported a fraying NOPD hat with a blue star and gray stitching. His mustache couldn't have been any more cop-like. His feet were bare, and he wore old blue jeans that were one size too big and a plain white T-shirt with a wrung-out neck. Judging from his red, leathery skin, the gray tint to his facial hair, and the crow's feet at the corner of his eyes, the man was in his late fifties.

Asher looked around at the number of plaques and ceremonial photographs on the wall—and the military camo Beretta sitting on the coffee table, abutting a pile of beer bottles. Each one of them with the label removed.

Last night's dream flashed through Asher's head: the figure on a balcony above the coffee shop, silver light reflecting from the badge.

"You have anyone to corroborate that story?" Asher asked.

The man gave Asher a dumbfounded expression. "Corrobo-who?"

Is this for real?

"Can anyone vouch for you? Is there anyone who was maybe here with you, or knew that you were here for the last day or two? You have any visitors?"

Asher knew that that alone wouldn't be enough. Even if he'd been here during the time of the murder, it happened right out front of his apartment. It wouldn't prove that he wasn't somehow involved.

"You hear anything? Any loud noises or screams?" Asher added.

"Screams? You mean, other than the voices?" the man said, shoving his index finger into his temple. "Ha." His laugh was both annoying and maniacal. "Ha, ha!"

Gene gave Asher a sideways glance.

"No and no," James said. "No one was here. No one other than me, myself, and I. Yeah, buddy."

The dream flashed through his head once again. Was this yet another coincidence? Asher hated coincidences; they belonged in movies and books.

James popped open a beer and held it out, offering a cold one to Asher. He dropped the metal bottlecap to the floor.

"No, thanks," Asher said. He removed a card from the inside of his jacket and held it out. "I'm not gonna waste too much of your time, but it'd be nice if you came down to the office and gave us a formal interview. If you were here, it'd be worth having the details on record, just to be safe."

James tilted back the bottle and downed half the beer before taking the card. He was quiet, now. No jokes. No laughing.

"That a problem?" Asher asked.

"I just told you, I was—"

"Thanks," Asher said. "It won't take long."

The man looked to the owner of the coffee shop, who shrugged.

"We'll see, Detective." James walked back to the door. "Is there anything else I can do for you?"

"Not that I can think of," Asher said.

James opened the door and stepped aside. His thumb tore at the label on the orange-brown bottle. Useful or not, involved or not, his sudden change in demeanor became a note in the back of Asher's head.

As Asher stepped out of the door, with one foot on the stairs and one still in the apartment, he turned back. "Actually, there is something." How would the guy react?

Pieces of the label fell to the floor as if he were standing in some dark alley—with not a care in the world. "And what's that, Detective?"

Asher pointed into the apartment. "What song was that?"

"The song?"

"Yeah. Who was that?"

He spoke with a curt cut to his voice. "Philip Sayce."

"And the song?"

But the man just stood there, itching to shut the door. It wasn't what he had said, though, that was of any importance. The fact that he was home, and no one could verify or refute it, wasn't helpful.

It was the pause in his willingness to talk.

"I guess you'll find out at the station," James said. "Well . . . maybe."

Asher turned down the stairs. "Much appreciated, Mr. Cormier."

Gene followed. Asher paused at the bottom step and glanced over his shoulder. Motionless and unspeaking, James's hatted silhouette filled the doorway, backlit by the smokey room.

Chapter 31

"What's so important?" Asher said. Agnes seldom requested that he stop by her office on account of it being "urgent"—her words, not his.

She lit a cigarette with a trembling hand, then tossed the lighter onto her desk. It slid across some papers and landed on the floor. "I want you to hear it from me before it gets back to you through someone else," she said.

"Hear it from you?"

Agnes was one of his few colleagues, albeit not with Homicide, who was honest to a fault with him—even loyal, he would go far as to say. Regardless of their political affairs, their personal opinions, their respective culpability to higher-ups, she always gave it to him straight. Few did, other than his closest friend on the forensics team.

"Yeah," she said, "don't kill me. I'm telling you this because I think you should know, love."

"Just come out with it."

She took a drag as she sat on the edge of her desk, the cigarette barely stuck to the corner of her lips. "Pierre reached out to me directly. He's eager to put it out there to the public that y'all have ID'd Cassandra's body, which means once I finalize the autopsy and sign the death certificate—"

"She'll be buried."

"No, she won't be buried; there's no one to claim the body. She'll be cremated."

"Did he say why? Well, I mean, I guess I know why. If your autopsy says that it's her, then it's her. There's no reason to drag it out. But why reach out to you? He can't tell you how to do your job."

"No, he can't. It was more of a request to wrap things up more than anything else, but the way it sounded, he's concerned about how it's gonna look if we sit on it any longer than we need to. And I don't blame him after everything that's happened. It sounds like he's just trying to move things along. He isn't looking to sweep it under the rug."

"Yeah, I know. I just wish he would've asked me to talk to you."

"If I had to guess, Pierre is just wanting to say once and for all that he has the body. That would close out the search for her, but Internal Affairs can continue with their investigation into what happened. That's a good thing."

"I know. Somebody's gotta get to the bottom of it."

Asher loathed asking for favors; it made him look weak. Incompetent.

"Look, I don't know what's going on in that head of yours," Agnes said, "but I can tell that—"

"Can you just buy me a little time? Please?"

Asher could see that she was being pulled in opposite directions: to close out the autopsy as quickly as possible in order to save face within the department while moving the case forward responsibly, but also to hold off on cremating the body so Asher himself could sleep at night, knowing that he wasn't screwing up any more than he already had. But if Agnes was so sure of her work, shouldn't the lead homicide detective who relied on her word be sure, too?

He had to do something. Things were moving too quickly.

"I'm heading over to see Pierre as soon as I leave here. Let me talk to him, and we can go from there. What about this latest victim—or maybe I should say, the *pieces* of this latest victim? That makes two more cases we've got going."

She nursed the cigarette, staring off to the corner of the room. "I'll get around to each and every slice of him soon enough. You two figure out whatever it is y'all got going on. I'll try to buy you a little time, but I can't guarantee anything." Only then did she look at him. "You already have her final postmortem report."

Chapter 32

Asher thrust open the door. Cigar smoke reeled in loose circles throughout the chief's office. "We need to talk."

Pierre looked up at him with the desk phone tucked between his ear and shoulder. "Yeah. I'll have to call you back," he said. "No, everything's fine. My daily headache just walked in."

Asher shut the door. "Oh, that's a good one."

The phone met its receiver. "I hope this is good," Pierre said.

At first, he just stood there like one of those gold-painted, living statues in the Quarter, frozen in place and waiting for someone to drop a dollar bill in the bucket, shrugging and folding his arms. Asher weighed his options. Keep his mouth shut and drive himself mad? Say something and let everyone else think that he is, in fact, mental?

But would he be considered foolish for keeping what he knew about Cass to himself? Or crazy when no one believed him?

There was only one way to find out.

"Don't have Agnes rush the cremation," Asher said.

"Oh, Jesus Christ. Not this."

"At least, not yet."

Pierre leaned back in his too-large, kingly chair and kicked up his feet. "Not this again. We've already been over this. If Agnes tells us that—"

"I think Cassandra's still alive." There, it was over with, like vomiting. Just the idea of saying it made his feet go numb, while his abdomen squeezed his stomach until it came out anyway. "I saw her, Chief." *No. Not the right words.* "Well, I didn't actually see her, I—"

"Whoa, whoa, whoa, slow the fuck down." He leaned forward, now. Outwardly curious. Perhaps confused. "What do you mean you 'saw her'? What the hell is this?"

"After the shooting. Well, after Sofia's funeral, at Café Du Monde. She was there. At least, one of the waiters said that a woman was there. She sent me the exact same breakfast that she always brought me when we were working together."

Pierre bowed his head, then rested his forehead on the desk and balled his fist in a pulse of heavy squeezes.

"What?" Asher said. "What is it?"

"Breakfast, Asher? Someone sent you breakfast, and that means Cassandra is out there somewhere? Am I getting this right?"

Okay—maybe he shouldn't have said a word. He should've kept his crazy to himself. It was easier to deal with when he himself was the only one to convince. He was good at that— catastrophizing away the logic.

"No. She sent me a black coffee and the one and only donut she used to bring me for breakfast nearly every morning. You tell me: who else would do that? I know how it sounds, Chief, but—"

"No, I'll give you that one. It is strange. And I surely hope you're wrong. But you know what?" The chief got to his feet and leaned forward with his palms planted on the desk.

Regret was seeping in. "No. I have no idea, Chief. Apparently, I never do."

"Not only have you been wrong about the woman before"—he leaned farther, almost falling forward over the desk—"but I'm not sure you've *ever* been right about her. About any of it."

It took Asher aback. Did Pierre want his help tying up loose ends? Did he not? Was he supposed to just shut up and go along for the ride at this point?

At least it was out there. At least now, Asher could say that he spoke up when shit did hit the fan.

And it always did.

Or maybe he just blew up the levy that was holding back the river of doubt that was all in his head. Either way, it was done.

"It had to have been her," Asher said. "And what about you? You think you're right, so I should just keep quiet and hope we're right about the body?"

"What else is there? Can you point me to a single fact that tells us for sure that she's alive? Where she is? If not, then telling me this shit is doing nothing but creating doubt where we're otherwise certain. Again . . . Agnes confirmed the ID. Now, unless you've actually seen her, or know where she's at, I don't wanna hear it. You know what I'm dealing with when it comes to the media right now?"

"Yeah, I'm sure what everyone thinks about us should be our top priority right—"

Pierre brought his volume down a notch, perhaps realizing that his old tactics of going off the deep end were growing less efficient with his lead detective.

Probably not.

"It has nothing to do with our reputation, Asher—and everything to do with the future of our department and getting this thing right. We've gotta do this one by the books; not that we usually don't, but we've got to now more than ever. For you *and* me."

"So you're not gonna entertain the idea, at least a little bit, in any way possible, that we might be wrong?" Asher wanted to make sure they were on the same page before he decided to never bring up the café again. At least, not to Pierre.

"Look," the chief said, "do whatever it is you gotta do. Explore it, forget about it." His voice was decisive now. "I just don't wanna know about it." He sat down. "At least . . . not until you have more than some personal anecdote."

Asher couldn't think of a single response, good or bad. The walls only grew closer, and the possibility of being even more wrong about Cassandra than they already were—whatever that meant—squeezed him until he was at a loss for breath.

"Well," Pierre said, "I trust that you'll do what needs to be done. But my hands are tied. Between the media wanting answers about the body, Agnes's report, and Internal Affairs, we can't sit on this. Not when our medical examiner is giving us answers."

"Okay. You tell me, then. What do you want me to do?"

"Easy," Pierre said. "Either bring me something that says Agnes is wrong, or let it go. Until then, I don't wanna hear about it. You've got two other cases to work now. So, I'm trusting you to do your job."

"And the body? Cremating the remains this soon is a good—"

"Again . . . do you have anything concrete to give me?" He held up a stack of papers. "Something more convincing than this autopsy?" Then he dropped them to the desk.

But Asher had dick. Nothing more than memories he couldn't trust, recollections of an ex-partner who had never been.

"No. I don't."

"Okay, then. That's what I thought." For some reason, Peirre was calm in his decision. It was strange.

Was Asher really that far off?

"You have one week," said the chief. "Then she's cremated."

Chapter 33

Still, she was everywhere. Like a sad rain that lingered in the air, days after it had stopped falling.

Asher shut the back door of his house and turned to the kitchen. Sofia was all he noticed—her coffee cup on the island, her blue-gray scarf hanging on the fleur-de-lis hook by the door, her slingback heels on the floor. A picture of her standing in front of Asher's Vette at the lakefront was stuck to the side of the fridge.

He waited for his wife to walk down the hallway in her robe. Her hair in a wet towel like a cotton beehive, caught in a light rain on a beautifully overcast evening.

Those days were gone, though.

Dead.

And all of her belongings could stay put, until his mind was free of Cassandra. It should've been the other way around. He knew how bad it sounded—focusing on work, and thus Cass, so he could move on from losing his wife. That guilt made it worse.

The sickening fact was, it was too soon to sit alone, in this house, with the fact that she was gone. He knew it. He thought about it. He acknowledged it when others asked how he was holding up.

But he wasn't ready to be alone with it, not here—much

less move what little of her remained throughout the house. Thinking about her while at home made him feel as if he were a temporary guest in someone else's house. Something didn't belong.

And it was him. He didn't belong, not alone in this house.

Asher walked past all of it and straight into his home office, then shut the door; it was the one room where he could escape the reminders.

He set down his coffee from Jean Lafitte onto his desk, along with his briefcase containing photos of the most recent homicides. He removed the files and began flipping through them. Then he placed them side by side.

One strangled, cuffed to the balcony, nude. The other stabbed, no longer in one piece. Head on a bench. Cut up in a way even the most seasoned of investigators would have deemed abnormal, extreme.

As he closed his briefcase and set it on the floor, then fanned out the two folders of photos in front of him, the corner of a lone image protruded from beneath one of the dossiers.

The Mississippi's edge. The blue tarp. The long, dark brown hair with the slightest touch of red.

Asher found the beads to the bracelet on his wrist and ran them through the tips of his fingers.

He slid out the photograph from beneath the folder with a single finger, stared at it for one second too long, then pushed it off of the table. It fluttered as it hit the floor in one fell swoop, jamming itself beneath the guitar stand holding his newest PRS. Beneath the Singlecut 594, and its now-rusting strings.

Chapter 34

You—

You watched the two of them enter the building. "Studio Black" hummed in black light above the front door of the art gallery, at the corner of Royal and some other street you couldn't name.

You'd never been here. Should you follow them inside?

Under the night, you peered through the tinted window. The suits and ties and gowns mulled about like those instinctive vacuums, bumping into this and that, then turning with indifference, each of them with a wine glass in hand and someone hooked to their arm.

You adjusted the stray hair over your eyes and zipped your hoodie—and hoped for the best.

It was *he* who drew you in.

You bounded for the door before it closed, and he held it open for you.

"Thank you," you said as you stepped inside behind them.

"No problem," said the attractive one, his back side perfect save for the hand of his acquaintance, which rested on the small of his back.

But not for long.

The host behind the podium handed the two men a brochure and smiled an affable greeting that faded once she turned toward you. Her eyes judged your attire. She could've at least tried to hide her disapproving, bushy brow, but she ostensibly made no effort. She held out one of the pamphlets.

"Thanks," you said.

The woman perused you from head to toe. She nodded, then showed you her back as if she was letting someone like you, dressed like you, enter the studio when she shouldn't have.

It was a good thing she did, because, well . . . *him.*

As you moved past the foyer, a tuxedo approached you with a shining tray of stemmed, red-filled glasses. The man was cordial—unlike the hag at the door.

He caught you off guard. "Cabernet, sir?" He had a straight posture, chin tucked, one arm bent behind him. His jaw was shaved to a glistening silk.

It was best to take a glass, blend in, somehow cover up the fact that you were underdressed. "You're a star," you said. You plucked a glass of red from the tray. "Cheers."

The man bowed and disappeared into the shifting crowd.

You stepped farther into the room of black-and-gray art that hung from the walls like stills of 1930's television, ballooned to life-size people and naturescapes. That was when you noticed it: the only color in the place was the wine. Your reality had been transformed into a trash polka dream.

You turned the corner, and the near-perfect specimen all but collided with your face.

"Oh, so sorry," he said. The hair, the tux, the swirling sea-green eyes. The complete lack of imperfection.

"No, no, that's my fault," you said. "My apologies."

He rested there and sipped his red, pointing at you with a finger of the hand holding the glass. "Guy at the door, yeah? I haven't seen you here before. You new here?"

You drew a sip, too. "Yes, I am." You left it at that while your eyes painted him, hoping he would notice you looking and return the favor. You loved it when they watched.

And he did; flirting in silence had always been your forte.

He extended his hand. "Charlie." You held it for as long as you could, neither of you squeezing, just holding one another with no hint of unease. Only flared noses and upturned lips.

"I'm Reese," you said.

"What a pleasure." Still holding. Shaking, now, in a rhythm that felt too good to be real. Then he yanked you in and spoke only to you. "Dressing up for this shit is overrated." He shook your hand against his stomach. Now it was his turn to take a look at you. "You're lucky—not many of us could get away with that kind of dress. Not in here." He released you, but there he stood. Practically pinned to you.

"You're a star," you said. The wooded, blackberry scent of alcohol drifted from his breath.

His nose widened. "I know."

The heat of his breathing fell over you; or maybe that was just your hope for later.

You said, "So, where'd your husband run off to?"

"Oh, no. No husband," he said. "Hell, no boyfriend. Just a plain ole friend who wishes they had taste. He's somewhere. Had to drag him here."

"Is that so?"

"The finest of studios," he said, raising his glass and gesturing to the room. "What do you think?"

"Yeah, it's nice, I guess."

"You guess?"

"Well, it's just the whole black-and-gray thing. Seems a bit, I don't know, bland?"

Charlie disagreed by nearly spitting the wine from his nose. "*Bland*. Is that so?"

"Well, I mean, there's nothing wrong with a bit of color here and there. Is there?"

Charlie's face straightened, looking almost serious-minded for the first time since you met him. He knocked back the bulk of his red, then rubbed his lips together as if he were working in some thin, bloody gloss. "A bit of color, huh?"

Somehow, he managed to squeeze in closer, the heat of his suit beading on his forehead. "Whether black is a color, *Reese*, is a matter of perspective."

You exchanged your own glass, swashing still, for his remaining two sips. "I guess I'm just a glass-half-full kind of guy, then." You pulled it off so casually, too.

Whether he drank from it, though, would determine if you had him. You could tell he was running through the options in his head, thinking about whatever "friend" it was who had wandered off, how they matched up to the dressed-down piece of potential in front of him, now.

If only your own parents had been this aware of you as a youth, while they sat in church each and every Sunday, praying to some imaginary fucker.

But prayers were bullshit. You knew that, now.

Yours had been ignored—Sunday after Sunday after Sunday.

Charlie took a sip.

"You like being alone . . . Charlie?"

That self-righteous, pious fucker in the clouds could sit back and watch yet again.

Only this time, you wouldn't be the one screaming.

Chapter 35

sher pulled back the bracelet and released it, snapping the beads against his wrist in a steady, pinching rhythm.

Justin broke the initial quiet. "Is that helping?"

Asher closed his eyes and pulled back the beads even farther until they broke free of his fingers and popped against his skin, tugging at the fine hairs there. "A little," he said. "It's a bit like the black box—sometimes it works, sometimes it doesn't. But when it does . . . it does."

"You're still using the black box, huh? That's good. Finding a way to rid your mind of what isn't useful, or even what's hurting you, is sometimes the only thing you can do."

He found it a caustic pill to swallow—his mind dreaming out of control at night, then actively forcing itself to go black by day. To think of nothing but that black void of an imaginary box. It was almost like his mind couldn't convince itself what was best. His conscience toying with his consciousness. Amusing.

But not really; it was more sad than anything.

"What's new?" Justin asked. "Any progress? Regression?"

"No. I've been having some dreams, but other than that, nothing's changed."

"Dreams? What kind of dreams?"

The kind that made no sense whatsoever.

"Strange ones. Dreams about work, mostly."

"Okay." Justin waited, crossed his legs. His pantleg rose above one of his quirky purple-and-gold dress socks. "Are they things about work that you're willing to share?" A blinding conflict to the rest of his typical business attire.

"We've got two new cases. Well, two new ones in addition to what we've already been dealing with after the whole Cassandra mess."

"We can come back to her if we need to. I wanna hear about these dreams."

"Basically, they have to do with the cases I'm working."

Justin started writing. That yellow legal pad. The messy cursive, obvious from across the way. "And? Are they dreams that you solve the cases? Is it stress over *not* solving them, perhaps?"

"No."

That'd be nice. Something normal, for once.

"I'm watching the murders happen," Asher said. "I can see the victim, who's killing them, the exact location where we found the body. All of it—detail for detail."

"You see the killer?"

"Yeah. Well, except for their face."

Justin frowned one of those isn't-that-convenient upside-down smirks, along with a dragging nod. "I bet that's comforting."

"Oh, yeah. Of course. It makes perfect sense."

"Yeah?"

"Not one bit."

More writing.

"I can't say that I'm surprised," Asher continued. "If I don't know who did it, I can't see who it is—not in a dream or anywhere else. Work has always been stressful. I guess what gets me is not knowing what it means."

"You just said it; it's work. It's stressful, and you're trying to catch whoever these people are. I'd imagine that working multiple cases that are so serious in nature would be a lot for most people, detective or not."

"Sure, but—"

"Unless there's something else." Justin was one of those people who could speak volumes with little effort, aided by his unmoving, eye-to-eye exchanges.

"Of course there's more," Asher said.

A slight lift of the therapist's brow.

Asher continued, "Every dream has a badge."

"A badge?" The certainty melted from Justin's face.

"Yeah. Like, a law enforcement badge. In one dream, the killer was wearing it. In another, it was someone on a balcony, watching me watch the killer. Sure, the killer's face isn't there—but law enforcement? I'd recognize NOPD. All of them. I might not be good with names, but I know faces. And that's what gets me. If they work for us, I've seen them. I've at least met them in passing."

"Huh . . ." Justin seemed at a loss for words; he was never speechless.

"Any idea what that could mean?" Asher said. "Hell, forget the details. What does any dream mean?"

"Well that's easy."

Easy? Asher couldn't tell whether Justin was being sincere or just joshing him. Justin couldn't possibly know what the dreams meant. Asher was purely talking, wishing for the best. Hoping to get something out of this session that could help bring the nightmares to an end.

If Justin could in any way know what they meant, it could help with the investigation. Or at least give Asher an idea. More likely, he was about to get some generalized form of an interpretation that meant jack shit.

"Dreams are your mind's way of returning to what you've already thought about during the day, while you're awake. The downside is that the dream could be useful, and based on fact, or it could be gum under the table—founded on some fantastical dramatization of something that crossed your mind for all of two seconds. But it *always* stems from something you're dealing with or thinking about during the day."

A generalization at its core.

"Yeah," Asher said. "I figured as much."

Justin leaned forward. Twisted the button. Opened the fitted jacket of his suit. "I might be reaching a bit here, but if you're having the same thing, or person, crop up in these dreams"—he pointed to the mirrorlike badge on Asher's hip, reflecting a silver glare that cut through the room in a thin, sharp plane—"I'd say that you already know who this person is."

The badge?

The balcony?

The dreams said nothing about active duty. Did they?

Chapter 36

Therapy before work always made the morning drag by—especially when the night before had been subjugated by thick coffee and late-night guitar. Asher couldn't help it, though. Ignoring a new set of strings was a blatant insult to god himself. Like bringing home a new puppy and kicking it out of bed.

He walked into the precinct and made a beeline for Xavier's desk.

"Well, it's about time," Xavier said. "What? No coffee for your better half?"

Asher sat down with his morning cup and nursed it. "Sorry. No time. Came in straight from the loony bin." His dry eyes grew sandier with each blink.

"Uh-huh. Excuses." Xavier shoved his foot into Asher's shin. "All I'm hearing are excuses."

"So, what's new? Any headway on our growing list of unlucky decedents?" He looked down at his dirtied shin with a sardonic glance. "What about the other one? You can't massage one and not the other."

Xavier crumpled a piece of paper and tossed it into Asher's face. "Smart-ass."

"Bitch-ass."

"Tight-ass."

Asher sipped his black, caffeinated syrup, then dropped his aviators onto the bridge of his nose.

"Actually, I do have something," Xavier said. He opened a file on his computer and swiveled the monitor in Asher's direction. "Meet our victim from down on Exchange Place—Claude Evans. A long-time member of New Orleans's thriving homeless population."

"And you figured this out by . . ."

Xavier flicked a photo of the man between his fingers, like some slight-of-hand card trick. "Ironically enough, the man's sister stopped by the Missing Persons department late last night asking about him. Said she was supposed to meet him for breakfast yesterday morning, and he didn't show. Couldn't find him afterward, either."

"Seriously? The guy had relatives meeting up for breakfast, and he was still on the streets? Sounds like one hell of a family dynamic."

"Or lack thereof. Like I said—ironic."

"You get her number?"

"Of course." Xavier tilted his head to the computer. "It's already in the system."

Asher removed the lid to his coffee and dropped it onto the desk, then sat back and swirled the drink just below his chin. Rocking in the chair. Slurping.

"This ain't no damn wine tasting," Xavier said, sliding the lid into the trash. He wiped the wet from the desk with his mitt of a hand. "You comfortable?"

Asher closed his eyes behind the reflective lenses. He could've passed out right then and there. "I should probably check it out, then."

"What?"

"You said he was part of the homeless community. I should hit the streets and ask around. Who knows? Maybe one of the others saw something. It won't hurt to take a look around."

"And the sister?"

Asher brushed it off with a lone shoulder. "Waste of time. Whatever she knows or doesn't know, I'm sure she's already given it to Missing Persons. Family don't run to the cops over someone they think is missing in less than twenty-four hours—unless they're ready to blab about every random suspicion they've got."

"Except this time, their suspicions check out."

"Yeah. And there ain't anything she's got that she didn't already give us, trust me. Speaking of"—a quick sip, better yet two—"you hear from Gene Lafourche yet?"

"Who?"

"Lafourche. The owner of Jean Lafitte's?"

"Oh. Yeah. No, I haven't."

"He should be sending their security footage over for you to take a look at. I checked it out at the shop, but it's gonna take some time to go through. And it needs some work."

"For sure."

Asher rubbed his eyes behind the aviators.

"You good?" Xavier said. "Looks like you need to take a beat."

He got up and dropped the now-empty cup into the trash. "Nope. All good."

"I don't think so. You need a night out."

"If anything, I need a night in. Hair of the dog. Does that work with caffeine?"

Xavier rose from his desk. "Good. It's settled, then. The

Lakefront Car Show is tonight. I'll stop by at seven."

"You're a royal pain in the ass, you know that?" Asher turned to step away, but as he did, Xavier clutched his arm. Asher looked down at his friend's ogre of a hand, gripping his bicep, holding him, keeping him from taking another step.

"I'm serious," Xavier said. "If you need more time off, you should take it, yeah? The chief wouldn't fight you on it."

Asher glanced at his arm yet again, and Xavier released him.

"Thank you, oh *wise* one. But trust me, if I need a shoulder to cry on, she'll look a lot nicer than some Hagrid-looking dope who insists on touching me in the workplace." Asher put on his best don't-get-soft face and sulked a sad frown.

"I'm glad you and I can have these talks," Xavier said, outwardly vexed that Asher was apparently incapable of taking advice when it came to his own well-being. "It makes me all . . . warm inside."

Asher removed his glasses and tucked them behind the top button of his somewhat open button-down. His face returned to indifference; his voice grew subdued. "Tell me," he said. He glanced around, this time sincere about who was nearby. "You *really* think it's her?"

Xavier only shook his head. His eyes laxed. "So, this is you? Doubting everyone and everything around you?"

"Oh, please. Don't give me that—"

"If this were any other case, you'd be satisfied with Agnes's report."

"If this were any other case, my wife would—" But he couldn't finish the thought. "If this were any other case," he continued, "I'd be the one in charge."

"Yeah," Xavier said with a sharpness to his words, "but it isn't. Cassandra's case happened *to* you, Asher. It wasn't dumped on your desk as an assignment. Let the higher-ups do their thing. We've got two other cases going right now, and—"

"Just do me a favor and take another look at the postmortem. Would it be that bad to keep an open mind about it? If it—"

"An open mind about what? That Agnes screwed up? It isn't *your* case. Internal Affairs has been called in for a reason. And the best thing that you can do right now is to solve the other cases we're working on. Why give them a reason to second-guess whether you're capable of doing your—"

"Thanks, but I already had therapy this morning." Asher turned, this time headstrong in his decision to leave. He pulled the aviators from his shirt, covered his eyes, and paced to the door, bypassing the thought of heading to his own office.

At least now, he preferred to be at home. At least there, the only doubts that he had to deal with were his own.

"Oh, and this time." He stopped at the door and spoke over his shoulder, only to yell so everyone could hear. "Clean that *pathetic* excuse of a Camaro!" He followed it with a quieter tone. "Us Corvette folks have an image to uphold."

"Seven-o'clock," Xavier shouted at his back.

Asher pushed his way through the precinct doors and toward the personless bank of elevators.

$$Chapter\ 37$$

The towering pale lights were scattered about the arena parking lot, outdoing the night's shadowy half-moon. They shone down onto the black and burgundy hood of the Vette, making it glisten. Asher shifted the car into reverse and backed into an empty space next to Xavier's Camaro.

Other classic cars of every make and model surrounded them, row upon row, for as far as Asher could see.

The last thing Asher felt like doing was sitting around at a car show when he could have been at the office—or better yet, at home, looking into the two cases that were very much ongoing. He needed a leg up before Pierre dropped a third one onto his desk. Better yet, before the chief caught his second wind and introduced Asher to some new, hotshot partner.

Department requirement or not, it wasn't going to happen.

Asher slid out of the Vette, inches from the ground. Xavier was opening the hood of his Camaro with a polishing rag thrown over his shoulder.

"Been here long?" Asher asked.

"Only a few."

Asher propped open the hood of his own car.

"You see?" Xavier said. "Those Vettes are nothing but a

nuisance. They're too small, the hoods open the wrong way. Oh, and don't forget about how they always"—he grinned—"finish last." He gestured over at Asher's vehicle. "At least that's the case with your '67, here."

"That right?" Asher pulled out his own rag from behind the driver's seat. "I thought it was nice guys like you who finish last?" He leaned over the engine compartment and searched for any last-minute blemishes under the black sky.

"You call it nice, I call it—"

"Well, what do we got here?" The voice was young.

Asher looked out from behind the car to find the guy from Justin's house, his nephew-in-law. Waylon, was it? The kid must've been a car enthusiast, too.

"How's it going?" Asher said.

"Hey."

Waylon rested there with his hands in his pockets, looking at the Vette with either envy or hatred; Asher couldn't tell which.

"You team Chevy?" Asher asked.

"Oh, yeah," Waylon said. "All the way." He pointed. "C2 in particular. This is the last year, huh? '67?"

"Oh yeah."

Waylon walked past Asher and to the open driver's-side door. He leaned forward, peered inside, and whistled, then turned his head to the owner. "Looks like a pretty penny."

"Well, I've chipped away at it over the years." Asher lifted his chin to his friend one parking spot over. "Waylon, this is Xavier. Xavier, Waylon."

Xavier spoke as he polished. "How's it going?"

But Waylon didn't respond, only pulled open the driver's door even farther and took a seat in the car. Both feet inside, hands at ten and two.

Asher looked over to Xavier, who returned his own look of curiosity. Or perhaps displeasure?

"Comfortable?" Asher said.

"Eh. I wouldn't say that." Waylon glanced over his shoulder to the small space behind the seats, then turned back. He ran his hand over the dashboard, rubbed his fingers together, then tapped his fingernail on the analog clock in the center console.

The clock Asher had yet to fix.

"That's a shame." Waylon slid out from behind the mahogany steering wheel and slammed the door shut as if the thing were a junker. The fiberglass rattled; the whole thing rocked. He stepped toward the front of the car and looked down at the engine. "Original?"

At first, it had appeared as though the kid knew his cars.

"Of course," Asher said. "Except for the new 383 and the blower." Maybe he didn't know cars. Not if he couldn't tell the difference between a new and original engine in the most popular year of Corvette.

Did Waylon really have such an off-center sense of self-confidence, or was he just trying to fit in? To be cordial, perhaps?

Waylon dimpled his chin with doubt, like some confused teen looking at his first pair of panties on their way down. Was it false confidence?

He moved between their cars, looking at the Camaro, now. "1968?"

"No," said Xavier. "'69"

Then a lingering silence. Ten seconds or so.

"So, how'd your session go this morning?" Waylon moved around the Camaro, looking but not looking, talking to Asher over his shoulder.

"I'm sorry?" Asher said, taken aback by the comment.

Waylon turned toward him. "Your session, with my uncle. How'd it go?"

Asher stopped what he was doing. His treatment was no one's business. What, the kid saw him at Justin's office, and now they're therapy buddies? Screw that.

"Hey, Asher." Xavier called from across the car. He pointed over his shoulder. "That beignet truck's here again. You up for it?"

Saved by the smell—Asher sensed his friend's effort to pull him away from the blatant oddity of the situation.

"Sure."

Waylon continued to stroll around the vehicles, shuffling back and forth between them as if deciding which one he preferred.

Asher tossed his rag behind the driver's seat and leaned down, reaching inside and locking the door. It didn't matter, really; everyone's windows stayed open at these shows, so anyone could reach inside if they wanted to. His only hope was that the kid, perhaps out the corner of his eye, saw him locking it. Or heard the click. A passive gesture telling him to move along.

Asher walked around to the front of the car and turned to the food truck with Xavier.

"They got good coffee, too." Waylon said.

They stopped and looked back.

His eyelids quivered, and the empty spheres beneath them rolled left, right, back, in an off-beat and anxious timing—that same tick Asher recalled from the first time they'd met. He welded them shut, squeezing, like something was stabbing at his corneas. Then he opened them as if he'd seen Madame LaLaurie herself.

Waylon waved, then strolled off and blended into the lot of grumbling cars and their owners.

Chapter 38

You—

"It's Reese, right?" The man shouted.

He stood shoulder-to-shoulder with you, placing his hand on the middle of your back. Not high enough to feel aggressive, nor just friendly even, but also not low enough that he was coming on too strong.

The bar was deafening. Some oversynthesized, hypnotic music played on loop from what sounded like fifty cabinets of speakers. Your teeth vibrated.

The last time you were in a club with a track that sounded like this, you were swaying in a bathroom stall with a small baggie of powdered ecstasy, wondering if you should snort it or put it on your tongue; it was your first time. Your golden, twenty-first birthday.

You had walked out of the restroom hoping no one would glimpse any powder at the tip of your nose.

Those were the days.

Now, you raised your drink in greeting and leaned in so he could hear you. "That's right." Then you pointed with the same hand. "Charlie, yeah?"

"You remember."

Of course you remembered; how could you forget such a fine specimen?

Someone nudged him from behind, causing him to spill a dribble of his drink down the front of his shirt. He turned around to say whatever it was that he needed, to yell or confront whatever drunken guy had stumbled.

That was when you went for it—more than a few drops into his drink on the bar. The place was so crawling, so drunken and stumbling, you could've announced it with a bull horn and not one soul would've been the wiser.

Charlie turned back and yelled in your ear. "Fucking assholes. No respect for any of *this*." Then he stepped back and ran his hand down his attire like some novice model.

You held him there for a couple hours at least. Talking, feeding him drinks, letting it seep into the crevasses of his system. Leading him on.

After a while, he leaned his head to the other side of the room. Then he grabbed your hand, pulling you behind him as he walked.

You tugged to stop him. "I don't dance." You tried releasing his grip, but he only held on tighter.

He rolled his eyes and cocked his hip. "Who said anything about dancing?" he shouted before pulling you in, until his pelvis met your own, and he ran his tongue up the side of your neck.

Charlie turned back toward the stairwell with you in tow.

It was quite the situation; from the way things were going, you wouldn't have to coerce the man as much as you had thought. Last time, it had taken nearly all evening to get the guy into an empty room. Dinner, drinks, meeting the friends, more drinks, more friends. Small talk.

Not this one. This was well-nigh . . . easy?

He led you up the stairs and into a massive VIP room. The music wasn't as loud as the first floor, but it would do.

In the back corner of the room, separated from the rest of the floor by a lavender velvet rope in front of a black curtain, was a small area with a couch and a table. He pulled you toward it and unlatched the rope, guiding you inside.

"Don't worry, they know me here," he said.

You couldn't help but smile.

VIP within VIP. Nice.

It wasn't long before you were on the couch, with Charlie on top of you. Straddled. Pushing against you. He undid the top button of your shirt, then reached for the second.

"Wait," you said, playing up the willingness in your voice. "You wanna play?"

He moved against you a bit more. "Of course I wanna play. I wouldn't have brought you up here if I didn't wanna play."

You rocked your hips to the side—and pulled the handcuffs from your back pocket.

"No," you continued, "I mean . . . *play*."

Charlie held out his wrists. As he did, his head dropped forward and his eyes closed for a split second, before he caught himself and his smile returned.

Surely, you were cast in some dream, tripping balls on how well you had imagined this would go, your subconscious playing it through in your head while you were passed out drunk after another night of searching for the right man and coming up short. It couldn't be this simple, not while you're awake and moving.

You placed the cuffs on each of his wrists, and he shoved himself against you even better than before. "Now what?" he said.

"Oh, you're a *star*, Charlie."

You grabbed him by the waist and rolled him off of you, onto his back. Then you got to your feet and stood over him. Him hard. You not. You'd take care of yourself later—once this was over and you had something worthwhile to think about.

"I don't feel so good." He coughed and clutched his stomach. His head glistened with the sweat of a heated club, made worse by what he had ingested.

You pulled back the corner of the curtain to see who, if anyone, was on the other side. But the one couple there, out on the balcony, quietly drinking like they were tourists in awe of such a city, was in the process of leaving. The room and adjoining terrace were empty.

Turning back, you saw Charlie now sitting up on the sofa. His hands were still cuffed in front of him. Like he was over the legal limit in the back of an NOPD cruiser. His eyes grew heavier, his face a faded sheet of white.

It'd be easier now, not having to worry about him overpowering you.

Of course, the alcohol helped, too.

"What'd you . . . what the hell did you do?" He coughed and pulled at the handcuffs. Too weak to stand, much less get his hands out of the steel restraints.

"Nothing, yet," you said. You downed the remainder of your Jäger and root beer, then slid the rope from your belt loops.

part two
DUALITY

Chapter 39

The explosion in Asher's head jolted him awake. He shot up, staring deep into the absolute darkness of the room. Black here, black there. Blacker. Unsure of where he was at. He looked over at his alarm clock, but it wasn't there. He went to throw his legs off the bed, but they hit a wall instead. He wasn't in his bed.

He was on the sofa in his home office.

Then another explosion went off, causing his chest to trip over its typical rhythm. Only it wasn't an explosion; it sounded like the back door.

"Asher!" The shout was more of a forceful whisper.

What time was it? Three? Four in the morning?

Another string of thuds sounded against the storm door out back. Asher swung his legs the other way, over the side without a wall blocking his exit, and felt his way to the light switch at the office door. He flicked the switch and grabbed his pistol from the foot of the couch, then made his way to the back door in the kitchen.

The cold steel of the pistol chilled his hand. As he turned the corner, a silhouette shifted behind the thin, pale curtain there. Moonlight dripped from the bottom of the window and down the edge of the door.

He thumbed the safety, moved to the side of the pane of glass, then eased back the curtain with the barrel of his .45.

"Hey, open up," Xavier said impatiently.

Asher hit the safety once more, then placed the pistol at the small of his back. He opened the door.

"No," Asher said with a bit of a bite, "I don't have trouble sleeping. Not one bit."

"Sorry," Xavier said, "but the chief couldn't reach you on your phone. And neither could I."

Asher let him in and shut the door. Xavier followed him down the hall and into his office.

"Well damn," Xavier said, looking around the room at the empty coffee cups, guitar on the floor, shoes and socks this way and that.

"Don't," Asher said. "Not now."

Xavier raised his hands in surrender. "I'm not gonna say a word."

Asher sat down on the sofa and started to slip on his socks and shoes from the day prior. "So, you woke me up just to shoot the shit, or are you gonna fill me in?"

"We've got another one," Xavier said.

Asher did nothing more than lower his head. "Yeah." He lifted his watch in front of him. "I should've known."

"But not just any other case," Xavier said. He leaned against the doorframe and rubbed his own bloodshot eyes.

"No?"

"No."

Asher sat back into the cushions and let his attention wander. Let the fabric hold him. He knew Xavier well enough that if he was showing up out of the blue, knocking on Asher's door in the dead of night, looking as if his dog of twenty years had just been flattened by a semi—it wasn't just another anything.

Asher stood. "Choked or diced?" he said.

Xavier grabbed his friend's jacket from the arm of the couch. "Choked." He handed it over as Asher hit the light, and they walked down the hallway together. "But it gets better."

Chapter 40

"You ain't lying," Asher said, Xavier at his side.

"I told you."

They'd paused in the middle of Bourbon Street, peering up at the balcony above Bourbon Pub Parade. Royal-purple shutters stood out against reddish-brown brick, even though the sun had yet to rise. A pride flag waved and popped in the hot wind, flapping in the midst of blue lights that flashed in circles across the surrounding buildings from the police cruisers below.

And the early-morning hours bled navy, as a body sat handcuffed to the terrace railing above.

Nude.

Asher noticed that, at least this time, NOPD had blocked off the streets quickly enough, and far enough, so they didn't have to deal with the public and the media. Not yet, anyway. It was still early, and the city had yet to stir.

As much as he tried, Asher couldn't pry his eyes from the intrigue of the scene, the theatricality of it: like standing out in the rain as one of Louisiana's hurricanes makes landfall, watching the Gulf crash over the retaining wall with this tree bending, that flag tearing. Wind banding around the corner of every building it could get its hands on. Howling.

The handcuffs above him gleamed a clean blue, attached to the railing and holding two lifeless wrists. The man's penis was flaccid and visible at the edge of the balcony floor, his pubic area shaved smooth. Legs spread. Head back.

"Come on," Xavier said. "Let's get up there."

As they exited the stairwell and entered the VIP room on the second floor, it was like stumbling behind the scenes of a magic trick. Bars in the Quarter were always set up to maximize the experience—dim lighting, flashing colors, loud music. And then you had people who added to the experience. A bustling staff, the shot girls, smokey rooms and bibulous customers. Tourists.

But not here.

The curtain was pulled back, so to speak. The house lights were up, the music off, no one around other than forensics, a few uniforms, and some lingering staff still in shock down on the first floor.

Xavier lifted the yellow-and-black tape that spanned the doorway, and Asher ducked beneath it, entering the room of empty beer bottles and unswept floors.

"This way," Xavier said.

He led Asher to one of the two smaller VIP areas at the back corner of the main room, set off from the rest of the space by rope and curtains. A uniform officer stood just outside the black drapes at the edge of the rooms, ensuring the staff didn't wander around, curious. One of Xavier's techs was snapping photographs out on the balcony.

The bar was typically a twenty-four-seven hotspot. But not now; what was usually a wild and bustling building was frozen still, as if time itself had ceased ticking entirely.

The room was basic and contained little to go on; a small

sofa, a glass table, mirrors covering the walls in every direction. Tobacco, cheap beer, and sweat lingered in the air. A bitter and humid taste sat in the back of Asher's throat.

"There isn't much in the room other than an ashtray with a few butts in it." Xavier pointed at a glass table in the middle of the floor. "We'll collect 'em for DNA."

"And the sofa?" Asher said.

"It's a cesspool. We'll process it, but it ain't gonna be a quick turnaround. Thing's covered in a mess of fibers, alcohol stains, and who knows what else."

Asher glanced around the rest of the room, his reflection staring back at him from the endless glass hanging from the walls. The mirrors were all framed by thick golden borders. For a bar, even for a VIP area, the space seemed . . . empty? Sure, the floors were grimy, the ashtray used, the sofa messy. But what was missing?

No empty cups. No napkins or clothing from the decedent. Witnesses?

Murder scenes weren't meant to be simple; they were messy. Chaotic. Confusing at best. Which, Asher supposed this one was, too. Only confusing in the sense that it went against the norm. They were left with very little to consider—aside from the body itself.

"Well, let's just make sure we're covering all our bases," Asher said. "There might not be much, but let's take care of the cigarette butts, the ashtray, sofa, and any prints that are more than a useless partial. There's probably dozens of prints scattered all over this place, but we've gotta do it." He turned to the couch. "I don't care if you have to wrap up the damn thing like a po-boy and drag it into the lab."

"I agree," Xavier said.

As Asher exited the small corner space and walked toward the balcony door, someone rushed into the main room in a panting haste.

"Sorry I'm late," John said. He nudged his uneven glasses up the bridge of his nose as he gripped his tattered notebook in the other hand. "Where you need me?" His breathing was arduous.

There was so much Asher wanted to say. So much he *could've* said. But it wasn't his place; John was Xavier's problem. A trainee who was proving late and sloppy right off the bat.

A shadow that was slowly fading into the background.

Xavier was all about chances, opportunities for the up-and-coming generation of forensics. But just like Asher, his patience would only stretch so thin before it frayed at the seams.

"Where do I need you? I need you *on time*," Xavier said. "Grab a camera." His voice was cutting. He pointed to the black case at the door.

But John—sweating and wide-eyed—looked to Asher for some reason.

It was almost as if he expected the detective to speak up. To step between them?

Chapter 41

"Kid's got some balls, huh?" Asher spoke to Xavier as they walked outside and onto the balcony. "A no-show on the previous one, and now he's late?"

"Well, he claims that he was sick for the stabbing case."

"Still . . ."

"Oh, I know. I know."

The scene itself was a spitting image of the first one: the decedent stripped bare, cuffed to the balcony with his legs spread-eagle, head back and looking up to the ceiling. Asher had zero reservations that this was the same guy, same killer.

John loitered to the side, grabbing pictures of whatever he could find, seemingly doing his best to stay out of the way, now.

Asher crouched next to the body. "Same ligature marks around the neck." He pointed. "He's cuffed the same. Posed the same." He spoke to Xavier. "We have an ID yet?"

"Yeah. Name is Charles Richard. The shot girl who found him said he was a regular."

"Huh . . ."

"What?"

Asher got up and scanned the balcony.

"A shot girl found him? And there's no drinks or any of

those little shot tubes up here? I ain't ever met no shot girl who cleans up—and with a body nearby?"

The corners of Xavier's mouth sank in uncertainty. "That's a good point, I guess."

"I don't like it," Asher said.

"What's to like?"

"So, she came up here with a tray of shots, saw a dead guy cuffed to the balcony with his dick out, and she just turned around and walked downstairs to tell someone?"

"What *should* she have done?"

"I don't know—dropped the tray, spilled a shot or two, set the tray down to run. Something. Hell, anything. It's too clean, you know?"

John spoke from inside of the room, through the open balcony door. "Who said she was carrying shots? Maybe she was just up here checking to see if they needed anything."

Asher ignored him. Xavier shut the door with his gloved hand.

The veranda was already well lit by the additional lights that Xavier's crew had thrown up, but Asher pulled his flashlight from the inside of his leather jacket for good measure. He shined it around each corner of the balcony, against the wall, then through the glass door and into the room.

"What are you thinking?" Xavier said.

It was all so textbook, exactly in line with the first murder. The gay bar, the balcony, the manner in which the decedent was posed. Like a carbon copy, a receipt from one of those manual credit card imprinters from the '80s.

Except—

"I'm guessing," Asher said, "that a company pen isn't gonna magically appear underneath some piece of furniture, or in a dark corner somewhere, and give us all the answers we need?"

He dragged his light through the glass door and over the floor inside.

"Yeah, I'm gonna go out on a limb and say, 'no,'" Xavier said.

A blinding light from a camera inside of the room flashed at the two of them. Not once, not twice, a slew of automatic shots.

"I swear to god," Asher said. "Where did you find this idiot? What the hell is he shooting? Us?"

Xavier bounced his hand as if he were dribbling an unseen ball. "Take it easy, man; the guy's new. He isn't walking where he shouldn't or going around touching shit. I told him to take some photos, so that's what he's doing. I'm not gonna stand over him the *entire* time."

"Uh-huh."

Asher rarely went out of his way to be a prick, or desperately nice for that matter. But something rubbed him the wrong way about the new guy. John was clumsy, to put it mildly. The exact opposite of detail oriented—whatever that was. Un-Agnes-like.

He had yet to screw up, other than the slight mishap of leaving his notes lying around and leaning against the balcony the other day. But those were neither here nor there.

Something worse would happen eventually, though. Asher could see it coming from a mile away. One botched piece of evidence was all it took.

"What about the sofa?" he asked.

"What about it?"

"You move it? Look under it? Is there anywhere inside that your guys haven't looked yet?"

"They're working on it," Xavier said.

Asher opened the door and walked inside. "I'll take that as a 'no,' then."

They returned to the small VIP area. Asher crouched next to the two-person couch there, in front of the glass table. He shined his light under it, but all he saw was a bottlecap and a dusty hair tie.

He slipped on a single blue, latex glove.

"Hey John," Xavier called into the main room.

He appeared beside them. "What's up?"

"Get down there. Grab a photo of whatever he's got."

John knelt in front of the sofa and adjusted the camera lens. Snapped a few pictures. Asher pulled the cap and hair tie from beneath the furniture. Xavier held open two separate evidence bags, and Asher placed them inside.

A long strand of red-brown hair hung, coiled, from the elastic hairband.

"Well, well," John said. He snapped another photo under the sofa, then fidgeted with the camera. "Looks like you've got some detective work to do, my friend."

Chapter 42

Instead of a body, it was pieces: limbs, a torso, organs already spilled so Agnes didn't need to remove them herself.

The head.

She stood over the autopsy table with her clipboard, assessing the puzzle of a homeless man who was pieced together like some unboxed and unassembled IKEA armoire.

"There he is," Agnes said to Asher, holding her eyes on the diagram in her hands.

"Here I am." He moved beside her and took in the damage, now under the morgue lights instead of in the middle of an obscure, faint alleyway in the dead of night.

He glanced over at the anatomy diagram in her hands, showing both dorsal and ventral views of a body. *How the hell does that work, when the parts are no longer together?*

"So, what do you do in this case?" Asher asked. "Draw a dotted line through everything that was cut off? That's a lot of lines."

"Actually, yes. Then I have a separate page for each one." She flipped through several pages beneath the typical outline of a body on the top sheet, each subsequent page blank save for the decedent's identifying information at the bottom.

He thought he'd caught her by surprise with such a sarcastic question, but the fact that he was right made it all the more satisfying, more comical.

Asher thought he'd give it one last try, just for shits and giggles. "So," he said. "How'd he die?"

Buttons were shiny—and Asher *loved* pushing that which shone. Like a crow homing in on a gum wrapper.

Agnes ceased writing, frozen. Blinking. Then she glanced over with fluttering eyes. "*Gee*, I'm not sure, Detective." Her voice was that of a scared schoolgirl, dramatic and overdone. "From what I can tell, he had one too many daiquiris and tripped." She turned and dropped the clipboard on her desk before grabbing one of the cigarettes that was already spilling from the open pack there.

"Good," Asher said. "I'm glad this was a cut-and-dry case of drunken negligence."

Agnes laughed, and so did he.

"Sorry about the mess," Asher said. "If it was up to me, they'd come preassembled."

Agnes lit up. "No worries, love." Then a drag. "It's part of the job."

"In all seriousness?"

"From what I can tell? Blood loss, prior to the obvious. If I find something else, I'll let you know, but I've already been through most of him. Nothing yet."

"Sounds good."

Asher debated bringing it up again. Surely, Pierre had reached out to Agnes after Asher's back-and-forth with him the other day.

How long did he really have?

"The chief say anything else about Cassandra?" Asher said.

"We talked about it briefly."

"Yeah, he called not long after you left, a couple days ago."

"What'd he say?"

"Well, it was more of what he didn't say than anything else, love. I'm not sure what the two of you have going on over there at the office, but over here, I can only drag my feet for so long before I've gotta answer to someone. And it ain't you."

"Gotcha."

"He asked if I could hold off on the cremation for another week or so."

"And what did you say?"

He couldn't stand being the go-between. Why couldn't the chief just have come to him in the first place? Now, Asher had to sit there and practically negotiate with Agnes, without knowing exactly what Pierre had said to her. As if Asher was incompetent.

"I told him I'd do what I can, but I can only make excuses for so long. The autopsy's done, and there's no reason to keep her here."

"Well, that's not entirely true. We do have—well, Internal Affairs has—a case to solve. We still don't know the whole story of how she worked her way into the department in the first place, nor the details of what she was up to over the last several years while she was on the payroll. There's still work to do."

"Sure," Agnes said, the smoke leaking from her nose like an afterthought, "but what's that got to do with her body?"

And for that, Asher had no answer. At least, not one that he was willing to share openly with just anyone as of yet.

"Yeah. I get that." Asher took a breath and rolled the bracelet on his wrist. "Just give me a few days. Then, she's all yours."

Agnes set the cigarette in the ashtray, then hopped up to sit on her desk. "Wait a minute. You don't have doubts about the autopsy, do you? Asher?"

"What? No. Hell, no."

That was lie. A blatant lie. But who didn't lie from time to time when it was necessary?

"Fine," she said. "But you're already two days in. After a week, she's cremated."

"I know."

Asher turned. Agnes stopped him.

"Oh, and love?"

"Yeah?"

"This new one y'all just sent over? That makes three." She picked up her cigarette and held it out in front of her, lighting the end while rolling it between her fingers like a joint. Lost in the burn.

As it turned out, Asher wasn't the only one who could push buttons.

Chapter 43

Xavier shut the door and walked to the side of Asher's desk. "I was able to narrow it down to about twenty minutes," he said.

"Twenty minutes?" Asher was surprised, but in a good way. "How long was the original footage that he sent over?"

"It was just over six hours. Stopped at midnight on the dot."

Asher gestured to the front of his desk. "Pull up a chair."

The two of them sat at Asher's desk. Asher opened the file that Xavier had sent him. He adjusted the monitor a bit in his friend's direction. If there was any chance of seeing the person on camera, this was it.

Asher maximized the video and hit play. At first, the street was empty, save for a roving squirrel and some trash, blowing along the edge of an adjacent building. "How long until—"

"Two seconds," Xavier said.

Sure enough, once the sun had settled, a pair of men entered the screen from the bottom right corner of the frame, walking down the alley from the direction of Conti Street. He let the entirety of the video play out to get the full picture. Then he dragged the timestamp back to the beginning.

"So, I'm guessing it's the two at the beginning of the footage who you think are worth looking into?" Asher said.

"Well, yeah—unless you think the old lady and her cane have something to do with dicing our guy up into a million pieces. I checked out all of it: the hours before and the hours after. Every minute and everyone. Nothing." Xavier pointed at the screen. "These two are the ones of interest, from what I can tell. If it's someone else, I'm not seeing it."

"It doesn't give us much to work with," Asher said.

"Don't come complaining to me. I'm not the one who gave us the footage."

Asher was right, though—it was in the air. Having nothing but a brief video of two dark and fuzzy faces walking down the alley wasn't much to go on. One of the men was wearing slacks and a sports coat, the other shorts and a T-shirt.

Asher looked to the screen. "Sunglasses at night?"

"Oh, don't act like you've never worn your shades after dark. I've seen it first-hand."

"Can you blow it up any more than this? Enhance the clarity?"

"Already have—and that's as good as it gets. Any more and the quality actually gets worse."

"Alright," Asher said. "So, what makes these two stand out?"

"You've already seen it. We can watch it again if you—"

"Just tell me. I can watch it again later if I need to." Asher hated guessing games.

Xavier grabbed the mouse and ran the video forward a bit. Pointed. "They enter the alley here, then they walk, taking their time, down the center of the street until they get here." More pointing. "But what do you notice?"

"Nothing, other than the fact that they're two dudes hanging out a bit too close to one another."

"What are they doing?" Xavier said. "Are they shopping? Taking pictures? Meeting someone? Eating? No, none of that. They're just standing there, side by side, looking farther down the alley and talking only to one another. Two guys, sitting there for far too long, just watching—in the direction of the murder."

"That could be anything. They could be tourists who have never been here before, just taking it all in. Who knows?"

Xavier ran the video forward some more. "Fine. But then they walk in the direction of the murder, once no one else comes in or out of the video for some time, then they exit the frame together as well. In the same direction they came from. Only this time"—he let their exit play out—"more frantic."

Indeed, the men practically jogged from the alleyway.

"Okay, so what now?"

To Asher, it was a needle in a rice field; they would've been better off tracking the shadows of two poltergeists on one of those ghost and vampire tours.

Asher continued, "This doesn't give us anything."

"Maybe," Xavier said. "But what *does* it give us?"

"What?"

"It gives us the obvious." Xavier grabbed the mouse and hovered the pixelated, white arrow over the first of the men. He held out his thumb. "Suspect one." Then he slid the arrow to the other figure and held up his thumb and index finger—right in front of the detective's face. "Suspect two."

Chapter 44

It wasn't like Justin to cancel their session—and it wasn't okay, either.

Asher had a sense, a gut reaction, that his therapist was hiding something; not only was their appointment canceled, but Justin had provided absolutely no reasoning behind it.

He threw the Vette into park. Forget the kill switch, he had no intention of dragging this out.

Asher strode into the foyer of Justin's home office. To his surprise, a young man in a suit was sitting there behind a corner desk, just inside of the entryway.

"Hello. Can I help you?" the man said.

"Yeah, I need to speak with Justin. Where is he?"

Voices, deep and quarrelsome, carried from Justin's office. They were growing louder, bouncing from the high ceilings and hardwood floors of the dated home.

"He's currently in a session with a patient. Is there something I can help you with?"

Who was this guy? And what the hell did Justin need with a receptionist? Was that even what he was?

"He canceled my appointment this morning, and I was wondering why. He's never canceled on me. I need to speak with him. Unless you can tell me why—"

"Oh, okay," said the man. "You must be Asher."

"Yeah."

"Justin decided to trim down his client list, and I'm sorry to say that he wasn't able to—"

"Are you shitting me? 'Trim down' his list? No, that's bullshit." Asher stepped toward the office, the voices inside growing louder, more cutting.

"No," said the man. "You can*not* go in there. Justin will be out soon. He's in the middle of an emergency session right now. You can't go in there."

"Oh, yeah?" Asher thrust open the door.

"No!" said the suit.

Asher stepped inside of the room—but Justin was nowhere to be found.

He didn't recognize her, but another therapist sat in the chair, legs crossed, frozen midsentence and writing on the notepad in her lap.

Across from her sat a patient. Unreadable.

Neither of them spoke. Their conversation paused, just lingering there.

"What's going on?" Asher said, although he wasn't all too sure to whom he was speaking. "What is this?"

Still, they didn't say a word.

"Asher, please," said the suit behind him. "Let's go. This is highly inappropriate."

"No answer?" Asher said. "Nothing? Where's Justin? I need to talk to him."

The therapist and her patient looked to one another, shrugging.

"Come on, I'll walk you out."

"No," Asher said. "I'm not going anywhere. *Where* is Justin?"

This didn't make any sense. Justin was the one person he was able to confide in. The one person who was there, day and night, willing to listen, ready to talk it out, to tell Asher the cold and hard truth that he needed to hear whether he liked it or not.

What was this? Some sick joke?

The man's voice behind him grew louder. "Let's . . . go. *Now.*"

"No," Asher said.

Just then, a car on the residential street out front sped past the home. A ray of light shattered through the window and reflected from the badge on the therapist's hip.

A silver badge.

The voice behind him grew louder yet. "*Now*, Asher."

"No."

He stepped farther into the room. If Justin wasn't here, then where was he? What was this?

Slowly, the therapist rose. She took a step toward him. Her face widened in a growing, animated grin. Jester-like.

"Asher!" said the suit.

He felt a tug at his shoulder, pulling him backward.

"Asher!"

Then another pull.

All he could see was that grin—lit by the glare of a silver badge on the woman's hip.

"Asher," the voice said. The chief shoved the detective's shoulder once more.

"What the fuck are you doing?" Pierre said. "Get the hell up."

Asher lifted his head from his desk, a cold dribble at the

corner of his lips.

The chief loomed over him. "Internal Affairs wants a word."

Chapter 45

sher took a seat at the head of the mile-long wooden table in the conference room.

"They'll be right in," Pierre said. "Good luck." Then he shut the door.

Be right in? What were they waiting on?

And who, exactly, were *they*?

This wasn't some interrogation, where a suspect sat at some tiny desk with two steel chairs in the corner of a claustrophobic and freezing room, with a camera blinking in the corner of the ceiling as the officer in charge turns the air to frostbite and watches the accused fidget and shiver from behind a CCTV monitor in the next room over; this was Asher. This was their lead detective.

And these people were his people—whether he had met them or not.

Five minutes slogged by. Then ten. Then—

"Good evening," a man said as he entered the room. He was holding a thick black binder, and another guy, notably fat, followed him in. Big guy shut the door then sat in the corner. Silent, like some pump-up dummy that had been overinflated.

"Good evening."

They shook hands. "Jazz Raleigh," said the man. No eye

contact. "Internal Affairs."

He was a half-normal-looking man, apart from the porno mustache and a wide tie that was about two inches too short for his dad bod of a stomach. He sat all the way at the other end of the conference table, about eight seats down.

The big guy offered no intro.

Asher half expected them to ease into it, to introduce why they were here and exactly what they were looking for with respect to the whole Cassandra farce. On the one hand, it was obvious: Asher's ex-partner had infiltrated the department over the course of several years, then, for personal reasons regarding her husband's parents having some sordid past with Asher's parents, conspired to murder Asher as part of some nonsensical revenge plot with her husband.

Asher didn't have much to add. He'd been oblivious, aside from what little Cassandra had spilled while her gun was pressed beneath his chin only weeks prior.

On the other hand, how had she done it? How had the partner of the lead detective of New Orleans's Homicide Unit managed to get hired as a psychologist-turned-investigator, when her motives were so impure? For this, Asher had nothing to offer whatsoever.

"Thank you for taking the time to meet with us, Detective. We appreciate it."

"No problem."

"I'll get straight to the point," Jazz said. "Our department is looking into the hiring of your former partner, in addition to the acquisition and closing of the cases y'all have worked over the course of her employment."

"Uh-huh."

"From what I hear, y'all have her body. Is that right?"

Possibly. Probably?

"We believe so. The examiner's office is still working on the autopsy and identification."

"And the cause of death is likely to be the fatal gunshot wound from a colleague"—he flipped to a certain page in the binder—"with . . . NOPD *forensics*? Did I read that correctly?"

"Perfectly."

Jazz paused. Shut the binder. Pushed it aside. The man folded his hands on the table and glared at him. "Mr. Huxley, if we—"

"*Detective* Huxley."

"Sorry. Detective Huxley, if we're gonna make any headway on understanding how your former partner was able to pull the blinds down over an entire homicide department, yourself included, it'd be great if you would assist us in doing so. Not to mention, I think it would be in your best interest."

"My best interest?"

"Under penalty of termination, yes."

What was he supposed to say? As far as motive, and what had happened years prior when the chief hired her, he was unable to explain what he didn't know.

"Of course," Asher said.

Jazz opened the binder again. The big guy in the corner folded his arms. He looked eager for a snack.

"Now," Jazz continued, "walk me through the last case that the two of you worked together."

"Which one are you referring to? The crabbing homicide out on Lake Pontchartrain, or the double homicides carried out by my ex-partner's husband and probably herself?"

"The crabbing homicide?"

"Yeah, that was a creative one. Husband caught his wife

messing around with his brother. Instead of divorcing and dealing with the family drama, the wife and brother murdered the husband. Filleted him and used him as crab bait in dozens of traps along the southside of the lake."

Jazz's faced drained of all color—not white, but colorless.

"Unfortunately for the new couple," Asher continued, "fishermen poaching one another's traps is more common around here than most people realize. Fish and Game had both of them in cuffs in less than twenty-four hours."

"And the poacher?"

Asher chuckled. "He got a warning."

Jazz's face hinted at the idea that Asher had taken an unwanted detour. Asher had figured that as IA of a homicide department, the man would appreciate the aside. Apparently not.

"Well," Jazz said, "I'm referring to the homicides carried out by your partner's husband."

"Oh. Well, why didn't you say so?"

He would keep his answers short and to-the-point; he wasn't about to implicate himself in some absurd collusion he had nothing to do with. He knew about his ex-partner's MO, and who she truly was, about as much as he understood nuclear physics. Sure, they had worked together for several years—but where could he even begin with trying to understand the woman now? How could he possibly sort through the layers and years of lies?

Did he even want to understand someone who had nearly ruined him, attempted to murder him, after that person might already be dead?

Would he have loved to see her pay? Sure. But at this point, what mattered and what didn't?

This Internal Affairs investigation, really more like

interrogation, was in no way kosher by Asher's eye. They should've been working alongside Homicide to figure this thing out, not running around accusing detectives and their superiors of misconduct, which was exactly what they were doing so far.

—

Two hours later, Asher exited the conference room—hungry, cold.

Pierre was waiting outside when they were done. "So, how'd it go?"

Asher slid on his leather jacket, bouncing his shoulders to adjust the fit. "Well, about as good as being accused under the table could go."

"Accused?"

"Well, 'How could you possibly not have known?' were their exact words."

The chief seemed unusually lax, after just having gone through his own meeting with IA before Asher's. Surely, his couldn't have gone much better.

Pierre slapped him on the shoulder and fashioned a mischievous grin. "Don't sweat it," he said. "I think we'll be just fine."

Chapter 46

Asher and Xavier stepped off of the elevator and entered the department lobby, the thud of their boots ricocheting from the marble floors and immense ceilings.

Asher paused midstride as he spied the frenzy of media lying in wait outside, beneath the building's awning. Their tripods were set up in front of their respective vans, the various insignia of local news channels plastered across the side of their vehicles.

Xavier stopped and turned back. "What is it?"

Asher knew exactly what it was, and it had nothing to do with the most recent homicides above the bars and down on Exchange Place.

"I ain't in the mood for this, man." He shot his thumb over his shoulder, toward the elevators. "Not after two hours of questioning."

"You do realize that you aren't *required* to say anything, right?"

"Oh, come on," Asher said. "Required and expected aren't that far off in our line of work, are they? If I ignore them, then it makes me look incompetent when I'm not."

"But aren't you?"

"What?"

"Incompetent." Xavier spoke dryly, but Asher could catch on to his friend's satirical prodding as if the man's thoughts were his own.

"Well, according to Internal Affairs I am."

"Yeah, along with an entire department of naïve colleagues, apparently."

"Ain't that right?"

"Come on," Xavier said. "Say whatever you have to, and ignore whatever you want. Fuck 'em."

They walked through the lobby and toward the double doors at the exit. Before they'd even finished pushing through, the questions came flying in.

"Detective Huxley!" A woman sprinted forward in her high heels, holding out a microphone like she was crossing the finish line of a track relay race, passing the baton. "Why is it that you still don't have an ID on the body that was found out at the river?" She shoved the mic into Asher's face. Xavier was apparently chopped liver. "Who's responsible here?"

Xavier did his best to fend off as many of them as he could, but the sheer number, a dozen or more, made it near impossible. He tried to stand in front of Asher, but somehow they managed to rudely work their way between them.

"The city's chief medical examiner is working on the ID and autopsy," Asher said. "As soon as she's done with her examination, we'll have an answer." He stepped out from beneath the building's overhang and walked toward his car. "No one is looking to jump the gun, here."

"Is that it?" another said. "It's the examiner's office who's responsible, then?"

"No," Asher said. "This is a collective effort. Our

department is working together with the medical examiner, in addition to Internal Affairs. Regardless of whether the decedent is our own, Homicide's internal review into what happened regarding my partner will continue."

A male reporter stepped between him and the Vette just before he reached the door.

"So, you're being looked into by Internal Affairs, and the public is supposed to believe that the investigation is a collective effort? When will the people have answers, Detective?" Not only was the man too close, invading his personal space with his rank, garlic-ridden breath, but he was now pressed against Asher's prize car.

Asher raised his hand, palm out. "Back *the fuck* up."

"Alright." Xavier jumped between them, easing the man out from between Asher and one of the few objects in life over which he grew quickly defensive. "Let's go," Xavier said to the reporter. "I suggest you quit while you're ahead."

Asher opened the car door, tossed his briefcase into the passenger seat, then slid into the vehicle. As he pulled out of the parking lot, the microphones followed him, shoved against the driver's window of the Vette.

Why did Asher suddenly feel guilty? In spite of everything that had happened with his ex-partner, none of this was his own doing.

Was it?

Chapter 47

You—

Where he had gotten the money for admission, you had no idea.

You were already inside of the Pharmacy Museum on Chartres Street, not far from Napoleon House, when you noticed the young and dirtied man step through the weathered French doors. The bell chimed.

He got in line to pay at the antique cash register.

You could sense that he felt out of place, like everyone would recognize he had no interest in the pharmacological, the historic—his attention swept the room as he fidgeted with the bag strung over his shoulder. An army-green cloth messenger bag that had lived its days on the demanding city streets. The man's face was unshaven and reddened from the Louisiana sun. Cracked. Tired. His thinning jeans and faded, plaid shirt had seen better days.

In a way, he reminded you of your younger self—finding your way into this store or that, any building or museum or restaurant, just to bask beneath the AC. Solely to encounter some sense of normalcy and to get off the streets and into the indoors, out of the thick heat.

He wasn't any old customer, though; the poor, former or current, recognized the poor. Yourself included.

And this man—he needed your help.

You watched from across the front room of the museum, next to the roped-off, original pharmacy counter in the back right corner. Behind the wooden counter and dated metal register were shelf upon dust-ridden shelf of decades-old glass medicine bottles in shades of dark brown, bottle green, and amber. Original logbooks, pharmacist tools, and more were littered about the space.

The man toiled over the crumpled bills in his hand and paid his entry at the front counter. But instead of grabbing one of the information pamphlets that guided visitors around the room in a numbered and orderly fashion, he bypassed the route altogether and made his way out back—straight into the courtyard and toward the fountain.

He brushed past you.

Help him. Help him the way no one helped you. The way Dad should've helped you, far too long ago. Don't be a coward.

You adjusted your tie.

His stench, his sluggish gate, his nervous disposition—all of it was too close of a memory to your younger self. Like a walking, antique mirror in great need of repair. In need of saving.

Not all reflections could be saved, though. Sometimes, the cracks were too deep. The voids too void to be filled.

You stepped out of the front room, past the hallway, and onto the back patio at the edge of the outdoor square, which was surrounded by two-story brick walls, red and laced with vines.

The young but tattered man sat down on the concrete ledge of the fountain, all the way at the back of the open-air space. A rusted, two-level water feature sat at its center, surrounded by greening water filled with spare change. Water trickled from the needly top of the fountain. The surface below hardly rippled.

You stepped behind a pillar beneath the patio, watching.

It was painful to see him like this.

The man set down his bag on the ledge, then removed something from inside of it. He pulled out a small, six-inch cut of French bread. He ate what was most likely his dinner, probably from some trash bin at the back door of a local restaurant.

As you walked toward him, he tore off a piece of the bread and dropped it on the ground next to one of the pigeons there. The bird hopped closer. He fed it more.

You unbuttoned your coat, which had always made you out to be more inviting.

More birds.

As you approached him, only a few feet out, he turned around and looked down into the water. The glare caught his rough, tired face in profile. White lines, like city streets on a map, danced over his untended beard. Then he set down the bread and reached deep into the water, soaking his arm, pulling up a handful of loose change. The dripping water soddened the bread.

He turned back and froze. Caught red-handed.

"How's it going, my friend?" You stuck out your hand. "Name's Ryker."

Chapter 48

erhaps it was time to come clean.

Hopefully, Xavier wouldn't fault Asher for having mentioned it to Pierre first. It had been a timing thing, a heat-of-the-moment sort of call. Lot of good it had done: Pierre had practically dismissed him entirely when he spilled his suspicions about Cassandra's death, and her supposed autopsy.

Perhaps Asher deserved it. Maybe there was nothing to spill. After all, it wasn't like he had some crazy, definitive secret he was keeping to himself. He hadn't even seen her at the café that day, after she jumped ship. It was a pure case of "he said, she said." Maybe the waiter had seen Asher and Cassandra there before. Maybe he was just jerking him around?

A few days later, Asher had returned to the café and showed the waiter a picture of Cassandra to verify that it was, in fact, her who sent him the breakfast that day. The guy couldn't say for sure, though. His memory of what the woman looked like was tenuous at best.

Asher may have spoken to the chief first, but if anyone was going to entertain the idea that Cassandra might still be out there, it was Xavier.

He pulled the Vette alongside his friend's Camaro in the

driveway. A thin layer of Southern pollen had blanketed Xavier's car like a fine mist on an October morning. He cracked the windows, then threw the car into park.

Smoke billowed from behind the home, out back on the deck, where Xavier was most likely grilling with a beer in hand. Asher walked out back.

Sure enough, Xavier stood over the grill, squinting in the onslaught of smoke as he flipped burgers.

"Should I call for the hose?" Asher said, stepping up and onto the deck. He grabbed the foiled tray from the table and handed it to the chef.

"Well that depends," Xavier said. "You like your burger well-done or charred?"

The man never could flip a patty. Ribs? Sure. Tenderloin? Absolutely. He could even finish a mouthwatering chicken breast to perfection, time and time again. But burgers? Whatever it was, well-done or burnt were the only options.

Xavier dropped them onto the tray, then set the food on the table.

"I'll grab your wine off the counter," Xavier said. He walked inside, then returned with a bottle of Cabernet and a fresh glass, setting them down in front of Asher. "It's all you."

Asher poured the red. "So tell me—anything new? You take a second look?"

He figured it was best to test the waters before diving in headfirst; currents were often deceptive.

"I did."

"And?"

"Not a thing."

They sat there and drank, ignoring the nearly black patties between them.

"What are you getting all caught up over, anyways?" Xavier said. "It's a little hard to review everything from the scene if I don't know what the hell I'm looking for."

"Well, if I knew what I was looking for, I wouldn't have asked you to take a second look."

It was a valid question. After all, he had requested a second review of Xavier's take on the scene, just like he had requested a second autopsy—without providing a reason for either of them.

"You wanna tell me what's going on? If I know what you're thinking, maybe I can help."

They sat in silence for the better part of a minute—Asher doubting what had happened that day at Café Du Monde, Xavier seemingly edgy over his friend not sharing whatever it was that was on his mind.

"Alright," Asher said. "But you're gonna think I'm crazy."

Xavier took a swig of beer.

"A few days after everything went down, after the shooting and then Sofia's funeral, I went to Café Du Monde for breakfast. I ordered, but when the waiter brought out the food, it was wrong."

Xavier seemed unimpressed. Waiting for more, he picked at the label on his bottle. "Okay . . ."

"He had a coffee and a box, instead. A large, black coffee—and a French cruller. What Cassandra always brought me in the mornings."

Now, Xavier's expression turned curious.

"He said that there was a lady at the register—who said that that was what I really wanted. I didn't think to do it in the moment, but I went back a few days later and showed him a picture of her. He didn't recognize her, but he couldn't give me a solid description of her either."

Another sip of beer.

"How would *you* take it?" Asher asked. "You'd say that was her, right? That Cassandra was there, at the café?"

Xavier broke eye contact and glanced around the yard, obviously doubtful of what he had just heard. He adjusted himself in the chair. "Maybe," he said. "But how? You saw her the last time I saw her—shot in the chest, hemorrhaging blood when she could barely walk. Hell, I'm the one who shot her. How the fuck she managed to stumbled out of that house is beyond me, man."

"Yeah, I know. Same. But do you think that there's any possibility that—"

"Personally, probably not. She's one lucky son of a bitch if she somehow managed to make it somewhere after being shot in the chest, bleeding the way she was bleeding."

"Sure. But we didn't find her. No one did."

"And the body from the river?"

Asher said nothing; there was nothing to say. He lifted his shoulders, held them, then dropped them at a languid pace.

Xavier set down his beer and stood up. He fiddled with the grill, extinguishing the briquettes with water and brushing the metal grates that were dripping with fat.

"Why are you telling me this?" Xavier said. "I mean, thanks for sharing, although you probably should've told someone sooner. I guess what I'm asking is—what are you wanting me to do about it? What do you want me to say? Is there something you're wanting to do? Without actually seeing her, or hearing from her yourself"—he gestured with the greasy brush—"what can you do?"

"Well, I guess that's why I'm telling you. I'm not sure what to do—or if there's anything *to* do."

"And the chief? You gonna tell him?"

"Already did. He said pretty much the same: I've been wrong about her before, and whatever I do, he doesn't wanna know about it. We've got a body, and we've got Agnes's postmortem."

Xavier set down the brush and picked up his beer. "Well, I can't say that he's wrong."

"I guess all I'm looking for is your opinion on whether there's something I should do about it."

"Yeah. Move on."

"Seriously?"

"Look, I'm all for the bitch getting what she's got coming, but the fact is . . . what've you got? A story from a waiter? I'm not trying to throw shade, but in order for us to do something, we've gotta have somewhere to start. Something to go off of, yeah?"

Asher felt better. Vaguely. At least, now, he had gotten it off his chest. The two people who needed to know, now knew.

"You of all people should know by now that I'm on board for whatever crazy shit you've got working, but based on what you're telling me, I'm not sure what that'd be." Xavier raised his beer, and they met glasses.

"Yeah. Me neither, man. Me neither."

Asher grabbed one of the less burnt burgers between them, and Xavier topped off his glass.

Chapter 49

It had been some time since Asher woke up with his alarm, thanks to the dreams and insomnia.

He poured his coffee into a to-go cup, then clipped his holstered pistol inside of his waistband, at the four-o'clock position of his back. He slipped on his leather jacket for an extra layer of concealment; his pistol printed more times than not, forming an outline through his shirt for everyone to see.

As law enforcement, that was one of his few unspoken fears: someone seeing that he was concealed carrying, then grabbing his gun before he could stop it. He wasn't required to conceal carry—he wore a badge on his hip, after all. Most of the other detectives open carried, wearing their piece in plain view. Unless they were undercover.

But not Asher; it just didn't feel right.

He grabbed his coffee and walked out of the kitchen door. But as he backed out of the driveway, he brought the Vette to a rumbling halt before reaching the road. The blower whined from under the hood.

Someone was parked across the street, in front of the house whose elderly owners shared a car—an old but well cared-for Crown Vic. Parked out there now was a discreet, all-white van. Like a painter's work van but with tinted windows.

Perhaps the neighbors had visitors?

Asher continued out of the driveway, then shifted the car into drive and crept to the stop sign. He looked left, then right. The Vette shook and pushed Asher back into his seat as he let up on the clutch and eased the gas.

He glanced in the rearview mirror.

The van cut a U-turn, following him.

Asher parked on the street in front of Justin's home office. The van came to a slow crawl about two houses back—then pulled to the side of the road. At first, no one got out.

His hands got all prickly, his senses on point.

He waited, but they just sat there.

Justin stepped out of his office and onto the front porch, to get some fresh air by the look of it. He let the sun wash over him. Then he lifted his hand to the Vette in greeting.

Asher did a second take in his side mirror—no one there. He opened his door and got out. No sooner had he shut the Vette than he heard a heavy door slide open.

A cameraman exited the unmarked van and paced toward him. Soon a reporter stood in front of him, adjusting her blouse.

"Detective!" the woman shouted in his face.

What the fuck—they're undercover, now, too? This is getting to be some TMZ shit.

Justin called from the porch. "You good?" He looked to the news duo, about two feet out from his property.

Asher lifted his hand as if to say, *I've got it.* Then he walked up to the front steps before turning back and addressing the two of them. "This is private property."

The cameraman stopped where the sidewalk ended, but the

woman stepped onto the lawn.

"Just give us one minute, Detective. When can we expect a formal statement regarding your partner, Miss Cass—"

"I already spoke to y'all yesterday." Asher didn't need to address them, but he still did.

"Not us," the woman said, balancing in her high heels on the spongy St. Augustine grass.

"Have a good one," Asher said.

"Is it true that you're being investigated for—"

"Like I said, this is private property."

She stepped back. Her heel snapped. The woman stumbled backward—and nearly fell into the street of passing cars.

"Don't make me call the " Asher cut himself off, clowning, toying with them in a way that he felt they deserved. "Oh, wait," he said. He glanced down at his badge with a where-did-that-come-from sort of faux bewilderment.

He turned around, and Justin gestured him inside.

The woman shouted from the edge of the road, fumbling one of her high heels, which was now broken in two. "It's part of your job, Detective!"

Justin shut the door behind them.

Chapter 50

"So, how long has that been going on?" Justin asked. They each took a seat in the office. No fire today—only the timbered scent of sandalwood smoldered from a glass warmer on the therapist's desk.

"And what's 'that'?" Asher said.

With an indolent chuckle, Justin lifted his chin to the door. "That. The reporters. This isn't a regular day for you, is it?"

"Not usually, no. But lately it's becoming all too frequent. Now that I think about it, this is the first time they've found me outside of work, though. Usually, they just swarm whatever scene we're at, then ambush us at the office."

"Sounds like quite the thrill."

Asher spoke with a blatant type of mockery. "Oh, it's the greatest thrill there is."

He was satisfied with having just enough friends to count on an injured hand with a missing finger or two—and as little attention from the media as possible, or anyone else for that matter. The quiet life. Simply . . . content.

"So how's the book?" Justin asked.

"The book?"

"Yeah. *Meditations*. Marcus Aurelius? The book I gave you? The one I said you should read to help with the derealization?"

"Oh, yeah. That one. I've been a little busy—I haven't gotten to it just yet. I will, though."

"We're always busy, Asher. Reading is like making the decision to have a child—it's never gonna feel like the right time, like you're free enough from your responsibilities. But once you make the decision to do it, it changes you for the better."

"Kids scare the shit out of me."

"For some reason, that doesn't surprise me."

They both chuckled a bit.

"Well," Justin continued, "I think you should start reading it whenever you get the chance. Even if you don't understand every line, and just make a first pass without giving it much thought, it's worth it. Then, later, you can go back to it. Or better yet, we can discuss it here."

"Of course."

Justin had never before put Asher on the spot, or made him feel outright guilty or anxious in one of their sessions. Not intentionally. But this was different—Asher felt some level of remorse for having not opened the book. Justin had given him his personal copy, insisting that it would help the derealization, even the general feelings of unease and depression surrounding Sofia's death, in addition to the day-to-day grind. It wasn't Justin's fault that Asher had put it on the backburner.

How could he have been so selfish as to not even crack it open to the first page?

"So, how are things? Last time, I think you had mentioned having these dreams about someone, and not knowing what they mean?"

"It's hard to say. This morning was the first time in days I didn't have one."

"And yesterday?"

Asher pinched the bracelet on his wrist, unaware that the fix was becoming instinctive. He only noticed that he was doing it once Justin's attention was drawn to the black-and-gold beads there.

"Yeah, well. I had a dream—but it wasn't at night. I fell asleep at the office."

"Was it like your other ones?"

"Yes and no. It wasn't a dream about any of the cases I'm working, or one of the scenes. It was actually here."

"What do you mean, 'here'?"

"Here—in your office."

The therapist's attention shifted to the things around them.

"What else?" Justin said.

"You had a receptionist."

Silence, followed by a nod. "Okay. That could easily be Waylon. He's helping me out, now."

"But you weren't here," Asher said.

"I was out for the day?"

"No. There was a female therapist in your place—it was no longer your practice."

"Huh."

Justin seemed so intrigued by the dream that he placed his notes on the table between them, freeing his thumbs for the twiddling. He looked more attentive than usual.

"What else?"

"She was a cop."

"Who?"

"The therapist."

"The *therapist* was a cop?" Now, he seemed really into it.

"Uh-huh."

"And what does that mean? I mean, how do you think that

connects to what we've discussed before, about your dreams being a continuation of what's going on during the day? Your mind returning to its leftovers, so to speak."

"I was hoping you could tell *me*."

Justin raised his hands, wide-eyed. "Well, I'm not a cop." He opened his coat to the absence of guns and badges. "Don't have the stomach for it, to be honest."

Asher had long-running suspicions about the phrase. Anyone who justified their words with "to be honest" had some underlying, perhaps subconscious, need for the expression. An ulterior motive?

"And I'm not a woman," Justin said.

Asher wasn't kidding, though. What did it mean? If Justin was right about what dreams pointed to, about the day's thoughts bleeding into the night, then Asher had the answer. Somewhere.

"And the patient?" Justin said.

That was a good question; Asher hadn't considered that one at all.

"No idea. For all I know, it could've been me."

A better question: why was Asher's conscience melding his work with therapy, *at* therapy? Sure, he had spoken to Justin about his career, but it wasn't that. It was something more.

Before, in the other dreams, those blank and blurry faces had only appeared at the scenes of homicides. The badge, too. Now, they were here—in one of the few places where Asher felt at ease anymore.

So, what had changed?

Chapter 51

Pierre burst through the door and dropped a stack of folders from head height onto the middle of Asher's desk. His work shot this way and that, as if from a furious, indoor wind.

"What is this?" Asher said.

"Applicants. You need a new partner; prospects are waiting for you in Interrogation Room 1."

"What?" Asher pushed the folders around, seeing precisely how many problems the chief had thrown in front of him. "Oh, hell no."

"It's not up for discussion. It's department policy that all detectives on the payroll have a partner—lead hotshot included." He walked out, leaving the door wide open. "I suggest you get on it." His words faded into the distance.

Asher sifted through the names. There were more than ten resumes here, attached to dozens of pages of cover letters and state questionnaires. The chief couldn't have given him more of a forewarning, some prep time, a better chance to object to the idea that Asher, somehow, should be involved in the hiring process? He had been in the office for all of five minutes.

He wanted a say in who his new partner was going to be, of course, but did he have the time to sift through every one of these applicants?

Asher grabbed the coffee that he had picked up on the ride in, the contents nearly full and, largely, still fresh—then made his way to the interrogation room with the heap of papers.

The room was packed. Asher tossed the stack of folders onto the table. He flipped through the applications, debating exactly how he should approach it. The one thing he was certain of was that there was no way in hell he was interviewing double digits. Not today.

He flicked off the lid of his coffee, like a bottlecap, and swirled the cup beneath his nose. He closed his eyes, sniffed, and made the worst face he could marshal.

"God*damn*," he said, wincing. He set the coffee back on the table, feigning as much disgust as he could manage to portray for the people in front of him. "Someone get me a fresh cup of coffee, would you?"

"I got you," said one of the younger applicants, jumping from his chair and striding to the door. "How do you like it?"

"Don't bother," Asher said. Then he grabbed the coffee from the table and took an obnoxious, slurping drink.

"What? You just said that you wanted a—"

"What I want is a colleague who stands up to me, not some glorified errand boy. Thanks for playing."

The young man batted his eyes in disbelief, shuffled back to his chair, then collected his belongings and exited the room.

"Who's next?" Asher said.

They all stared at one another, doe-eyed in the headlights of a tractor trailer, barreling down I-10 in the pouring rain.

Asher shuffled the folders with a casino wash, closed his

eyes, and plucked one from the middle of the pile. "Perfect. Who is . . . Jessica Babin?"

A redhead with baby blues raised here hand. "Here."

"Grab a seat." Asher gestured to the chair across the way. "The rest of you can wait out in the hallway."

They exited the room, and the woman sat at the other end of the table.

Asher paced.

"I appreciate the opportunity. After five years with Slidell PD, I'm ready to—"

"Hypothetical," Asher said. He lost himself in the one-way mirror beside them. "After weeks of working a string of double-homicides, you decide to move in on your prime suspect. Thing is—he's sleeping with your wife, who happens to be there with him. You show up with your partner, and things go south."

"Wait, I'm not a lesbian."

"Does it matter? Do you think she's being held hostage because her naughty place is just that good?"

"I don't know. It's your story."

"No," Asher continued. "Things go south, and the person who you thought was your partner turns out to be the suspect's wife. Now, both the suspect and your crooked partner are holding you and your own wife hostage." Asher turned from the mirror and stared dead at her. "Go."

"Wait it out. Talk 'em down," she said. "The last thing you should do in a hostage situation is make the abductor feel rushed. Or better yet, like they're not in control of the situation."

"Nope. Tried that. Your wife dies, and your partner dies, too; at the very least, she skips town and you never hear from her again."

She leaned forward with her hands on the metal tabletop.

Flat, like she's bracing herself for the thought that's on its way. "No. I've dealt with these situations in the field. Captors never respond well to pressure."

"Wrong. If you wait it out, you talk to them, you try to put them at ease—that gives them time to think."

"And then, you have time to plan."

"So you walked in there without a plan?"

For that, she had no words.

"Yeah," Asher said. "That's what I was afraid of." He closed her file and handed it back to her.

"Wait, seriously? That's it? You're not gonna ask me about—"

"Sorry. Department has a very strict 'don't get shot' clause. You understand."

He opened the door, to a hallway of applicants who were undoubtedly just as bleak.

Chapter 52

You—

You watched the homeless man sit on a bench in front of Faulkner House Books on Pirates Alley. Several hours had passed since you handed him the bag of beignets and iced coffee. Now, it was nothing more than a waiting game; from what you could tell, there were mere seconds left on the clock.

You sat beneath a green awning just around the corner on Cabildo Alley, at a small table outside the door to Pirates Alley Café and Olde Absinthe House. A few dozen feet away. Your closeness to the poor man was innocuous enough.

Until it was time.

He had finished the coffee, but now, he opened the bag of fried dough and powdered sugar once more for a second fix, and relaxed on the bench as he consumed another of the irresistible, sweet squares. Addictive, they were. Sugar fell to the gray stone at his feet, scattered by the wind, never to be seen or tasted again.

The man soon placed what he couldn't finish of the beignets back into the bag and lay down on the bench. He removed a book from his dark-green messenger bag and held it above him to the sky, and he began reading.

If you had to guess, his decision to read across from the bookstore was the man's con to have somewhere to rest undisturbed. Otherwise, any one of the store owners along the alley might have suggested he "move along."

It took another twenty minutes or so before you could discern that the beignets were beginning to do their job. The man coughed and rolled from side to side on the bench, unable to get comfortable, pulling his knees to his chest as his face tensed in agony. To him, it was probably the coffee; Café Beignet practically served rocket fuel in a cup.

It wasn't the coffee, though. Well . . . not exactly.

The adrift man shot to his feet and broke through the gate that led to the back of St. Anthony's Garden, the entry located a few feet from his bench. He clutched his stomach and spewed vomit.

Unbeknownst to tourists, and probably many of the locals as well, St. Anthony's Garden was largely a vanishing place for the homeless. A place for them to sleep, to interact among themselves, to barter one-on-one without the attention of the Quarter.

To shoot up.

Lucky for you, most days the garden was empty before dark. The inside of it was obscured by flora planted along the perimeter. Only one angle allowed passersby to view the middle portion of the garden without entering it: a twenty-foot gap in the bushes along Royal Street. The rest, along Pere Antoine Alley on one side and Pirates Alley on the other, was grown over with little visibility. The fourth side, and rear of the garden, adjoined the back of St. Louis Cathedral.

You followed him inside. He leaned against one of the trees on the boundary of the garden, shielded by the surrounding overgrowth, and continued to be sick. He dropped to his knees.

Your steps were overshadowed by the sound of his stomach emptying into the brush. And the clip-clop of hooves on a nearby street.

It was easy, then, to slip the crook of your arm beneath his chin from behind, trapping his neck between your forearms, cinching. You felt the blood thump against your skin. Slowing. Struggling. His body jerked, his hands grabbed, feet sliding.

"It's gonna be okay, my friend. It's *all* gonna be okay."

Then he went slack.

The man's pulse faded as his head fell limp over your arm. He tried his darndest to fight it, but . . . the beignets. The oh-so-"strong" coffee.

For you, taking away his pain wasn't enough, though. Not after what he had gone through. Not after what your own father had made you suffer—at the hands of these very same city streets.

—

You reached into the man's pockets, still worn by his lower half, and removed what was inside: some dirty napkins, change, a few bills, a lighter. You dropped all of it to the ground, except for the some-odd ten dollars in crumpled money. Then you made sure to close the gate on your way out.

No one suspected, no one stopped you. Not a single ask. Typical city streets—no one would even notice that he was gone, if they never noticed him in the first place. At least, not until the pieces of the poor man were found. Someone might care, then.

You walked to the front of the cathedral.

Keep your head up, Ryker—that's one less person suffering out here.

Chapter 53

Asher stepped into the hallway, and the redhead marched heatedly out of the precinct without looking back.

"Alright, then," Asher said. "Next up is . . . Mike Laurent."

A towering man in black jeans and a tight-fitting jacket, which covered his black V-neck shirt, got up and walked into the room. He greeted the detective with a nod as he passed by.

Asher shut the door. "Have a seat."

The man sat not at the opposite end of the table but in the chair closest to Asher. He rested formally with his hands folded, outwardly intense. Shoulders back. Mouth flat. Asher leaned against the mirror.

"From what I hear, you're the one to work with," said the applicant. "The famous Detective Huxley."

"Famous? Or *in*famous?"

"Famous, of course. You work against the grain, have your own style of investigation, you break the rules where they need to be broken. Somehow, you managed to work your way out of being murdered by your own partner—*while* being held at gunpoint. At least, that's the rumor."

"Yeah, well, you shouldn't believe everything you see on the news."

"Who said anything about the news?"

Asher grabbed his file from the table and gave it a once-over. The guy was ex-SWAT-turned-patrolman.

"What happened?" Asher said. "You got tired of serving warrants and being pelted in the head by rioters?"

"Not exactly."

"Then why the move from SWAT? Rolling around Covington in an outdated cruiser and writing speeding tickets can't be any more rewarding than what you were doing before. What changed?"

"The stress," he said. "Was it exciting? Sure, most of the time. Interesting? Maybe. But the constant pressure to perform nonstop got old after a while. There was no intrigue to it. No challenge. Just get up and go."

"And you think that investigating murders, visiting homicides and staring at dead people, is gonna bring down the blood pressure?"

"For sure."

Asher's gaze widened. His mouth went lax. "Yeah . . ."

Just then, Asher noticed the pistol inside the man's jacket, hanging from a leather shoulder holster. Asher pointed to it.

"What you carry?" Asher said.

"Sig Sauer, P226. At least, that's my off-duty choice."

"Can I have a look?"

For some reason, he seemed hesitant to hand over the gun, but he had to, if he wanted the job.

"Sure." The guy removed the gun—and did the worst thing possible for the interview. He grabbed it by the slide and held it out, the grips facing Asher. At first, Asher considered that alone to be bad enough. But then—

"You always carry like that?"

He continued to hold it backward, pointed at himself. "What, the shoulder holster? Yeah, I'm used to it."

"No," Asher said. "The safety."

The man turned the gun and looked at the safety—the thumb safety that was off, with the gun poised to fire.

"Oh," the guy said. "No. Not always." With a slight quiver in his hands, he inadvertently turned the gun on the detective in front of him—and *then* he engaged the safety.

"Carry a 1911," Asher said, "and what you just did wouldn't have been nearly as bad."

"What do you mean?"

Grip safety, idiot.

He grabbed the next folder from the table, then opened the door. "Up next, we have"—he scanned the resume—"Trey Trahan."

Laurent walked past him and out of the room. "Safe travels," Asher said.

Trahan walked in and sat in the same chair, closest to the detective. He seemed competent enough, dressed in dark blue pants, a grayish button-down shirt and tie, his black hair slicked back. He was dressed for the occasion, which was more than Asher could say for a few of the applicants out in the hallway.

"Two down, huh?" the man said.

"Oh, don't cheapen the process, now," Asher said. "Errand boy counts, too."

"That's right. I forgot about him."

Asher flipped through his application. It was textbook: started out as a uniform, moved up to a supervisory role, graduated to detective. Accolades included. The only question was—why the need to transfer? Why go from one detective role to another, unless he was being driven out of his current role by something in particular?

Or someone.

"Tell me," Asher said. "Why the move? It looks like you're already with homicide out in Baton Rouge. Trouble in paradise?"

"What makes you say that?"

Asher flipped to the back of his resume, then dropped it onto the table. "'References available upon request'? What's that about? You think I don't know your boss?"

He shifted in the chair. "I'm sure you do. I just thought it would be—"

"The only reason people put that on their application is because they're hoping no one will contact a certain person. Or, if it's really bad, certain people. So, which is it?"

They locked eyes, Trahan seemingly waiting for Asher to bluff and confess that he was only joking, Asher not joking at all but intrigued as to what could be so bad that a detective from Baton Rouge was persuaded to leave their precinct and apply for a more demanding position.

Either he's an idiot or he's got balls.

The man was reluctant, but he eventually spilled it. "I've got three little ones at home with another one on the way." He glanced off to the side, either in anger or in grief; Asher couldn't tell. "I've been in my position over there for nearly five years now, and they keep dumping more and more cases in my lap, knowing good and well what I've got going on at home. I've got a wife who's about to lose it because I'm never there, three children who hardly see me, and a personal life that's practically—"

"So, you're clearly not bad at your job, you're moving up the ladder after five years of work, and you're wondering why you're being assigned more cases?" Holding back was in no way one of Asher's virtues. "And that's, what? The city's fault? People should just stop dying?"

"Of course that's not what I'm saying. I just need to—"

"No, what you're saying is that you'd rather be at home playing house than doing your job." Asher picked up the man's folder, closed it, then pushed it into the bottom of the pile. "As it turns out," he continued, "the better you get at what you do, the more of that thing you're gonna be assigned to do. Come on—you can't tell me you didn't see that one coming. That's working-for-someone-else 101."

"What are you saying? In order to work in homicide, anywhere, I should just abandon my family and work twenty-four seven?"

"Oh, god, no. That's a horrible thing to say. What I'm saying is that your wife should learn to keep her legs closed if she can't handle the little tykes."

And that had the effect he hoped. The guy was so shocked he left without a word.

Asher was bluffing—he had no idea who the man's boss was.

Chapter 54

sher addressed the remaining applicants out in the hall. "Take five."

The idiocy was tiring.

He walked past them to Xavier's desk, where his friend was still messing with that CCTV footage from Jean Lafitte Trading Company.

"I thought you said it wasn't good enough to get anything out of it?" Asher said.

"No, I said that I couldn't enhance it any more than I already have to get a good look at their faces. But that doesn't mean that we didn't miss something."

"You ain't gonna let it go, are you?"

"Hi, I'm Xavier. It's nice to meet you. Of course I'm not letting it go—it's one of the only legs up we've got right now. Why should I?"

"Good point. Keep me posted, then."

"How are the interviews going?"

"So you heard, huh?"

"Of course I heard. Pierre sent out an email to the whole department, warning them."

"Warning them of what?"

"That you're gonna be in a bad mood for the next day or

two, and to stay clear of you entirely."

"Are you serious right now? What the hell is he—"

"Oh, chill out, man. I'm just fucking with you." Xavier appeared all too satisfied with his own little personal quip; he was usually on the receiving end. "But he did tell me that you'd be busier than usual talking with potential recruits, so you might not be available as much today."

"Yeah, well, change of plans." He dropped the remainder of applications onto Xavier's desk. "I need you to take over the interviews for the time being. I've gotta get down to the coroner's office. Not to mention, if I don't get away from the dumbassery for at least a little while, I'm gonna fly off the handle. Thanks in advance." He turned away.

"Whoa, whoa, whoa. Hold up."

Asher spoke over his shoulder. "You know the kind of partner I need better than I do. I have faith in you, man."

"This isn't my job, Asher." Xavier's voice climbed a bit, both in tone and volume. "I'm not kidding. This isn't funny, man."

It wasn't Xavier's job—not in the least. But Asher needed to step away from it all, even if only for a short while. If anyone could handle it without running to the chief and blabbing about fairness, it was Xavier.

"And I'm not joking," Asher said. "Have fun with it." He walked out of the doors and toward the bank of elevators. He could hear Xavier still rambling on behind him, back in the office.

Chapter 55

Agnes was seated at one of the several light microscopes across from her desk when Asher walked into the office. The room was surprisingly tranquil: no bodies were visible in the adjoining morgue, no typing, no buzz of autopsy equipment or saws. Even the stench of formalin had faded to a minor consideration.

Only the lowly sound of Brian Stoltz's "I Been Up All Night" played in the background—one of his countless blues tracks with a cutting, funky edge to it, from *East of Rampart Street*. Asher knew the song well. It was about not sleeping, waiting for your girl to call, rolling oversized joints and sipping black-on-black coffee.

"Well, it ain't dark yet, woman." He looked at his watch. "What are you listening to? You plan on hotboxing this place?"

She dropped her head and pursed her lips to the side, giving him a sideways, oh-please glance. "Sorry to disappoint you, love, but you're a little late. Me and Ann from accounting already smoked a bowl." She pointed to the coffee pot behind her desk. "But there's some stone-black coffee if you're looking for a fix."

"Damn," Asher said. "Always late to the party." He grabbed a Styrofoam cup and poured himself some coffee. "What you got going on?"

Bitter and black. Ground-chicory perfection.

"Quite a bit, actually," she said. "I'm working on our second decedent from the balconies. I'm assuming they're connected, yeah?"

"That's what we're thinking."

"Well, the tox screen is clean—other than the alcohol in his system."

"And the pieces of our man out on Exchange Place?"

"Same. He's clean. No alcohol in his workup at all."

She stopped what she was doing at the scope and grabbed a folder. "Here," she said, handing him the file. "There's some pulmonary edema in our ripper victim, but that—"

"Our 'ripper' victim?"

"Sure. It rolls off the tongue a bit easier than 'the decedent who was stabbed and gutted on Exchange Place,' does it not?"

"Alright, then. Ripper guy it is."

"Like I was saying, there's edema all throughout the lung tissue. As many times as he was stabbed, it's most likely secondary to the knife wounds."

"Remind me again—edema is . . ."

"A buildup of interstitial fluid. Usually, it's mostly water. In this case, it's heavily tainted with blood, and a lot more than usual, too; the guy's lungs look like they were dipped in a bloodied froth. Even under the microscope, the alveoli—the microscopic air sacs in the lungs—were severely congested with a pinkish fluid. Sometimes, it can be difficult to pinpoint the exact cause. But here? I'd say it's the obvious."

"A few dozen stab wounds. Sure."

Asher flipped through more of the pictures. She narrated. "I also found small hemorrhages on the skin, in addition to larger, more obvious ones internally. The body, or I should say, the 'pieces' of the body, are a mess. Because he was stabbed so many times, it's damn near impossible to tell up from down."

"Sure. Makes sense. The number of stab wounds led to internal hemorrhaging from the lacerations, as well as hemorrhages under the skin once blood started to pool internally. Anything else?"

"Other than the obvious dismemberment, there's nothing crazy on the autopsy itself. As messy as it is, those are some clean cuts, though. Really, it all comes down to blood loss early on in whatever confrontation took place."

"And our second decedent from the balcony?"

"Same as the first—asphyxiation from being strangled." Agnes moved from her seat and gestured to the microscope. "But, there's this."

He sat down and rested his eyes at the edge of the eyepieces. "What am I looking at?"

"Remember those rope fibers I found embedded in the throat lacerations of the first decedent, at Good Friends Bar?"

This was it—the break he had been looking for. Rope, in general, was made from a dizzying number of materials, both naturally sourced and synthetic. Cotton, nylon, polyester; the list went on. If he could identify the material and, therefore, the type and brand of rope, he could track down where it was sold, and then who had bought it within a certain period of time—giving him a list of possible suspects.

At least, in theory.

"So, what type of fibers are they?"

"Hemp. The coloring, tensile strength, diameter of the strands, their shape in cross section—it all checks out. But what I'd really like to know, and I'm sure you would too, is—"

They spoke in unison. "Where is the rope?"

"Precisely," she said.

"Well, damn," Asher said. "This is good. I can use this."

"I figured. At least, now, you have something more to go on than just some pen."

"Absolutely."

Agnes turned off the light on the microscope and walked to the coat rack behind her desk. She removed her lab coat and hung it there. "I should have the official postmortem on balcony number two for you soon, but as far as today goes, I'm beat." She pulled loose the hair tie that held back her dreads, letting them fall over her shoulders. Then she turned off the computer.

It was something Asher had always admired in Agnes—her ability to be both detail-oriented but also cognizant of how hard she pushed herself. Sure, she was chief medical examiner, but she wasn't going to kill herself just to do her job well.

"Say," Asher began, "I know you're busy trying to wrap this one up, but I was wondering, if you have some time over the next day or two, if you would—"

"No."

"No?"

"No. I'm not taking another look at your girl's autopsy. Y'all already have the postmortem report." She threw her bag over her shoulder. A look of resolve, but also pity, crossed her face. "Sorry, love, but there's nothing else for me to look at."

Before she walked away, she removed a key from her key ring—and placed it on her desk in plain view. "It's getting late."

She walked to the door and stopped.

He recognized it. The master key to the morgue freezers.

Agnes turned back. "You should get some rest."

Asher looked to the key, then back at her. "Sure—"

But just like that, she was gone.

Chapter 56

"I'll take it from here," Asher said as he walked through the door of the interrogation room. Xavier was just about to sit down with another applicant.

"Be my guest," Xavier said. He didn't move, though. He sat there at the table, seemingly intent on staying for the interview he was about to start on his friend's behalf.

The applicant—an attractive woman with sinful dimples and ash hair falling over her chest—leaned forward and shook Asher's hand. "Remi Bordelon," she said. "It's nice to meet you."

"Asher Huxley."

Her neck and hands were glass, coruscating somewhere between ivory and alabaster under the pure white light of the room. Her nostril was pierced with a small rose gold ring. Asher failed to point out the fact that this was a job interview and she probably should've taken it out.

She had that girl next door look about her but with a modern touch. Her larger-than-life librarian glasses sat low on the bridge of her nose. She adjusted the collar of her peacoat, which was practically the same coat as Pierre's, only the feminine version—and she wore it better.

Fitted to a T.

Asher opened her file. "So, you're leaving the criminal psychology division out in Baton Rouge?"

"Yes."

"And why is that?"

"I'm looking for something more; I'm tired of working in a cubicle. I think it'd be more rewarding to be out on the streets and involved in the active part of the investigations, instead of just profiling and interviewing offenders here and there."

Asher looked to Xavier. Presumably he, too, felt some semblance of déjà vu. He had this thing that he did when he felt some sort of way around strangers. A tell, of sorts. Xavier picked at the already fraying skin against his thumbnail until it throbbed a deep cherry red.

"And you think your experience in psychology has prepared you for that?" Asher said.

"I do."

Over the next twenty minutes, they had a productive back-and-forth. Even Xavier chimed in from time to time, asking questions Asher had yet to explore himself. Overall, the interview was a resounding success. From what the detective could discern, the woman might be a decent fit. At least she was a far better option than any of the other applicants so far.

If it weren't for the obvious—that she reminded him of Cass.

"Well," Asher said, "I appreciate your time. We still have other applicants to interview, but either way, we'll be in touch."

"Of course," she said. "I look forward to hearing from you." Then she walked out of the room.

"Well, what do you think?" Xavier said. "I'd say she's the best one so far."

The truth was, Asher had no intention of bringing another psychologist onto the team. Not after Cassandra. Not to mention, Pierre would probably have a conniption fit if Asher tried to do so; no one was looking for a repeat performance. Another disaster.

But why did Pierre include her as an applicant, then? Was the chief testing him? Seeing if he would run back to what was familiar?

The fact that she was a criminal psychologist, at its core, could've been useful; it had been helpful years ago when Pierre hired his first partner. But it was too much, too soon.

He slipped her folder into the bottom of the pile. "No."

"No? You're not gonna hire her because she reminds you too much of . . . her? You think that's a legitimate reason?"

"It doesn't matter what I think, or what you think, or if she's a good fit. But it does matter what everyone else will see."

"Oh yeah? And what's that?"

"Exactly what you and I saw—something that should've never happened."

To that, Xavier had no response.

Asher had convinced the remaining applicants to head home— after he polled them on who was willing to work for free, collectively, until Asher could decide who was the best fit. As it turned out, not one of them was willing to openly compete for the job.

It was a good thing, too, because Asher wasn't willing to be followed around by any of them, much less several of them at the same time.

The chief stopped him as he walked out of the office.

"So, how'd it go?" Pierre said.

"Great," Asher said, lying through his teeth for the sake of remaining partnerless. "Perhaps, too good, actually."

"That's good news, then."

"I'll need some time to mull it over. You know . . . make sure I'm giving everyone a fair shake. Due diligence and all."

Asher had no intention of mulling it over, nor making a decision. They'd been horrible, for the most part.

"I expect an answer sooner rather than later." The chief turned away. "You know . . . department policy and all."

Asher left and rode the elevator down to the lobby and exited the building, ready to be home, as far away as possible from the idea of having a partner ever again.

He approached his car. Just as he grabbed the door handle, he noticed someone standing beneath the overhang of the building, leaning against the wall. He'd walked right past them. They weren't just standing around, though, taking in the evening weather, or relishing a hard-earned smoke break. No.

It was a man, dressed in work boots and a windbreaker. A young man, open stance, arms folded. Glaring. Not hiding it in the least.

Asher glanced around. There was no one else in sight.

The side profile of the man, caught in the dropping, bleeding sun, was what jumped out. John's thin, rectangular glasses reflected the weakening daylight in bands of shooting gold.

Chapter 57

No matter how hard Asher tried, he still couldn't make out her face. Like a shadow that promised, no matter what, to give way to the spreading morning light—only to lie repeatedly.

It wasn't the distance, or that something barred his view of her; she was right there. But regardless of his efforts, of his straining eyes under artificial lights, he was incapable of discerning her empty, shadowed face.

So close, yet so muddled.

He stepped farther into the room—before he noticed not one but *two* patients sitting across from her. He didn't know either of them. How could he? With no faces, there was no one to recognize.

Then she bolted to her feet and bounded toward him. That badge shone from her hip in shards of argent. She strode nearer. Faster. Until she was lunging straight at him, with reaching hands.

Asher drew his pistol from his back and thumbed the safety, then pulled the trigger.

Nothing happened.

He squeezed again and again, stepping back. He wasn't strong enough. The smooth, hairpin trigger refused to break.

Her hands, with those cold and rigid fingers, gaunt and white, found his neck like a vise. He fell backward, pulling her down, and that blank and blurry face stretched and screamed an inch from his own.

Swallowing all of him.

He leapt awake as Xavier shook him from his slumber. He was soaking wet, on the sofa in his office.

"What the hell, man?" Xavier said. "I could hear you screaming from outside. I had to use my key to get in."

The chilling indoor air collided with Asher's sweating skin. "What is it? What's going on?"

"You need to get up—we've got another one."

Chapter 58

Asher needed his morning go-get-'em, so they stopped by Jean Lafitte on the way.

The moment they walked into the shop, the barista greeted Asher with those freckles and an innocent bounce in her step. "Good morning, Detective. Are you having the usual this morning?"

"Please."

"And your friend?" she said, giving Xavier a little wave from her shoulder.

"Well, that depends," Xavier said. "What's 'the usual'?"

"The black stuff," said Asher.

The barista pulled two cups from behind the counter. She spoke to Xavier. "Your friend prefers a good café noir."

"You see?" Xavier said to Asher. "Why can't you just learn the lingo like a normal addict?"

"Extra shot of black," Asher said. "And I'm sorry. I know he looks like an ogre"—he turned his back to his friend and whispered to the barista, leaning a bit over the counter—"but he's really just a spoiled teddy bear."

"Excuse me?" Xavier said. He turned toward her. "Sorry. My loser friend here has forgotten his manners." Held up his hand. "Xavier."

"Emily." And she waved again.

He spoke quieter, now. "He gets a little cranky before his morning feeding," said Asher.

Xavier grabbed him by the shoulder of his leather jacket and yanked him back. "Just the normal for me, please." Emily was now standing behind the huffing machine, which devoured a clear funnel of beans like it was nothing.

"Coming right up."

"How's it going, Detective?" The owner greeted Asher as he walked up behind the counter with a box of Pirate King Coffee.

"Oh, you know," Asher said. "Just hanging in there."

"I hear that. Y'all get the footage I sent over?" Gene asked.

"As a matter of fact, we did. Thank you."

"Of course. Hopefully, it does y'all some good."

"Unfortunately, I can't say that it has. But that's no fault of your own, of course. Those CCTV cameras are only so good in the dark, especially if they aren't set up for low light."

"Well, that's unfortunate."

"Yeah, we ran through all of it, frame by frame." He pointed over his shoulder. "Xavier here was able to identify two men who might be of interest, who were coming and going at just the right time, acting a little weird—but that's about it."

Emily set down the first of their drinks. "You're up, Detective."

"Thanks."

"Can't y'all do some fancy computer stuff?" Gene said. "You know . . . tweak it a little so it's easier to see or something?"

"Yeah," Xavier said. "We did exactly that. But we can only enhance it so much before it's grainy and useless altogether."

She set down Xavier's coffee, too. "I appreciate it," he said. He pulled out his wallet and sifted through the bills inside.

"Don't bother," Asher said, in kindness but with a hint of sardonicism. "She won't touch it."

"What?"

"If you wanna pay, you gotta hide it somewhere. Or shove it in the tip jar before you make a break for it."

Emily winked.

Asher smiled.

Xavier removed a five from his wallet and held it, crumpled beneath his cup. "We'll keep working at it, though," he said to Gene.

"For sure," Asher said. He popped Xavier in his chest with the back of his hand. "This guy ain't gonna let it go that easy. We'll figure it out."

"Well, that's good to hear," said Gene. "Somebody's gotta catch the son of a bitch. Shit happens, but you'd freak out if you saw how much our sales have dipped after all of that. There's just fewer people coming down here." He began placing the bags of coffee on a rack in front of the counter. "Whatever y'all need, just let me know. Stop by anytime, you hear? My star girl right here'll take care of you."

"Yes, sir," Asher said. He lifted his cup. "Y'all have a good one. Give us a call if anything comes up."

"Will do," Gene said.

Xavier addressed Emily behind the counter. "Say, can I get one of those to-go menus?" He gestured to the far end of the counter, behind her. "That way, I don't have to rely on this piece of work for my morning brew." A tilt of his head referenced Asher.

"Of course." She turned.

Xavier slipped the five under a stack of cups next to the register.

"Here you go," she said. "I'll see y'all soon."

"Yes, ma'am," Xavier said.

As they walked outside and turned toward Conti Street, a voice intoned from behind them. "Have a good one, Detective." It came from above.

They turned back, looking to the balcony above the shop—where James Cormier was standing.

"Good morning," Asher said.

"Uh-huh."

"Am I gonna see you down at the station sometime soon?" Asher said. "It'd be nice to get that statement from you."

A silence lingered there like a morning fog on the Causeway.

James took a swig of his beer, then turned to his apartment. "Yeah, buddy." He spoke with a derisive bite over his shoulder.

Chapter 59

"So . . . where's that ten- or eleven-pound thing that's usually attached to a person's shoulders? The uh . . ." Xavier snapped his fingers, searching the air for an answer.

"The head?" Asher said with a faux uncertainty.

Xavier pointed at him. "That's it. The head. It's called the head."

Asher scanned the area, then spied it about thirty feet away—watching them from the stoop of Touchdown Jesus; more formally, it was the Sacred Heart of Jesus behind St. Anthony's Garden. His arms were outstretched to the sky in typical savior fashion, forming an impressive the-goal-is-good shadow on the back of St. Louis Cathedral after sundown, front-lit by a blinding white spotlight at his feet.

"By the look of it"—Asher gestured to the towering, judgmental sculpture—"our head is hedging its bets with the afterlife. Perhaps a little too late, though, don't you think?"

"*Jesus,*" Xavier said.

The two of them grew wide-eyed, appreciating the satire of the moment. "Really?" said Asher.

"Oh, please," Xavier said. "You of all people couldn't be any less offended by a religious crack of all comments."

"Wow. It's almost like we've met before."

The scene was all too familiar: the decedent had been stabbed countless times, then partitioned into numerous pieces, dismembered and displayed from the inside out amid the thick brush at the perimeter of the garden. Then there was the head—watching from over there at the feet of the divine.

"Where's your boy at?" Asher said.

"Who?"

"Your boy, John."

"Oh, yeah." Displeasure bathed his face. "He's at home, sick apparently."

"Again?" Asher said.

"That's what he says. He started to feel better for a little bit, then he took a downhill turn."

"What's the guy doing, running around licking toilet seats?"

The body, in all of its parts, lay beneath a live oak at the edge of the garden, resting around the trunk of the tree as if on display. Showcased in some abstract amateur art gallery. All that was missing were the little tags beneath each of the installments, noting the name of the artist and their style of work.

The medium was obvious.

"So, who are we looking at?" Asher said.

"You mean, besides the next Dahmer?" Xavier reached into the back pockets of the legs—which, impressively, weren't attached to the rest of the body but somehow managed to remain in the same pair of jeans. Held to nothing, to no waist or hips, by a brown leather belt. "Not sure," he said. His latexed hands came up empty.

"If I had to guess," Asher said, "based on the second-hand clothes, lack of ID, and the first stabbing that's undoubtedly related—"

"Another one of the homeless?"

"Unfortunately."

Asher walked to the head that sat lonely on the ledge of Touchdown Jesus. "But why you?" he said to himself. "Don't y'all already have it rough enough?"

What he did notice were the cuts. Or rather, the gash. Singular.

Unlike the first victim, who was decapitated in what appeared to be hectic fashion, with numerous sloppy incisions to the neck and throat in order to sever the head, this one was different; here, the separation was clean. Almost flawless. Of course, it had certainly taken more than one cut to decapitate the victim, but this was almost . . . surgical? At least, it was cleaner than the other.

But what did it mean, if anything?

He heard Xavier approach him from behind.

"I've gotta talk to the homeless in the area," Asher said. "If this is one of them, they've gotta know something. There's no way that two wanderers are taken out in spectacular fashion on a whim. Not to mention, this close together—when *and* where."

"You've mentioned doing that before," Xavier said. "So, why haven't you?"

"Detective!" a woman called out from Pirates Alley, on the other side of the fence.

Asher continued, "In case you haven't noticed, I've been a little busy on account of working *another* serial homicide"—he looked to the body beneath the tree—"in addition to this one. Now, we've got two serial murder cases on our hands."

"Not quite," Xavier said. "If we're lucky, they stop here—no victim number three, no serial killer."

"Yeah, well, I'm not holding my breath."

"When are you gonna step down, Detective?" the woman yelled again from the road, somehow having managed to bypass the uniforms on the outskirts of the garden. "Aren't you under investigation by your own department?"

Asher called to one of the officers on the other side of the gate. "Get her out of here! She's walking through part of my scene, for fuck's sake."

The officer snapped back, "No one said anything about the alleyway being part of the scene, Huxley."

"Get her the hell out of here," he repeated. "Unless you think whoever did this was dropped in with a goddamn Blackhawk, the streets on all three sides need to be blocked off. Now."

"We're on it," called out another officer. They mumbled among one another, rolling out yellow tape like they were on the clock.

Asher lingered between the head and the other remains of the decedent, looking between them. Xavier began his usual camera work, taking photos of anything and everything relevant.

The morning had a peculiar feel about it: aside from the body, he and Xavier were the only ones inside of the garden, so far. The rest of NOPD bustled on the outside, securing the roads and running interference. The garden felt so abandoned. Yet somehow, it weighed heavily.

On Asher's shoulders alone, he felt.

"What is it?" Xavier said.

Two cases. Four bodies.

He reached for his bracelet—but it wasn't there. The calm of the garden enveloped him. Smothered him. Squeezed him. The birds grew deafening, the heat hotter. The surrounding green began to spin like some rogue carnival ride.

"Hey, man. You good?" His friend's voice grew faint, distant.

A black box, Asher. Just hold it in your head—front and center. Empty and pitch-black. Nothing else. Nothing in, nothing out.

He drew a breath until his lungs felt as if they would tear, then he let it out over eight slow seconds.

There's nothing else. He let his eyes fall shut. *One box. Black. Empty. Everything else is just a distract—*

"Y'all find 'em yet?" The voice reached out from behind him in the thickest of Cajun accents, on the other side of the garden from Pere Antoine Alley. "If y'all ain't got 'em, I might be able to—"

An officer approached the man and began talking, possibly escorting him from the grounds. Asher could hardly make out either of them through the vegetation, nor hear what they were saying. The figures moved swiftly from the gate. Then another shout.

"I think I saw 'em!"

And the white of a clerical collar stepped past an opening in the brush.

Chapter 60

"Hold up," Asher said to the officer. He walked to the other side of the garden and stopped at the gate.

A sweating, jittery man in all black approached the entrance. The uniformed officer stood behind him in the alleyway. The man reached his arm through the bars and shook Asher's hand.

"Brother Emanual Ryan," the man said.

The click of Xavier's camera moved about the garden behind Asher, along with the acapella of scattering birds.

"How's it going?" Asher said.

"Sorry to bother ya." He glanced back over his shoulder at the officer he'd been struggling with, who was keeping a close eye on him from the road. "I heard what happened, and I thought ya might wanna know that someone stopped by the cathedral last night around dark and made a donation. An anonymous payment in the drop box."

"Is that not normal?"

He moved closer. "I ain't get a good look at 'em, but it just didn't feel right, ya know?"

"Okay."

The man wiped the perspiration from his brow and checked behind him. "Whoever it was, they were in a hurry. Frantic."

The way Brother Emanual was acting, it appeared as though he too had somewhere to be.

"They dropped some change in the donation slot at the front door, then took off."

"Okay," Asher said. "And this was around what time?"

"I'm not entirely sure. Around sunset?"

"Alright."

"I guess what I'm saying is the guy just seemed a bit sketchy, ya know? It was late, he was in a hurry, almost paranoid, dropping money in an overnight donation slot when he looked so uneasy."

"Only certain demeanors donate?"

Apparently, that was the wrong question; the man scowled.

"Not quite, Detective." He fidgeted some more. His forehead glistened. "But can't ya tell—haven't ya ever just had that feeling, that thing in ya gut that goes haywire when ya see someone acting, moving, in a certain way—when someone is just . . . off?"

"Sure," Asher said, "but being 'off' isn't much for us to go on. Nor is it a crime."

"Well, it was getting dark, so I can't give ya much else. He wasn't a big guy, but he seemed paranoid, like he was in a hurry. That's about all I've got. I just thought ya should know. Maybe someone else noticed him?"

Asher pulled a card from the inside of his jacket, then handed it over. "If you think of anything else, feel free to reach out."

The brother huffed as he took the card, as if the detective should've done more with his vague sense of concern. But as Asher turned away, another question came to mind. Perhaps a more pertinent one.

"Say," he said curiously, "are you always at the cathedral so late?"

The man placed the card into his pants pocket. "No," he said. "I'm not. But I was there all night, praying, just like I have been almost every night here lately. I'm nearing the end of my seminary training." He dried the moisture from his head once more, this time with his sleeve—the heat was thickening. "Is that a crime?"

"Of course not," Asher said.

But the cathedral closed well before dark—and the donation slot was outside.

Chapter 61

"**N**ice job, dickhead." Pierre was chewing out his lead detective, but in a surprisingly docile tone of voice. "What could've possibly enticed you to threaten someone from the media? And this isn't the first time we've had a complaint filed against you." The chief held up a two count. "First, you put your hands on a dead woman's husband while your ex-partner so conveniently stepped out of the room, and now you've got it out for reporters?"

"Hey, you get in between a man and his muscle car—"

"Oh, shut the hell up." Pierre leaned down and turned his computer monitor toward the detective. "It just came in this morning—the board of commissioners received a formal complaint regarding your little run-in with your news friend."

"Oh, come on. I'm getting a slap on the wrist because some legacy media jerkoff wants a soundbite? I've got better things to do with my time."

The chief decapitated the torpedo with his chrome cigar cutter, then placed it unlit between his lips. The end fell to his desk like a head from a guillotine, lost amid the never-ending mountains of papers. "No. Now, *we* have better things to do with our time." He rolled it there, between his teeth, seemingly weighing his options.

"Well I'm not apologizing, if that's where this is headed. Idiots will be idiots; although, I'm not sure how I attract so many of them."

"I'm not asking you to apologize."

Like Asher needed something else thrown at his feet, wasting his time. First Internal Affairs, now this. What ever happened to the good ole days of simply hitting the streets and leaving the bureaucratic theater up to the chief?

Pierre continued, "Now, both of us are scheduled to appear before the board to discuss exactly what happened, and what the 'necessary course of action' should be." His air quotes were angry.

"Necessary action?"

"Yeah. In other words, what's your punishment? That is, *if* Internal Affairs doesn't demand your resignation, first. Don't worry, though."

"Worry? Who's worried?"

The whole thing was a farce. Asher had lost his wife, was nearly murdered by his colleague, attacked by the media left and right, and now *he* was the one being held responsible? For what? Being screwed over by his own partner, his own department? Then the media attacking him for it?

Purely nonsensical.

That was the hard truth, though: at the end of the day, someone was always held responsible. In the public eye, accountability and justice didn't always align—especially now, in the days of clicks, likes, and dwindling job security. As long as someone paid the price—

"I'm having Andrea from HR send over an online training module."

"Do what?"

"Chill out. It's just a media training course that can be completed entirely online."

"Of course. I mean, what else do I have to do?"

Pierre set flame to the cigar and nursed it, meeting Asher in front of his desk.

Asher turned and opened the door. "I'm not doing it. I'm not gonna be treated like a rookie because some reporter—"

"I don't really care. And yes, you will do this. I don't give a shit if you let the videos play in the other room while you're rubbing one out in the shower. Complete the course and ace the assessments."

"Or?"

"Don't make me give you an ultimatum, Asher. I'm trying to help you, here. Take care of this one simple task, and I'll handle the rest."

It hadn't registered to this extent before. But in the moment, Asher realized: Pierre was dealing with the fallout over his former partner to a greater extent than Asher—other than losing Sofia, of course. How was he not? Not only had Cassandra been the department's newfound recruit, but Pierre had hired her. Regardless of what was going to happen, Pierre would end up taking the fall to some extent, negligent or not.

Maybe it was in Asher's best interest to help the chief help him.

Who knew—perhaps Internal Affairs and the media would come to their senses and realize the chief had had no ill intent in hiring her. And why was the media so interested in holding Asher himself accountable? For what? It should've been *him* in a pine box.

Not his wife.

Chapter 62

As soon as Asher stepped into his office and closed the door, something gripped his throat like one of those dead-of-night visions: the walls shifted, the ceiling caved under the weight of his thoughts, his skin exuded a wet cold, and his pulse fluttered under a string of shallow inhalations.

Like he was being submerged, shoved down inchmeal into an ice bath on an empty stomach, unable to breath out, only in. Cold and faint.

Trembling.

He dialed Justin. The line rang and rang, followed by, "You've reached the office of—" Asher hit the red icon, then was about to dial the number again.

The office door flung open to reveal his mountain of a friend.

Asher did his best to hide it, to stand up straight with his shoulders back. To exude strength and confidence. But who was he kidding? Xavier could read him like a bibliophile with a newly purchased paperback fix, on the sofa under a tin roof, pelted by rain on a Saturday morning.

With ease.

"You good, man?" Xavier held open the door with an

inquiring look about him. No work—purely checking up on his friend.

"What's up?"

"You got a minute?"

Asher fell into his chair. "Sure."

Xavier shut the door behind him and took a seat. A tense sort of guise shaped his mouth. "Well, I just wanted to check up on you is all. You hangin' in there?"

"Yeah, well, that depends on what you mean by 'hangin' in there.' Feels more like I'm being hung out to dry, to be honest."

"It's a lot. In a way, that's what I wanted to talk to you about."

"What's that?"

Asher could read him, too—like one of his interrogations in a string of murder-suicides, the suspect fidgeting at the foot of the table, hesitant to speak without a lawyer present.

"I wanted to say sorry," Xavier said.

Didn't see that one coming.

"Sorry? For what?"

"Doubting you. For not giving you the chance to voice your concerns about Cassandra and the autopsy."

"Don't worry about that."

"Seriously—you good? I mean, do you really think that she might still be alive, after everything that's happened?"

Yes. No.

"I'm not sure what to think anymore, man. I'm the only one entertaining the idea, so more likely than not, I'm flat-out wrong. Or maybe I'm just going crazy."

"Or," Xavier said, "maybe this is just your way of processing everything that you've gone through over the last several weeks. It'd be a lot for anyone." He paused. Then he picked up again on a more serious note. "You know, I've been thinking about it. And I've been having these daydreams. These scenarios that play out repeatedly in my head, no matter where I'm at. No matter what I'm doing. They just keep coming like a nasty reminder of what happened. In particular, what could've happened."

No. Not you, too.

"What if I hadn't pulled the trigger?" Xavier continued. "What if . . . what if you could've talked her down? Talked *both* of them down? Maybe then, Sof—"

"We've been over this. Don't do that to yourself, man. Please. It ain't worth it."

Asher needed someone to lean on. He needed Xavier like he needed sleep. A normal night of it. If someone as calm and collected as his closest friend was having doubts about that day, then who was the grounded one? Who was Asher going to rely on if it all fell apart?

Again.

"Yeah," Xavier said. "I've been trying not to, but it seems like the harder I try, the more I think about it. The more I wish I hadn't made that decision for you. For us. For everyone. The more I think about it, the more I feel it was a fuckup on my end."

Asher wasn't sure what to say to that; no one should've been carrying that burden.

No one but Asher.

"Regardless, I know you're going through more than anyone else," Xavier said. "So, I'm here for it. Even if that means we chase down some insane hunch that'll ultimately lead to nothing. I'm all in. Hell, it wouldn't be the first time I've encouraged your crazy."

"So, I am crazy?" Asher said.

"Oh, come on. We both know that you fell off the wagon a long time ago, Detective." Xavier cut a deep smile.

It helped, knowing he wasn't in it alone. Pierre was wrapped up with Internal Affairs, so there was common ground there as well. And evidently Xavier, like Asher, was still thinking about how it all played out on that rainy day, in that narrow and crowded hallway.

Glinting barrels pointed this way and that.

"Well, I'm not sure where to go from here," Asher said.

"You don't need to be sure. In the end, it wasn't you who hired her."

They knew what that meant, but the chief couldn't have known that she'd go off the rails, either.

Xavier continued, "Something tells me that if your hunch is right, she ain't the type of woman to just sit around and wait for you to—"

A few taps on the door preceded its opening.

"Hey, y'all." John stood in the doorway with a file folder. He started in with Xavier. "I've been looking all over for you. I've got those lab results you've been—"

"The door was closed for a reason," said Asher.

Xavier backed up his friend, perhaps sensing the moment had been cut short. "You can wait outside."

John said nothing as he eased shut the sad, groaning door, taking his good time.

Chapter 63

Xavier was right: it was time to see what the homeless were up to.

Asher figured he would start where the second ripper victim had been found at St. Anthony's Garden, then work his way to Exchange Place, where the first stabbing had occurred in front of Jean Lafitte Trading Company. There was no way that it was a mere coincidence that both victims were living on the streets; someone, somewhere, had to have known them.

Better yet, someone surely had a lead of some sort.

Something.

Much of the city's destitute tended to gather around Jackson Square and the neighboring streets—where tourists were drawn to Café Du Monde, the cathedral, Bourbon Street, and other well-known sights. More visitors meant more handouts. More money.

It was a proximity thing—and it delivered day after day.

It wasn't difficult for Asher to locate other members of the homeless community. The problem was that, in general, such individuals had no interest in speaking with, nor aiding, law enforcement. Why would they? NOPD had no interest in helping them. At least, that was the impression of the homeless, thanks to the imposters who lessened the trust of locals.

Asher walked down Pirates Alley first, showing a headshot of the second ripper victim to passersby. A few wanderers lingered on the backside of St. Anthony's Garden, but the majority of people were either locals who were off to whatever night job they were late for or tourists, moseying along while shopping the work of street artists.

In the end, no one could identify the latter victim of the two stabbings; he also showed around a picture of Claude Evans, the first ripper victim, to drum up any leads there as well. Even though one of the homeless recognized the unknown man, they didn't have any information other than that they'd "seen him around."

Perhaps the homeless would've been more cooperative if they weren't given a bad rap by the overwhelming number of hustlers—the stolen valor rolling around in their brand-new wheelchairs with their sad cardboard war signs, the faux monks slipping bracelets onto people's wrists, then demanding payment with their backpacks full of money slung over their shoulder, the seemingly distraught and sick calling for an ambulance only for a comfortable night's sleep and a hot meal.

The list went on.

It wasn't that NOPD didn't want to help the city's homeless. The sad fact was that they couldn't waste limited resources on helping everyone who was living on the streets when a good number of them were professional cons. Good at it, too.

Asher pushed forward anyway—all it took was one lead. Just one piece of information to point him in the right direction.

The city was beginning to die down, or perhaps "ramp up" was a better descriptor of the night life. A red-orange sun had begun to melt on the other side of St. Louis Cathedral, and those lime-green hand grenades were flooding the city streets like neon tracers from a rifle.

Touchdown Jesus began to raise his hands and call yet another goal.

It wasn't all bad, though, when it came to the city streets and the homeless. Fortunately, there were those who genuinely tried, and succeeded, in helping those in need; that was the heart of the Crescent City. Southern hospitality at its best. But for the naïve, many of the tourists, the half-full glasses of the world, that was also the deceptive aspect of New Orleans—its ability to draw in the out-of-towners for a quick buck.

Like most locals, Asher could distinguish between the truly less fortunate, out on the street because it was the only home they had known in recent years, and those who were out on the corners in theatrical fashion, working their signs and cups for money they could have done without. He focused on the former—the quiet ones, the ones on the outskirts of where tourists gathered.

As he approached Exchange Place, fewer people lingered there in the alleyway. Maybe Gene Lafourche was right—perhaps the murder had given the road a bad rap. But murders in New Orleans were nothing new. And much of the traffic throughout the Quarter was out-of-towners, not locals. So, how could one crime cause such a drop in business?

And why hadn't such a cut in foot traffic occurred near the second ripper murder? Was it because of the draw of the cathedral? Maybe the immediate area surrounding Jackson Square felt safer, more populated? It made little sense to the keen detective.

What Asher did know was that if he wanted to get to the

heart of the homeless population and tease apart what was really going on under the surface, there was one person he should probably make a point to see.

Even though she was a last resort, as far as homeless sources were concerned.

Chapter 64

sher left Exchange Place and made his way to Marie Laveau's House of Voodoo on Bourbon Street.

After walking to the bespoke, decades-old shop, he found her standing there in front of the redbrick steps, pacing in abrupt strides. Swaying. The moment she laid eyes on Asher, she began shaking her head and wagging her finger in his direction. Her matted, dirty-blond hair reached down to the back of her knees. The bottom of her demure, black-and-white dress was wet and tattered where it dragged the hurried city streets.

"Oh, no," Mami said. "Don't ya come any closer dan dat, Detective." Her finger waved furiously, her other hand planted firmly on her hip. She panted, but that was just the years of fried food and sedentary routine talking.

Asher raised his hands to show he had no ill intent.

"Ya only come see Miss Mami when ya need something. Don't ya, Mr. Policeman?" She stomped back and forth with her hands waving above her head, flapping her chin. She wiped her sweating face with a handkerchief, then reached high into the sky and begged the gods for help.

"Oh, come on, Mami—we both know that ain't true," Asher said. "You're my favorite queen on this side of the

Mississippi. You know that."

Mami was a large woman with a complexion as dark as dark could be. Her chest threatened to break free from her dress, and she was always barefoot—a dangerous gamble on a street infamously known for the chance puddle of vomit or scattering broken glass, especially as the night grew deeper and the drunken tipsier.

She wobbled toward him.

"Like hell dat ain't true," she said. "What is it, now? Ya need a numba? An address? Or maybe ya want me to wear one of those wire tings, so ya can invade my privacy dat way."

"Of course not, Mami. What? An old friend can't stop by to check up on you? See how you're doing from time to time?" Asher stepped closer. "How you been?"

She smiled, and her gold tooth shone even under the shade of a dripping sun. "Like crawfish in a pot, I'm right where I belong, Mr. Policeman." She leaned in with a big eye. "But ya probably already knew dat, now, didn't ya?"

"And what makes you say that?"

"Well, ya found me."

Her skin glistened in the green and blue neon lights of the adjacent bars, their signs buzzing and flickering ever so faintly in an effort to stay alive.

"Yeah, I did. But you're reliable, that's all. I knew you'd be here," Asher said.

The woman put her back against the building and ran the handkerchief down her neck. "Come on, I ain't got all day now. Let's get dis over with so ya can be on ya way, and I can get back to my exercise."

Asher stepped in front of her and faced the building. He removed the two photos of the ripper victims from inside of his jacket, then held them in front of her. "You recognize these two?"

She wiped her face once more then tucked the cloth down into her struggling bra. "No." She spoke in a brisk cadence, with resolve, but she'd hardly looked at the pictures.

"Come on, Mami," Asher said. "Two seconds is all it takes." He held the pictures higher, up to her eyes, so she was forced to take a second look.

Mami was a good woman. Over the years, she had come to know everything that went on in the Quarter from Jackson Square to North Rampart and from Toulouse to St. Ann Street—her territory, so to speak. She walked those streets day and night, finding a way to make it by taking odd jobs or returning favors here and there.

In doing so, she saw things. She heard things. Things she probably shouldn't have. But after NOPD was able to squeeze some facts out of her following a robbery turned murder, as well as a drug deal gone sideways, they've been using her as the local go-to ever since. She knew things, and she was incapable of lying.

That was just how she was—unapologetically honest. And that meant telling the cops precisely how she felt about the homeless problem in the city and what she deemed to be their incompetence when it came to solving it. After all, she was living it.

Mami pointed to the picture of Claude Evans. "Now, dat one, I've never seen before." She turned her attention to the photograph of the second ripper victim. "But him . . ." She squinted in the late evening.

Asher inched the picture closer to her face.

"I see him walking up 'n down Chartres all the time, always

braggin' about how he found some magical lot with free money. Ha. Now, I know the Quarter, Mr. Policeman. And I can tell ya right now, ain't no such place 'round here. There's plenty of magical tings goin' on when it comes to *losing* money when ya trying to make it in a city like dis, but scooping it up for free like it's at the bottom of some wishing well? Mami don't think so, Detective. No, sir."

"Are you sure?" Asher said. "Is there anything else? A name, perhaps?"

"Ya see?" Mami said. "Always wanting more, ain't ya?" She pushed off of the wall and pulled the handkerchief from her bosom, folding it in two and patting her forehead.

"I just wanna be sure. I can't really go into it now, Mami, but—"

"Come to think of it," she said, "I ain't seen dat man in some time. What happened? What ain't ya telling Mami?"

"This man," Asher said, looking at the picture, "was just murdered. And all we've got to go on is this picture."

Mami clutched her throat in shock. "Murdered? Now, who would wanna hurt a poor ole man on the streets? Don't we deal with enough around here already, scrounging up just enough change for dis or dat?"

"That's why I'm here," Asher said. "That's what I'm trying to figure out."

Her attention wandered into the street. Her panting returned. "Well, ya know me, Mr. Policeman—and now ya know what I know."

It wasn't much, but it was something. Maybe Asher could walk Chartres Street to get a feel for what it could mean.

"Thanks, Mami." Asher slipped her a ten in good faith. "I'll be seeing you."

"Oh, no, Mr. Policeman. Oh, no." She tucked the money deep between her sweating breasts. "Next time, ya can buy Mami dinner, first."

Asher waved goodbye; Mami didn't.

Chapter 65

sher began walking back to where he had parked the Vette behind Café Du Monde. It was dark now, and the streets were crawling.

For a moment, he paused. Out in the open. And the feeling of working alone, of being partnerless, fell over him there in the night.

On his way back, he continued to show around the pictures of the two decedents who were stabbed to death and then beheaded. Dismembered. The photos were close-ups of their faces; it would've been in poor taste to show anything else, any detail below the chin.

As he hit St. Ann Street and turned toward the café, he approached an elderly man lying on one of the benches on the east side of Jackson Square.

Asher held out the photos. His badge was visible on his hip. "Good evening," he said to the man. "Do you happen to know these two gentleman?"

The disheveled man sat upright and grabbed the pictures from Asher's hands. "Well, let's take a look," he grumbled.

The man was clearly homeless—the soles of his shoes were scarcely hanging on, his shirt was torn in more than one place, and he hadn't shaved in some time. His skin was leathery from the Louisiana sun. Not to mention the miasma. A mix of perspiration and something sour.

His hands trembled as he examined the photographs.

Almost immediately, he handed back the picture of Claude Evans. "Ain't seen him before." But he continued to study the other picture, the unnamed, second ripper victim that Mami had recognized.

It intrigued Asher how multiple people seemed to have crossed paths with the unnamed victim at one point or another, while few recognized Mr. Evans, the one they'd already ID'd.

"Yeah, I've seen him around," the man said. "Mostly right here on Chartres." He pointed westward. "It's been a minute, though." He handed back the picture and held out his hand. "Name's Billy," he said, and they shook hands.

"Detective Huxley," said Asher. "You don't happen to know his name, do you?"

"No, sir. I tend to keep to myself if you know what I mean."

"Oh, yeah?"

"Yeah." He looked around. "Too many people with too many questions. That's one thing about being out here alone— too many people putting their nose where it don't belong. Everybody I run into wants my backstory. 'So . . . how'd you end up on the street? What happened?' Everyone saying that they can help, when all they really want is a handout."

"Your backstory, huh?"

The man leaned in, looking up at Asher. "Now, you tell me: who in the world wants to hear my sob story about how I lost my wife, and how my kids—" His face grew bitter. His bottom lip curling. "Well, let's just say my kids are somewhere else."

"That's none of my business, but I do appreciate your time." Asher felt bad, but if he stopped to consider the unfortunate circumstances that had led to every homeless person ending up on the streets, well, he wouldn't have time for anything else. There was no point in getting dragged into it, now. He placed the photos back into his jacket and gave the man a thank-you nod.

"Say . . ." The man stopped him. "I can help, you know."

"I'm sorry?"

He pointed to Asher's jacket, where the pictures lay hidden. "I can help. I can keep an eye out for you. You know, let you know if I see or hear anything worth your while."

It was getting late. "Sure." He continued his walk back to the car.

Billy called out to his back. "I'm on it, Detective."

It was curious—the homeless had certain inclinations toward law enforcement. And helping wasn't usually one of them.

Chapter 66

Per usual, Asher hadn't been able to sleep—the dreams hunted him through all hours of the night, refusing to leave him be until the now-widowed detective awoke to the sound of his own gasping.

Clammy.

So, he had left early for his appointment with Justin.

The foyer of the home office was dead silent, save for the creaking of hardwood floors beneath Asher's boots. Justin's office door was cracked open, and from what Asher could see, he wasn't here. He decided to get some coffee going while waiting—but as he opened the cabinet, he noticed there was none.

He was early; waiting was fine. Waiting without his caffeine though? Not fine at all.

Asher rapped on the kitchen door of the main house, hoping that either Justin or someone else would open up and have the answer to his coffeeless morning. At first, no one responded, but as he lifted his hand again, Tammy opened it and greeted him, dressed in blue running shorts and a Yoda T-shirt that read, "Not The Day Today Is."

"Oh, hey Asher. Come on in." She nudged open the door and walked into the kitchen. Asher followed. "Let me guess . . .

no coffee?" She pushed herself up and onto to her tiptoes as she reached high in a cabinet.

"You guessed it," Asher said.

"Justin ran out on a family emergency, but he should be back any minute." She set a yellow can on the counter. "I hope Coffee and Chicory is okay."

"Ha. It's almost like we've met before."

"Perfect." Tammy grabbed a few napkins from the counter and placed them on top of the can as well. "Oh, sorry." She gestured to the young man sitting at the end of the island. "This is Adam."

The guy greeted Asher with unmoving, headstone eyes as he peered up from his leaning tower of pancakes.

"How's it going?" Asher said. He reached out to shake his hand, but he was met with a bent elbow instead.

"Sorry," said Adam. "Not into the whole touching while eating thing."

Asher bumped elbows with him instead. "No worries."

Adam's brown hair was untamed and waved without purpose; somehow, it fit him. His boney hand trembled with an extended pinky as he sipped his coffee. The first thing Asher thought of was one of those custom flame paint jobs that had become so popular on vintage motorcycles and classic muscle cars—Adam was like that. Fidgeting, tapping, restless, even though he was going nowhere. In a hurry, with nowhere to be.

Moving while still.

Adam slid from his chair and patted his mouth with a delicate napkin. "Well, I better get going," he said. "Things to see, people to do." He bid Tammy adieu with an air kiss on either side of her cheek. "Same time tomorrow?"

"Sounds good," she said.

The stack of pancakes remained there, teetering, soaking in a puddle of maple that oozed down the sides of the hardly eaten breakfast. Adam downed the remainder of his coffee and set the cup in the sink. Then he walked to the outside door across the kitchen.

"Nice to meet you," Asher said.

All he got in return was a soft "Uh-huh." No gesture other than easing the door shut as he left.

"Sorry," Tammy said. "Lots going on."

"No worries." Asher grabbed the coffee and turned back to the foyer. "I appreciate it."

As he left the kitchen, Tammy moved into the doorway and leaned against the frame there. "Hey," she said, in somewhat of a guarded and secretive voice. It threw Asher for a loop, considering they hardly knew each other. Hell, they didn't know each other at all; their only link was Justin.

Asher turned back. "Yeah?"

She glanced around the corner, down the hallway, folding her arms. "Can you do me a favor?"

He was too curious to say no. "Sure."

She took a single step toward him. "Don't say anything to Justin about Adam stopping by for breakfast." Her focus shifted between his eyes. "You know . . . family dynamics and all." The smile that followed was crooked, but somehow convincing.

"Yeah, no problem."

Why in the world was he so quick to agree? They were hardly even acquaintances.

Keeping something from Justin, anything that put Asher in the middle of his therapist's marriage, or any family matter, was a mistake. But saying no to his wife would've put him square in the middle of whatever this was regardless.

Asher instantly regretted it. Hopefully, her ask was innocent enough.

Tammy reached out and touched his arm. "Thanks, Asher. Lord knows this house has seen enough drama to last a lifetime." She walked back into the kitchen before easing the door shut behind her.

Chapter 67

"Sorry about that," Justin said. "I like to have coffee ready to go for when people get here." He took a seat in his chair. Asher sat across from him on the sofa. "In laws are something else, huh?"

"No worries. I'd just feel bad for you if I had to do without my morning fix."

"Ha. Well, good news is I get to throw you out after an hour."

Asher valued his time with Justin: their sessions were truly two-sided. Any semblance of "how does that make you feel?" and Asher would've thrown himself out. Did they always agree? Certainly not. But Asher left his appointments feeling as if he'd taken a step forward—later followed by one or two steps back, on occasion.

But progress was key, no matter the setbacks.

His fear was that he'd become dependent on these visits, though. In the end, he needed to function alongside the catastrophizing, under feelings of the unreal and the disconnect from the world around him. His career included. He was coming to realize that eliminating those feelings was a pipe dream.

The goal was to live in spite of them—not without them.

"So," Justin continued, "what's new?"

"Oh, not much. Just living the dream."

"Living the dream, huh?" He adjusted his tie. "I'm curious . . . what does that mean exactly, given our discussion about your *actual* dreams the last time."

"Sorry. I should've been more specific: I'm just . . . living the nightmare."

"Ah. There it is. Now we're getting somewhere."

Asher couldn't get past his interaction with Tammy. What was going on, there? He could see it, occupying the space between him and Justin; something was on the therapist's mind, and it wasn't anything good.

Justin spoke with indifference. "You wanna elaborate—"

"No. I don't wanna talk about me today."

"Okay." He released a frustrated huff, although he probably hadn't meant to. "And why is that? What would you like to talk about?"

"You," Asher said.

Justin clicked his pen and set it down on the coffee table, on top of his notepad. "You know we don't do that, Asher. Our time together is about you. To help you, not me."

"Well, the way I see it, our sessions are for the betterment of me, and you're the one helping me, ergo, what's going on with you matters. At least, I think it does, if I'm the one sitting here with you, taking advice from you. See? I'm being totally selfish."

Justin only stared at him, trying to squirm his way out from beneath Asher's request. But would he say no, if that was what his patient wanted?

"I think we should talk about Sofia," Justin said.

"What about her?"

"You've gotta talk about what happened, Asher. It won't just go away, no matter how hard you try to forget it."

"You think I'm trying to forget about her?"

"No. But I think you're trying to forget about what happened to her. You may not see it, but in a way, that's kind of the same thing. Don't you think?"

"No."

The truth was that Asher needed a distraction—something to ponder, other than the hell he'd been dragged through over the last several weeks. He needed to feel something other than the memory of betrayal, of loss, and the reality of his current tragedy.

He craved normalcy. To know that Justin, too, had his own inhibitions. Like a normal human being—whatever that was.

Ironically enough, the derealization, as Justin called it, had always hit at the most inopportune of times, when it made Asher feel at his worst. And now, sitting here with the therapist, he was looking for exactly that—a distraction, a way to dissociate from what he'd be forced to come to terms with at one point or another.

His partner had hung him out to dry. His wife was dead. He needed a black box, so to speak. One stronger than what he was able to conjure in his own head.

"And what could you possibly wanna know about me?" Justin said. "What about me is gonna help you?"

"I don't know—but I'm tired of talking about the same thing." He paused for Justin's objection, but there wasn't one. "I got here early," Asher continued. "You weren't here."

"No, I wasn't. And I'm sorry. I had a family emergency."

"Yeah, that's what Tammy said. How are you able to disconnect the two?"

"What's that?"

"What you do here versus what's going on out there."

Asher leaned his head to the door. "You mentioned your in-laws when we sat down. What's going on with—"

"Asher." Justin leaned forward and clasped his hands. "We can't do this."

"What's that?"

"This." He gestured between them, a single finger running back and forth like a fallen metronome. "I'm here for *you*, not me. If I need help, I'll get it."

"Oh, I know. This isn't about you. I need someone to talk to, and talking about how fucked up my life is right now isn't helping me."

"And talking about what's screwed up in my life will?"

Asher said nothing, only crossed his legs and clasped his hands. Answering by not answering.

"And?" Justin said. "What makes you think that my life"—he stood and walked toward the unburning fireplace—"is in any way something to talk about?"

You work from home? You're a neat freak? You're in the midst of a "family emergency"?

Your wife is asking me to keep secrets?

"Maybe if you tell me what's going on," Asher said, "and how you're handling it, it'll help both of us."

The office door opened. It was Tammy, dressed like she was on her way out, her purse slung over her shoulder. "Hey, sorry to interrupt." Her voice was hurried. Shaky. "I need you."

Asher said not a word; there was no need. The distraction was nice. But on the other hand, what about him? This was his time—regardless of the topic.

Chapter 68

sher's venture down the city side streets had proven only somewhat useful.

"What the hell does that mean?" Asher asked. They were sitting at Xavier's desk in the precinct.

"A 'magical lot with free money,' huh?" Xavier said. "I have no idea what that means." He danced his pencil on the table. "So . . . who'd you hear that from?"

"Mami."

"Well, shit," Xavier said with a dissatisfied laugh. "Why didn't you lead with that?"

Reaching out to the homeless had been Xavier's idea to begin with, and he'd brought it up on more than one occasion. What was the issue now?

"I did say that," Asher said. "But what's the problem? It's information, ain't it? It's better than what everyone else has given me—which is nothing."

"Oh, it's something. Of all people, you're gonna place your bets with Mami?"

"The department reaches out to her all the time. What? You don't think it's relevant?"

Xavier's laugh grew deeper. "A magical place that's handing out free money? Why don't we walk the streets looking for the pink Clydesdale with a horn of glitter sticking out of its head?"

"I would—but I don't have the time to build a stable, nor do I have the space to house it. Besides, everyone knows that you start off with a pony first to make sure you'd be an appropriate equine parent." His voice grew over-the-top in an obvious way. "Duh." Mocking.

Asher received only a scowl in return.

"Look," he continued, "it's something."

"Alright. I'll think on it—but no promises. If we can get an ID on this second stabbing, though, I think we'll be in good shape. Then we can start making connections. Personally, I say you reach out to that priest again."

"Maybe. He didn't seem to have much for us in the way of useful information the first time I spoke with him. I doubt another visit will do any good; he's got my card."

"I'll tell ya what"—Xavier shut down his computer and began gathering his belongings—"I'm gonna head out to Jackson Square and talk to some of the business owners down on St. Ann and St. Peter, see if they have any CCTV footage they're willing to share."

"Sure," Asher said. "It worked with Jean Lafitte."

"A little. At least now, we can keep an eye out for the same two guys. Well . . . the same look, the same behavior. It'd be great if we had faces to go off of."

"Yeah, it would. Say . . . you ever got around to looking at that bottle cap and hair sample from the VIP room?"

"Oh, from Bourbon Pub Parade?"

"Uh-huh."

"Yeah, but all we got is DNA from the hair. It won't do us much good if we don't know who we're looking for. There's no match in CODIS, so . . ."

"Well, damn."

"Besides," Xavier said, "what are the chances that that hair is from the one person we're looking for, out of everyone who's visited that one room? It's unlikely at best. And highly circumstantial, regardless."

Asher rocked in the rolling chair, considering their options. They had leads. He could taste it—something was there, that powdery drip in the back of his throat.

But what was it?

Whatever it was, it was too obscure for him to see as of yet. It'd come, though. At some point, he'd find it as if it had been walking alongside him all along.

"Alright," Asher said. "You get out of here and get us some more footage. Keep me posted on that DNA profile, will you? Maybe we'll get lucky."

"Sure thing."

They parted ways.

As Asher walked to his own office, turning the corner with his eyes painting the ground, mulling over the scant evidence from both the balcony cases and the ripper victims, the two of them collided. Head-on.

"Really?" John said.

"Well, back at ya," said Asher.

John looked behind him at Xavier, and addressed Asher as he picked up the paperwork he'd dropped on the floor. "Still sending that man out to do all of your legwork, huh?"

"Come again?"

"Xavier—you have him out on the streets quite a bit for a forensics lead, yeah?"

Where the hell was this coming from? Had he missed something?

"We get off on the wrong foot?" Asher said.

"Of course not." John attempted to organize the papers he'd picked up, shuffling through them with an angry hand. "I just can't help but notice that everyone's job around here is getting more and more difficult by the day, Detective. Don't you agree? Two cases, no serious leads on either one of them . . ."

Asher stepped in to him, surely closer than John felt was even remotely okay. "As an equal, I don't *have* Xavier do anything." Asher leaned into his ear, his speech low but calculated. "You should really stick to the rookie stuff. Who knows? Maybe one day, your opinion will matter."

"Hey, numbnuts," the chief called from his office door across the way. "Get in here."

Asher stepped back, turning to Pierre's office while keeping a disparaging eye on the new guy over his shoulder.

"What the hell was that all about?" the chief asked as he approached.

"You tell me," Asher said. "New guy confidence? Idiocy? A false sense of big dick energy? Who knows? Whatever it is, it ain't gonna get him far around here, I'll tell you that."

They stepped inside, leaving the door open. Pierre picked up the corded desk phone and handed it to Asher. "It's Midnight Murder Walks. They have info on your decedent, Charles Richard?"

"Midnight Murder Walks? And that is . . . ?"

The chief responded by pressing the flashing, red hold button on the phone's receiver.

"Detective Huxley speaking."

Chapter 69

The company office was a can't-breathe hole in the wall: put the key in the front door and shatter the back window. The all-brick room was painted a peeling midnight black, the wood flooring original and splintered. Cold air raged from the rusting floor vents. They shone with condensation.

"Good afternoon," a man said as Asher walked through the ringing front door, struck by the damp smell of the place.

A dull, ochre glow melted from a small chandelier above, making it look as if it were swinging, but it wasn't. It was hardly hanging from the mended and plastered ceiling.

Asher pulled back his leather jacket and discreetly flashed his badge. "Detective Huxley. I'm looking for—"

"Kendric, one of the GMs here." The man lifted his hand in greeting, then stepped out from behind the counter. "I'm the one you spoke with on the phone. Thanks for stopping by." He stabbed at his near-perfect afro with a chrome pick comb.

"Yeah, no problem."

They shook hands.

"So, what can I do for you?" Asher continued. He glanced around. "We can talk privately if we need to." Another employee stood in the corner like a deaf shadow, minding his own.

"No, that's okay. We can talk here."

"Alright."

"You're definitely the detective in charge of the Charles Richard case, right?"

"Uh-huh."

"Well, it might be nothing, or maybe it's something—I don't know—but I just wanted to make sure that someone important hears it from me personally."

"Okay . . ."

The man was a straight shooter, based on his widened stance and his wherewithal to realize that he should speak with someone important, not just some low-level paper pusher who'd probably file a report and slip it into the bottom of some backlogged desk drawer. That, alone, made Asher intrigued by what he had to say.

"Well," Kendric continued, "my boss, Charles Richard, who was also the owner, was heavy into the bar scene out in the Quarter. I'm out there almost every weekend, and I'd see him walking in and out of places all the time. Mostly around the corner of Bourbon and St. Ann."

"Okay."

There was more; there had to be. Asher could tell by the way he fidgeted with his comb that he was only just getting started. And suddenly, Asher had a sense that things were about to get interesting. The hair on the back of his neck stood on end.

"In particular," Kendric said, "I'd see him a lot with Cam Spencer."

And there it was.

"We weren't usually in the same bar or anything, but—"

"Wait . . . Cam Spencer, as in the owner of The Walking Murder Tours?"

"Yeah. That's him."

"Okay, then."

"I'd always see Charles hanging out with Cam, hopping from one bar to the next down St. Ann Street or on Bourbon, too, from time to time. I'm not sure why, or how it's relevant, or *if* it's relevant, but I thought you should know."

"Yeah, of course."

It was something—but more than anything, the obvious was of greater importance.

"To be honest," Asher said, "talking on the phone with you was the first time I'd heard that Charles owned Midnight Murder Walks. That alone is important, since Cam Spencer owned a tour company as well."

"For sure," said Kendric. "That's the main reason I wanted to talk to y'all. Like I said, it might be nothing, maybe they were just friends, but I thought that that connection would at least be worth mentioning. But, you know, a lot of the tour companies around here keep in touch. They're all out for the same business, you know?"

"Yeah, of course. Either way, it's an important piece of information. It gives us some common ground to work with."

If it was nothing, then it was a coincidence. But it couldn't have been—there were no coincidences in this line of work. Not like that.

Two tour companies keeping in touch? Sure.

Their bosses knowing one another, working together on the business end of things? Of course.

But the fact that Cam Spencer and Charles Richard not only hung out together outside of work, but were both murdered in the same fashion? No way. The tour business had a role to play in what had happened to the company owners.

What that role was, and to what extent it pointed to a single suspect, was yet to be seen.

Then, of course, the kicker: they were both murdered at gay bars. And Cam Spencer had kids. With his wife.

<h1 style="text-align:center">Chapter 70</h1>

You—

You lingered at the back of your walking tour, which was making its way down St. Ann Street. Next stop? Napoleon's Itch.

The guide walked backward at the head of the group, occasionally glancing over his shoulder to avoid the crumbling sidewalk and puddles of god knew what—as if the city were bursting at the seams beneath your feet. "Not only does St. Ann Street host some of the most well-known bars in the French Quarter, but just two blocks ahead, between Burgundy and North Rampart, is the original location of Marie Laveau's home—where the queen of Voodoo herself lived with her children in the mid- to late-nineteenth century."

A Criminal's Pub Crawl was one of the few walking tours that would pass by the bars you had yet to case. Not only that, but the guide promised to show the group the inside of what he considered "the hottest watering holes in town." Whatever that meant.

"And here we have it, ladies." The guide staged his best enthusiasm for a crowd that was clearly more out-of-towners than locals. Their cameras. Their wide eyes. The bar was nothing special, but local tour guides had their own way of making it so. "The one, the only—Napoleon's Itch."

There was something about him, the guide in his skinny jeans and bleached, haphazard hair. His black shirt that was one size too small. Something familiar but also off-kilter.

You followed the group through the white doors and into the relatively small space. An alien-green glow lit up the rows of bottles behind the bar. A red "CASH ONLY" sign hung from the ceiling above the liquor.

"Take your time," the guide said to the group. "Grab a drink, socialize. This is the first stop of many."

You approached him and placed your hand on the small of his back. "This place is really something," you said. You fluttered your eyes for good measure.

He'd take the bait; they always did.

"I know, right." His voice was velvet.

Then you noticed it—the way that lump in his throat moved up and down when he talked. Glaringly familiar.

You had tried, over the years, to erase him from your memory. To forget that you'd ever had a sibling who looked out for you about as much as a stranger in a seedy alley.

Nothing worked, though; in the end, you saw him everywhere. In the faces of strangers, in the dark corners of your dreams, in the twisted grins of passing children whom you've never laid eyes on. They were all him: the memory of what he'd forced onto you, with no sense of remorse or a lone regret.

"I'm Reese," you said to the guide, standing between him and the rest of the group. Demanding his attention.

"Thank goodness," he said with a criminal grin. He'd already introduced himself at the beginning of the tour, but he reciprocated, placing his hand in the center of your back. Not still, but rubbing. Slow. Just enough to reassure you that he was interested.

You leaned into his ear. "Oh, you're a star, hun."

The way he felt you, with his fingers scratching, massaging, that line where your jeans ended and your skin began, back there where only the two of you could notice—it welcomed a rage you had only felt, and could never shake, under the hands of an older sibling.

Chapter 71

The wails of children escaped the room and filled the hallway.

Well, this should be interesting. Asher opened the door and stepped inside.

"Good evening," he said to the woman in a honey pencil skirt and matching high heels, a bib thrown over her shoulder as she chased the older of two children around the room.

"Hi, Detective." She crouched and reached under the table. "Sorry about this." She pulled the toddler toward her as he jerked away. Her baby rocked in a car seat on the floor. "I had to come straight over from the daycare."

"No worries," Asher said. "I imagine you've got a lot on your plate right now." He offered an extended hand. "I'm Asher Huxley."

Of course her world was turned upside down; she was Cam Spencer's wife.

"Janice," she said, taking his hand as the child pulled at her other.

"I apologize," he said. "I had no idea that you'd have your children with you. If you'd like, we can reschedule for a later date. I'd hate to discuss certain things in front of them."

"No, no. It's totally fine. Really." She juggled the older one.

"There's no one else to watch them. Besides, this one's preoccupied with being in a new place, anyway."

Asher could truly have said that he knew what it was like—losing a spouse. Even he noticed his tendency to approach these situations with a bit more consideration than perhaps he would've before. Before Sofia was taken from him, in front of him, in the most horrific of ways.

Only, the woman in front of him had two kids, and he couldn't even begin to fathom what that added to her anguish.

That sharp catch clawed at the back of his throat.

"I won't take up too much of your time," Asher continued, doing his best to keep his emotions in check. "I just have a few questions about your husband, if that's okay."

"Of course." She sat in one of the two metal chairs and rested the toddler on her knee. Asher couldn't tell if the bouncing was for her or the baby.

"Well, I appreciate it." He sat down as well. He lowered his voice, given the child in front of him. "So, as I said before, your husband was found on the balcony of a bar in the Quarter—a place called Good Friends Bar."

"Yeah. I remember."

The toddler reached for the table and failed. Cried.

"Do you know anything about the place? Why he would've been there, or if there's anyone who had it out for him, perhaps?"

"No, not at all." She rocked the car seat with her foot. "I mean, he'd started going out a lot over the last week or so." Her shoulders dropped to a saddened posture. "Here lately, it's almost like he's been more concerned with his night life than with his family. He never used to be like that."

"What was he like?"

"Quiet. Kept to himself. Content with the life we'd built. I have no idea what changed recently, but it doesn't surprise me that he was out in the Quarter. Of course, what happened surprises me quite a bit." Her eyes began to water.

"Of course."

She pulled a bottle from the diaper bag on the table, then handed it to the baby. The toddler on her leg wasn't having it—fighting in her arms, slapping, turning cherry red in his effort to escape his mother's grasp.

"So, do y'all having anything? Any information about what happened?" she said.

Asher wasn't entirely sure how to broach the subject, or whether it was worth discussing at all.

"Not necessarily," Asher said, "but there are a few things that might be relevant. Some things we're looking into."

"Okay."

"This might be nothing at all, but are you familiar with Good Friends Bar? Have you ever been there, or do you know much about the place?"

"No, not really. I mean, I've heard the name, but I don't really know anything about it."

Was she really gonna make him do this in front of the kid?

"So, Good Friends Bar . . . actually . . . Good Friends Bar"—he felt the hundred stares of a packed audience radiating from the toddler in front of him—"falls on the lavender line. Now, that doesn't necessarily mean anything—it's not like only *certain people* are allowed inside or anything like that. Straight men visit those bars with their friends all the time. But what I'm wondering is—"

That was when it hit her—and the flood gates opened from her bloodshot eyes. "Why my husband was there if he's married?

If he's got two kids waiting for him at home?" Her chin quivered. The toddler took notice.

Asher nodded shallowly. Just asking the question made him feel like an ass, but it was necessary. No potential lead could be excluded—no matter how sensitive or unlikely or ridiculous it seemed. No matter how petty. All it took was one step forward to make a difference. Just one piece of information could break the whole thing open. That went for any case.

But she didn't need to say a word—he could tell by the hurt, by the mascara-tainted water now flowing down the gentle curve of her cheeks.

She had no idea.

"Well," she said in an unsteady voice. "Unfortunately, your guess is as good as mine."

Asher handed her a tissue from the box on his side of the table. She pulled the toddler closer and wrapped her arms around him, smelling his hair.

"Okay," Asher said. "Is there anything else, anything at all, that we should know about your husband?"

Asher wavered on whether or not to tell her about Charles Richard, but he decided against it. He was keeping that one in his back pocket. She probably knew who he was because of her husband's business, or at the very least that he also owned a tour company; but the fact that her husband was regularly seen with him was something Asher wasn't ready to offer up just yet. Not without her volunteering the information.

Chances were, there was something to it. If there was, he didn't want anyone—no matter how seemingly innocent they might have come across—getting spooked.

She pondered his question but offered nothing in response. "No. I don't think so."

"Okay, well if there's anything else that you do remember, feel free to—"

"Just promise me," she said. The kids were quiet, now. She was struggling, stammering, to rein in her crying. "Just figure out who did this. Please?"

Chapter 72

Asher sat on the couch in his home office, away from the memories of his wife that were littered throughout the rest of the home. He cradled *Meditations* in his lap and kicked his feet up onto the ottoman.

Since Sofia's death, his anxiety had changed in a way he'd never expected—the panic attacks and insipid laundry list of symptoms had lessened, although they hadn't vanished entirely. Instead, this new thing lingered and followed him around no matter the circumstances, regardless of where he ventured or how he otherwise felt.

The derealization—it was something new. And Asher was no fan of the new.

He wasn't sure how, or whether it made any sense, but perhaps Sofia's passing had made him realize how trivial his worry had been all along. Was it worth it? Worrying over that which was out of his control, over the uncertainty of a future that he would meet whether he liked it or not?

Not according to Marcus Aurelius.

One day, the detective would be dead and gone—along with everyone and everything he'd ever loved or remotely cared about. Why should he waste time worrying about what he couldn't grasp?

Maybe losing Sofia was the source of his diminished anxiety, the worry he'd come to loath so well. Or maybe his worry had only changed shape, now that his world was no longer the same. At least, not here. Not in this home.

Asher cracked open the book to where he'd left off the night prior, but then a knock sounded at the front door. He set it down on the end table and stood.

"Who is it?" he asked.

"Your chief," Pierre said.

What was the chief doing here so late? He never showed up here at all, much less late at night.

Asher opened the door to find Pierre standing there on the porch in his peacoat, a cigar rolling between his teeth, teasing the edge of his mustache. "Can I come in?"

Asher stepped aside. "Yeah, sure."

Without saying much, Pierre began walking around the living room, like he was assessing the intricacies of a new homicide. He paused between the kitchen and den, staring at Sofia's unwashed coffee cup, still sitting on the island.

Her lipstick on the rim of the mug was poised like a knife's edge against a delicate thread under the kitchen lights. If he washed it, perhaps the world would stop spinning altogether. Perhaps Asher might crash down along with everything he'd ever known.

"Getting a lot done around the house lately?" Surely, Pierre could see that that wasn't the case; the home was frozen in time, from when life seemed more rational.

"Oh, yeah," Asher said sarcastically. "I can't sit still."

Pierre continued pacing. "I won't keep you—I just wanted to stop by and see how you were holding up."

"Can I get you anything?" Asher walked into the kitchen and grabbed a bottle of water from the fridge. "Coffee? Water?"

"No, I'm good. Thanks." The chief puffed on his cigar as he walked into the kitchen, then tapped the ashes into the sink.

What was going on?

Pierre leaned back against the counter with the torpedo between the tips of his fingers. "So . . ." He blew on the smoldering end of it, forming a ball of glowing embers that floated away into nothing.

"So . . ."

"Are you . . ." Pierre started. "Are you good?" His eyes found the coffee cup yet again.

"I'm fine, Chief." Asher downed a bit of the water. "I am fine, I've been fine, and I'll be fine. Really." He peeled the wrapper from the bottle and tossed it onto the counter.

"You sure about that?"

"Of course I'm sure."

"Really?"

"Yep."

"Okay . . . okay," Pierre said. "Well, I just wanted to make sure that you're . . . getting past this whole thing and moving forward, is all. Cleaning up, you know?"

"Yeah. Sure."

"You know . . . that you're cherishing the memories. Not dwelling."

"Uh-huh."

"Okay, then," said Pierre.

He walked to the coffee cup, stood next to it, glanced at it, looked to Asher, took a drag. Then he nodded as if to say, *Then what is this?* He pulled a set of papers from the inside of his peacoat and dropped them onto the island, next to the coffee mug. "I'm sure you haven't forgotten, but tomorrow morning is our little meeting with the board of commissioners."

In fact, Asher had forgotten.

"I'm assuming you've started that media training that Andrea sent over?" Pierre said.

He hadn't.

"Uh-huh."

"Good," Pierre said. "Then you should have nothing to worry about."

Looked like the rest of Asher's night was spoken for.

Pierre took one last drag, then extinguished his cigar on the edge of the kitchen sink. He placed what was left of it inside of his coat. "Be sure to look over these." He pointed to the paperwork on the counter. "There's some notes in there on the complaint that was filed against you, in addition to what I plan on submitting to the board tomorrow, on behalf of the department."

"Yeah, I'll give it a look."

"Good."

The real exchange went unspoken: Pierre was worried that his lead detective was off the rails, and Asher insisted that he had it all under control.

The chief walked to the front door. "You'll be fine, Asher. It'll all work out in the end." He opened the door and stepped onto the porch, then turned back. "Take care of yourself, you hear?" He gestured inside, to the obvious disarray of Asher's private life. "And be sure to get some sleep. We've got an early morning."

"Will do." Asher shut the door behind him.

Chapter 73

he New Orleans Police Board of Commissioners was comprised of seven members: the city manager, the police commissioner, the civilian manager, and four civilian members (two appointed, two elected). They sat behind a large semicircle bench at the head of the room, touting their fancy thronelike chairs and microphones and golden nameplates.

The room felt like a court, and it was blazing hot. Humid. The country, state, and city flags hung motionless behind the members of the board, covering nearly the whole of the wood-paneled wall. Asher and Pierre took up real estate at a table in the center of the room. A handful of spectators, media included, sat behind them.

"Good morning," said Commissioner Beau. She was a small but spirited thing.

"Good morning," Pierre said.

Asher added, "Morning," while fighting back a yawn.

"Let's go ahead and get started, shall we?" the commissioner continued. "Detective Huxley, you've had a citizen complaint levied against you by a Miss Carla Pichon, stating that you, and I quote, 'raised a hand to a working member of FOX News Media as a physical threat, with the intention to cause bodily harm,' end quote, in the parking lot of the civic New Orleans Police Department on—"

"I'm sorry, Miss Beau"—the chief rose from his chair—"if I may. I would like to point out that—"

"Can the detective not speak for himself, Chief? I would like to remind you that, although this is an informal hearing, it's not you who is the subject of this complaint. It's Detective Huxley."

Pierre looked to Asher, perhaps waiting to see if he would speak up for himself or let him handle it on his behalf. But Asher felt that if the chief was that intent on speaking up for him, on pointing out something that might help, then why not let him roll with it?

"Yes, ma'am. I completely understand," said Pierre. "But before we get into the meat of things, I would just like to make two quick points, which might save us all a little time here this morning."

The commissioner removed her glasses and sat back with a reluctant look about her. "Make it quick, Chief. This doesn't need to be a drawn-out, overly complicated meeting."

"Yes, ma'am." Pierre buttoned his coat, even though the room felt like a sauna under a desert heat lamp. "First of all, I'd like to point out that the individual who confronted my detective, and stood between him and his own vehicle, preventing him from leaving NOPD grounds, is not the person who filed the complaint. This letter"—he held up the paperwork—"was filed by someone else entirely and, from what I understand, is another member of that very same legacy media outlet. Second—"

The commissioner disagreed with a lift of her hand, halting the chief's comments. "Chief, I understand what you're saying, but it's my job to remind you that *anyone*, whether they're a government official, a citizen of Orleans Parish who is *not* employed by the city or state, or anyone else for that matter, is allowed to file a written complaint against your department—and that includes whether or not that individual is the subject of said complaint. What's your second point, please?"

Pierre cleared his throat and shifted his shoulders, as if he were itching in his own skin. "Second, I'd like to bring up the fact that Detective Huxley has already begun media training through our HR liaison in the department. Even though, I might add, nothing materialized from the interaction between Mr. Huxley and the member of the media he's said to have 'threatened.'" He brought out the air quotes. "Nothing actually happened here, Commissioner."

"I understand, Chief, but—"

"Furthermore, I'm not entirely sure why we're here in the first place. I mean, is there something that the board is looking for me or my detective to accomplish here? If anything, it's Detective Huxley who should be filing a complaint against Fox News because their reporters can't seem to respect the personal space of my detectives."

The room fell silent. Other members of the board seemed bored stiff.

Asher could hear the chief breathing, each exhale growing heavier, more irritated. It was nice having a boss like Pierre to stand up for him, even if he did ride Asher's tail more often than not.

"Is that all, Chief?" the commissioner said.

"I'm sorry, Miss Beau, but at what point does the media go too far? Are they just allowed to run free and harass the members of our department at will?"

"I understand where you're coming from," she said, "but regardless of what did or did not occur, when a complaint is filed against an NOPD detective, we're required *by law*—just to be clear—to convene a meeting of this board."

"Yes, ma'am," the chief said. He sat down.

"Now, Detective Huxley," she continued, "as I'm looking here at this written notice, in addition to your departmental file, I see that this is not the only inquiry that seems to be following you around these days." She didn't bother to look at him. Not even a glance.

Suddenly, Asher felt as though the commissioner had not been entirely forthcoming in her statement that the hearing was all but formal. And that—*that* rubbed him the wrong way.

He saw it now: this was really a hearing on his role, or lack thereof, in the Cassandra debacle. Regardless of what ended up happening with Internal Affairs, the whole mess with his ex-partner would follow him around, haunting him, for as long as he remained in law enforcement.

And there was not a single thing he could do about it.

Asher answered the commissioner with a voice meant to tickle his own twisted sense of humor. "Well, what can I say—these days, I'm all about pleasing the people, ma'am."

Chapter 74

You—

It had been nearly two hours since you bought him his first drink—and by your eye, that should've been plenty of time. The dance floor, the whole bar itself, was as packed as ever. Deafening.

You leaned into his ear. "You wanna head upstairs?" The smell of sweat and bourbon wafted from his wet skin.

His nose rustled your ear as he leaned back into you. "Yes, sir." And his breath made your skin form those chilling bumps, raising the hair on your arms and chest. As if the rope was already tightening.

You led him upstairs and into the private lounge. They called it the red salon—red velvet furniture, deep-red lighting, maroon carpet. Even the tables and artwork on the walls were a blood red. The glassware and fixtures, too.

You thought back to several months ago and how disorienting it had been the first time you were here. A one-night stand had shown you the place after you stumbled into the bar at 2 a.m., drunk off your ass from a round of hurricanes. Few people knew the place existed.

That was what made it so perfect.

Between the lighting, the booze, and the drugs—the molly in particular, which flooded the bar on a nightly basis—no one paid attention to the two of you. No servers, no upstairs bar, no security.

The room was its own private world. A place to get it all out. To release what you'd kept pent up inside you for so long, now.

Here, you could work under the guise of loud music and little light.

"How's this?" you said, showing him into the room. You flipped the sign at the door to read "OCCUPIED." Another reason why it was so ideal, the perfect room to get in and get out; it was a first-come, first-served private party.

You locked the door.

He pushed you down onto the sofa and straddled you, taking your drink and setting it on the table next to his own. Unbeknownst to him, you had little intention of going any further.

As he kissed you, you slid the cuffs from your back pocket. He had no clue, no suspicion as to what he was in for. That your lips would be the last he'd ever touch.

You clamped the first cuff on his wrist.

"What the fuck, Reese?" He seemed more taken aback, more angry, than you had anticipated. "What are you doing?"

"Let's play," you said with a coercive tease in your voice. You pulled him closer and reached for his other arm, but he pulled away.

This wasn't how it was supposed to happen. The drink—where was his drink? You looked to his glass on the table. It was empty. At best, he seemed a bit tipsy, but that was it.

But how?

He moved to get up, the one handcuff dangling from his wrist. "Fuck this, man. I don't know what the hell you *think* was gonna happen, but—"

You gave him no time to react at all: you grabbed the cuff that hung at his side and pulled him down. Elbowed him in the face. Then you realized—downstairs, you'd tweaked the wrong drink.

His now-flattened nose leaked a thick crimson that sputtered down his chin and bled into his white shirt, even redder under the glow of the red salon.

He stumbled backward, then landed against the wall and slid to the floor. A look of disbelief washed over his face as he smeared the edge of his hand beneath his nose. Eyes caught in the headlights. Momentarily distracted by his own blood trickling over his fingers like a leaking faucet.

You stripped the rope from your belt loops.

Before he could gather what was happening, before he could recognize the situation that had already begun to unfold, a situation that would make a broken nose feel like a happy ending, you cinched the cord around his neck and yanked him down. Your knee on his chest.

Unlike the others, he was actually fighting. He kicked. He tried talking, only to choke on the blood.

There was no time for the garrote—you'd have to do this the old-fashioned way. By brute force.

Lucky for you, his ability to react was a fraction of his old self, dampened by the alcohol. But as you pulled on opposite ends of the rope, he kicked—and the glass door to the balcony shattered over the two of you.

Oh, you're a star, hun. Such a bright and dying star.

You wrenched the cord tighter.

Someone yelled from the street below. "Hey, you alright up there?"

You pulled. He shook.

Red sprayed from his nose in choking, illegitimate breaths that disappeared into the red carpet beneath you.

Your arms strained, and his legs trembled one last time—until his body fell limp under a blanket of shattered red glass.

You leaned down to his red-washed face and loosened the rope, before sliding it from beneath his neck.

Then you ran from the bloodied salon without ever looking back.

Chapter 75

"Forgive my detective, Miss Beau." Pierre stared at Asher with an angry eye. "I wasn't gonna bring this up, although I'm sure that the board is already aware of this matter to some extent, but Detective Huxley has been dealing with some personal matters here, lately."

Asher stood up and dropped the laid-back demeanor. "Don't. There's no reason to bring my personal life into this. Not here."

"You wanna have a job when we walk out of here, don't you?" The chief spoke low. "Besides, what happened with Sofia isn't entirely personal, is it?"

Asher clenched his jaw; as much as it hurt, the man had a point.

"What are we doing here, Chief?" The commissioner was growing impatient.

"Sorry, Miss Beau," Pierre continued, "but I think it's important to note that Detective Huxley has only just recently lost his wife in the midst of a recent case—*because* of a recent case. So, all I'm asking"—he gestured to Asher—"sorry, all *we're* asking, is that the board take into account the recent events that the detective has been subjected to."

"Yes, Chief," said the commissioner.

But did they really know? Were they truly aware that Sofia's murder was, at least to Asher, far more damaging, more horrific, than the betrayal of a partner?

The board moved as if they were ready to get in and get out of the meeting. To prove a point and to move on.

But then—

"I apologize," said the chief, "but I have just one last point to make, and then I'll shut up."

The panel chuckled, and so did the reporters behind them with their notepads and tape recorders. Breaking character for only a moment.

"Fine," the commissioner said, swearing with a raised hand. "But I hope this is good—because you're absolutely right. This *is* your last point before I lose the last of my patience."

"Of course," Pierre said. "You have my word."

The whole room fell silent, perhaps wondering what the chief could possibly have to say on top of "the detective's wife was recently killed, so give him a break."

"This has already been disclosed in a recent meeting of mine with Internal Affairs," Pierre said, "but I feel the need to bring it in front of the board as well, provided that . . . well . . . for obvious reasons."

The civilian manager, Liam Johnson, leaned forward and braced his arms flat on the table. His eyes darted between the chief and Asher.

Pierre continued. "Mr. Johnson is currently under investigation for his role in—"

"I don't think so, sir." Commissioner Beau interrupted him. "This hearing is, in fact, not going in that direction. We are not here to discuss the work of anyone on this panel, nor anyone else in the room for that matter, other than Detective Huxley."

"Oh," Pierre said, "yes, ma'am. I completely understand. Only . . . you insisted on bringing up the fact that Detective Huxley is also being investigated for what happened with his former partner. So it's only fitting, then, that we address that matter directly so the rest of the board will be up to speed."

"I think it's time to move on," said the commissioner.

But for the chief, it certainly was not.

"Well, if we take a look at the official record," Pierre said, holding up the file, "we'll see that the person who levied this complaint is, in fact, none other than the wife of Mr. Johnson, here." Pierre pointed the folder directly at him.

At first, the commissioner said nothing.

Pierre dropped the folder to the table with a slap. "*You* are the one who brought this up, Miss Beau, so let's go with it, shall we? Don't you think this is something worth mentioning, Commissioner? Or were you gonna leave out that small piece of information?"

Liam Johnson shot up from his chair. "This is ridiculous."

The next line hit Asher like one of those decades-old potholes on a New Orleans street.

"Mr. Johnson is the one who recommended Detective Huxley's ex-partner to *my* homicide team, and now Mr. Johnson's wife just so happens to be the one who filed a complaint against Detective Huxley? When she isn't even the one who interacted with him in the parking lot? Come on," Pierre said. "If we're bringing up other inquiries that have nothing to do with the reason we're all here, which I think is inappropriate to begin with, then we should at least lay out all the cards."

Well, that makes sense. No wonder the chief was so confident after his interview with Internal Affairs.

Pierre seemed to have been saving that little tidbit of information for a rainy day, and now the skies were beginning to open.

"Look, Chief," said the commissioner, "I don't know what's going on here between Mr. Johnson and your department—and, quite frankly, this whole thing is headed in a bad direction—but we need to be very clear on something. Nothing justifies one of your detectives threatening someone. Anyone, for that matter."

"Of course," Pierre said.

"And Detective," the commissioner continued, "I don't care if it's verbal, a gesture, a sideways glance, or an inappropriate thought, I don't wanna see this back in front of the board again."

To his surprise, the rest of the board members remained mute. Not one of them chimed in. From the looks on their faces, none of them wanted to get involved in whatever this was. Not even the city manager dared say a word.

Miss Beau continued, "I expect you to provide us with a certificate of completion from your media training by the end of the month, Detective. Another incident, and the board will be forced to consider a period of suspension." She closed the folder in front of her. "Depending on the severity of the matter, of course."

Commissioner Beau stood from her chair, then stepped down from behind the bench. Each of the board members followed her—except for Liam Johnson. He just sat there, staring a hole through the chief, as if his career had just gone up in flames.

Pierre glared back, unmoving.

"Well, that was quite a production," Asher said.

The chief grabbed his belongings from the desk. "Like I said the other day—don't sweat it." He turned away. "Let's go. Lunch is on me."

Chapter 76

The moment they stepped outside, Pierre's phone rang.

Whenever the chief was in a good mood, he had a way of answering the phone that sounded like a spry combination of "yeah" and "hello." He pulled a cigar from the inside of his jacket and placed it between his teeth. "Yellow," he said into the phone.

They paused under the building's overhang.

"Oh, come the fuck on," Pierre said. His voice shifted from upbeat cheer to pissed in all of a split second. "You've gotta be kidding me. Where at?"

Just then, Asher's phone did a silent dance of its own. He placed the aviators over his eyes and pulled the phone from his pocket. Michael Myers's picture appeared on the screen, framed by a running blue light.

"Talk to me," Asher said. Agnes only rang him when it was something important.

"You've gotta come down here," she said. Her voice cracked. "Like . . . now."

"Why? What's up?"

Pierre began pacing, shaking his head. "What do you mean, different?"

"I'm here looking at your second ripper victim, and there's something you gotta see," Agnes said. "Something we didn't catch with the first one."

"Like what?"

"Just get down here; it's best you take a look at it in person."

Asher looked at his watch. His stomach twisted into a gripping knot.

He hated guessing games—it was either really good or really bad. The humid air around him squeezed his every breath, and the sun shifted over the parking lot, making the shadows crawl. His vision grew narrow. The pulse throbbed in his neck, and his mouth was dry.

"I'll be there in twenty," he said.

The chief hung up at the same time. "Who was that?" he asked.

"Agnes. Said she's got something I need to see. Sorry about lunch—I think I need to head on over there."

"Well,"—Pierre lit the cigar, pulling breath after breath until it was smoldering good—"that was your boy, Xavier."

"Oh, yeah?"

"Yeah. Don't take too long over there at the coroner's office." He let the smoke bleed from his nose. "Looks like one of our suspects is getting sloppy."

part three
REVELATIONS

Chapter 77

Pieces of the homeless John Doe lay on a steel table, drawn out from box A5.

Agnes pulled back the opaque, plastic cover and positioned the man's head for Asher to see. She pointed to the base of it, where it had been severed, separated from the rest of the stabbed and mutilated body.

"So, just by looking at the laceration," she said, "it's clear that whatever was used to stab and dismember the first victim was also used here. Something unusually sharp. Surgical, even. The obvious difference between the two decedents is how clean the work is." She set down a photograph of the first homeless victim—the severed head of Claude Evans.

"Okay," Asher said. "So, why the difference, then?"

"More likely than not, it's one of two things: either he was in a rush with the first decedent and took his time with the second, or he attacked victim number one from the front and the second one from behind; cuts from behind are typically cleaner, since the attacker can hold the head steady by grabbing their hair or forehead. From the front, it's a free-for-all."

As well as Asher had come to know Agnes, he could sense there was more to it. Something she was leading up to. She didn't drag him all the way down here just to say there was a difference in how the victims were attacked.

Not when she had insisted he see the body in person.

"Now," she continued, "remember how I told you there was edema in the lungs of our first ripper victim, but it wasn't all that clear why, because of the stabbing?"

"Uh-huh."

"Well, our second one, here, shows signs of it, too."

"Okay."

"Like I said before, it could just be secondary to the knife wounds, which wouldn't be all that surprising. But what *is* noteworthy is what I called you down here for."

She picked up the picture of the first stabbing victim and placed it next to the head on the table. Agnes was all about effect—showing Asher what she was referencing before bothering to explain it. A guessing game. Could he draw a conclusion on his own?

"What am I looking at?" Asher said.

"The not so obvious, hidden by the obvious," she said.

"Well, I'll go out on a limb and say the obvious part is how clean the beheading is."

"Uh-huh. What isn't so obvious is what's hidden beneath the lacerations. In particular, what's hidden because of the sloppy job on the first of the two victims." She adjusted the picture.

Whatever it was, it had to have been—

"Oh, wow," Asher said.

"And there you have it," Agnes said, gesturing to the subtle bruising just below the chin, intersecting with the clean and glaring cut. "There's bruising, which wasn't so easy to see with the first one."

"Yeah, I see it, now—but what does that mean? Wouldn't

there be bruising from the knife wounds?"

"No, not necessarily. I mean, it's possible but not likely. Not like this." Then she brought the photograph of Claude Evans closer to the head of the second victim on the table. "These bruises are consistent with manual strangulation. Someone's hands." Pointing. "Their fingers."

"I thought they looked familiar."

"Right? We've seen this before."

Asher found it interesting—but also puzzling. If anything, it muddled his idea of the killer. He didn't quite see how it helped the case in any useful way.

Not yet.

"That's the thing, love," Agnes continued. "If we add bruising on the neck to the edema in the lungs . . . it *could* point to another cause of death entirely. The stab wounds are still relevant, obviously. But given the strangulation marks, I can't entirely rule out asphyxiation, now, either."

Well isn't that a peach.

"It's just something to think about, hun." Agnes stepped back and lit a cigarette. "The main reason I bring it up is because if these two were strangled before being stabbed, then that begs the question: why slit their throats if they're already dead?"

"You tell me—you're the medical examiner."

"Oh, no," she said. "I'm the how; you're the why. Motive is all you. I just give you the facts—what you do with them is entirely up to you. One possibility is that they're botched strangulations that turned into stabbings. But for both of them? I don't know."

About a minute of silence followed.

"What I did hear," she said, "is that you've got an official serial killer on your hands, now. Another balcony?"

"That's what I'm told. I'm about to head over there now."

The bruising on the ripper victims was certainly something. Unfortunately, it was unclear what it meant, as were the faint and delicate marks themselves.

Agnes's question, though, made the detective think twice.

If they were asphyxiated, then why stab them? What am I missing?

Were these failed strangulations turned stabbings? Or did Agnes find exactly what someone had meant for her to find?

Chapter 78

s Asher approached the balcony to Napoleon's Itch, the obvious hit him square in the chest: no victim was cuffed to the railing, posed for the city streets to see as tourists and the like passed with their cameras and open mouths.

And that one unexpected change in the case transformed everything around him into an unreal place, where he was nothing more than an observer, thrust from reality into some banal movie from which he couldn't walk away.

He felt detached. Helpless. Was he even qualified to be here?

"Hey, Asher." A call from the balcony.

No matter where he focused, it was all a murky screen, playing out in front of him with indifference. Not good, not bad; he felt nothing. Other than the solitude of being separated from the world around him.

"You coming up?"

The detective had no choice—this was his job, his way of life. In a sense, it was all he had.

He ran the bracelet on his wrist over his fingertips and stared off into the street, until it all came into focus. The smell of the wet brick, moisture filling the air. The trotting of hooves in the distance. Brass horns. A puddle at the edge of the road rippled with the vibrations of a town that never slept.

It brought him back to what was real, enough to move forward and do the job that he, somehow, needed to get done. Because she knew he could. Because Sofia—once upon a time, when he could still touch her—had encouraged him to dump everything he had into his newfound career.

She had been certain of his ability, when no one else was.

"Yeah," he said, speaking to Xavier above him. "I'm on my way up."

And so it continued.

Asher entered the small, private room. Red light from within and ambient light from outside mixed at the far end of the space. A man's body lay on the floor, covered with broken glass from the shattered balcony door.

"You got an ID?" Asher said.

Xavier handed him a tattered leather wallet. "Yeah. Name's Delphin Stanley. Someone passing by on the street heard the glass shatter, and then what sounded like a scuffle. Just after midnight last night."

A single empty rocks glass and a half-empty bottle of Jäger sat on a table next to the sofa. Other than that? There wasn't much inside of the room—save for the bed of glass and the body in the middle of the floor.

"At least he's making it interesting," Asher said. "I was starting to get bored there for a second."

"Tell me about it," said Xavier.

Asher knelt next to the body. "What are you thinking?"

"Looks the same to me," Xavier said. "You know, other than the lack of cuffs and not posing him outside. By the look of it, something went south."

"Strangled?"

"I'd say so, yeah."

Even under the dim red lighting of the room, Asher could make out the pattern of a twisted rope around the man's neck. Bruising. Eyes half-open, glassy.

"Just like before," Asher said, "let's make sure that we look at the sofa, as well as the glass on the table."

"Already on it."

Asher moved outside and onto the balcony. From what he could see, nothing was out of place. The wrought-iron table and chairs were set neatly against the building. Cushions in place. An ashtray rested at the center of the table, seemingly clean. Only glass littered the balcony floor.

"Make sure you print this tray, too," he called inside.

"Got it," Xavier said.

Of all things in the room—the sofa, the rocks glass and bottle, the broken glass door—it all came back to the body and where it rested. The fact that the assailant hadn't had the time to pose it was new.

And new was good, in this instance.

"I heard Agnes called you on your way over," Xavier said.

"Yeah. Turns out, she's second-guessing the cause of death on the stabbings. After a second pass, it looks like they might've been strangled."

Xavier paused with the camera around his neck. "Really? Strangled?" Then he looked at the dead guy on the floor. "How in the world does that make any sense whatsoever? If they were strangled, then—"

"Why do what he did?"

"Exactly."

"Who knows? Anger? Control? The inability to stop once

he got started? It doesn't matter. All that's ever mattered is that we stop him; there is nothing else."

A knock at the door. "Hey, Detective."

Asher glanced that way to see John standing in the doorway. "That person who heard what happened is outside, waiting for you. They'd like a word."

John walked into the room before setting a work case down on the floor. Then he stretched on a pair of blue latex gloves.

"Feeling better?" Asher said. It came out normal, although he was aiming for a hint of derision.

John shifted his attention to Xavier. "Yeah. Why?"

But Xavier wasn't going to speak for him.

Asher checked his watch, then walked past John and to the door.

Chapter 79

The woman juggled her bag of beignets alongside a steaming coffee. Powder fell from her lips as she took a puffing, white bite—chewing reservedly, moving her hand in front of her mouth as she noticed the detective walking toward her.

"I see you've got the right idea," Asher said.

"Oh, yeah." She spoke with a mouthful. "Just felt like the right time, you know?"

"For beignets? It's always the right time. I'm Detective Huxley with the homicide department." He moved to shake hands but changed his mind.

"Sorry," she said with her hands full. "I'm Andy."

"No worries, Andy."

Then he wondered—

"You haven't been standing here the entire time, have you? Since last night?"

"What?" She looked confused at first, then seemingly caught on to what he was getting at. "Oh. No. Most definitely not."

"Good." He felt sorry for her—surely, this had taken her by surprise. Walking the Quarter that late at night, probably with better, more exciting things to do in a city like this. And certainly at her age; she appeared young, in her mid-twenties maybe.

"I gave one of the officers my number when they first came out, then headed home for a quick shower and a cat nap. Said they'd call me."

"I see."

"Then grabbed some sustenance for the hangover"—she held up the bag and coffee from Café Du Monde—"right before they called me back. Said I needed to speak with someone more official, in person."

"Gotcha. It worked out, then." He waited while she continued to eat. She had not a care in the world, from what he gathered. "So, what happened, exactly?"

With her mouth full, she said, "It was around twelve thirty, one in the morning, when I was walking back to my room on Ursulines—The Haunted Hotel?"

"Yeah, sure."

"That place gives me the creeps. Started hearing shit, so I went out for a few drinks until I could barely keep my eyes open. Figured I'd have a few, that way a little noise here and there wouldn't bother me, you know?"

"And where were you coming from?" He pulled a small yellow notepad from his back pocket. Clicked the pen.

"The Cat's Meow. Left some friends and called it a night." Took a sip of her coffee. "Right when I got in front of the place, just below the balcony, I heard a bunch of glass shatter. Like a window or a door or something. Then some fighting."

"Fighting?"

"Yeah—stuff getting knocked around, shouting."

"Okay."

It wasn't much to go on. He was hoping the woman had actually seen something. Anything. Noises meant practically nothing—unless the killer was shouting his confession as he ran off.

"Is there anything . . . perhaps more specific? A description or something that could help us identify someone?"

"No, not—" She paused midbite. "Well, I'm not entirely sure because I only caught a glimpse of someone when they were standing just inside the door, but if it was him, he looked fairly skinny? Dark hair? I'm not sure, 'cause it was so dim. But, yeah, he wasn't big at all. Pretty thin."

She was right: it was a tenuous description at best. Not only had she not seen him well enough for a reliable ID, but by her own account, she had been drinking.

Asher handed her his card.

On the other hand, if her recollection was correct, the description did match the one he'd gotten from the bartender at Good Friends Bar, after they found the first victim. Still, it was a watered-down version of an apt picture of the man.

"Well, I appreciate it," he said. "Let me know if you think of anything else."

He considered having her come into the precinct and work with an artist to get a halfway decent sketch of the guy. But at this point, it probably would do more harm than good.

How many skinny guys with dark hair—chaotic hair, according to the prior description—were running around in New Orleans?

Chapter 80

They were done processing the scene—and Asher needed to take a beat.

He and Xavier left Napoleon's Itch and walked down St. Ann Street toward Good Friends Bar. Strolling. Talking. Wandering and letting their ideas on the cases float to the surface.

Asher needed to get up and get moving, somewhere. He couldn't just sit around and think on it any longer; the more he walked, the more the thoughts came and went. Filtering out the old and ushering in the new.

And the movement helped with the anxiety, with that feeling of being encased by the unreal with nowhere to go.

"Well, that makes three," Xavier said.

"Uh-huh."

"So . . . what are you thinking?"

The sun had begun to wilt behind the French skyline, the balconies lit by a dying, burnt orange. Ferns hung from the wrought-iron terraces, their fronds curling in the city warmth.

"To be honest?" Asher said. "I'm thinking about how much I hate coincidences."

In particular, it was what Agnes had told him about the stabbings—this idea that the decedents were strangled before being stabbed was an anomaly he couldn't stave off. Until he made sense of it, there was no way he could sit still.

"What's the coincidence?" Xavier said.

To a greater degree, what were the chances that Asher would've been assigned not one but two high-profile cases after returning, both of which turned out to be strangulations?

And repeat offenses, at that.

"The cause of death," Asher said. "All three of the balcony cases are asphyxiations, and with Agnes going back and changing her mind on the stabbings, now those are, too. At least, that's what she's leaning toward."

"Okay," Xavier said. "So what? You thought you'd come back, get assigned one case, and never see the same cause of death again?"

"Of course not."

They reached Good Friends Bar. Asher stopped and looked up to the balcony, then back to where they'd come from, toward Napoleon's Itch—across the street from Bourbon Pub Parade.

"Three murders, less than two weeks apart, all within the same block," Asher said. He glanced around, the gears turning.

"Yeah. So?"

He thought back to the stabbings and where the bodies had been found, not far from where they were now.

"And the other case . . . the two stabbings. Those are what? The closest, one block from here? The other one, four blocks?"

"Yeah?"

Asher wasn't all that sure what he was getting at, but it helped to talk it through. To think out loud, so Xavier could tell him how ridiculous it all was. So Asher could shoot him down and flesh out the idea anyway.

At least, that was the usual path of resistance. Their process.

"What if we're missing something else entirely?" Asher said. "What if Agnes finding those strangulation marks on the stabbing victims is something more than just botched strangulations?"

"Okay. And?"

"And what if that's the key—what if these cases are deeply personal for whoever's committing them? Cuffing the victims to the balcony, stabbing and dismembering the others? What if the strangulations are just . . ."

"Just what?"

"I don't know." He was unsure where that was headed. "Just . . . never mind. Forget it."

They turned around and made their way back toward Jackson Square, stopping on Pirates Alley, where the second stabbing had taken place. He wasn't sure why, but Asher felt the need to map it out on foot, to retrace the city streets that connected the two sets of cases.

The five murders.

"When's the last time we worked two homicide cases that were this close?" Asher said.

"What do you mean?"

"I mean, literally. Have we ever had two ongoing investigations that were on top of each other like this, geographically? The balcony cases are all right here down St. Ann, behind the cathedral. And the stabbings were, what? Right next to the church, then a few blocks away on Exchange Place?" He looked west.

"Yeah. So? This is the busiest tourist spot in the city. It can't be all that shocking; it was bound to happen sooner or later."

"Maybe."

They walked farther, turning down Chartres Street and

heading toward Jean Lafitte Trading Company.

"Just because the two cases are repeat strangulations doesn't mean they're connected," Xavier said. "Nor does it mean that the killings are personal. Offenders strangle their victims for all sorts of reasons—sexual pleasure included. Shit, that's probably at the top of the list. Look at all of the most popular serial killers. It all comes back to sexual gratification for the majority of them."

"True."

They turned down Conti then onto Exchange Place, stopping there at the corner. Asher thought back to the first stabbing, which had occurred right here, in front of the coffee shop.

He ran through each of the murders in his head.

"*That* . . . isn't a coincidence. There's no way." Asher stared off down the street in somewhat of a haze, looking deeper into nothing as if he were seized by some drug-induced stupor.

"What are you talking about? What's 'that' that can't be a coincidence?"

Asher turned back to where they'd come from, back in the direction of the cathedral. "The two cases—which one was first? What was the first murder?"

"The strangulation. Above Good Friends Bar. Why?"

"And the second?"

"The stabbing, right here on Exchange Place." Xavier leaned his head in front of Asher to get his attention. "You good?"

"And the third?" Asher said. "That was Bourbon Pub Parade?"

It was right there on the tip of his tongue; he could taste it. Like that first shot of espresso right before the sun rises.

"What . . ." Xavier looked back and forth, between the coffee shop and the direction of the cathedral, like he was watching the murders take place right there in front of them. "You think the fact that they alternate means something?"

Chapter 81

sher walked into Justin's office—and the door slammed shut behind him, caught in a crosswind of ice-cold drafts.

The woman stood slowly from the chair and dropped her notepad to the table, but there was no sound; the room had no volume. Like a feature film stuck on mute. Not even a subtitle.

She stepped toward him.

Asher reached for the door handle behind him without ever looking back; he couldn't take his eyes off of her. She held his gaze, unblinking, as she stepped toward him yet again. She was so cold, yet gorgeous all the same.

Then he noticed them—the two men in the chairs across from her, quiet, still. They watched with blank and blurry faces as she moved toward him, their arms flat and motionless on the arms of the seats.

She pushed closer.

Who were they? What were they doing here at Asher's appointment?

And where was Justin?

He turned the doorknob behind him, but it was locked. He twisted the bolt—and it twisted back. The metal cold. Freezing his skin.

What is this?

She stepped closer, with longer strides now. A badge shone from her hip as her skeletal, white hands reached toward him in what felt like slow motion.

Still, the two men moved not an inch. Then he noticed the similarities between them. The exactness, to be precise. A hair-for-hair copy of one another—the same grin, the same build, same clothing.

The two of them wore the same facial features, trait for trait. Blank stare for blank stare. Strangely, Asher was unable to see their faces. How was that possible?

Who were they?

The woman lunged toward him with those grasping white hands. Skin and bones. Her mouth screaming, with not a single sound passing her lips.

Who were they? Were they brothers? Relatives?

Twins?

She fell toward him, on top of him, and they fell backward together through the now-open door. Then that thing glared from the edge of her face.

That vibrant green piercing through her left eyebrow. The barbell Asher knew all too well.

He awoke, frozen in bed with dry, burning eyes. A catch in his throat.

And still, he had no answers.

Chapter 82

ells rang at the top of the door, and Emily greeted him from behind the counter with a gleeful morning pep. "Good morning, Detective."

"Morning," Asher said.

"Large café noir?"

His eyes weighed heavily. "Please. And an extra shot would be great."

"Yes, sir."

Asher sat at the table nearest to the window. It was early, but the city streets were already stirring under an early golden sheen that cut the rooftops in two.

As he scanned the alley, he envisioned the first stabbing, there: the body strewn about in bloodied pieces like some sick showing, the man's head resting on the bench as if it were merely people-watching on a lazy day.

What was he missing?

If the decedent had been strangled, as Agnes suggested, then he'd most likely died in the doorway of that shop, from where he was dragged beforehand—before things had taken more of a macabre turn when he was dismembered.

But why?

Was it a cover? If so, why hide the strangulation? What could possibly have been so personal about the cause of death that the killer would've tried covering it up?

Or was it a lack of control—killing, then needing more until whatever driving force was satiated?

"Here you go," Emily said, setting the coffee in front of him. She tapped the tabletop, then turned away. "Let me know if I can get you anything else, Detective."

"I appreciate it," he said. His focus was consumed by the anomaly on the street. A few people walked by as if nothing had ever happened there. As if someone hadn't been murdered in cold blood and left out in the open, right there on the stone beneath their feet only days prior.

He hung around for a good ten minutes before deciding to leave for therapy. He pulled a five-dollar bill from his wallet, folded it in half, and tucked it beneath the napkin holder at the center of the table. As he headed for the door, he called to Emily, "Thanks again. Have a good one." He lifted his coffee in farewell.

Her smile beamed.

When he stepped outside, he was immediately cut off by a walking tour. A group of ten or so people with their maps and cellphones flowed around him, as the guide said something or another about the pirate himself, Jean Lafitte.

Someone at the back of the group handed him a brochure in passing. "Be sure to check us out," the man said. He was someone with the tour company, for sure.

"Will do," Asher said.

As Asher walked from the storefront, he considered tossing the ad into the trash, but when he opened it for a closer look, he decided against it. He set his coffee on the edge of a planter in the middle of the alley.

Inside of the flier was a list of attractions, places visited six days a week by the walking tour, three to four times a day. Each of the stops included a picture, a location, and a few bullet points on its history. At the top of the list was LaLaurie Mansion—supposedly one of the most haunted houses in New Orleans, where Delphine LaLaurie was investigated for the horrific and brutal treatment of her slaves. Asher didn't buy into the supernatural; it was an interesting story, nonetheless.

Next in line was the New Orleans Pharmacy Museum, which showcased the world of nineteenth-century medicine and healthcare. Constructed in the early 1800s, the building operated as the apothecary of the country's first licensed pharmacist. A photograph of a large, dark amber medicine bottle, spilling a clear liquid over a dirtied table, was printed next to the building's history.

Last was the New Orleans Historic Voodoo Museum—a fifty-year-old gallery meant to educate visitors on the culture of New Orleans's Voodoo legacy. The small but one-off museum featured everything from Voodoo readers and practitioners to a self-guided tour through tiny rooms of rich art and folklore. For sure, it had come to be one of the most unique places in town.

Over the years, Asher had visited each and every one of the city's most popular sights and attractions, including those listed in the pamphlet. Of course, being a long-time resident, he'd seen everything in between as well. Every alley, every backdoor entrance.

It was part and parcel of the job—and that was a leg up when it came time to make connections between decedents or suspects. Not all detectives were created equal in that regard.

But as he scanned the brochure, it gave him an idea: he had

walked the streets below the balconies, the second floors of the bars where the victims had been strangled. The locations that were undoubtedly selected with a careful eye by the killer. But what about the link between the victims themselves?

The decedents, at least the first two who were strangled, had owned tour companies. Perhaps visiting not only the companies themselves but where they toured would spark something inside of him.

Surely, the fact that they were both business owners in the same line of work was no accident. What better place to start?

As he closed the pamphlet and tucked it inside his jacket, something caught his attention from above. A feeling of sorts, like he was being watched the whole time, since he'd set foot in the alleyway.

The hair on the edge of his hands stood erect.

He looked up to see James Cormier leaning over the railing of his balcony, nursing a morning beer. The man gestured "hey" with his bottle. Followed by a twisted grin that drowned in the yellow morning light.

Chapter 83

sher was hearing voices.

From the foyer, it sounded like Justin was in a session with another patient, which was unexpected since Asher was usually his first client of the day. He forewent taking a seat and lingered just outside the office door. Curious.

He knew that he shouldn't, but he couldn't help listening in. More than anything, he was surprised that he could hear them. It was an old house, though. The walls, through echoes and layers of plaster, appeared paper-thin.

As he listened closer, the voices—well, it almost sounded like three of them. A couple, perchance? Marriage counseling?

He moved closer to the door and leaned against the wall. But he only caught pieces of the conversation. "Get ahead . . . emotional changes . . ."

He shouldn't have been standing there. It was wrong, eavesdropping on someone else's—

The door opened.

"Oh . . . Good morning, Asher." Justin seemed surprised to see him there. At least, so near the office door.

"Morning," Asher said.

Justin stepped out of the room with Waylon in tow.

"Hey, Asher." The young man seemed cheerful. A good session? "Good to see you again."

"How's it going?" Asher said.

Waylon bypassed the small talk and made his way to the main house, out through the kitchen door, moving as if he had somewhere to be.

"We all ready?" Justin said.

They entered the room for Asher's appointment.

—

"These dreams are killing me," Asher said. "It's getting to the point to where I dread falling asleep."

"And the latest one?" Justin asked. "Was it different from the ones that came before?"

"No . . . Yes . . . I don't know."

"Well, what was different?"

What? You mean, besides the fact that you no longer had a receptionist out there? His attention floated to the office door.

"Nothing, really," Asher said. "Other than, this time, there were two of them sitting across the way."

"Two of who?"

"Two patients, in the room with the therapist." Asher pointed to the chair in which Justin was sitting. "It was the same therapist as before, sitting right there."

"Okay. So . . . who is she?"

He needed to get it out, like a sickness, to tell someone what was driving him mad. Justin himself had said that Asher's dreams reflected his daytime thoughts—apparently, she was on his mind more than he realized. "Cassandra," he said.

"Cassandra?"

"Yeah."

"You sure?"

He pointed to the corner of his eyebrow. "Had a piercing. So, yeah."

"Well, I'm glad it's finally coming together for you. It makes perfect sense to me."

"It does?"

"Sure." A faint smile crossed his lips. "Cassandra was a clinical psychologist at one point, wasn't she?"

She was. But that didn't help him: he needed a way to stop it, to rid his mind of her once and for all. He wanted to think about her, to dream about her, about as much as he wanted to lose another partner.

Or watch another wife die in front of him with a gun to his head.

"And the two of them? The patients who looked like spitting images of one another?" Asher said.

"Spitting images?"

"Yeah. They were exact copies of each other. How do you explain that one, *Doc*?"

"Like . . . twins?"

Asher shrugged. "You tell me."

"Well, my guess is that you've already got the answer. Remember? What are you dealing with during the day, when you're stressed or busy or angry? One way or another, it's all connected. You've got the answer right up here." He tapped the side of his head. "But if you're having these dreams on a regular basis . . . My guess? . . ." He leaned forward. "You're having trouble letting go. You *need* to let go, Asher—or your own worry will pick you apart, piece by piece."

"Well, jeez. And all this time I was worried it might be something depressing."

Chapter 84

Leaving therapy, Asher slid into the Vette and dialed Xavier. He needed some investigative fix—a push in the right direction or a piece of evidence that would point him to someone in particular.

He had an idea on where to go from here, regardless of the forensics.

Just sitting there in the Vette relaxed him: the classic vinyl smell of the '60s, a bucket seat that held him like a worn-out pair of jeans, the look of a cockpit straight from some state-of-the-art navy jet. The quiet was unmatched, before the satisfying shaking and rumbling of the engine would commence, once he'd turn the ignition to start the 383.

It was his own private time machine. His bliss.

Xavier picked up on the fourth ring. "What's up?" He sounded busy.

"Hey, where you at?" Asher said.

"I'm back at the precinct. Just got done meeting with Pierre, about to call up Agnes. What you up to?"

"Leaving a doctor's appointment. Say, were you able to take a look at what we collected from the Delphin Stanley scene? I know it's a long shot, but I'm hoping—"

"Actually, yeah. Well, we've still got some work to do, but

we're making good progress on it."

"What'd you find? Please tell me you've got something. And don't tease me."

Silence flooded the line; quiet from his best friend was rarely a good thing. Xavier was the open type as far as Asher's people went. In part, that's what Asher loved about him—his ability to be honest to his face, no matter the difficulty of the conversation. But when Xavier went quiet, that only meant one thing.

His friend was choosing his words wisely.

"We're all done processing the bottle and the rocks glass— I'm sorry to say, but there's nothing there, man. At least, there's no prints. None that are good enough to use, anyway. I've got someone running DNA on the glass right now. But how that turns out is gonna depend on the PCR and whether it's from someone who's already in the system."

"Damn. Is there anything else? What about the furniture?"

"Yeah, we're working on it. I've got some fibers from the couch that I just got done looking at, so that's what I'm working on now. I think they might match the ones Agnes found on our first balcony victim."

If it was a match, that'd certainly be a step in the right direction. Then, if they could track down where the fibers had come from, it would at least narrow down the search.

But a match was almost a necessity. They had fibers from the first of the balcony victims—but to match them to multiple murders would be the shoo-in he was looking for.

"Well, keep me posted," Asher said. "Are you heading over there to see her right now?"

"If she's around, yeah. I'm about to call her up."

His idea was to follow not only the killer, but the victims. It was an old trick he'd learned from another detective when he'd first joined the unit, back before he was comfortable in his own skin, with his own methods of investigating.

On the outside, it might have seemed like a no-brainer—investigating the background of the victims in addition to the offender, side by side. But from what Asher had seen when he first joined the unit, most detectives didn't do it that way. They focused on the crimes themselves, the killers in particular. As a result, the victims were usually an afterthought.

What he'd come to find was that, more times than not, if he could look into the background and activities of the decedents, it'd lead him straight to one or more commonalities among them—and, therefore, to the killer himself. Or herself.

"Alright," Asher said. "Let me know what she says."

"Will do."

"If they're a match, then that's what we need to hit hard. Start looking for a manufacturer and then a point of sale."

"For sure," Xavier said. "If she's able to take a look, we should have an answer within twenty-four hours."

"Sounds like a plan."

"Where you headed now?"

"I've got an idea," Asher said.

"Uh-oh."

"Yeah, well, I've come into possession of a certain flier that might be of some use—a pamphlet from one of the local tour companies. It's not one that we're dealing with now, but if these tour owners are in some way connected, then it's a start. I think I'm gonna visit a few of the tour's stops and see what I can dig up."

"For sure."

"Oh, and Xavier?"

"Yeah?"

"Keep thinking about our homeless cases. If this is headed in the direction that we think, getting ahead of this next stabbing is gonna be our best bet."

Chapter 85

Asher stepped through the narrow green French doors and into the Pharmacy Museum. A young woman was taking payments behind an antique cash register at the counter, in front of a floor-to-ceiling wall of old bottles filled with medicinal herbs and endless remedies. He couldn't tell if they were real or not.

"Hi, how many?" she said. A receipt book on the counter in front of her.

"Good afternoon." Asher tastefully flashed the badge on his hip, concealed by the bottom of his leather jacket. "Is there a manager I can speak to?"

He could tell she was wrapped up in the work, unbothered by his presence. Busy. She asked another employee to watch the counter and admit the two customers behind him. "Follow me," she said.

She walked him to the back of the room, adjoining the courtyard out back and near a small door labeled "EMPLOYEES ONLY." She knocked, and a middle-aged man answered.

"Hey, there's a cop out here wanting to talk to you," she said quietly.

He glanced past her to Asher. "Who?"

"A cop," she reiterated.

The man opened the door with a deft quickness and stepped into the museum, his demeanor now formal. "Hi, can I help you?" His voice lagged with concern.

They shook hands. "I'm Detective Huxley with the New Orleans Homicide Unit. You have a minute?"

"Yeah, sure. I'm Micah. What can I do for you?"

Asher removed a folded printout of the three balcony victims from the inside of his jacket, their pictures side by side along with their names and ages. "You recognize any of these men?"

At first, Micah hesitated, seemingly nervous to say that he did recognize them, skeptical to get involved in whatever this was—but that was most people's response when they didn't know the victims personally. They were nervous of being suspected themselves.

Who wouldn't be?

"Yeah," the man said. He adjusted his all-black trucker hat and ran his hand over his graying goatee. "They own or work for some of the tours that come through here. I heard about what happened to Cam and Charles." His voice lingered on the third name. "And . . . Delphin?"

"You knew him?"

"I knew *of* him, yeah. All three of them? They're all—"

"What tour did Delphin own?"

"Um . . . he wasn't an owner. He was a tour guide for A Criminal's Pub Crawl. Why?"

"Not sure," Asher said. "You know of any reason why the three of them in particular would've been targeted by someone? Something other than the tour business that may have linked them in some way? Someone who may have—"

"No," Micah said. "Not at all. Nothing like that."

"Are there any employees who may have known them? Or someone who might have some information that they're willing to provide us? If so, I'd like to speak with them, if that's okay with you," Asher said. "If not, I can always reach out when they're not on the clock."

"No, I don't mind at all. Let me introduce you to Brad—he's been here the longest. Kid's here seven days a week. Even when we're closed, he's here working. If there's anything you should know, he's the one you need to talk to. Just one sec."

Micah looked for him in the courtyard, then in the front of the museum. "Hey, Brad. Come here." He waved over a young guy who was organizing one of the display cases up front.

The manager turned back to Asher, almost as an aside. "Man's *obsessed* with this stuff." He gestured to the room.

The young guy met them at the end of the counter, at a glass display case that ran from the front of the museum to a pharmacy stand at the back of the room. He seemed to be about a hundred pounds soaking wet. Pockmarks filled his face, beneath a see-through layer of straw-colored peach fuzz.

He twirled a vintage thermometer in his hand, the glass thick and cloudy after having passed through an endless number of unwashed hands.

With Micah looking on, they discussed pretty much what Asher and the manager had already covered—the decedents, the tours, what did and didn't connect them. Although the employee claimed to have seen the decedents in passing, either talking to Micah or coming through with their tours, he insisted that he didn't know them personally. And there was nothing that alerted Asher that he had known the victims outside of work.

Asher provided them with his card and told them to reach out if anything came up, or if they happened to recall anything useful. Something just didn't sit right with him, though.

It was no coincidence; all three of the victims were associated with tours that came through here, and that meant something. Now, he just needed to figure out where that tidbit of information fit into the larger picture. And from the way things were going, this guy Micah, the manager, wasn't going to be of any assistance.

Not voluntarily.

Asher walked to the door, feeling like he'd just been sucker punched back-to-back. Like he was the butt of some joke he wasn't privy to. He knew, deep down, that he was in the right place. And the fact that he couldn't put it together as of yet made him feel as though he were watching it all play out around him, blurred—like he was an oblivious victim-to-come in some low-budget horror flick, and the audience knew something he didn't.

As he reached the door, he noticed a glass display case at the front entrance—holding an antique, ochre prescription bottle of tiny nearly round seeds next to a laminated page. The display conveyed the use of various herbs used to fight inflammation throughout the nineteenth century.

He bent forward, curious as to what exactly was inside of the bottle. The small label on the container came into focus. "HEMP SEEDS," the label read. Next to it sat a large spool of dated, fraying rope—dark brown and cut at one end, unraveling.

Hemp rope.

Chapter 86

Piece by splintered piece, it was coming together. All three of the balcony victims were involved in the tour business in some way, shape, or form; that was number one. Two, seeing an old spool of hemp rope, the same type of rope used to strangle the balcony victims, the rope that would never be traced to a modern-day manufacturer—because there was none—told Asher he was in the right place.

Still, something didn't fit. If Agnes's hunch was right, what was missing? What was the link between these cases? The tours and rope only connected the balcony victims. What about the stabbings?

Outside, he turned his back to the sun and called Agnes.

"Hey," Asher said. "You busy?"

"I think I can spare a minute or two. What's up?"

"I'm over here on Chartres at the Pharmacy Museum. I've got a question for you."

Agnes was not only obsessively detail-oriented in her work, she was also fascinated with history. In particular, medical history. And that played right into her hand as a medical examiner.

"So, I'm thinking about what you said," Asher continued.

"That our stabbing victims might have been strangled first."

"Okay . . ."

"Is there anything else, anything at all, that points to the stabbing decedents being strangled first? Or is it just the bruising and edema?"

"Not that I can tell. Why?"

"You sure?"

"I mean, sometimes, we see that the hyoid bone in the neck is fractured, but that's only in about 50 percent of strangulations. So, it's not too surprising that I don't see it with our current cases. Why?"

Damn.

"What are you getting at, hun?" Agnes continued.

"You said that, based on the condition of the bodies, and the fact that the balcony victims showed no other signs of bruising or defensive wounds, that they might've been sedated somehow, yeah? That there was likely little to no struggle?"

"That's what it looks like."

Asher agreed, based on the crime scenes themselves. So, what was it? What was he overlooking?

"You're the history buff when it comes to medicine," Asher said. "You tell me—what was used back in the day, a century ago, that could be used as a sedative? What's a good, hard-to-trace toxin that could be used to render someone manageable?"

Agnes laughed into his ear. "Really, love? You got a pen and paper? We might be here a while. Or maybe you can narrow it down for your girl?"

He thought back to the museum and what he'd seen there. "Anything common but also hard to trace." The museum was filled with an endless array of old medicines, the majority of which would probably make anyone sick, nowadays. But what about the kid, Brad? The manager himself had said that he was always there. *Obsessed.* "What about thermometers? What was used in thermometers back in the day?"

Surely, that was an easy one for someone like Agnes. "Mercury, mostly. But thallium was used, too. Sometimes, they were mixed, depending on the thermometer and what it was used for. Why?"

"I think the balcony victims can be traced back to the Pharmacy Museum," Asher said. "I need a favor. Can you test for mercury and thallium in our victims?"

"Which ones?"

"All of them—the ripper and balcony victims. If they *are* connected somehow, through strangulation, or being so close together in their location and when they occurred, maybe that's it. Maybe they're being drugged in the same way, strangled, and then the rest is just smoke. Or a difference between the two offenders. I'm not sure."

"Yeah, I can test for it," she said. "The quickest test for both of those would be a urine spot test. The only problem with those assays is the high incidence of false positives."

"Will you do it, though? The initial tox screens were all clean, so maybe we should starting looking at what *isn't* in your typical toxicology report."

"I mean, sure—if you think it's worth the time. I should have some samples left over that I can use. It'll take me about twenty-four hours to get you the results, though."

"I don't care—I just need this done as soon as possible. Like . . . now. If we're right about this, then our next stabbing should be on our front doorstep in no time."

"I'm on it," she said. "I'll have the results tomorrow."

Chapter 87

"So, who's it gonna be?" Pierre said. "I'm not crazy about the fact that you're working alone."

"Yeah, well, I need some more time," Asher said. "I have to review the applicants I've already interviewed and then—"

"What's there to review? You need that much time to figure it out?"

"To figure out who I'm gonna trust having my back on the street? Yeah. I do."

Asher was stalling; he didn't want any of them. Only Remi, the last woman he'd interviewed, might fit the bill—but again, her background was in criminal psychology.

His plan was to buy some time so that he could find an appropriate colleague on his own. Someone who was in line with his particular style of investigating, who could handle his "informal" approach to the work—as Judy in the Press Office had once said, according to Xavier.

"I'd like to find someone myself, who's gonna be a good fit for me."

"What, the applicants I gave you aren't good enough?"

"No. No, that's not it. I just . . . I didn't feel like they were a good fit. If I'm gonna be working with someone day in and day out, trusting them with both my well-being and my coffee order, I'd at least like it to be someone I can tolerate. You know, someone who can handle—"

"Your insanity?"

"Well, I wasn't gonna put it quite like that."

Before Sofia's passing, Asher would've never pushed back to this extent. The chief would've shot it down in a split second, demanding he choose an applicant who was in the pool that he'd already provided. Pierre was the boss, after all. But now, after everything Asher had been through, especially with the chief firing and then rehiring him, Asher figured that he had more pull, a bit more say in getting things done the way he wanted.

Asher wasn't blind to what had changed in their relationship over the last few weeks. If Pierre didn't trust him, or at the very least didn't value his opinion, then he never would've hired him back.

"Like I said before," the chief said, "it's department policy. You have to have a partner—and you need one sooner rather than later."

"I know. And I'll find one. It just needs to be the right person. I never had a say in the matter when it came to Cassandra."

"I know you didn't. You were in a new position, and I did what I felt was best—and that's on me."

"Well . . . this time, it doesn't have to be. Not entirely. Let me find someone, and you can have the final say as always. I don't think that's an unreasonable request."

The chief swiveled in his chair, his head tilted back, looking up to the water-stained tiles of the drop ceiling. "Fine," he said. "I'll tell you what—you can keep looking as long as you reconsider the applicants you've already interviewed and you find someone on a reasonable timeline. The second this gets dragged out any longer than I think is necessary, much longer than it *already has*, I'm assigning you someone myself."

"Of course," Asher said. "I get it."

"Now get busy so I can stop worrying every time I see you without—"

"*Aw*, really, Chief?" Asher started to sit down. "Are you saying that you worry about me when I'm—"

"Get the hell out of here." Pierre threw his pencil at him and did something that Asher had rarely seen the man do, over the years he'd served under him.

He grinned.

Chapter 88

Asher shut the door to the Vette, and a cloud of blackbirds scattered from an oak tree at the center of the cemetery, vanishing into a morning fog that bleared the canopy of hardwoods like an unfinished painting. From the same oak tree as before, as if her funeral had been only yesterday.

He headed for the bald cypress at the far corner of the yard, smelling the delicate grasslike scent of the sunflowers in his hand along the way. Sofia's resting place was alone among the others; that was just the way she'd wanted it. By herself, under the shade of an elderly tree.

But as he drew nearer, that catch in the back of his throat returned. The lump. Choking. Robbing his ability to draw a decent breath.

He stopped.

This was the first time he'd visited her since that day, when she was lowered into that hole, never to be seen or heard from again. As if the rug of purpose had been pulled right out from beneath his feet. By that woman.

By Cassandra.

He gripped the bouquet tighter, feeling the stems crunch beneath his fingers—before remembering the real reason why he was here. It was for Sofia, who deserved all of his attention. Not her. Not the mistake who'd put his wife here, alone, beneath a bed of soil, for him to visit only on occasion, from a distance of six feet.

He pushed forward, loosening his grip on the stems. They were all he could offer her, now. He shoved the anger back down.

Sofia deserved his attention, not her.

As he reached the grave, he placed the flowers, the blooms of many suns, into the metal vase to the side of her black headstone. Then he sat on a bench to the side of her—the one he'd had made for her and only her.

"Hey, babe." His voice broke a little, but she was the only one around to hear it. "Sorry it took me so long to stop by. It's been crazy." He forced a smile, although deep down, a million emotions other than joy filled him to the brim.

Not anxiety, though—the grief replaced that feeling.

He had so much to say, so there was no point in dragging it out. He needed to get it all out before the feelings grew into something he'd be unable to control, and he'd have no choice but to leave her here. Alone.

"I'm sorry." He spoke over the lump. He swallowed it repeatedly but it returned, there in his shaking and brittle voice. "I should've done more. I should've been more—more of a husband . . . more of a friend . . . more of . . . I don't know. Someone who was around?"

He wanted to blame it all on them, on his ex-partner and her husband. The people who were literally and plainly responsible for Sofia's death. But he knew the truth: he had a hand in it. A loose and distant role that centered around his inability to leave his job at the front door.

That was the very thing that'd driven her away in the end.

Cassandra began to weasel her way back into the memories. Asher gripped the edge of the bench—but the harder he tried to forget her and what she'd done, the more detail of that very day came to mind. That hallway. The four of them there. The cold of the barrel pressed beneath his chin.

"Anyway," he continued, "I just wanted to stop by and say that I'm sorry." He sat in silence for a moment, thinking of how to say it in a way that actually meant something. "I know it doesn't change anything, it doesn't . . . mean what it would've meant then . . . but, I'm sorry. I wasn't around. I wasn't there for you, and I should've been. I was such a lousy husband."

He left his seat and sat on the wet grass, to the side of her headstone. He leaned against it and pictured the black box in an effort to rid his mind of the rest.

No one else belonged here.

He closed his eyes and emptied the box of everything but the touch of the stone beside him.

"I'm sorry," he said. "I'm sorry. What you did . . . what I *caused* you to do . . . it's not your fault. None of it's your fault. That's on me." He felt the wet of the grass seep through his clothing and touch his legs. The wet of the tears down his cheeks. "But you should know . . . I hold none of it against you, you hear? That's on me. It's *all* on me."

He rocked there, holding the black box in his mind, fighting for his time alone with his wife.

"But you should know that I'm trying. I'm working on me, now. With Justin. With Pierre. Xavier. I'm doing everything that I can to make it right and be a better me." He opened his eyes. "But it'd be a lot better if I had you here. Who else is gonna give me a hard time?" Now, he smiled because he meant it. Because he felt it. "Who else is gonna be there, Sofia?"

She didn't respond. He sat there. Waiting. Filled with regret and loathing for the life that he'd now found himself living—thanks to his inability to set aside the job.

Sure, Sofia should never have done what she did. She should never have entertained the idea of another man, someone else to fill the void that he'd created. But at the same time, Asher knew that the only way forward was to take accountability for his role in all of it. In the downfall of their marriage, and in the needless death of his wife.

He got to his feet. "I need these cases to work out, Sofia. They have to . . . But more than anything"—he blotted the corner of his eye with a tacky and humid leather sleeve—"I need you here with me."

Asher stood there with only the birds, looking over his wife's grave. The dirt still appeared fresh. No grass, nothing. Only a sad mound covered her. His wife, the woman he'd once held, the woman he'd once kissed, once showered with, once held with her hair against his nose and made love to at three in the morning in a sea of pillows—was in a pine box, covered in dirt.

Interred.

How was *anything* worth doing, now?

Then he walked away from her—for what he knew would be another of far too many goodbyes.

Chapter 89

Asher stood in front of the bank of elevators, waiting for a lift to his office. His silver badge reflected in the steel sheen of the elevator door, his image dead-center of the entrance.

He needed this one: if the tox screens from Agnes pointed to some irregularity, either mercury or thallium that was sitting around at the Pharmacy Museum in old vials or thermometers, he'd have what he needed for a closer look. The more he thought about it, the more it ate away at him—that spool of hemp rope in plain sight.

A group of uniformed officers and a few others waited behind him in the lobby. The up arrow on the wall glowed a burning orange, while the digital number above the doors counted down with a loud tick. Three . . . two . . . then a chime.

He was lost in his own reflection as the doors opened—his image splitting in two. Like those patients in his dream, in front of the therapist with her badge. One patient appearing as two.

His reflection vanished entirely, and the doors remained wide.

The others pushed past him in their nine-to-five hurry. "Excuse me," said a few of them, seemingly irritated in their cutting tones of voice. They crammed themselves into the steel space like sardines on a sweaty day, staring at him as he stood there, lost in some trance.

One of the men held out his cane, keeping the gate ajar a moment longer. "You coming?" he said. But Asher was lost in what it all meant—his dreams flooded back to him for some reason, feeling all too real. "Sir?" the man repeated. "Are you getting on?"

"What?" Asher said, absorbed in his own thoughts.

The man's cane still held back the sliding doors. "You getting on?"

"Oh," Asher said. "No." He stepped back from the elevator, and the man lowered his cane.

Is that what the dreams are—a memory of her from back then? A conversation about a patient?

When Cassandra had first been hired as Asher's partner, she'd insisted on keeping the identities and stories of her former patients quiet. Even though she was no longer running her own private practice as a psychologist, she respected the doctor-patient confidentiality of her work.

In time, however, there was a single patient Cassandra had mentioned to Asher in passing. Not once, but twice. A case that supposedly "wouldn't let go," even after she'd left her practice to pursue a career in homicide. In her own words, it haunted her, no matter how hard she tried to rid herself of the experience, of her self-professed failure. In the long run, it drowned her in guilt.

The doors shut, and the two of him grew together as one in the reflection of the polished metal. A line, where the door parted, cut him neatly from head to toe. Associating his halves once more.

Or so it appeared.

The patient Cassandra had mentioned to him was one of

the only patients she was unable to treat successfully—her biggest challenge as a private psychologist. Asher ravaged his memory in search of what exactly she'd said about that person in particular.

What was their name?

He simply couldn't recall who the patient was, nor the specifics of the case. But he did remember how disturbed she'd been. There was something relevant in those dreams—in the identical patients across from her.

Dissociating? Splitting? What was the word she'd used so long ago?

No one in the dreams had muttered a word.

Asher sifted through his memory of their fleeting conversations from years prior, but all that came to mind was Cassandra's frustration. Something about her inexperience surrounding a condition?

But what did that have to do with anything?

Then his phone rang with the *Halloween* theme song, as his reflection was cut in two once again.

Chapter 90

You—

Churchgoers trickled down Pere Antoine Alley in the midmorning. You stood against closed doors in the crook of a shallow brick archway, to the side of a black lamp post holding a red-and-white sign that read, "CHURCH QUIET ZONE."

Maybe that was why the vagrant man had chosen to sleep in this alley in particular—few people, quiet people.

Maybe they were *giving* folk, perchance?

Hardly. You knew that from experience, thanks to that ridiculous thing they called "family" that had kept you out here. Thanks to a parent who had never been, not in any true sense of the word.

Your suit and tie were strangling you in the Southern humidity. You slid your sports coat from your arms and placed it in the crook of your elbow, then loosened the skinny charcoal tie—no better way to spend a perfectly good one hundred dollars than on the perfect tie.

Just outside the gate to St. Anthony's Garden, the poor man picked up his cardboard bed and dusted from it the discomfort of another night in the Quarter. As he did, a number of people walked by him: individuals too lost in their cellphones or earbuds to notice the hurting man or the other people walking in front of them;

couples sharing a meal or holding hands as if the world around them were a never-ending void; walking tours snapping pictures of the church and architecture around him, as if the needy were only something to remain out of frame in their next bedside photo. Not one person so much as acknowledged him, helped him, said, "Hey, how's it going?"

And that gutted you.

Why? Because you knew good and well how it felt to be him, albeit when you were far younger. Under the thumb of a fleeting "father."

Come on, Ryker. Do better. Be the man you know yourself to be, deep down. Don't be like one of them.

Do better, my friend. You can do better.

The man knelt down and used a tiny handheld broom to dust the cement where his bed typically lay. He appeared far more attentive to his space than other wanderers in the area, like he'd used this spot on a regular basis. Then he shook out a ragged, old blanket that had faded to a burnt orange beneath the searing sun.

You couldn't bear to watch it any longer—the painful routine of this desolate man, all but wasting away in such an alive city. The Crescent City. The famous city of New Orleans that was supposed to be the hub of Southern hospitality.

You let out a heavy breath and let your shoulders fall a little—and took the first step toward him.

The man needed you, the way you had needed your family what felt like only yesterday. The way you had needed your father after Mom died. No one had helped you then, but you could help him now. You had a skill that few others had: the ability to see the future that men like him would have to endure. That was, if you stood by and did nothing.

But that wasn't you—he needed you.

You held out your hand as you reached him. "Ryker," you said with a smile. "How's it going?"

He hesitated, holding out his hand as his expression remained empty. The same expression, you imagined, he'd worn day in and day out. Rain or shine.

Who could've blamed him?

He shook your hand with a brittle grip. "Hey." Then he turned back to cleaning his spot on the street, glancing at your new suit from the corner of his eye.

"When is the last time you ate something?" you said. "A hot meal."

The old man laughed and smiled a hurtful smile. "A hot meal? That's funny, son." He mumbled to himself. "A hot meal. Yeah. Right."

"Well," you said, "is there anything I can do for you? Can I get you anything? I'd like to help. Let me help you."

He hung his blanket over the railing of the garden, then turned toward you—and you saw that emptiness deepen in the man's posture, along with a tense brow. He said nothing.

"Here," you said, removing your wallet from your slacks. "Let me help." You pulled a ten-dollar bill from inside and held it out for the taking.

The man reached out and latched on to the money, his hand freezing there, seemingly hesitant to pull it back toward him. You let go.

He held the money up to the sky, looking it over as if you were playing some sick joke on him. He grabbed the ends and popped it in his hands like he was checking that it was real—like it'd vanish at any moment.

You gestured to the ground. "Is this your usual spot?" Then you returned the bulging wallet to its rightful place. "Is this where I can find you?"

"Find me?"

Perhaps that was a poor choice of words. "Of course, my friend. Maybe this doesn't have to be the last time we meet."

But he never looked away from the bill, only nodded and went back to cleaning his bed. Where you'd return to find him again.

To help him.

Chapter 91

Asher answered the phone, still staring at his reflection in the elevator door.

"Talk to me."

"You sitting down?" Agnes said. "If not, you might wanna grab a hold of something."

That was all she needed to say—he didn't need to hear the results. He had that gut feeling. That thing that flushed through him and made his shoulders drop, his breathing slow, expression lax if only for the briefest of moments.

He let himself fall back against the wall. "Don't tease me, now."

Unless it was bad news; then she could hang up and forget she'd ever called.

"They're positive, Asher."

"Seriously? Positive for what?"

"Well, it's a mix of mercury *and* thallium—but I did a follow-up after the urine spot tests. The levels of mercury aren't really a cause for concern. I mean, any mercury is bad when you're talking about ingesting it, but from what I can see, these levels aren't enough to have any effect on someone in the short-term. They're hovering around the high end of normal or below."

Normal? What the fuck is normal when it comes to ingesting mercury?

"You could make the argument that it's just your everyday background exposure," she said.

"And the thallium?"

"That's the interesting part—the thallium levels are off the charts. They had enough thallium in them to cause some serious problems in a matter of hours."

"What kind of problems?"

"In the short term? Exactly what you'd expect from most toxins. Nausea, vomiting, stomach pain, lightheadedness. Basic issues that'd only get worse at such a high dose."

"So . . . do you think someone could be using something from the Pharmacy Museum?"

For a moment, her voice fell silent. Admittedly, it was a long-shot type of question, but nonetheless an intriguing one.

"There's no way I can know that for sure," Agnes said, "but it's possible. Like I said before, those antique thermometers you were asking about used mercury or a combination of mercury and thallium in some instances. But hell, it could be from something else entirely, if you're talking about the museum— that place is chock-full of all kinds of harmful shit. What's got you hung up on thermometers? That's a strange thing to be looking at to begin with, ain't it?"

"Yeah, it is," he said. "But the Pharmacy Museum has an entire spool of hemp rope, Agnes. It's sitting right there in a fucking display case at the front door. Not to mention, our balcony victims can all be traced back there, either as owners of tour companies or working as tour guides. I don't know . . . when I went there in person, I noticed they had a decent collection of old thermometers. And if they're actual artifacts, then whatever's in them can't be good. Like you said—the place is crawling with a million things that'd probably kill you. Thallium included."

It made sense, but Asher was doing his best not to jump the gun. The test results pushed him that much further in the direction of the museum. He just wasn't keen on the details, as of yet.

"Well," she said, "regardless of where it's coming from, I've got something else that's gonna make you twitch."

Forget sitting down—he started pacing the lobby of the precinct.

"And?" he said.

"All of the victims had relatively the same amount of mercury and thallium in their system—except for one. And I'm sure you can guess who I'm talking about."

"Our last balcony victim?"

"You got it, hun."

Of course—the decedent who hadn't been posed. But why? Why was that one different from the others?

"Look," she said, "like I said before, I don't usually trust the results of these urine spot tests because they give so many false positives, but in this case? We've got four out of five hits, and the one sample that came up negative is already an outlier for other reasons. I have no idea where the thallium came from, but it's at least a cause for inquiry. And this links both sets of murders."

She was right—it didn't matter where exactly the thallium had come from. Not yet. That'd be important later on, once Asher had someone in custody. What mattered now was that, most likely, it had come from the Pharmacy Museum. Surely, of all the crap that place had on display, thallium was somewhere in the building.

If it wasn't, then Asher had stumbled across one hell of a coincidence. And, well, coincidences weren't a thing. Not for him.

"I agree," he said. "It's gotta be there somewhere." He turned and walked out of the precinct. "And I'll have the answer soon enough."

Chapter 92

The Pharmacy Museum was tranquil, all but desolate, and the hair on Asher's arms stood on end as a nervous stitch snaked its way down the center of his back.

He walked through the entrance, and Micah greeted him from behind the counter. Messing with that vintage cash register. "Oh, hey." He pointed at Asher. "It's, uh ... Mr. ... Detective—"

"Huxley," Asher said.

"Ah, that's right." He shut the register and gave Asher his undivided attention. "What can I do for you, Detective?" He wore that same trucker hat from before.

"I'm looking for that employee I spoke to before. I think his name was—"

"Brad?"

"Yeah," Asher said. "Is he around by any chance?"

Micah suddenly looked like a puppy that'd just been clipped by a speeding car, caught in the headlights of an approaching big rig on a flashing, storming night. Shook with too great of uncertainty to make heads or tails of what was happening.

"Um, no," he said. "He's off today. Why? Is something wrong? Did he do something?"

He's off? The one who's "obsessed" with this stuff and "here seven days a week"? How convenient.

"It's nothing in particular," Asher said. "I just need to speak with him again . . . see if he has some additional information I'm looking for."

In fact, it was particular—but Asher could do without Brad for the time being. Whatever the staff had access to, so did Micah.

And if he played his cards right, Asher would have access, too.

"Well, I can tell him you stopped by," Micah said. "Is there something else I can help you with, while you're here?"

"Actually, there is," Asher said. He treaded carefully—the employee was only a hunch. Everyone was suspect until he had reason to home in on one person.

The manager included.

"You mind showing me around a bit?" Asher said. "I've seen what everyone else sees coming through here on the tours and walking through the exhibits. Can you show me what everyone else doesn't see?"

"And that would be?"

"The employee-only stuff? Stock rooms? Unfinished exhibits?" Asher walked to the end of the counter, away from the girl at the register, who was now taking payment from an incoming couple. He tilted his head for Micah to join him. "I need to see the exhibits or artifacts that contain any toxins y'all have lying around. Stuff that's off the exhibit floor, in particular."

The man's puppy dog brow shifted to more of a cornered rottweiler sort of glare. Defensive.

"*If* you don't mind," Asher said. "Otherwise . . ." The

unspoken prospect of a warrant lingered between them.

Micah seemed cooperative enough, though. "Yeah, of course." He pointed to a stairwell between the indoor exhibits and the courtyard out back. "Right this way."

He brought Asher to the third floor, which was roped off at the top of a creaking, winding staircase. The old, worn-out treads spoke beneath the detective's feet as they ascended, circling past the second floor. At the top, the space opened to a large and seedy stockroom, littered with endless piles of seemingly random artifacts—some of it ordinary, some of it a bit macabre. Torturous-looking stuff that was likely typical of 1800s medicine.

"This is pretty much it," Micah said. "Feel free to take a look around, let me know if you have any questions. Nothing's really under lock and key; we're constantly getting stuff in all the time, then loaning things out to other museums or colleges. It's very much a living collection, so to speak."

"What about thallium?" Asher said. He was more specific, now that he had the manager alone. "Any idea where that'd be if you have it? Or any other samples that could be considered toxic?"

Micah lifted his chin to a glass case in the far corner of the room, closed but unlocked by the look of it. Inside were a number of aged glass medicine bottles and syringes, each one tagged with relevant information: date of acquisition, owner/lender, origin, etc.

"The only thallium that we have is a handful of salts and liquids"—he opened the case for Asher to look inside—"which are all labeled and permanently sealed." He pointed to another box across the way, sooty and open beneath a cracked window. "We've got thermometers, too, but I'm not sure which ones contain what. Most of those contain mercury, I would think."

"You keep records of all this stuff?" Asher asked.

"Records? Like, what? A logbook or something?"

"Yeah, like a logbook . . . or something."

Micah laughed off the detective's mockery. "Well, kinda. But only for the stuff that's restricted or banned by either OSHA or the EPA. We submit quarterly reports on our inventory for all that. Everything else just comes and goes, you know? Like I said—it's very much a living collection."

"Right," Asher said. It was a start. If the thallium was coming from here, it should've been reflected in the museum's records—*if* they were accurate and up to date.

Not only were a number of the glass bottles here not full, several of them were near empty.

"If you don't mind, I'm gonna need copies of your logbooks," Asher said.

"Yeah, no problem."

Asher looked around a bit more, but nothing else caught his attention. They walked downstairs to the first floor and to the front counter there.

"Do me a favor?" Asher said.

"Yeah, sure."

"Keep me posted on your inventory and let me know if anything comes up missing—in particular, those samples upstairs."

They shook hands. "Of course," said Micah.

Asher squeezed for good measure. "I'll need to reconcile what's coming and going for those, once I get that logbook from you." He held his grip until the owner agreed once again.

Micah gave him a shallow grin. Asher placed his card on the counter, then turned to the front door. "Have a good one," he said over his shoulder.

But as he did, it nearly knocked the breath out of him—like jumping from the swing and landing on his back as a kid: that spool of hemp rope. It was missing from the display case.

Oh, yeah. Isn't that a peach.

Asher turned back to the owner, pointing over his shoulder. "Say, Micah? That spool of rope over there in the window—who has access to that?"

"What, the hemp display? Everyone. Employees are adjusting exhibits all the time. Why?"

"It's gone."

Micah fiddled with a receipt book on the counter. "Yeah. So?"

Asher did a double take. The hemp rope, gone. The employee, Brad, conveniently "off."

Micah glanced up from his work, seemingly allergic to Asher's intentional, heavy glare.

"Actually"—Asher walked past the counter, dragging his feet to address the owner one last time—"I'm gonna hang out for a bit, if you don't mind." He gestured out back to the courtyard.

Chapter 93

Hours had passed, and nothing had happened.

Asher sat there in the courtyard of the Pharmacy Museum, at a table next to the fountain out back. He had a clear view straight through the building and to the display case at the front door—where the spool of hemp rope had yet to be returned.

Or maybe it was gone for good? If that were the case, it was a perfectly good opportunity that had slipped through his fingers.

He should've known better than to let it go missing, wherever it was.

If the rope was being used in the balcony murders, there was still no guarantee that he could prove it—*if* it was returned. Would the spool be the exact rope that had been used to strangle each of the victims? Or would it merely be the supply, so to speak? Where the ligatures had come from?

It'd be the difference between a murder weapon versus a strong case of circumstantial evidence.

You're getting ahead of yourself, Asher. Be patient, now.

That ringtone began playing, muffled, from the inside of his jacket.

He answered. "Hello?" He kept a close eye on the display

case across the way, inside of the building.

"Hey, hun," Agnes said. "Where you at?"

"At the Pharmacy Museum."

"Oh, really? What are you doing there? You got a minute?"

As far as these cases were concerned, he had all the time in the world—devoted 100 percent, day and night. As far as the victims? His time was wearing thin.

The end of someone's life was now past due.

"Yeah, of course. What's up?" he said.

"I'm just calling to let you know that the chief is wanting to wrap things up with Cassandra's remains. He wants the death certificate signed sooner rather than later. Like, now, to be more precise."

"What? Why?"

"He called me earlier and said your time is up. No one has claimed the body, so he wants the whole thing finalized and her remains cremated—or so he's asking, I should say."

Again? Pierre had reached out to Agnes instead of his lead detective? Again?

"Well, that's nice. Did y'all talk about me the *whole* time? Maybe one of these days I can listen in on one of these conversations y'all like having about me while I'm not around."

"Hey, I'm not the one who called, looking to stir up shit with you or anyone else, hun. I'm just relaying the message."

"Yeah, I know. Sorry. I knew this would happen sooner or later."

"Well, don't get too worked up over it. Look on the bright side—it's behind you, and now you can focus on your current cases. Hopefully, Internal Affairs can do their thing and either put together a decent case against her and her husband, or hand it back to you guys to do the investigation yourselves. She might be dead, but there's still a case to be had."

Agnes was right. It was time to move on, but that didn't make the news any easier.

"Alright," Asher said. "Thanks for letting me know. I'll talk to Pierre soon enough."

"Sure thing, love. Keep me posted on the others."

"Will do." He hung up.

The museum was growing busy, now. His once-clear view of the display case was dwindling with the passing of tours and customers walking between the exhibits. Maybe it was time to call it a day.

Asher adjusted himself in the uncomfortable metal chair, as a glimmer of daylight danced on the surface of the water in the fountain next to him. He hadn't noticed it when he sat down. Surely, that was it—what Mami was talking about with the second ripper victim, the homeless man.

"A magical lot with free money," he whispered to himself.

Son of a bitch. He was taking money from the fountain. This has to be what she was talking about. If this is the place where the homeless guy was grabbing spare change, where the second ripper victim was—

Asher's phone rang, and he sprang from the chair. "Goddamn it," he said aloud. The people lounging around the yard glanced his way.

He answered testily. "Yeah?"

"Hey," Xavier said. "I catch you at a bad time?"

Of course he had.

"No, what's up?"

"I've got those lab results on the Delphin Stanley case. The DNA from the rocks glass matches our victim. So, not much help there."

"Great. What else? Tell me you've got something else."

"Yeah, we do. We've got fibers from the sofa—and they match perfectly with the ones from our first balcony victim, Cam Spencer. Fiber evidence is always a bit hit and miss, especially with a jury, but they're as much of a match as you can hope for."

"Perfect. You reach out to Agnes yet?" Asher said. "Y'all should probably get together and make sure y'all are on the same page. The more, the merrier."

"For sure," Xavier said. "I'll run the samples over there for her to confirm."

He removed his aviators. Squinting. Did another take, then a third. No way.

"Hey, I'll talk to you later." He hung up before Xavier had a chance to speak.

The rope—it was back in the display case. Surrounded by people left and right, strolling past the exhibit in every which direction. But what made Asher dart from the courtyard and through the museum was the sports coat and backpack, heading out the front door. Someone looking over their shoulder.

Head down. Hat low.

Chapter 94

You—

Now that you were off the clock, it was time for a bite to eat. You turned the corner and headed for the po-boy shop on St. Louis Street. You had promised that poor man you'd return to help him, and you had every intention of keeping your word.

People living up to their word was a rare thing these days. You had no plan on falling into that same trap: able to help but turning a blind eye when someone needed it most. To this day, you carried the scars of what that felt like as a child—empty promises that defined the relationship with your own family. In the end, you were lucky enough to escape these unforgiving streets.

But not him; he needed you.

You walked into the small but busy shop and ordered at the cash-only counter.

"Hey, Ryker," the lady said from behind the register. "What can I get you?"

The place was a gem: a hole-in-the-wall that was a clandestine culinary masterpiece, sporting red-and-white checkered tablecloths, Styrofoam cups, and plasticware. Just as it should've been. It was homestyle Southern cooking that was to die for. Quick and wholesome comfort food at its best.

"Let's do some seafood gumbo and boudin balls," you said.

Those were for you. "And then a shrimp po-boy and a large tea." That was for him. "Dressed." No way he'd turn down the shrimp. Not to mention, this was the best sweet tea within a square mile of here. Period.

You paid, then waited for the food at a nearby table—thinking of how much he must be hurting, out here on the city streets. All alone. Hungry.

What if he, just like you, had family nearby? People who were around but did little to ease the pain. A mother or father who'd done nothing to hold up their end of the parent-son relationship.

In no time at all, the lady handed you two bags of food. You filled a cup with sweet tea and headed for the exit.

"Until next time," she said.

You turned your back and pushed through the door. "Thank you, my friend." Then you stepped outside and headed for the cathedral, eager to reach him before long.

You would've hated for his last meal to be a cold one.

Chapter 95

The man in the hat took a left at the corner and headed down St. Louis Street.

The sun was drowning below the rooftops—and the shadow of a neighboring balcony cast Asher in a dim light as he stopped at the corner and watched him. The person entered a restaurant, but Asher wasn't going in after him. He'd keep his distance.

The last thing he wanted was to let this one slip through his fingers; he needed this. For the department. For Pierre. For Xavier.

He needed this one for himself—to prove that he could, in fact, move on from Cassandra's hell. From nearly losing his career for good.

From losing Sofia.

Asher waited there at the corner as to not draw attention to himself. He had all the time in the world, but the dark was growing closer now.

About ten minutes had passed before the man in the hat stepped out from the restaurant. He turned back from the way he'd came, in the direction of the Pharmacy Museum. His backpack was slung over his shoulder—and he was headed straight for Asher.

As the man rounded the corner, Asher turned to the building and put his back between them. The man brushed against him. Asher's pistol was right there beneath his leather jacket.

"My bad," the man mumbled in the growing night, and kept walking.

He continued farther down the road until he reached Jackson Square, with Asher not far behind him. Then he turned down Pirates Alley alongside the cathedral and stopped on a bench, just outside Faulkner House Books.

It was darker, now. Even though the man's face was right there, the night refused to give him up. As if the dying sun dimmed—just for him.

Asher waited less than a block away, near the front of the cathedral. The man pulled something from his bag. Perhaps food from where he'd just left? He sat there, fidgeting with it. Unwrapping it.

But not eating.

—

The man in the hat had returned the food to his backpack and was now walking around the garden toward Pere Antoine Alley. Asher kept his distance. Who the hell was he?

The man had come from the Pharmacy Museum, so maybe Asher would have better luck going back there and asking Micah if he knew who he was. Surely, it was an employee if they were handling one of the displays. But then again, what if he left the man here alone and something happened?

What if this was Asher's chance to put an end to whatever this was? Or maybe it was all in his head. Maybe the rope was nothing. Perhaps it was all one big coincidence.

Yeah. Sure, Asher. And maybe Cassandra was really a good woman.

Asher stopped at the corner of Royal and Pere Antoine Alley. There's no way he was letting the guy out of his sight. Not this late in the game.

The man in the hat approached a homeless gentleman nearer to the garden, sitting on a piece of cardboard with his back against the fence, seemingly lost in the ambience of jazz that lingered on the city streets.

On the other hand, Asher could just get it over with and approach the guy. Save himself the worry altogether. Ask what he was doing at the museum and what was going on with the rope.

But the more he thought about it, the risks far outweighed the reward. If it was nothing, and the guy was just some random employee and the rope was a fluke, then he'd just look crazy. And Asher would've only played the fool and lost an evening of running around with nothing to show for it. Fair enough; that was part of the job.

On the off chance that this was the guy, and the rope was *the* rope—he only had one choice if he stopped to question him.

Arrest him.

Otherwise, he would be showing his hand. Then who knew what would happen? The murders might stop, he could disappear, or come after Asher himself.

End up taking more victims out of spite?

There were too many cases in the past where law enforcement felt they were getting close, and the murders just up and stopped: Zodiac, Jack the Ripper, the Axeman of New Orleans. No way Asher was adding his name to the list of cops who couldn't deliver. Not with a case—with two cases—that were this big.

He needed this one.

Just when Asher was leaning toward heading back to the museum, toward questioning Micah so he didn't blow his cover with a possible suspect, the man handed what looked like a drink and food to the homeless man. Then he turned around and walked toward Asher once more before heading back to the bench on the other side of the garden. The detective remained back, in the shadows of Royal.

That was all it took. Asher had made up his mind; he wasn't going anywhere. Not when he'd seen what he just saw.

Now, he needed to make the decision—did he have enough to bring the guy in for questioning?

Or better yet, if the balcony and ripper cases were, in fact, connected . . . was Asher himself the one who was being watched?

Chapter 96

You—

The hunger was driving you up the walls—surely, no worse than what it was doing to that poor man on the other side of the garden, though. Hopefully, he was still there.

He needed you.

You pulled the po-boy from your backpack and unwrapped it after taking a seat on the bench. The shrimp had done their job the first go 'round, and there was no doubt that they'd work now, as well; no one on the street turned down free seafood. Not in this city. Not shrimp of all things.

You prepped the sandwich and rewrapped it just as it was—the piece of white masking tape holding the paper together and all. Then you returned it to the brown paper bag, even folding it crease by crease to its former shape.

You dosed the drink, too. That was where the real effect was able to shine through. Only so much could be done with food before the texture was no longer the same. But something to drink? That was far easier, more potent for sure. All you needed was a leg up on the physical side of things.

You'd done your research, so you knew that it didn't mix well with water. Nonetheless, it was colorless. Tasteless.

A good swirl, and no one was the wiser.

You made your way around the garden to Pere Antoine Alley, where you hoped the homeless man was still resting. You promised him you'd be back, and you intended on keeping that promise.

Look at how you turned out—perfectly fine on the outside, normal by the eye of passersby. Sharp dressed with a jacket and tie that killed. But on the inside? You were fucked up six ways to Sunday. No one should've gone through what you had been forced to endure.

This poor man included.

Sure enough, he was there, sitting on his now-clean cardboard bed and leaning back against the garden fence. Head back, looking up to a darkening sky with deep breaths.

He's lucky to have you, Ryker. He needs you, and now it's time to help him. Help him the way no one helped you when you needed it most. Be a friend to those who have none, my friend. Just be a friend.

"Well, there you are, my friend." Your smile was sure to brighten his day, to make the whole process that much easier.

The man opened his eyes and looked up to you with a half grin. "Oh. You're back?" He spoke with a blend of surprise and perhaps pleasure. Hopefully, he was happy to see you.

You dropped the backpack from your shoulder and removed the bag of food from inside of it. Then you handed it to him, along with the drink. "I told you I'd be back. I only hope I'm not disturbing you."

He reached out and took them from you, although a bit hesitant. Seemingly unsure of why you, of all people, were bringing him a free meal. "Um . . . thanks," he said.

"Of course, my friend. Just promise me one thing."

"Okay . . ."

"You enjoy that tonight." You zipped the bag and slid it over your shoulder. "That's for you and only you, you hear?"

He pulled the sandwich out of the greasy bag and held it to the tip of his nose. Closing his eyes. Ostensibly, there was no need to unwrap it. "Absolutely," he said. He drew a deep breath with closed eyes and flaring nostrils. "Thank you. I have no idea what I did to deserve this, but thank you."

"Don't mention it," you said. "Sometimes, we just need a leg up is all."

He unwrapped it and stole a savoring bite. A few extra shrimp fell from the toasted bread and landed on his lap—and that was the beginning of the end.

You gestured to the drink beside him. "Don't let that tea go to waste, now. It's only gonna sweat more and more out here in this heat, yeah?"

He grabbed the cup in haste, drawing a well-deserved sip.

"Now that's a proper meal," you said. "Enjoy it, my friend." Then you turned away, speaking to yourself and no one else. "You never know when it could be your last."

Fulfilled by your good deed for the day, you made your way back to the bench around the corner.

It never ceased to amaze you, what a little gesture could do for someone's day.

Chapter 97

Asher hung out on Royal Street for the better part of an hour, watching the man in the hat and sports coat eating while sitting on a bench in the dark. His hat dipped below his eyes, slouching, legs crossed. Like some old man reading a '50s newspaper. It seemed as though this guy, whoever he was, had not a care in the world.

Either this was painfully ordinary to a man like him, or the detective had missed the mark. Regardless, he'd had that rope out of the display case; now he was out here, feeding the homeless.

Getting it wrong? Sure. Asher had gone down that road more often than he cared to think about. But this wasn't that. Too much was adding up.

Who was he?

If only he would take off the hat. If only the sun would rise again in spectacular, blinding fashion. Maybe then, and only then, he would have the answer as to who this was, without having to risk it all on approaching the guy. If he could only glimpse his face.

But who was he kidding? Asher was going to have to wait it out. He knew—for better or for worse—that he might be in it for the long haul, wading deep into the night. He only hoped that he wasn't making a fool of himself. That he wasn't blinded by something obvious.

Again.

Cassandra's face crossed his mind. And with just as much ease, it vanished. Leaving Asher grinding his teeth.

The clock was ticking, and Asher was still playing back-and-forth with the idea of heading back to the museum.

It didn't look like the guy was moving anytime soon, so it was time to check on the homeless guy around the corner. Asher hoped he wasn't shooting himself in the foot by stepping away, but by his eye, he had no choice in the matter.

Maybe he should call Xavier. But whoever this man was, he probably would be gone by the time Xavier got here and was brought up to speed. He couldn't risk it.

It was too late.

Asher turned back to the alley and headed for the other side of the garden. As he did, he couldn't help but feel as though he were being watched. He paused there in the dark on Royal Street, between two lamp posts whose light reached only so far into the night. He glanced back.

This was New Orleans, though, buzzing with people every which way he looked—street artists and their customers, a corner brass band and their audience, more homeless, cooks taking a smoke break behind their restaurants, delivery trucks blocking half the road as their drivers carted dollies of refrigerated goods through the back doors of cafés and eateries.

Of course he was being watched—the only question was by whom.

He continued down Pere Antoine Alley and toward the man on his cardboard bed. He was sitting back against the fence, seemingly drained by another day on the city streets, sipping his drink with heavy eyes. Asher kept his distance at the corner, looking between the man in the alley and where he'd just come from on Royal.

He waited there for a moment, then made the decision to turn back. As he did, the poor man set his drink on the ground and lay down—curling into a ball with his knees cradled against his chest.

Asher felt as though he were in a pickle between second and third, between the man in the hat and a possible victim. Darting back and forth between the odds that it was all in his head, or he was about to round the base and bring home this whole case.

The homeless man tossed and turned. At the very least, he was still breathing.

Asher turned back to Royal Street—and nearly straight into the path of the hatted man. He crossed the road and dipped behind the tailgate of a delivery truck. He wasn't going crazy. In fact, he was right where he needed to be.

Maybe?

The man in the hat turned down the alleyway and toward the guy on his cardboard bed. He took his time, wading through the shadows that shifted and blackened just for him.

He moved like the forewarning that he was. Every time Asher felt like he'd catch a glimpse of his face, the edge of darkness held tight to the man and the brim of his hat.

Chapter 98

You—

The better part of an hour had passed by the time you finished dinner. Which meant that the poor man across the way was likely done as well.

If all went as planned, he had enjoyed the food. Who wouldn't have been ecstatic with a shrimp po-boy as their last meal? The boys on death row couldn't have had it that good. Could they have gotten a po-boy in their final hours? Probably. But a *New Orleans shrimp po-boy?*

Doubtful.

You'd traveled. You'd been out to the West Coast. You'd seen what they called "seafood." Even up north around the Great Lakes—order barbeque shrimp and you were given tiny, steamed shrimp with a cup of sauce on the side. Just the thought of such a crime churned your stomach into the tightest of garrotes.

But not here, not now. You had given the man the best there was to offer in a city like this. Anyone in his position would've been grateful.

You tossed the trash in a nearby can and hooked your backpack onto your shoulder, then made your way down Royal Street to the other side of the garden.

You thought about the man and his background in life. Who he could've been. Were his parents still alive? Did he have an ex-wife who was secretly happy that he was out here, making her look good after he'd cheated on her and she kicked him out of their house that they'd built together over the course of decades? Did he have kids?

What if he was out here on the streets while his adult children were somewhere else in the city, going on with their mundane, nine-to-five schedules—just like you and your own deadbeat dad? You had no idea where, but your father was out here somewhere.

It didn't matter, though. You wouldn't piss on him if he was doused in gasoline and lit on fire on the steps of the courthouse. He deserved it; you were only disappointed in yourself that you couldn't manage to do it by your own hand. Hell, maybe you were turning out just as pathetic as he was.

"Thank god for genetics," you mumbled, and rolled your eyes.

You stopped at the corner of Royal and Pere Antoine Alley. Sure enough, the man was still lying there on his cardboard bed, curled up with his knees to his chest. It was working.

You ended up waiting, though; you needed him alone. So, you stood there in the alley, against a building and inside the shadows, until the man stirred and stumbled to his feet.

You moved forward. Quiet. Hidden. You glanced back to the head of the alleyway. No one was there, but Royal was buzzing. You'd have to be quick.

The man braced himself against the garden fence with one hand and threw up, holding his stomach with the other. Rocking as he reached for the gate.

This is it, Ryker—he needs you. He needs you like a son needs his father. Help him, my friend. He needs you to help him.

You lingered there in the dark, against the building. Then, sure enough, he opened the garden gate and stumbled inside of the secluded space. You strode forward and passed his makeshift bed and the drink you'd given him not long ago, and that crumpled and now-empty bag of food.

His grumbling and heaving mixed with the ambience of even louder brass horns and shouting, with the nightlife. The bass of music from nearby bars thumped deep in your chest. It excited you, made you feel that much more alive. You stepped through the gate and into the garden of shadowy statues and unmoving plants.

It was a familiar scene: the last place in the entire city they would've thought to look for you.

But where'd he go?

<h1 style="text-align:center">Chapter 99</h1>

The homeless man stumbled to his feet—and hurled the dinner from his stomach, against the garden gate.

Asher's reservations about what was taking place were beginning to fade. The picture was growing clearer: the homeless man was ill, and the person responsible was watching him from within the alley of shadows.

Right there in front of him.

The only question, now, was how Asher should go about intervening. Did he have probable cause to detain him? Was giving someone a free meal enough to put the guy in cuffs? He needed more than just a hunch. Asher may have been able to piece together what was happening—but legally, he needed to be able to spell it out so there was no doubt.

Judge. Jury. The DA. Others needed to put the pieces together as well.

On the other hand, he couldn't just sit back and watch. If this was the guy, then Asher knew good and well what was about to happen, and preventing another homicide trumped any and all concern he may have had about doing this or that by the book.

The poor man stumbled through the gate and into the

garden, and the suspect followed.

That was it—it was time to make the call.

Asher dialed Xavier and told him where he was, where he needed to meet him and why. More likely than not, he wouldn't get here in time. But if things went sideways, at least Xavier would know where to find him. For better or for worse.

Asher hung up, then moved from behind the delivery truck and crossed the street, following the blankets of darkness cast by the balconies above. He reached the small gate at the back corner of the garden, behind the cathedral.

He followed the two of them into the unknown. Into the space that felt completely isolated, like a whole other world, barred from the view of those meandering their way through the rest of the Quarter.

Asher drew his pistol from the small of his back and thumbed the safety. It clicked. He wiped the humidity from his brow. As he inched farther into the garden, that feeling of disconnect only strengthened—that sense of the unreal with which he'd been battling. Like he was going through the motions, not feeling, not thinking. Not deciding, just doing.

He lifted the .45, and the white light illuminating Touchdown Jesus ignited the orange-and-black spheres of the bracelet on his wrist. He took note of their shape. Their color.

He drew a deep breath, then released it, bit by bit, as he crept forward in the dim yard. The shadows of endless plants and statues were smeared across the damp grass and cement walkways, crisscrossing like the New Orleans streets themselves.

Where the hell were they?

He heard a faint growl from across the garden. A repeated heaving. Asher wasn't dumb enough to walk straight there, though. Out in the open for someone to notice if they were looking. No—he'd work his way along the perimeter and toward the noise on the other side. That was his compass, the man's pain growing louder in the dark.

He had a small flashlight, but that wouldn't do him any good either. Lighting his way would only announce that he was here in the first place, so he followed what little light he could garner from the two spotlights inside of the garden—and the glow of a city beyond it.

Asher needed to take his time; he needed to hurry.

The sound grew nearer. Louder. Followed by the snapping of a twig not far in front of him, as he rounded the first corner of the fence. He continued alongside Royal, then turned the second corner. Sticking tight to the shrubs against the fence line.

People walked and talked a mere four feet from him on the other side of the fence line—but no one suspected he was there. Or that anyone at all was inside of the garden at this hour.

The Quarter was too loud, and the garden was too peaceful. Too dark.

As he continued through the bushes and toward the cathedral, toward the back of the garden on the opposite side from where he'd entered, the homeless man's pain grew louder. Asher pushed forward with his gun at the ready. He had almost reached the back corner when he paused.

He heard another rustle—only this time, it came from behind him.

The hatted figure lunged at his would-be victim, gripping the man's throat and pinning him against the wall of the cathedral. Asher holstered his gun as he sprinted toward them. He wrapped his arm around the guy's neck and leveraged the thin man's weight against his hip, throwing him to the ground.

But as soon as the suspect was down, he tripped Asher, then

reached into his backpack before Asher knew what hit him.

They were both on the ground now. A scalpel in the other man's hand. Gleaming white. All else black.

The man jumped on top of Asher and straddled him, thrusting downward with the blade. Asher caught his arm with both hands and swept him onto his back, holding his wrist to the ground.

"Drop it," Asher yelled. "Now." He slammed the man's hand onto the concrete.

"Fuck you," the guy said.

The voice—it was familiar.

Asher let go with one of his hands and elbowed the guy in the face as hard as he could. His head bounced from the cement. The scalpel fell from his hand.

The man laughed.

A stream of cerise sparkled as it flowed down the side of the man's face and onto the cement path beneath them.

"Asher!" He heard Xavier rush through the gate and toward them, the white beam of his flashlight cutting across the black of the garden. "Where you at?"

"Right here," Asher said. A bit of relief echoed from his voice. Panting. He rolled the suspect onto his stomach and pulled his hands together behind his back—one knee on his neck. Asher cuffed him.

Xavier and his light found them there in the center of the garden, at the foot of Jesus with his arms reaching for a punctured sky. Asher pulled the hat from the person's head and tossed it to the side.

"What'd you get into?" Xavier said. "Who is it?"

The scene, once unreal and movie-like in the detective's head, came into focus as clear as if they were sitting beneath the

July sun. Xavier's light paused over the kid's face, blood streaming from the wide-open gash above his brow. Over one of those hooded spheres of an eye Asher had met face-to-face on more than one occasion.

Above Waylon's eye—like an empty black bead in the night.

part four
INSANITY

Chapter 100

Justin's nephew sat in the back of the cruiser, holding a full-fledged conversation with himself, glaring at the steel divider in front of him that separated his plastic bench seat from the front of the patrol car. A seatbelt held him back. His hands remained cuffed behind him.

Asher set Waylon's backpack on the hood of the car. Navy lights strobed from myriad police units that barricaded all access points to St. Anthony's Garden and a block in every direction. Yellow-and-black tape crossed the two alleyways, flanking either side of the garden with a uniform posted at each gated entrance.

He wasn't messing about—every square inch of the garden and surrounding streets would be canvased front to back. Showing up to a scene post hoc was one thing. Being involved in it? Asher and forensics were on the same page; nothing would be left to chance. Every available tech Xavier had was out there working to find and catalog anything and everything they presumed was relevant to both the ripper cases and what had happened with Asher only minutes prior. All of it would be mapped out in grave detail.

There was something about the attempted murder of a cop that sent the entire force into overdrive.

"You good?" Xavier said to Asher. He set the scalpel, now

bagged as evidence, onto the hood of the car. The disposable blade was brand new, shining and out-of-the-box sharp. Even so, if it had been used in any of the stabbings and then scrubbed, forensics would find out. It might have looked clean, but that didn't mean it was.

Blood could only hide for so long.

The handle was so aged and rusted that it was littered with divots from where years of moisture had eroded the metal. It was a beautiful juxtaposition that had nearly taken Asher for a big ride, a final ride—if the kid had managed to stab him. Who knew how many pieces he would've been in right now, scattered around like some anatomical puzzle?

Asher nodded to his friend that he was okay as he watched the homeless man being lifted on a stretcher into the back of an ambulance. An officer shut the doors, then slapped the side of the vehicle. It sped off.

"So," Xavier continued, "you gonna tell me who this kid is? I usually don't see you this shaken up. I mean, granted he just tried to kill you, but rarely do I see you this—"

"He's my therapist's nephew," Asher said. "And I'm fine." He held a small flashlight between his teeth and peered into the backpack. He couldn't believe what he was saying. Someone he'd met on more than one occasion, spoken to, shaken hands with, someone who was related to *his own shrink*—was the person responsible for the murder of two innocent people, and now the attempted murder of a third. Not to mention Asher himself.

Still, it weighed on the detective's mind: who was he working with?

He gestured to Xavier for a box of gloves across the hood of the cruiser. Xavier slid them his way, then Asher stretched on a pair of blue latex gloves. He gave the second one a good pull and released it, letting it pop against his wrist as he shot Xavier a crazed look. "Bend over."

"Seriously?" Xavier said. "Your therapist's nephew? Well . . . at least y'all's sessions won't be so boring. Y'all should have plenty to talk about, now."

Asher pulled a filthy, dark amber bottle of clear liquid from the bag and set it on the hood. Whatever was inside swashed in the flashing blue lights, like a miniature ocean of the unknown. But not for long. Xavier would know what was inside of it before the night was over; the man never slept after something like this.

Xavier bagged and tagged the bottle. "Any guesses as to what it is?"

"I've got a few ideas," Asher said. "Whatever it is, I can guarantee you, we'll find it at the Pharmacy Museum."

"I'm on it," Xavier said.

"Well I'll be damned." The voice approached them from behind. "You actually pulled it off." Even with the kid in handcuffs, John was still a smart-ass. He patted Asher on the back, and Asher gave him a sideways glance.

Usually, he appreciated sardonicism. But with John, for whatever reason, he just didn't. It rubbed him the wrong way. Probably because he was new and inexperienced, and so young.

"Nice of you to show up," Asher said. "I thought for sure you'd be sick this evening."

To that, John had no response.

"Why don't you go help the rest of the team," Xavier said. "There's a lot to cover."

The trainee tipped his imaginary hat, then walked off. It seemed as though Xavier had become the mediator between them.

"What?" Xavier said to Asher. "You can't be on the

receiving end of the attitude? You can only dish it out?"

"It's not the attitude itself that bugs me," Asher said. "It's gotta be earned. Besides, you know I keep my circle tight. I deal with you"—he lifted his chin to the rest of forensics—"not them."

"Speaking of who you're willing to deal with," Xavier said, "where's the chief?" He checked his watch. "He should've been here by now."

"What? You don't think I can handle things myself? I got us this far."

"No. It's not that at all. I just thought that maybe you could use an extra hand so you can question the kid. If we're talking about two cases that are somehow related, it's probably best to get moving on that sooner rather than later, yeah?"

"He'll be here soon enough," Asher said. "Besides, I'm not questioning him out here. We're heading back to the precinct for that one. Mano a mano. That's the only way."

"Do me a favor and get that one on tape—that's gonna be a popcorn-with-extra-butter type of show."

"Yeah, well, that's assuming he talks."

Asher glanced through the windshield and into the back seat of the cruiser. The kid was still at it, rambling to himself in the most accusatory of ways. Like he was having an argument with his past self about the mistake he'd made by being caught.

Whether he was in any way remorseful for having murdered two innocent people was another story altogether.

Asher shined his light back into the bag, careful not to get ahead of himself and grab something he shouldn't. Not to be poked by some needle, or cut but another scalpel or a loose blade. He jostled the backpack and shifted what was inside.

"What else you got?" Xavier said, outwardly eager to wrap

up searching the bag so he could tend to the rest of a waiting scene. They were outside, so time was ticking.

How's this for what else?

Asher turned the bag upside down, and a pair of handcuffs fell to the hood of the car. That got the kid's attention.

The windshield was bathed in a shifting blue like a wall of water between them, where Waylon was handcuffed on the other side, in the back seat of the patrol car. He glared at the detective through the flashing glass. Unmoving.

The kid's slow grin spread like a fungus in the Southern humidity, far and wide.

# Chapter 101

Waylon sat in the interrogation room with his hands cuffed to the table, rocking in the metal chair.

Asher stood in the hallway with Pierre, discussing what had happened and explaining why his lead detective was already familiar with their prime suspect. Asher glimpsed the kid through the narrow pane of glass in the door, talking to his reflection in the one-way mirror to the side of him.

"Your therapist's nephew?" Pierre said. "You realize how this looks, right? First, your partner tries to murder you and then goes missing, and now our prime suspect in these stabbings is someone you know?"

"I don't *know* him," Asher said. "I met him, like, a couple times. I know *of* him."

"Yeah. I'm sure that's how the media's gonna spin it."

"Fuck the media; I'm tired of the media. You know how much time we've wasted trying to paint a picture of what the media, what Internal Affairs, what some board of administrators, thinks of everything that's happened here? I don't give a shit anymore, I really don't. They're all idiots."

Pierre stepped closer, rolling a smoldering cigar between his teeth. "Well, you should care."

"Oh yeah? And why is that?"

"Because your job depends on it; *our* jobs depend on it." Pierre moved to the door of the interrogation room and peered inside at the kid. "I don't care how you do it, Asher . . . just get ahead of this thing." The cloud of cigar smoke broke against the glass. The chief was seemingly enamored by how such a young man, how such a small guy, could've pulled off what he had managed to accomplish. "If you don't, the media shitstorm that's coming our way, in the middle of an *internal investigation*, is gonna fuck both of us."

"And by 'get ahead of it,' you mean . . ."

"You and Agnes think these cases are related. Figure it out." Then Pierre walked through the side door of the room—to a viewing area behind a pane of one-way glass.

Asher dialed Justin.

"Asher?" Justin answered. "Everything alright?"

He couldn't pinpoint it, but Asher felt some sort of obligation to let Justin know what had happened with as little worry as possible—in a way that'd let him know what was going on without freaking him out any more than necessary.

"Hey, Justin," Asher said. "You got a minute?"

"Um, yeah. Sure. I guess so. You okay?"

How the hell was he supposed to explain this?

"Yeah, well, not really. Can you get down here to the precinct? We've got your nephew, Waylon, here. He'll get a phone call, but I figured—"

"Wait, what? Slow down. You have who, there? My nephew?"

"Yeah. Waylon? I figured I'd give you a call myself. We've only had him down here for a few minutes. He'll get a phone call here soon, but like I said—he isn't going anywhere. I wanted to see if you—"

"What do you mean he's 'not going anywhere'?"

That was the first time Asher had ever heard that level of irritability in his therapist's voice. Ever. Justin was the collected type, the cool-headed one. Put together. It made sense, though; until now, Asher had only spoken to him in a professional setting.

He knew that he shouldn't take it personally, but he couldn't help it.

"Well, I know this is gonna be hard to believe . . . but . . . we've got Waylon on attempted murder, and we'll be—"

"What? *Attempted murder?* What are you talking about, Asher? Waylon? *My* nephew, Waylon? Are you sure we're talking about the same person? The young guy you met in my office? *That* Waylon?"

Maybe he shouldn't have told him at all—at least, not over the phone.

"Like I said," Asher continued, "I know it's a bit of a shock, and there's a lot to unpack, but yeah. I still have to talk to him, but he's also gonna have other, more serious charges as well."

Justin laughed over the line—an unbelieving, crazed, no-way-in-hell sort of chuckle. Hoarse and broken. Emotions coming through. "Oh, come on, Asher. Give me a break. Look, from what I know, you're a damn good detective, but . . . no. There's no way that we're talking about the same kid."

Waylon may have looked like a kid, but he was far from it—years off as a matter of fact.

"I know it's late, but is there any way that you can get down here sometime soon. I plan on speaking with him here in a minute, and then he'll have to be processed. But there's only so much I can say over the phone."

Asher could hear Tammy asking questions in the background. Justin's voice grew muffled through what was clearly a covered speaker. Asher waited.

"Yeah, Asher. We'll be there shortly. I'll call you when we get there."

"Just tell them at the front desk that you're here to see me when you get here. I'll most likely be in there with him when you get here, so just come back and have a seat in the waiting area. I'll let them know you're coming."

"Fine. Oh, you said something else. What did you mean when you said that he's gonna have more serious charges? What could possibly be worse than attempted murder, Asher?" Tammy's rambling continued in the background.

Worse than attempted murder? The cold memory of Cassandra's pistol, pressed beneath Asher's chin only weeks prior, returned with a vengeance. The sight of Sofia, held at gunpoint. The echo of a deafening pop as Cassandra fell backward. Followed by another piercing crack in the hallway of that hellish house.

Sofia's blood had painted the wall before her head ever hit the floor.

That metallic smell in the air.

Worse than attempted murder? Asher could have come up with at least one thing that was worse than attempted murder.

"Just let the people up front know that you're here to see me."

Chapter 102

Asher entered the interrogation room.

He glanced at the one-way mirror as he made his way to the table, but Waylon's reflection stared back at him. Without question, the chief was watching the two of them from the other side.

It was showtime.

"How you holding up?" Asher said. He dropped some paperwork onto the table and took a seat across from him.

Waylon chuckled to himself as he blinked in a peculiar rhythm, repeating, as if something wicked were eating his eyes from the inside out. "Holding up?" Then he brought together his cuffed hands and clapped in a slow, snobbish pulse. "Well, aren't you the *star* detective. Look at you, taking care of your captors and all."

"Alright, then." Asher wanted to get to the core of things before Justin arrived, before some lawyer came through the door and advised the kid to keep his mouth shut. "You've already been read your rights, including your right to legal counsel—so you're not obligated to answer any of my questions. As a matter of fact, you don't have to say anything."

Waylon lifted his hands, palms up, a few inches from the table top as if to say, *What's your point?*

Asher dropped an evidence bag with the handcuffs onto the table between them—next to the scalpel and bottle of liquid that were also bagged; Xavier had already collected a sample of the solution for analysis. Then he slid a folder between them. He opened it to printouts of the fiber analysis and the spool of hemp rope.

Asher pressed RECORD on the camera, fixed to a tripod next to the table. He went through the typical permissions that he needed to have on the record, asking Waylon if he consented to an interview and whether he was aware of his rights.

"So," Asher said, "before we talk about the obvious, the . . . attempted murder and all, I wanna know why. And let's cut through the smoke and mirrors: the evidence is pretty damning as it is. If you talk now, maybe it'll help you out at the trial."

Waylon ignored what was in front of him—except for the folder. He pulled it closer and rested his hands flat on the table, leaning forward and looking it over. He gave the evidence a slow nod, then sat back in the chair with his arms still on the table.

He cleared his throat and looked into the mirror beside them.

"Tell me something, Detective. You have any siblings?"

"This ain't a Q&A. If you think I'm gonna sit here and indulge your ego that wants to play with me by dragging this out, you're sorely mistaken."

"Play? Oh, I think we've already established that I can play. You're sitting here asking me questions because you got the *what*, but not the *why*. That right?"

The last thing Asher ever entertained was indulging his arrests—giving them power over the conversation led to nothing good, in his experience.

He pulled the folder in front of him, closed it, then got to his feet. "You'll be processed then given your phone call. Someone'll be by later to assign counsel if you don't already have someone." He turned for the door.

"Fishing." Waylon's voice came off as reluctant but willing. His type were all the same: they needed the attention. For the case to be about them, their story, what horrible things they'd done. They needed the credit.

"Do what?"

"Fishing."

Asher let go of the door handle and turned back to the table. He dropped the folder and sat down once again. "You murdered innocent people because of . . . fishing?"

"Well . . ." He pulled the folder back in front of him and opened it. He turned it around to the detective and pushed it toward him, pointing to the photo of the hemp rope. "People always want a reason, and you're no different. We've gotta blame it on something. Don't we?"

Fair enough—Waylon had his interest.

He sat back. Anger was taking over Waylon's desire to screw with the man in front of him. Memories of something heavy were coming through, something traumatic. The recollection of something he clearly hadn't shared with anyone for some time, if ever.

"Okay," he said. "Fishing. What about it?"

"Well, I'm guessing your people were able to figure out that the victims were strangled." He laid his index finger over the chain of his cuffs, then twisted until his skin shifted to a throbbing royal purple. "But it'd help your case even more if you knew that it was a tourniquet knot that did the trick." He tightened the chain around his finger, then let up, twisted, then eased up, playing with what would've been clearly painful for anyone else. "Simple—but effective."

The pen from under the bed?

"Yeah. Sure. Those are used in fishing all the time."

"Don't be a smart-ass, Detective." Waylon leaned forward beneath the white light that shifted ever so little above them. "They deserved it. Every one of those fuckers deserves it. Shit, they probably molested *their* little brothers, too, when they were kids. Probably went to the same dumbass fishing camp and learned the same dumbass knots as my own brother."

He leaned farther. The light above them accentuated the kid's beady and piercing, dark eyes.

"Weekend after weekend, year after year, he'd come home and brag about learning this and that. That's all he ever talked about—that fucking camp. But me? Oh, no. Not me. Not little ole me. No . . . it didn't matter what I did. I never lived up to *his* accomplishments."

A brief quiet lingered.

"Those were the days," he continued with sarcasm. "I had to listen to my parents doting on that fucker day in and day out. Day and night. Talking about nothing but that goddamn camp. 'Oh, that's *amazing,* son. We're *so proud* of you.' Over and over and fucking over. And then the weekends—"

He appeared lost in his reflection beside him, in a daze that grabbed him and refused to let go.

"Oh, the weekends. Mom and dad just left us there at home. You believe that shit? Together. Alone." He looked back at Asher, ostensibly eager to watch his face put two and two together. "What about you, Detective . . . You ever been touched by another man?"

Asher had been here before. His best move? Keep quiet. Let it all play out while the information was still coming. So he shook his head with no expression at all. Outwardly unbiased.

"Yeah," Waylon continued. "I didn't think so."

Something troubling was going on with this guy's mental health. It wasn't surprising, though; nearly every homicide that came through here had something or another to do with mental health issues. Childhood trauma, abuse, depression. The list was endless.

But as their conversation continued, Asher thought back to Cassandra and that story she'd shared with him about her most trying patient. Like most doctors, she'd taken the confidentiality of her patients seriously.

Why couldn't he shake the thought of her?

"Look . . . you're right," Waylon said. "I'm sorry. If you think it'll help, then I'm willing to talk." His eyes shifted over what sat on the table between them.

Asher grabbed the folder to step out for some fresh air. To let Waylon think it over. "If you confess—willingly, that is—and show even the slightest bit of remorse . . . then, yeah. It'll help. I can't guarantee anything, but it should help you."

"Alright," he said. "I gotcha. And look, I'm sorry. I didn't mean to get off on the wrong foot." Waylon held out his hand. "Name's Reese."

Chapter 103

sher closed the door behind him and stepped into the hallway. What in the world was that? The memory of his exchange with Cassandra flooded him—the one patient she'd ever mentioned back when they started working together. Was that distant recollection of their conversation trying to tell him something, or pointing to someone in particular?

Then there was her role as a therapist in his wretched nightmares, the identical "patients" across from her in what appeared to be Justin's office.

Was his memory drawn to Waylon, of all people?

Asher thought of Cassandra's frustration with her inability to effectively treat a certain branch of conditions, a certain area of research with which she'd never been trained well, to her own admission. He thought of those patients across from her in his dreams. Of the *one* patient that appeared as two. What had she said to Asher back when they first started working together?

Something about a condition that was confusingly changed to "dissociative identity disorder." Was that the dissociating? The splitting?

Or was Asher mistaken, thinking about his own issues with derealization? Hadn't Justin mentioned that Asher's issues fell under the purview of some sort of dissociation?

He looked back to the door of the interview room. Waylon was fixated on himself in the one-way mirror, rocking. Talking to himself while that seemingly nervous tick of his eyes was going haywire. Like some sinister boy robot on the fritz.

Why couldn't Asher shake Cassandra from his memory, after she'd caused him so much pain? Or maybe that was the reason: the pain.

Pierre stepped out of the viewing room. "Well," he said, "that was interesting. What are you thinking?"

"That's a good question. To be honest, I'm not sure. What I do know is that the kid needs some serious help. What's interesting, though, is the fact that he not only had that pair of cuffs in his bag—but he just admitted to strangling our balcony victims."

"And you believe him?"

"Maybe? I mean, we've got him on the stabbings for sure." Asher leaned against the wall. "I need a minute to think."

If he was lying, then why? If he was lying, how would he know about the rope? The public only knew that the balcony victims were strangled; they'd never released the details on how so.

"I'm not so sure we should be looking for another suspect at all," Asher said.

It was a good thing he'd gotten the interview on video thus far; testimony, even coming from a detective, had its limits in front of a jury.

"Hey Asher!" Justin paced down the hallway with Tammy in tow. "Wait up."

And now it's really about to get interesting.

"You made it," Asher said.

"Of course we made it," said Justin. He and his wife were panting as if they'd just run Legends of the Hidden Temple at the front desk. "What's going on?"

"How's he doing?" Tammy added in a broken slur.

"Let me know when you're heading back in there," Pierre said. Then he walked in the direction of his office.

"Let's step over here," Asher said, moving away from the door of the interrogation room. "Him seeing y'all is only gonna make things harder on all three of you."

"So, what's really going on?" Justin said. "What exactly is he here for?"

"Like I said over the phone, he's being charged with two counts of attempted murder, but to be honest, that's the least of his—"

"*Two* counts?" Tammy said. "What the hell did he do? And how do you know for sure?"

"Well . . . the attempted murder charges are actually the straightforward part—for one, I caught Waylon attacking someone who's living out on the street."

"*What?*" Tammy said.

Justin clasped his hands behind his head. "And two?"

Asher could already feel the grimy awkwardness of his predicament, caught in the middle like he was the reason for their nephew being here—while at the same time doing his best to soften the blow. But would they blame him in the end?

"Me," Asher said. "We got into a physical altercation when I tried to stop him. Even if I wanted to forget it ever happened, it doesn't matter; he'll be charged with the attempted murder of a law enforcement official either way. That one's out of my hands entirely."

Tammy breathed in with a string of deep, rapid gasps as she

covered her mouth—and there she held them. Asher knew the feeling, that lump she couldn't swallow.

"Wait. Hold up," Justin said. He spun around and ran his hand down his face. He clasped his throat.

Tammy sat on a nearby bench and leaned forward with her head in her hands.

"What else?" Justin said. "On the phone—you said there was more?"

Giving the news to anyone in this situation would've been bad enough. But to Justin and his wife? Their nephew was alive, and yet Asher felt as though he were delivering the news that he'd just died on the operating table.

"Like I was saying, the attempted murder charges are the least of his worries. Some of the evidence that we've collected on a string of homicides has been traced back to him as well."

Tammy broke down, albeit in silence. She sobbed to herself as Justin's face went slack.

"At first, it was largely circumstantial," Asher said, "but after tonight, between the attempted homicide and what I've got from his bag . . . he's looking at a minimum of two additional charges of first-degree murder. Possibly others."

Justin huffed, unbelieving. "Others."

"I'm sorry," Asher said. "Really, I'll do everything I can to—"

"You've gotta do something," Tammy said. "He has no one else. We're all he's got. His father Billy is out on the streets, he has been for years; he no longer talks to his brother Adam because . . . well, that's a lot to unpack. Please, there's gotta be *something* that you can do."

In the end, there'd only be so much Asher could do for anyone under these circumstances. At the very least, he could try to figure out the *why*, with the help of Waylon's aunt and uncle.

Asher turned to Justin. "I know this is probably something that you're reluctant to share, but it'd really help Waylon, and me too, if you can tell me: have you ever treated Waylon for DID? Or any other dissociative disorders?"

Justin unbuttoned his suit. "No. Why would you ask that?" Sweat bled from the fabric beneath his arms.

"Well, there's cause to charge him on two cases that we're working, which is gonna include more than two homicides. At first, I was thinking that maybe we should be looking for another suspect, an accomplice. But based on my conversation with him so far, I'm worried that this has something to do with his mental health. Again, I can't force you to share anything, but if there's something—"

"No, nothing like that," Justin said. "I mean, I've only recently started treating him for bipolar disorder, but I've seen absolutely nothing to suggest an alternative diagnosis."

"Okay," Asher said. "That's okay."

"Justin—" Tammy's voice managed to get it out in pieces and choked-up fragments. "You need to say something. Tell him, Justin."

"Tell me what?"

"Well . . . he's been treated by an endless number of psychologists, and psychiatrists, in the past for mood swings and behavioral issues. But no one's really been able to help him. At least, not with any long-term solution that actually works. You really think that's relevant in some way?"

The color drained from Justin's face as if he'd bled out right there in the hallway. "Wait . . . is this . . . my fault?"

Chapter 104

Then it was back to the interrogation room.

As much as Asher felt for Justin and Tammy's predicament, he wasn't letting them see Waylon; whatever the murderer had to say, he could say to the detective he'd tried to stab. At this point, only a lawyer would be allowed to see him—and Asher had no idea when that would be. That was something Justin and his wife were trying to figure out.

Waylon was an adult; he'd make his own decisions. Legally, the wants of his aunt and uncle were irrelevant.

As long as Waylon was willing to talk, Asher would be there to get it on the record, on video.

"So?" Asher said as he walked into the room. "Is there anything else you wanna share, now that you've clarified—"

Waylon stuck out his hand, and his face transformed into something formal, almost older. Asher couldn't put his finger on it—maybe it was his posture or the way that he tilted his head. Whatever it was, he no longer looked like the younger man, the kid some saw him as.

"Well," Waylon said, "the least you can do is introduce yourself, my friend. Especially after you just made me sit here while you're shooting the shit out there in the hallway."

Asher leaned across the table and shook his hand. "Detective Huxley," he said, unsure of how to address whatever this was.

"Name's Ryker," he said. Then he folded his hands in front of him like a little schoolboy sitting at his desk, doing his damnedest to oblige the nun and her ruler at the chalkboard.

Asher hit RECORD on the camera and took a seat. He covered the typical spiel about rights and lawyers once again. He had to get it on the record every time he started a new line of questioning.

With Waylon or Reese or Ryker or whoever.

But before Asher could start in on the real questions, he realized who he was talking to.

"Sorry about the, uh"—Waylon made a downward stabbing gesture with his hand, rattling his restraints against the steel table—"you know. Heat of the moment and all."

"No worries at all . . . friend," Asher said. "Everything worked out just as it should've."

Waylon lifted his hands to emphasize that he was currently chained to a table after being caught red-handed at the unthinkable. So, "just as it should've," at least for him, might have been a bit over-the-top.

But Asher stood his ground. "Like I said—just as it should've." Then he adjusted the evidence bags between them to gauge the kid's reaction. Waylon's sideways smile pointed to the scalpel.

"Well, let's get down to it," Asher continued. "I think it's fair to say that we've got enough evidence to charge you with the obvious. You know . . ." And he made the same downward stabbing gesture. "Not to mention what you were attempting to do when I rolled up. You care to share?"

He only shrugged.

Whatever this was, whoever this was, they had something in common, whether they realized it or not. If this was even real. If so, they shared the same body, the same childish core man who'd given birth to them. Would the same reasoning that worked earlier work now?

"As you very well know," Asher said, "I can't force you to say anything. But the more you confess to now, the more it'll help you later on down the road—when you'll inevitably stand trial. So, if you're willing to talk about it, I think it'll—"

"And what exactly are you wanting me to confess to, Detective? You were there, you saw things for yourself. Shit, you almost *were* one of those things. Ain't that enough?"

"No. No, no, no." Asher called his bluff. He remained calm and spoke as if he knew something the guy had yet to confess. "I think you know what I'm asking . . . Ryker." Saying the name felt beyond strange. "That man you attacked tonight"—he moved the scalpel closer to the other side of the table—"wasn't the first. Let's be honest, here. Anything other than the truth is only gonna come back to haunt you when you're in that courtroom, when your peers are hanging on every word that comes out of your mouth."

Waylon leaned forward, clasping his hands between them. He pushed the scalpel aside without giving it so much as a second glance. "That'd be perfect, wouldn't it? For you, that is. What? You want me to sit here and give you some sob story about my childhood—something totally *Dahmer*esque? How's this?"

He sat up straight, rolled back his shoulders, then pushed a stray tuft of hair back toward his ear. Waylon glared straight into the camera with an overdone, satirical tone of voice.

At the very least, even if Asher didn't get a serious, clean confession out of him for the stabbings, he'd have it on record: the kid was batshit. *If* this wasn't some ploy. Only sessions with a trained psychologist were going to determine that.

But here and now? Asher planned on getting everything out of him while he had the chance.

Waylon's voice grew sardonic. "There once was a happy family—until Mommy died of cancer. Daddy couldn't hold a job, so he and his two sons lived on the street." He spoke to the camera as if it were a friend. "Year after year of empty promises, and one of those kids grew hopeless. He wanted out, and that's exactly what he did. He got out. He cleaned himself up, dusted off the scruff, and made something of himself—all on his own. Unfortunately for him . . . what hung around was the resentment. The memories."

Waylon shifted his attention from the camera to the man across from him. He leaned forward. "Something like that, Detective?"

"Only if it's relevant," Asher said. He wasn't going to back off, not when he had full access to their prime suspect. "Is that it? One of the kids grows a pair, gets a job, and gets back at Daddy for all the horrible days?"

"Well," Waylon said. He inched forward in his chair and lifted his hands between them, his elbows on the table. "Pops always said to work with my hands."

And the son of a bitch winked. He didn't care that he was here; he'd done exactly what he wanted. He'd found a way to deal with the anger, and he wasn't sorry. At least, not about what he'd done. Perhaps he was sorry that he'd been caught. Most of them were.

"But perhaps you're right, Detective." Waylon leaned back

and returned his hands to their original place on the table, folded and formal between them. "As long as that kid is off the streets, he can't hurt Daddy now, can he . . . my friend?"

<h1 style="text-align:center">Chapter 105</h1>

sher stepped into the viewing room, where Pierre had been watching the show from behind the one-way glass. "I need a favor," Asher said.

"Alright."

"I need a warrant for his place. As I'm sure you can tell from watching, I've got no idea who the fuck I'm talking to from one minute to the next, so I'm not entirely sure what I can trust and what I can't. I've got no idea who has access to his place."

At this point, it was after midnight. Asher knew how much the chief didn't care for waking up judges in the middle of the night to ask for favors, but this was too big to ignore.

"Well, if you're gonna do it, it needs to be done right. Take forensics with you." Pierre stood from his seat and unlocked his cell phone. "You can be the one to organize everyone on that side of things."

"Of course," Asher said. "I'll get together with Xavier. I hate to pull everyone out of bed at this hour, but I don't think this one can wait. There's no telling what the kid's got lying around that could make all this a lot easier."

The chief hit "call" and lifted the phone to his ear. "You'll have a warrant within the hour."

As Asher returned to the hallway, Xavier and John were just now getting back from the scene. He met them at Xavier's desk.

They looked exhausted. "Just sitting on your ass as always, huh?" Asher couldn't help but poke the bear.

Xavier gave him the bird as he downed half a bottle of water.

"Yeah, well, the night ain't over," Asher said. "It's time to get to work."

"I'm just getting warmed up," Xavier said.

John tilted his head as if to say, *Y'all are crazy.*

Xavier finished the water like it was nothing. "I'm about to get going on that sample from the bottle. Based on what you've said about the pharmacy, I think I can—"

"Nope," Asher said. "Don't get comfortable. I'm heading over to Waylon's place as soon as I get the green light from the chief—and he wants you and your team to tag along."

"Now that's what I'm talking about," Xavier said. He slapped John in the chest with the back of his hand. "It's showtime."

The mentee melted into his own puddle of exhaustion.

Chapter 106

Waylon's apartment resembled that of a modest professor. Eclectic.

Dimmed by yellow Edison bulbs. Two bedrooms. Black-and-gray art of New Orleans adorning the living room walls. Original hardwood floors and shiplap ceilings made the world echo. Steps, voices, the tension of old wood beneath their feet; all of it ricocheted between the all-but-empty living room and kitchen.

Something thick and gray hung in the air.

Xavier photographed every square inch of the place while his team searched for anything that they could've linked to the murders.

"Are we looking for something in particular?" Xavier said to Asher.

"Not really. Just anything that could be relevant to our two cases. You know . . . more of the rope, any chemical solutions, cuffs . . . a giant sign that reads, 'I LOVE MURDERERS BECAUSE I MURDER, TOO.' You know . . . the usual paraphernalia."

"And you're convinced the DA can put together a case for the stabbings? I know you're pretty confident on the balcony murders, now that you've got the rope from the Pharmacy

Museum—not to mention the toxin that we can probably trace back there, too. And the cuffs from his bag."

"I am." Asher held up a box of disposable scalpel blades that he'd found tucked behind a head of lettuce in the refrigerator. "Because we've got a matching set. Maybe?"

"Oh, that's nice. That's really nice."

"Chances are, it'll be a fresh blade on the scalpel that we've already got back at the precinct. But . . ."

"But there's a good chance that there's traces of blood on the handle itself."

"Exactly. And I'll bet you any money that the brand and style of these blades will match the one on the scalpel that we've already got."

Asher handed over the box, and Xavier bagged and tagged it.

"So . . ." Xavier wavered in his speech, seemingly hesitant whether he should say what he was about to utter anyway. Or whether he should say what Asher would pull out of him now that he'd already begun the thought aloud.

"Yeah? So . . ."

"You don't feel some kind of way about all of this? With this kid being your therapist's nephew and all?"

"Of course I do."

"And what way is that?"

John and another one of Xavier's men walked down the hallway and into the bedrooms.

"Well, he's being charged with two counts of attempted murder," Asher said, "as well as the murders of each victim in the stabbings *and* balcony cases. The DA should be able to pull it all together with what we've already got. So, there's not really anything I can do about that—not that I'd want to if I could."

"Asher, I've known you for too long not to recognize your bullshit."

What could he say? One part of him felt bad for the kid. The other part? He wished he could be part of the firing squad.

"It's not bullshit," Asher said. "To be honest, it's sad. I told Justin, my therapist, that I'd try to find anything that could help with an insanity plea. More likely than not, his lawyer—whoever that ends up being—will go for the typical insanity defense; they always do with cases like this. And I already planned on searching the place anyway."

"And you don't find that a bit . . . counterproductive? You're searching for evidence to help prosecute him while also looking for what can acquit him through a mental health defense?"

"Not at all," Asher said. "All I care about is the truth, that he gets what's coming his way. If it's all a ploy, then he deserves a guilty verdict and whatever comes along with it."

"And if he's a mental case?"

"Well . . . then he deserves whatever comes along with that, too."

Xavier went quiet. John stepped out of one of the bedrooms and called to the front of the apartment. "Hey, y'all might wanna come take a look at this."

With everything that was going on, Asher didn't need his best friend questioning his motives. Not now. Asher walked past him and toward the hall. "All I care about is that we've got him—and that he's prosecuted based on the evidence. Regardless of the defense, of the outcome in a courtroom, it's our job to find the truth; what the DA does with it is up to the DA."

He continued on to the bedrooms.

"What is it?" Asher asked John as he walked into the first room.

"You tell me," John said.

"Holy shit." Asher paused in the middle of the bedroom and did a double take. "Hey, Xavier, get in here."

The walls were decorated with black-and-gray art, just like the living room. Only here, the art wasn't New Orleans cityscapes and monuments.

It was hand-drawn pencil sketches of human anatomy—dismembered, hacked body parts.

Xavier walked into the room. "What the fuck?"

"Right?" Asher added.

"Well, it isn't a giant sign," Xavier said, "but it's definitely something."

"Make sure you get pictures," Asher said. "Collect one of them as part of the warrant and photograph the rest."

Another of the forensics techs spoke from the doorway. "That ain't all." They crossed the hallway and stepped into the other bedroom.

"Oh *yeah*." Asher said.

Xavier added, "Is this just sick, or is it somehow relevant to our cases?"

"Oh, it's relevant," Asher said.

The second bedroom was also covered in grayscale pencil art—of naked men and their intercourse. No holds barred.

No one else in the room had the full story on Asher's interrogation of the kid; Xavier had the bullet points. To them, it was probably unclear what it all meant, merely twisted in a sick sort of way. To Asher, it was clear. The art could be used in one of two ways.

On one hand, it could be leveraged to support innocence

by reason of insanity: a graphic obsession with human anatomy that stemmed from anger and/or a desire for violence, alongside a deep-seated interest in homosexuality and erotica stemming from childhood trauma. On the other hand, both of the collections could support the prosecution—the premeditation necessary with a charge of first-degree murder.

"You know what, go ahead and collect them," Asher said. "All of them."

Chapter 107

The rest of the forensics team had left; Xavier stayed behind with Asher.

He wasn't ready to concede that he'd searched the place well enough. Between the spare scalpel blades and the drawings, they'd certainly stumbled across more key evidence that was useful—but Asher couldn't leave until he felt that he'd exhausted every inch of the kid's apartment and then some.

Asher paced the hallway, thinking of anywhere he'd hide things himself if he lived in a place like this. Air vents. Light fixtures. Faux outlets.

As he stopped between the two bedrooms and checked one of the floor vents in the hallway, he heard a faint sound coming from the back of the apartment. So quiet, in fact, that he turned off his flashlight and squinted—as if that would've somehow aided his hearing. Like turning down the radio to see better while driving on a stormy night.

"What is it?" Xavier said from the living room.

"Shh." Asher took a step toward the back of the apartment. The only other room that they'd searched besides the kitchen, living room, bathroom, and two bedrooms was the laundry room off the back of the hallway. "You hear that?"

"No. What?"

Asher moved into the laundry room and clicked his light back on. "That," he said, pointing his light to the ceiling.

Xavier walked into the room and put his head down, closing his eyes to listen. "Is that music?"

"I don't know."

"We're surrounded by other apartments. It's probably just someone next door."

"What about that?" Asher narrowed his beam of light and focused it on one of the ceiling tiles in the corner, above the washer. "You see that?"

"What?"

"That," Asher said. "That tile doesn't line up with the rest of them—and it's worn." He shut the lid on the washer and climbed on top of it. With a delicate hand, he eased the tile upward and held his light between his teeth. Then he set the piece of ceiling down in the space above them.

The sound, the music as it turned out, grew louder once he'd moved the tile.

"Is that . . . Jonny Lang?" Xavier said. "'Matchbox'?"

Asher drew his pistol from his back and thumbed the safety, leading with the barrel as he poked his head through the ceiling. "It's a record player." After looking around, he pulled himself into the room by the wooden ceiling joists just above the tiles.

"You need me up there?" Xavier said.

Asher whispered. "Yeah—if your ogre ass can fit through the ceiling."

"Funny. Very funny, man."

Once Asher was up there, his jaw all but hit the floor. The room was something along the lines of a claustrophobic, crude living space, too small to call an apartment. Or a studio, even. It was more of an abandoned walk-in closet. A small cot, half bath, and desk in front of the unlocked hexagonal attic window were the extent of its contents. A full but fading moon hung in the glass like a pitted eye, watching. The sweet, pungent odor of mothballs mixed with the musty air. The whole space had a gray feel about it.

Xavier made his way up there with a light of his own. "What the hell?"

"Tell me about it."

Asher moved to the desk and swept his light over its contents. He lifted the needle on the record player and set it in place to the side. The vinyl spun itself out and drew to a dying halt.

"This kid just keeps getting more interesting," Xavier said. He shined his light over and beneath the cot in the corner, but there was nothing to see.

Asher browsed the papers strewn about the desk, stacked and organized next to an empty to-go cup—"CAFÉ BEIGNET" on the side of it. The folders were dated with frayed, dirty edges.

"What you got?" Xavier said.

Asher opened one of the manilla folders, then pushed the papers aside with the barrel of his .45. They were files, handwritten notes and typed assessments dating back many years. But they all had something in common.

Asher's stomach plummeted, and his feet fell numb. A coldness poured over him from head to toe, and the sweat bled from his pores like a squeezed sponge—as if his body were rejecting the mere sight of what he held in his hand that was now shaking.

He glanced around the room with his light.

"What?" Xavier said.

He handed the paper over, and Xavier shined his light over it. Asher ran his finger down the file and pointed to the patient name at the bottom.

"Waylon Blanchard," it read.

Chapter 108

"I don't get it," Xavier said. "These are patient notes? From what? There's piles of them."

Asher grabbed another of the folders and sifted through it. He held it in front of Xavier and pointed to the provider name at the top of one of the documents.

To the name and office logo—of Cassandra's private practice from years past.

"Oh . . . shit." Xavier dropped the paper onto the desk. He looked back down through the ceiling through which they'd climbed. He swept his light over the room. Wiped the sweat from his neck. "What now? What is this, then?"

Asher was enamored by it, albeit shrouded in anger. Disgust. He turned back to the desk and continued sifting through the folders of paperwork, scanning the sessions and dates.

What drew Asher's eye wasn't so much the in-session therapy notes themselves; the private, handwritten notes between Cassandra and her patient were far more intriguing. At a brief glance, all of it came back to Cassandra's struggle with understanding and treating one thing: multiple personality, or DID.

Dissociative identity disorder.

She couldn't fix Waylon as a doctor—so she wanted to be there for him? To make up for it outside of the office?

"How does this make any sense?" Xavier said.

"I was right. I'd been right all along."

"Right? Right about what?"

"About Cassandra—she didn't bleed out, man. She didn't skip town or run away. No." Asher swept his light over the room. "I was right. *Fuck*, I knew it."

"What are you talking about?" Xavier said. "What? What were you right about?"

Asher shook his head. Kicked the leg of the table with everything he had. "You son of a bitch. I was right the entire time, man. I should've listened to my gut . . . *Fuck*."

"You did, Asher. There's nothing else you could've—"

"It wasn't her, Xavier. Everyone believed the body that washed up was Cassandra—because that's *exactly* what she wanted us to believe. And it worked. You can create a piercing, you can fashion a gunshot wound . . . and, yeah, it was her ID. Her clothing, probably, too. She knew what she was doing. I should've listed to my gut."

"Do what?"

"If you need a place to hole up, what better person to run to than someone who wants you there. Or better yet, someone who has no one else, who's been abandoned by everyone else. If Cassandra was Waylon's therapist at one point, and he kept in touch with her outside of therapy, of course this is where she ran to; he needed her, and she used the hell out of him. *Fuck*."

"Um, sure. Maybe?" Xavier said. "How the hell does that have anything to do with the cases we're working?"

"That's what we've gotta figure out," Asher said. "Maybe Waylon knew about Cassandra's end game with me and figured, 'hell, if my own therapist can do it . . .' Who knows, man? What says that she even knew about what he was doing? Maybe he was just the one person she could run to who'd keep their mouth shut. And if he really is batshit, it would've made it all the easier for her to get what she wanted . . . The fucking woman's alive, man."

"So, why don't you use this as leverage with the kid to—" Xavier's attention grew lost in the attic window, unlatched and blown open a fraction of an inch by a one-off breeze in the fading night. Daylight had begun to brush the dark aside in soft strokes of childish blue.

"What?" Asher said. "What is it?"

He pointed with his light. "There."

A figure darted from the adjacent fire escape across the alleyway, hopping to another balcony and down a connecting set of stairs.

"Stay here," Asher said. He dropped from the ceiling and back down to the washing machine.

"And do what?" Xavier called.

Asher spoke as he climbed down and darted from the laundry room. "No one gets in or out." He made it downstairs in a string of short bounds then fled the apartment. But by the time he made it out the door, they were gone.

Cassandra was nowhere to be found.

Again.

Asher stood there as the moon faded into a bluing sky, and the edges of daylight teased the rooftops. His catastrophizing was not only becoming reality, it would soon grow legs and spread beyond his own worry and into the world around him: the department, the city. Who knew where she was headed or why? Or when?

Asher's phone rang. "Hey," Xavier said, "should I call for backup?"

"No," Asher said. "Do you think it was her?"

"Of course it was her, man. You saw what I saw, didn't you?"

"*Shit.*" Asher flung his light against some brick wall, and it shattered more elegantly than his world was crumbling around him. "Don't call *anyone*. We're heading back to the precinct."

Chapter 109

sher and Xavier entered the precinct together and were immediately struck by the clamor of clicks and voices coming from the lobby newsroom.

"I didn't know we had visitors scheduled for this morning," Xavier said.

Asher shuddered. "That makes two of us."

They walked into the conference room, and he felt as if he'd been thrust into the lights-camera-action of a feature horror film. Peak conflict.

The place was packed, and Pierre stood behind the bushel of microphones at the podium. "Yes, ma'am?" he said, pointing to a reporter in the front row.

The two friends stood at the back of the room, looking on. It was better for everyone involved if no one knew Asher was there; he hadn't exactly been on good terms with the media in recent days.

"Does the department have any updates regarding the recent stabbings, as well as the bar murders in the French Quarter? And can you clarify that NOPD does, in fact, have someone in custody as of yesterday evening?"

"Yes, ma'am," Pierre said. "Our homicide team has arrested

a Mr. Waylon Blanchard, the person we believe to be responsible for the absolutely *horrific* stabbings of Mr. Claude Evans and, to date, an unidentified male whom we're working to ID as soon as possible; a photograph and description of that individual are available on our department website. We'd greatly appreciate the public's cooperation on that matter if you do have any relevant information for us. However, what our team has come to discover is that the aforementioned cases are, in fact, one and the same."

The room erupted into a sea of soft-spoken gasps and frantic writing, as attendees adjusted their posture and double-checked their tape recorders and cameras.

The woman in the front row, decked out in her freshly pressed red pant suit, chimed in again. "So, the one and only suspect in those cases is currently detained?"

"Yes," the chief said. "Thanks to our lead detective"—he gestured to Asher at the back of the room—"we've been able to put both of these cases to rest. And we'll be happy to release any further information regarding our investigation as the DA deems appropriate. Not only is our prime suspect in custody, but we've obtained a recorded confession as well."

Thanks, Chief. Thanks a fucking lot. Asher lowered his head and gave Xavier a glance, hoping they could duck out.

"Additionally," Pierre continued, "we also have an update on our former detective, who's very much been the topic of discussion as of late."

Now, it was Xavier's turn to grimace in Asher's direction. *Don't do it, Chief. Please don't do it.*

"I'd like to announce that we've officially identified the decedent found at the Love Wins pier as our former detective, Miss Cassandra Lejeune, who was involved in the hostage situation and shooting several weeks back. Therefore, we assure the media and the city of New Orleans that they can rest easy, knowing that this trained and dangerous individual is now off of our city streets for good."

Another reporter in the back—an older, hunched-over man with wiry glasses and a wrinkled tweed jacket, stood with surprising agility. "And when are we gonna have answers on what happened with that? Have any reports been filed on the nature of what she did within the department and how she was hired by NOPD in the first place?"

"No, sir," Pierre said. "Not yet. But it *will* happen. We currently have an internal investigation looking into exactly that, and I'll release that report as soon as the inquiry is closed. That request for information is currently out of my hands and is being looked into by a third party. As of now, that's all we have. Thank you."

The room exploded with shouts and unaddressed questions.

Asher slapped Xavier in the chest with the back of his hand. "Buckle up." He tilted his head to the bank of elevators.

The chief hurled his rocks glass of Jack Daniels against the wall, and the ice and crystal shattered into a flurry of clear shards. The whiskey dripped down the wall like those claw marks down Asher's back, in the shower with his then-alive wife, only weeks prior.

That was before Sofia had been taken from him.

This was now.

"What the *fuck*, dickhead?" Pierre pulled at his tie until it fell from his neck.

"You're gonna put this on me?" Asher said. "I'm the only one who had doubts about this thing the entire time. And now you're gonna blame *me*, of all people?"

"I'll blame whoever the hell I want to."

Xavier had never defended Asher openly to Pierre before, not like this. Apparently, he felt strong enough to chime in. "Chief, he put away two cases in one day. Don't you think the man deserves a little—"

"And you can shut the hell up." Pierre pointed straight at him. "All you do is enable him. Both of y'all are a damn pain in my ass."

"Chief," Asher said. "We've got Blanchard."

"You really think that means something right now? Do you? He knew your partner, Asher, and you didn't know jack shit about it. Did you?"

"I do now. And how was I supposed to know about that?"

"That's all you did," Pierre said. "You traded one nut job for another—and fucked me in the process. Thank you for that."

Asher contemplated stopping there, but he couldn't manage to pull himself together in time. He'd survived his wife, survived Cassandra's attempt at putting a bullet in his head, coming back to the job, solving both of his assigned cases after returning.

Anyone with eyes could see that he'd done everything in his power to forgo jumping the gun on getting the woman's ID wrong; now, only two people needed to take the fall for that one.

"And *I'm* the one who ID'd the body and signed the death certificate?" Asher said. "*I'm* the one who pushed to have the body cremated and shoved under the rug? Oh wait . . . actually . . ." He turned around and braced himself against the wall, then hung his head to ease the pull at the back of his neck.

"Yeah. I got it, dickhead." Pierre dropped into his chair.

No matter what Asher did, it was never enough. He wondered if it ever would be.

He was growing to learn, though, that at least with Pierre, he could only do so much. He was only human. And that meant doing the best he could with what he had in front of him.

It meant moving forward—when every achievement felt like a step back.

"So," Xavier said. "What's the call?"

Asher pushed off the wall and turned back, and the two of them stood in front of the chief's desk, arms folded, waiting for their orders.

For the detective, it was all two-fold. Asher was right, and he'd done his job well: Cassandra was alive, and the kid was in custody. On the flip side?

Cassandra was alive—when she was supposedly dead.

"I don't care how you do it." Pierre lit a cigar. Savored it. Got comfortable in his oversized leather chair.

Asher could see it: the chief was on the edge of losing it, his fingernails splitting straight down the middle as he held tight to a sinking department.

"Find her," Pierre continued. "Bring her in. Or put it to rest. Quite frankly . . . I don't care. Just do it quietly." He tapped the embers from his torpedo. Adjusted the ashtray. "And if you can't"—he looked to Asher—"if this gets beyond this room . . . well . . ." He took another drag, then let the smoke bleed from his nose. "All three of us are gonna be looking for new careers." He propped his feet onto the desk. "You've got twenty-four hours."

Chapter 110

It was late morning, and Asher had been up and at it for over twenty-four hours.

With the clock ticking, there was no time for slumber, no time to stop and think about what would become of his career if he wasn't able to find Cassandra and put a stop to this never-ending nightmare, this perpetual loop. But if he was to keep going, he at least needed to run by the house to change clothes and grab a bite to eat.

He'd stop by Jean Lafitte Trading Company for coffee on the way out; some things were necessary for him to get through it all, his one and only fix included.

Asher threw the Vette into park and made his way inside. He didn't bother with the lights, just headed straight for the bedroom and changed into something fresh. Something more appropriate for the sure hell that would be the entirety of his day.

Or the next few hours, if he was lucky.

Clean clothes, clean start. For Asher, the better he dressed, the better he felt, regardless of whether he was seeing double after being awake and still working more than a day later.

He slid on a new pair of jeans, a black button-down, his leather jacket, and black work boots. Then he returned his pistol to its home at the four-o'clock position of his back, inside of his waistband.

Even through his shirt, the cold of the .45 felt nice against his sweating skin.

He walked out of the bedroom and into the kitchen as he checked his watch. He needed to get moving—he was meeting Xavier for coffee in twenty. Opening the fridge, he grabbed some leftover, two-day-old bacon, threw a few pieces onto some bread, and called it a meal.

But as he grabbed his keys and turned for the door, something didn't quite belong. How had he not noticed it before? He'd walked right past it, twice.

Past the black flip phone on the counter.

It vibrated, turning in short bursts. Where had it come from?

Asher drew his pistol and thumbed the safety as he aimed the gun at the kitchen door, then into the living room. Back to the door.

The phone continued to tremble—pulsing like his blood beneath the fabric of his shirt. The phone crawled to the edge of the counter, almost falling to the kitchen floor.

He grabbed it and stepped back. The pulse of the phone met that of his palm, the two rhythms colliding in an offbeat timing. His heart outpaced the call, growing faster with each tremor of the plastic in his hand.

Asher's thumb eased back the hammer on his pistol.

One click. Then two.

He flipped open the phone and placed it against his ear, but he said nothing. At first, only the ambience of horns and drums, of a distant siren and rambling, reached his ear in the dead silence of the home. Then a voice he'd hoped to never hear from again spoke to him over the line, as if that house, that hallway, that barrel beneath his chin had never been.

"Long day at work, hun?"

Then he saw it: Sofia's coffee cup, upside down on a hand towel. Clean and drying next to the kitchen sink.

About the Author

KB Fisher is an independent author of mystery thrillers. He lives with his family in the Southeast United States and is a native of Slidell, Louisiana.

One of the most valuable things a reader can do for an author is to provide an honest review of their work. Please visit the book's review page on Amazon or Goodreads to do so.

Email: authorKBFisher@gmail.com
Website: authorKBFisher.com

www.ingramcontent.com/pod-product-compliance
Lightning Source LLC
Chambersburg PA
CBHW070304310726

48976CB00005B/1568